EBUR

ALL THE RI

Priyanka R Khanna grew up in Mu..........graduated from Hamilton College in Clinton, New York. After graduation, she worked in the public relations department of *Hearst* Magazines in New York. She returned to Mumbai and joined the launch team of *Vogue India*, where she spent fifteen years as the fashion features director, overseeing fashion-related content across digital and print.

Khanna, who was first published in *The Hindu* at the age of sixteen, continues to write and speak on art and design, fashion and culture.

She lives in Mumbai, with her husband and two children.

This is her first novel.

ALL THE RIGHT PEOPLE

A NOVEL

PRIYANKA R KHANNA

EBURY
PRESS

An imprint of Penguin Random House

EBURY PRESS

USA | Canada | UK | Ireland | Australia
New Zealand | India | South Africa | China

Ebury Press is part of the Penguin Random House group of companies
whose addresses can be found at global.penguinrandomhouse.com

Published by Penguin Random House India Pvt. Ltd
4th Floor, Capital Tower 1, MG Road,
Gurugram 122 002, Haryana, India

First published in India in Ebury Press by Penguin Random House India 2022

Copyright © Priyanka R Khanna 2022

10 9 8 7 6 5 4 3 2 1

This is a work of fiction. Names, characters, places and incidents are either the
product of the author's imagination or are used fictitiously, and any resemblance
to any actual person, living or dead, events or locales is entirely coincidental.

ISBN 9780143453017

Typeset in Bembo Std by Manipal Technologies Limited, Manipal
Printed at Thomson Press India Ltd, New Delhi

www.penguin.co.in

To Jyoti and Subash Khanna,
who continue to raise the bar as parents and people

PROLOGUE

MUMBAI DAILY	12 MAY 2016 p. 2

RETAIL RAJA'S DAUGHTER'S BIG FAT JET-SET WEDDING

By Surbhi Shukla There's rich and then there's nouveau riche. No prizes for guessing which category Mohan Mehta falls into. But it's just semantics, when you've got the big-time dollars to spend. The news out of Malabar Hill is that the rolling-in-the-dough Retail Raja is going all out to ensure his precious daughter Tara's wedding—scheduled to be held at Monte Carlo's famed Hotel de Paris later this year—will be out of this world.

It was only a few months ago that Tara's hunk of a hubby-to-be Nakul Puri (rich and good-looking—some girls have all the luck!) got down on one knee in a hot air balloon over Napa Valley, with a stunning five-carat diamond from Graff. Don't just take our word for it, the bride documented the entire proposal on her blog—along with outfit details, of course. Private-*shivate*. If you got it you flaunt it, right?

The dashing Puri is the son of London society queen Anjali Puri, the ultimate hostess with the mostest. Her claim to fame, besides the family millions, is her annual tea with the Duchess, that all of the BBDD's (British-Born Designer Desis) in London will sell an heirloom to get into.

'The theme for this wedding is Keeping up with the Puris, of course,' one Birkin babe sniffed, perusing the red, velvet-lined box that delivered the wedding card along with treats from (where else?) Fortnum & Mason.

We hear that the bride's outfits have been keeping couturiers on their toes. She has been requesting matching looks for her bridesmaids who, of course, include her besties: the elusive billionairess Aria Mistry, daughter of Rusi, and the pint-sized politico-firecracker Shaan Singh, daughter of, yes, Arjun Singh. This weekend, the girls are whisking off the bride on Mistry's private jet to Mykonos, for a spot of fun in the sun. What happens in Myko stays in Myko? Not a chance, when this diarist is around.

But back to the wedding. Sources tell me that the Mehtas have hired the wedding planner responsible for Tom Cruise's nuptials, roped in Cirque du Soleil to perform, and Bollywood superstar Rohan Rawal will make an appearance at the four-day affair. It certainly helps when daddy has him on a six-figure contract. With over 1000 guests being flown in from all parts of the globe, it's going to be a wedding that will go down in the books.

'That's not a wedding, dahling, that's a circus.' Birkin babe adds, taking a delicate bite out of her glacé de fruit. 'But then, that's the difference between mass and class.'

1

Mumbai, Chhatrapati Shivaji International Airport

'We really should send that bitch Surbhi Shukla a copy of our boarding cards.' Shaan Singh slumped down in her first-class seat, across the aisle from Aria Mistry, happily accepting a glass of champagne from the flight attendant.

'That tabloid?' Aria was dismissive. 'Don't even give her the satisfaction.' Aria shifted her focus back to her elaborate in-flight routine. She smoothed her shoulder-length brown hair back into a neat ponytail, slid on disposable rubber gloves and proceeded to spray sanitizer liberally all over the seat, ensuring every last corner was wiped down. Shaan sat back, watching the very familiar scene unfold—Aria would make her way to the bathroom, where she would change into a robe and pyjamas, slide on her eye mask and get ready to sleep, all before take-off. They'd been on so many flights together, and yet every time Shaan couldn't help but be amused by her friend's fear of disease and disorder.

'You know, they say, that the armrest and tray table are the dirtiest parts of the plane,' muttered Aria, moving on to Shaan's seat now.

'Now, see, *that's* the stuff that should be in the newspaper. I mean, at least she should get the facts right—we're changing TWO planes to get to Mykonos.'

The friends were on their way to the Greek islands for a five-day bachelorette that Shaan had planned down to the last debauched detail for the third member of their crew, Tara Mehta.

Shaan paused, her face contorting into a frown.

'I wish we could have just flown private,' a grin appeared on her face. 'I can never understand your need to be low-key. I mean, the plane is just sitting there?'

Aria shot her a withering look. 'You're STILL talking about that article?' she ignored the rest of Shaan's commentary, snapping off her gloves. 'Anyway, like I said, it's a tabloid, it's not even in proper English! It's gossipy, tea-party conversation. Who reads that besides you and Tara?'

She laughed, a sly smile spreading across her face. 'Incidentally, our new Corp Comm head insists on sending me every clipping that mentions Mistry & Sons. I had to finally tell her to take Surbhi's column off the mailing list. It's old news—my two friends turn to it first thing every morning and *always* keep me in the loop.'

'Excuse me, I read the political news first,' Shaan retorted. 'THEN I turn to the gossip.'

'Darling, the news happens in your living room. NOTHING, in this country, happens without your father knowing about it first.'

Shaan cocked an eyebrow.

'This is true. But this Surbhi is something else. A bitch in school, a raging bitch now!'

'Speaking of mature behaviour,' Aria rolled her eyes at the now inebriated bride, who was stumbling between seats, much to the flight attendant's consternation.

'WOOHOO! Myko, HERE we come!' Ishita, one of Tara's friends, yelled as the pilot began his announcement.

Aria winced. 'Really, Shaan, can you do something? This behaviour is just unacceptable. These girls are drunk, loud and plain annoying.'

Shaan was about to speak as Aria cut her off. 'I know!' Aria raised her hand. 'She is the bride and it's her bachelorette. But there are other people on this plane, who would probably like to sleep. I feel like I should personally apologize to them.'

Shaan just laughed. 'Only you, Aria Mistry, would think of apologizing for something that isn't even your fault. Trust me, the amount of champagne these lushes have had, the minute we take off, they'll be knocked out. And, by the way, aren't you proud of my restraint?'

Aria exhaled. 'Can we go easy on the partying though, Shaan? In fact,' she drew out the words, 'I had a thought. A friend was just telling me about this cycling tour of Athens that takes you to all the ancient sites. Maybe we could skip out of Mykonos for the day . . .'

Shaan stared at her.

'Okay, fine, then there's this brilliant chef who does this organic tasting menu, foraged from the countryside and everything is slow-cooked over a fire. It's impossible to get a table, but let me—'

'Biking. Five-course *ghas poos* tandoor dinners. We may as well sit around and play rummy in our kaftans all day,' Shaan signalled for a refill on her champagne. 'Tara is getting

MARRIED. And you know what that means—one guy for the REST. OF. HER. LIFE. So, for the next few days, let's drink, let's dance, let's hang around at the clubs, let's sit in the sun, let's flirt with some pretty boys. We'll celebrate her downfall, Myko style. Because after this, there'll be no benders, no more wildo days,' Shaan sighed. 'Nothing to look forward to, except going grey in that British museum, with the very propah Nakul, drinking tea and nibbling on scones,' she added in a faux English accent, raising her pinky finger in emphasis.

'Yes, but—'

'Leave the planning to me, Aria,' she yawned. 'Now, look at what you've done. You've even *bored* me to sleep.'

Aria shot her friend a withering look.

'And see, what did I tell you, she's passed out, too,' Shaan chuckled, gesturing to Tara, curled up under a Louis Vuitton monogram shawl. 'Aww, look at our sweet little Star. Did you ever think that the pudgy little thing, with her uniform reaching her ankles, would be this sexy fashionista?'

Aria closed her eyes, as the plane made its way to 35,000 feet. Outside the window, the monsoon-heavy dark clouds took her back to a similar rainy day, when Tara Mehta had walked into their classroom and into their lives.

~

1995, Mumbai

It seemed even the skies were mourning the end of the summer holidays.

As the rains lashed the stained-glass windows, students trampled in, leaving upturned umbrellas on the now slick corridor outside the classroom, shaking off big fat droplets of water from brightly coloured, patterned raincoats, and hanging up school bags on the backs of the wooden chairs.

'Settle down, settle DOWN!' their class teacher Miss Choksey, yelled above the din. 'For god's sake, Harsh and Romil, this is a classroom, not the gymnasium, get DOWN!' she pulled down her naughtiest students, who'd clambered on to the wooden desks and were tossing around a tennis ball.

The bell rang shrilly. 'Now, children, let's get to our seats,' she continued. 'Nyrika and Ria, you can continue your little chat session later,' she said archly to the two best friends who had their heads together whispering.

'Good morning, Miss Choksey,' the class sang out in unison.

The mid-morning lull was just settling in when the headmistress strode into the classroom. Behind her was a bespectacled new student, nervously fiddling with a red Barham House sash.

'Good morning, class,' said their headmistress, as a murmur filled the room, and the children pushed back their chairs to stand in greeting.

'A new student joins us today,' she patted the trembling girl's shoulder. 'Class, this is Tara Mehta. I would like you to all welcome her. Say hello, dear,' she gently nudged her to the front.

Tara mumbled incoherently at the sea of new faces, blinking back the tears that threatened to spill over, her eyes glued to the floor.

'Poor thing,' Aria Mistry whispered to her best friend, who was also her seat mate, Shaan Singh. 'She looks so scared.'

'Isn't she wearing her uniform too long?' Shaan replied, wrinkling her nose.

'Aria,' Miss Choksey called out. 'I would like you, as class monitor, to take care of Tara, yes?' she smiled at her favourite student, who nodded enthusiastically.

'Now, let's get back to geometry. Tara, have a seat over there, and take out your pencil box and notebook. As I was saying, the equilateral triangle has three equal sides, the isosceles . . .'

At breaktime, Aria, ever diligent, waved Tara over introducing her to some of the other girls. Aneesa eyed her somewhat curiously, before going back to her elaborate doodling; Ria and Nyrika sang out hello in unison and then went back to whispering, a curly-haired girl named Nisha smiled and offered Tara a buttery cheese sandwich and some salty *jaali* wafers, which Tara gratefully accepted and proffered her tiffin of homemade chakli to the others.

'Your dad was in Barham?' Shaan gestured to the red house sash she was wearing.

'No, my father went to Ramji Asar High School for Boys,' Tara said.

'Where's that?' Shaan tilted her head, barrelling forth, without waiting for an answer. 'Anyway, Aria is in Savage, which is green house, because her father was in Savage. I'm in Wilson, blue house, but my father didn't go to school here, he went to a boarding school called Doon.' Shaan chattered on about the different coloured houses, named after the school's founding fathers.

'And I'm in Palmer, just because I'm mellow like yellow like jello,' a lanky boy Kunal attempted to rap, grabbing a few wafers. Shaan just rolled her eyes at the interruption.

'Do you know how to make friendship bands?'

Tara nodded. She wanted to ask why the houses were so important, but she didn't want to embarrass herself on the first day.

'You can make some with us, then,' Shaan stated. 'You should come to Aria's house on Saturday,'

Aria smiled at Tara, primly wiping her mouth with the lace-edged napkin that always accompanied her pink snack box. 'Yes, ask your mother. We are going to make brownies and friendship bands for the rest of the class.'

And that's how Tara showed up at Windsor Villa the following weekend.

'This is just *your* house?' Tara's eyes widened as she took in the mansion, which stood at the edge of a long driveway. 'Only you live here?'

Shaan giggled at Tara's amazement.

It was the fanciest house Tara had ever been to— the gleaming marble hallways, the ornate chandeliers, the majestic staircase, the lush green lawn that was bigger than the neighbourhood park and the bright blue swimming pool that seemed to end right where the Arabian Sea began.

'Yes, four humans and six dogs! And that's why you have to call her Princess Aria,' Shaan slid down the oak banister. 'Make sure you bow to her every time she walks into the room,' she winked.

'Ignore her. And let's go to my room. I want to show you this new game my cousin Ayesha sent me from America, it's called Dream Phone.' Aria leapt up the stairs two at a time.

Later, as the girls sat on Aria's canopied bed ('A proper princess bed like in Sleeping Beauty!' Tara would later tell her mother), eating cheesy toast, fries and warm-out-of-the-oven brownies, Aria's father walked into her room.

'Hello darling, hello Shaan,' Ruṣi Mistry kissed his daughter on the head.

'And who might you be, young lady?' his voice boomed, as he smiled down at Tara.

'This is our new friend Tara, Papa. She's the third angle of our triangle,' Aria replied, solemnly.

~

They became a tight-knit trio. Aria-Shaan-Tara. Their names blending together, rattled off in one breath, by their parents, classmates and teachers. With all the naivete of youth and privilege, they defined their own world and their individual roles—Aria, the voice of reason, measured, driven; Shaan, passionate, impulsive, rebellious; Tara, large-hearted, impressionable, eager to please. They were fiercely protective of each other, their loyalty unquestioned.

Their hemlines grew shorter, their list of crushes longer. They went from slumber parties to school socials, first kisses to heartbreaks, from watching *Masoom* to swooning over Richard Gere in *Pretty Woman*. They hankered for independence, for the freedom they believed came with adulthood; they planned for the future—college, marriage, children. They fought over boys, over borrowed clothes, over perceived slights. They saw their bodies changing, their parents ageing, they saw fortunes rise, the city they called home changing its name and its identity, metamorphosing at a speed they couldn't comprehend. They let others in, only at the periphery, their status as a trio sacrosanct. It was them versus the world.

If Tara's transition into a new school and a new world was somewhat seamless, she had Shaan and Aria to thank for it. In class, when the boys at the back aimed spitballs at her, Aria gave them a solid dressing down. In senior school, too embarrassed to ask Riyad, her crush, to the school social, Shaan stepped in—not giving the hapless boy much choice in the matter. When Tara was in danger of failing the grade, Aria helped tutor her till she passed the class.

In return, the girls, especially Shaan, earned Tara's boundless gratitude and wide-eyed awe. As a teen, when Shaan skipped school to lounge around the pool at the Bombay Gymkhana, she convinced Tara to do the same, resulting in both being suspended for a week. It was with Shaan that Tara went to her first rave in Goa, it was Shaan who taught Tara how to roll her first joint. Unsuccessful in trying to convince Aria to indulge in any of her escapades, Shaan found a worthy, pliable sidekick, while Aria only looked up from her unyielding schedule of school, tuitions, piano and tennis lessons to shake her head in disapproval at their latest antics.

That was until Shaan moved to Delhi in tenth grade. On the urging of a Doon School buddy, her father, Arjun Singh, who hailed from a minor royal family, had retired from his corporate career for one in politics; trading his corner office for his home constituency on the banks of the Ganga. After years of splitting time in two cities, he realized the need to make Delhi his power base, to establish himself in the larger political landscape.

To leave her friends at such a crucial time in their lives was heartbreaking for Shaan. And she was determined that they stay constantly connected.

'So, girls, this is the plan,' said Aria, always ready with a list for any eventuality, after the three had cried for hours at Shaan's impending departure.

They were sitting in Shaan's bedroom, clothes and books strewn across the floor, the cardboard boxes she was meant to be packing stacked in the corner, lying empty.

The schedule

- 9 p.m. Daily Call: Aria will conference call. If for any reason someone is not available, we fix an alternative time. Discuss all that happened in the day.
- Computers on, once we are home from school, so we can always chat if anyone is free.
- Once every month, Shaan will come to Bombay.
- Once every two months, Aria and Tara will go to Delhi.
- Christmas and New Year's, Shaan to stay at Aria's and go to Alibaug.
- No big decisions shall be made without notifying the others.

Three years till COLLEGE!
Near or Far, Best Friends Always and Forever.

She handed the girls a print of this schedule and made them sign their names.

'To pin on your boards,' she said with a hint of pride, as Shaan burst out laughing. It soon turned to tears.

'What will I do Ari-poo, without your lists, your next-level Parsi OCD, those insane chocolate tarts that you make?' she cried, tears rolling down her cheeks.

And yet the three managed to grow together, even apart. Shaan's departure left a physical space and a realization that she was the stubborn, steadfast, sticky glue that held them together. Aria and Tara, though still close, found themselves opening up to different relationships, new friends, new boyfriends, new interests.

Then came graduation. And college. Tara in London, Shaan in Washington DC and Aria in Boston. Thanksgiving breaks together—New Orleans, London, Paris. Summers and Christmas back home in Mumbai and Delhi. Breakups and new loves. First jobs and graduate programmes. New apartments and moving back home. Engagements and bachelorettes.

Which is exactly where they were now.

2

September 2016, Monaco

'What on god's green earth . . .?' Rusi Mistry thought to himself rather disdainfully as he walked through a long corridor into the evening's venue with wife Meher and daughters Aria and Leah.

'This evening is divided into different experience zones, each created with the aim of heightening and tingling every sense,' a throaty hostess explained, guiding them into the cavernous main ballroom, which had been transformed for the night into a tropical forest.

Every inch of the Belle Epoque-designed room was covered in lush green foliage and brilliantly hued tropical flowers; palm trees had been transported indoors, adding further drama to the room's high, arched ceilings; suspended from wires and silk ropes, aerialists and acrobatic dancers nimbly flew, displaying their body's athletic prowess, while a mariachi band played tinny versions of classic Hindi songs.

Through the Amazonian ballroom, they walked into a specially created nightclub. In continuation with the tropical theme, life-size fluorescent animals lined the mirrored dance floor, the foil balloons that covered the ceiling undulating with the pulsating disco lights.

There was a separate room for desserts, multi-tier Godiva chocolate fountains holding centrestage, and yet another room for the 170-dish-long buffet that spanned the world's cuisines—Peruvian, Japanese, Modern French, Italian, Chinese and of course Indian. 'It will be unusual, desi with a twist,' the chef had promised, chuckling that by the end of the night, the guests would gather in droves for his famous blue cheese and truffle dusted kulchas and creamy dal makhani.

'Toto, we're not in France any more,' twenty-five-year-old Leah, smirked. 'And is it just me, or does it also smell like rain?'

'Smart, SMART girl, you are. We made special perfume to smell like the Amazon forest.' Leah turned to see their hosts, Mohan Mehta and wife Bina, glowering son Rishabh in tow.

In a jazzy, green velvet sherwani, gleaming ruby buttons straining over a protruding belly, Mohan smiled broadly, breathing in deeply, as if to underscore his point, before stretching his arms out in greeting.

'Welcome, WELCOME! You like?' he looked up at Rusi for approval. 'Tara loves South of America. So I thought, for the wedding, I bring South of America to South of France!!' He chuckled at his own wit.

'Wouldn't it have been easier to just get her married in Brazil?' asked Leah, looking around at the room, which was quite the spectacle even for the standard-issue grand Indian celebration.

'Always so funny, Leah *beta* . . . Aria, so nice you are also looking,' Mohan pulled her cheeks lightly, like he used to when she was a little girl. 'So happy, you all could grace us with the pleasure of your company.'

Before Mohan could go on, Meher stepped in, enveloping Bina in a warm hug. 'Shall we go say hello to our beautiful Tara?' She steered the mother of the bride towards the LED-lit stage, festooned with oversized butterflies, which would have given even the Kodak Theatre a run for its money.

Aria led the way to her friend, embracing her.

'Wow, T. It's beginning. Are you nervous?' she whispered.

Tara shook her head, the smile never leaving her face. 'I can't believe it's . . . finally here, Ari. Everything is going so perfectly I have to pinch myself. I don't want to, um . . . jinx it,' the flurry of hellos and air kisses, interrupting their conversation.

'*Thoo thoo*, Tara is looking like a real princess, isn't it?' Bina stroked her daughter's tonged hair.

'You're looking lovely too Bina,' Meher said. 'Such an elegant sari.' Bina's face broke into a delighted smile. 'I *toh* told Manish, I want to look classic beauty, like Waheedaji, for my daughter's wedding.'

Even with the flamboyance of the evening's setting, Tara had ensured that all eyes would be on her. After all, it wasn't just for the guests who were present. Her every look was to be chronicled on her blog and for her 25,000 followers on Instagram.

She'd flown across the world shopping for a trousseau. She'd hopped on the Euro Star to Paris to buy her lingerie at Sabbia Rosa and her linens at D. Porthault. In Beirut, she'd commissioned Elie Saab to design a couture look. 'Oh my god, you guys,' she'd FaceTimed Aria and Shaan, while in fittings, 'The designer just told me that Jennifer Lopez's stylist is legit obsessed with this outfit and wants to book it for her next music video!' Back home, she'd spent hours with Manish Malhotra and Sabyasachi, making sure that every panel of her lehengas was created to her exacting standards.

'You know, this is a wedding, not a fashion show,' Shaan said, not for the first time, as Tara dragged her from one appointment to another. 'Are you more excited to be marrying Nakul or the fact that your wedding is going to be in *Vogue*?'

Tara ignored the jibe, far too wrapped up in preening and posing in front of the mirror, admiring her sculpted back in the tiny blouse.

And all her effort had paid off. The shimmering sequin sari-inspired gown by Elie Saab, with a feathered trail, fit every inch of her five feet nine inches' frame perfectly. A custom-designed Colombian emerald and diamond choker complemented the champagne-hued dress; she'd left her highlighted hair in loose waves, her eyes, heavily lined in kohl, her cheekbones contoured to look even sharper. She looked sensational and was keenly aware of it, ensuring that at every moment the photographers were shooting her from her best angle.

'You look so beautiful, darling,' Meher kissed Tara on both cheeks, and the ladies chatted casually, oohing and aahing over her outfit, the decor and jewellery.

'Aunty Meher, did you like the welcome hampers in your suite? I made sure that they included the lemon biscuits, I know they are Uncle Rusi's favourite.'

'You've thought of every little detail, Tara. Even the fragrance of this room! I'm so amazed—everything is impeccable, darling, now you mustn't worry. Enjoy every moment!'

'Yes, all must enjoy. Don't leave early, Rusi . . . Bunty, what are you doing, get everyone drinks?' Mohan snapped at his son Rishabh, who disinterestedly beckoned over one of the many blonde women in long dresses, each of whom carried trays of drinks suspended from their necks.

'There's surprise performances—mind-blowing I tell you, and very . . .' Here Mohan emphatically gestured counting money, before handing over glasses of Dom Perignon to the Mistrys.

The ties that bound the Mehtas and the Mistrys were dual-fold: wealth and privilege—'Money shouts, wealth whispers' ringing far too true in this case. And the close friendship between the daughters, Aria and Tara, extended to an easy rapport between the mothers, Bina and Meher, who had spent hours together volunteering for the PTA and attending after-school activities with their firstborns. Unlike her husband, Meher was willing to overlook Mohan's arriviste attitude for the most part, especially since she was so fond of both mother and daughter.

And now, nearly twenty years later, here they all were, halfway across the world at the four-day extravaganza that was to be Tara's wedding. It was only day one, and Rusi was already on edge. The bride was a sweet child, and that's really why he had come (Meher had also been quite insistent, that for Aria's sake, he make an appearance) but the blatant excess that now characterized Indian weddings rankled him immensely.

'Tropical rainforests, Cirque du Soleil acts, Bollywood performers—where is the class, the elegance, the sanctimony of marriage?' Rusi would rail at his wife, after attending yet another grand Indian wedding. His own wedding to Meher, almost thirty years ago, had been a discreet affair. There were no ice-bars, dancing waiters, mile-long buffets; that's not to say that any expense had been spared, but none that had been spoken about. He hoped his daughters would find nice, well-brought-up men who hailed from similar value systems. There would be none of this show-sha nonsense.

~

'Need help with that?'

Aria turned, juggling two champagne glasses and dropping her Bottega Veneta knot clutch, as she tried to see who had spoken to her.

'You know, I've been watching you all evening,' Rohan Rawal picked up the bag, but not before giving Aria the once-over.

'Great pick-up line. Not in the *least* bit creepy,' Leah grabbed a glass from her sister.

Tall, in a fitted silver suit, with a white shirt opened at the collar, hair falling over his right eye, a cigarette dangling from the left corner of his smirking mouth, Rohan looked Aria up and down. He wasn't lying. She hadn't been difficult to notice. In a room filled with overdressed, over-coiffed women, she stood out for her natural, classic beauty. Dressed elegantly, in a sophisticated navy column dress that lengthened her muscular five-feet-seven frame, her shoulder-length brown hair in a low knot, ears and wrist glittering with delicate diamonds, she carried herself with a sense of poise. She'd inherited her father's height and his rose-tinged colouring, but her light brown hair and aquiline nose was all her mother.

'There's something about her,' he'd later confide in his agent. 'It's not that she's a super hottie, but there's something . . . something that's just *mad* sexy.'

Rohan was leaner in person and possibly even better looking than on screen. Though Aria hadn't watched any of his films, she knew from the billboards that dotted the country that he was a well-known actor. Even if she hadn't recognized him, the tittering of the girls behind her would have been somewhat of a clue. But she refused to let on.

'Excuse me,' Aria's tone was icy. 'You are?'

'Your knight in shining armour,' he grinned, handing back her bag.

'Shining you are,' Aria looked pointedly at his suit, that gave the effect of being crafted out of kitchen foil. 'But what makes you think I need saving?' Aria arched an eyebrow.

'Well, besides the few minutes you spent with the bride, you've scrolled through your phone a million times already this evening. When that banker boy was trying to talk to you, you were totally spaced . . . And your face didn't crack ANYTHING even resembling a smile during the performances. You looked like you would much rather be having a root canal. It's meant to be a party, you know—CHILL, babe!'

'No arguments there,' laughed Leah, who enjoyed nothing more than watching her uptight sister being put in place.

'Calling a woman you don't even know 'babe' is offensive,' Aria retorted.

Rohan put his hands up in apology.

'Did you stop to think that maybe it was your thrilling performance and that *completely* superfluous striptease that did me in?' Aria found herself saying, as much to her surprise as to Leah's. 'I think you forget that this is a wedding, NOT the Moulin Rouge.'

Earlier in the evening, Rohan had emerged on stage, flanked by a row of Carnivale dancers in elaborate, brightly coloured headgear and barely-there costumes. At the end of the show, he'd stripped to reveal his glistening, oiled chest and chiselled abs to a cacophony of cat calls; the aunties he'd flirted shamelessly with through the night were only too happy to shower him in multiple Euro notes. For Mohan Mehta, it had been his money's worth and promised to be a talking point for many months to come.

'Aw snap,' he laughed. Not that she would ever let on, but even Aria, with all her harrumphing, wasn't oblivious to the way his eyes crinkled when he smiled.

'You can huff and puff all you want, SoBo girl, but the thing is,'—he stepped closer till he was whispering in her ear, their shoulders lightly brushing—'you clearly noticed *everything*, which means that you couldn't take your eyes off me too.'

~

'Meher!' Rusi bellowed. 'Meher! Meher!'

'Is there a reason to shout?' His wife walked into the suite's bedroom. 'I can hear just fine.'

'I can't take this BLOODY thing off!' He fiddled with the buttons on his sherwani. 'What are these damn designers doing these days? And who the hell insists on an Indian dress code?'

As Meher walked over, her husband looked at her with an appraising eye. Tall and slim, with hazel eyes, Meher's chocolate brown hair fell straight around her shoulders, her alabaster skin dusted with a hint of blush and a soft rose-pink lipstick. Dressed in an off-white Shahab Durazi sari, accessorized with a delicate line of solitaires, she remained by far the most elegant woman in any room, in thought and in carriage. Even now, over three decades after they met, he couldn't help but wonder at how she managed to still look like the same girl—just with deeper laugh lines—that he used to share Campa Cola floats with at the Willingdon Club post a swim.

He smiled tenderly, as she unhooked the buttons. In so many ways, she had always been a better person than he was— kinder, friendlier, more easy-going. And she had passed these qualities on to Leah, while he had made Aria his from the day she had been born.

'Did you notice how everyone was behaving with that actor boy? How can these be adults and people we associate with?' Rusi pried the last button off, the relief palpable on his face. 'You're well-respected individuals heading some of the country's most important companies and institutions, and yet, you see one star, and you act like your main focus in life is to be part of a Bollywood dance troupe?'

'Oh Rusi. It was just harmless fun, it's a celebration. And I have to say, the boy is quite charismatic. He's also young, remember what you were like at that age?' Meher shook her head, amused as always at her husband's indignation.

'Remember?' he exclaimed, as he slid off the jacket. 'I haven't reached dementia yet. And no, I don't remember what it was to behave so boorishly. We had our fun, but within reason. Meher, he was sauntering around in that godawful silver suit, with his drunk cronies, lighting up cigarettes when it's against the law to smoke indoors! It was like he OWNED the place. Don't you think he should have had some respect for the elders in the room? We're no chumps, you know. He must be Aria's age, and if I had a son, I would not tolerate such behaviour. And then he goes and . . .'

'If you had a son, the poor boy would have to be a saint to please you. Look at Aria, I worry that her only mission in life is to make sure you are happy.'

'Well, she has big shoes to fill. This family has a legacy, which is not something that should be forgotten. She is the great granddaughter of Sir Rusi Pestonji Mistry. If she is to change the company's name to Mistry & Daughters, she has a lot to learn.'

Meher sighed. She had long resigned herself to the fact that this was one argument she could never win but she genuinely worried for the burdens he placed on their older daughter's shoulders.

She loved her husband, but sometimes he could be so unforgiving—it was all black and white when it came to his moral code.

It was what had first attracted twenty-year-old Meher Bawa, a sentiment that her mother had echoed. 'He is a man of morals, Meher. Of culture. Of good upbringing. These are qualities that will see you through even the most difficult moments of your life.' But over the years, his idea of right and wrong, that very morality she had admired, had become set in stone, with little room for deviation.

'She'll get there, Rusi. She just needs to live a little, that's all I'm saying.'

~

On what seemed like its thirtieth attempt, a shrill ring finally cut through Rohan Rawal's dreamy sleep. He reached across to the nightstand, fumbling around for the phone and his cigarettes. 'Darlin',' he drawled as a female voice screamed into his ear.

'This is my UMPTEENTH call, and I am NOT your darling,' his manager admonished. 'You are now three hours late and the father of the bride—who is paying you to attend this wedding, may I remind you—is threatening to pull his money.'

'Arré . . . Divi, don't be angry,' Rohan put on his best schoolboy voice. 'I was such a hit last night, he got more than his money's worth.'

'His money's worth extends until the day after tomorrow, and includes a signed contract. This is not a guy you want to screw around with. Not only does his company have you on an unheard-of commercial contract, but he's paid you a ridiculous sum to attend this wedding. Seriously, Rohan, you have to stop fucking around!'

Rohan grinned. Divya Dalal, Bollywood's first ever official agent, headed Imagine, the country's biggest talent agency. *Entertainment* Magazine had anointed her as one of the country's top ten most influential women five years in a row, and here she was, berating him for the child he really was. Her handholding actor days were over, but she didn't have much of a choice with him—it wasn't his fault that all her junior female agents had been too smitten to be effective and the men, well, he had reduced them to boys.

Rohan Rawal was India's superbrat and he milked his appeal for all it was worth. At twenty-eight, he already had three Rs 50-crore films in his arsenal, a five-year cola contract, a smattering of endorsements and heartthrob status, having dated his way through a string of starlets. Plucked from obscurity—otherwise known as a Barista in Versova—by Divya's eagle eye for talent, he had managed to hold his own against the phalanx of star sons that currently held sway in the industry, becoming an even bigger star than his single mother, a travel agent, had ever imagined.

Divya, who in the course of his career, had become one of his closest confidants, had big plans, including a Hollywood launch, hoping to make him the first mainstream crossover male actor. But as Rohan kept telling her, they had all the time in the world. For the moment, he was enjoying the adulation and success. He was already 'India's Sexiest Man Alive'; the rest of the world would have to wait a little longer.

'Diviiii . . . you know you love me. I'm telling you, I'm on my best behaviour with all these limited-edition Dior hags,' he guffawed. 'But I gotta tell you, I met a girl last night . . . ooh Diviii,' he stretched, his grey sweatpants sliding down his taut stomach. 'She's somethin' else.'

'May I remind you, you say that about *every* pretty little thing who comes your way.' He could just picture her rolling her eyes. 'Rohan, come on, ya, let's get a little serious, behave yourself for the next few days, attend all the events, stay a while, mind your Ps and Qs, and then after the contractual obligations to MohanSons are done, let's move on to focusing on the film, please.'

'She's the opposite of frivolous, let me tell you. She's as uptight as it gets,' he laughed, remembering the look on Aria's face. 'Anyway, just for you, I'm on my way now.' Hanging up before she could say another word, he leaned back against the pillows, rang his spot boy for a morning espresso, lit a cigarette and smiled.

Maybe, for once, he would listen to Divya and head to the party soon. Who knew what surprises waited there?

~

Whether it was the feeling of sand beneath her feet, the second mimosa, or that she was with her closest friends, Aria was feeling infinitely more relaxed at Tara's 'White Beach Brunch' that morning. She looked on affectionately as her very animated friend held court.

'So, we finish dinner at Wasabi and then he says, "Come baby, I want to take you for a ride in my new Bentley convertible." *Maine toh keh diya, "Betaji*, I have three Bentleys in the garage, *kuch bata jo mere ghar pe nahi hai!"*' Shaan laughed, taking another puff of her e-cigarette as she regaled a rapt crowd with more of her dating exploits. 'I tell you, I've met all of *Dilli ke mashoor* Mumma's boys.' She paused for effect, adjusting the neckline of her strapless dress and pushing her oversized gold rimmed sunglasses on top of her head. '*Us din se, maine usey rakhi tie karna shuru kar diya.*'

She winked at Aria, who just shook her head, having heard a version of this story multiple times. With her inky black curls and a full-figure that she dressed to showcase every curve, the diminutive Shaan had no concept of what it would take to be a wallflower. The daughter of one of the country's most influential politicians, the fast-talking Shaan revelled in the confidence that came with her family's power. While she may have inherited her father's savvy, his diplomacy had skipped a generation. 'You need a filter,' Aria and Tara would groan, when Shaan mouthed off yet again. It was only because of her father's clout—he was famous for keeping politicians,

Bollygarchs and plutocrats out of jail, even when his party wasn't in power—that she managed to get away with social murder.

She flitted around the world, collecting people and stories that were then liberally embellished and recounted. Even Aria, who clocked up enough frequent flier miles to support an airline, could barely keep up. It was Istanbul one day, Ibiza the next, armed with a plane full of new friends; London after that; and then, with a whole new crew, Los Angeles. Shaan lived by the axiom 'work hard, play *harder*'. While most of her days were spent by her father's side, campaigning like a good daughter of India, her nights were in search of a good time.

Over the years, Shaan had become more Delhi than Mumbai, revelling in her father's growing influence, her behaviour and stories inflected with the blustery, brash mannerisms of the capital's power Punjabis. She enjoyed nothing more than intimidating simpering society girls; their fascination and fear commingling when it came to Shaan's conflicting personalities and she in turn, made no bones about her impatience with them.

'She's like Jekyll and Hyde,' remarked Tarana Chopra, of Chopra Dairy Farms, who made the colossal error of inviting Shaan to her single ladies' cooking class, held every Monday afternoon, which was then followed by a gossip-filled high tea; an invitation Shaan had gone on to ridicule at every chance. '*Ek din, sweet; doosri din, sherni.*'

'She came to my baby shower and caused such a scene,' Parul Gupta of Gupta Fashions had complained. 'All because poor Vineeta was telling us about how her new Filipino nanny expected to eat on the dining table with the rest of the family. I mean, that is so awkward, *hain na*? But Shaan took it to another level, about classism, human decency . . . etc., etc. What does she know? She isn't even *married*. Poor Vineeta was in *tears*.'

'Who knows which part of her will show up to your party? But only between you and me, *haan*,' another babbled to Tara, in London, nervous about word getting back to Shaan. Tara, a great believer in planetary alignment, simply replied that Shaan was a Gemini, her signature explanation when it came to her friend's many idiosyncrasies. Shaan could be incredibly fun, loyal to a fault, passionate and deeply empathetic, but she could also be volatile and impatient, and not one to suffer fools gladly.

'Arré, who is that piece of makhan?' Shaan shielded her eyes from the glare to decipher the identity of the figure approaching the bar, fist-bumping and hugging a few guests on his way.

Wearing a white tee that showed off every sinewy muscle, and a pair of white jeans, Rohan was only too aware that he was turning heads as he bounded into the beach club, a blonde woman on each arm, his entourage fanned out behind him. As he passed by the table, he disentangled himself from his arm candy, lowering his mirrored aviators and shouted loudly, '*Ay Dilli wali*, Shaan Singh, Cannes *mein kiske kaan kha rahi hai*?'

Shaan squealed, leaping towards him, as he engulfed her in a bear hug. 'What are you doing here? Who allowed you into this posh wedding?' She pummelled him playfully. 'And who have you picked up along the way?' she raised an eyebrow at the now pouting blondes.

'Some of us have to pay for our own charters, you know,' he teased her right back.

'*Bechara*. Okay, come meet my bestest friend.'

Shaan led him to Aria, who was watching their exchange, open-mouthed.

'Rohan, meet Aria. Aria, this is Rohan, you know who he is, na?'

'AaaaRiiiiAA,' Rohan dragged out the syllables in her name, the smirk back on his face. 'You and Merger Memsahib are best friends? *Ho nahi sakta*!' His forehead creased in mock confusion. 'Do you know what an Excel sheet looks like? And does she even know what a party is?'

'You know each other?'

'She's a fan.' Rohan laughed at Aria's evident annoyance.

Before a sputtering Aria could retort, Shaan, as she was known to do, switched tack mid-conversation.

'Oh shootttt, I'm such a ditz. I forgot you were performing last night . . . I can't believe I missed it! But *kya kare*, PMO calls and *humein toh bhagna hoga*,' she sighed dramatically.

'Aria, Rohan and I had the most ridiculous time together in Ibiza last year. It was four days of complete depravity—thanks to this guy,' she playfully punched Rohan again. 'I barely remember any of it. What ever happened to Karishma? God, what drama, with those photos!'

At a party in Ibiza, Rohan and his then-girlfriend, Karishma, an upcoming starlet, had been recognized and surreptitiously photographed, causing a tizzy on every front page in India. Caught in her itsy-bitsy bikini and in a very intimate moment with Rohan, Karishma's publicists had gone into overdrive, trying to smash the story, but ended up creating an even bigger viral sensation.

At the moment, the tabloids were playing the guessing game—are they, aren't they? And Rohan, a notorious bachelor, was enjoying every moment of this cat-and-mouse charade.

'Shush with those stories, you'll shock the princess,' he laughed at Aria's incredulous expression.

'Don't be mean to her,' Shaan put her arms around Aria, protectively. 'It's not easy being perfect all the time.'

~

Later that evening, when the bride, groom and most of the guests had called it a night, Aria and Shaan walked over to a cafe on the promenade for an early dinner. It had been weeks since they'd last seen each other, and Aria was looking forward to some one-on-one time with her best friend. They'd just ordered and Aria was telling Shaan about a new hospitality project, when Shaan began waving her arm frantically.

'What do you nee . . .' Aria turned, annoyed. Shirtless, in a pair of neon blue running shorts and a t-shirt hanging out of his rear pocket, Rohan jogged over to the table, his chest glistening with perspiration. Accompanying him was yet another perky blonde, this one in a silver sports bra with cut outs that revealed more than it concealed.

Not him again, Aria groaned inwardly. Was there any occasion that he didn't have his shirt off? And where did he keep finding these women?

'How you have the energy to run after those tequila shots . . . I don't even know?' Shaan shook her head.

'This body is a temple, honey,' he drawled, winking at them both. 'It doesn't just build itself, y'know?'

'*Uff, kuch bhi.* Build, *shuild.* Now, *aa ja*, we just ordered,' Shaan left no room for discussion, ignoring the murderous look Aria shot at her. 'Uhh, will your . . . friend . . . like to join us too?' Shaan gestured to the woman, who was jogging on the spot, her head bopping to the music playing through her earpods.

'Ro . . . HAN?!' she removed an earpod, gesturing to the road in front of them.

'Uh, uh . . . honey, you go ahead. I'm going to hang with my friends.'

Somewhat miffed, she managed to paste on a smile. 'Call me later. I'll be waiting,' she added coquettishly.

'You forgot her name, didn't you?' Shaan let out a squeal of laughter as Rohan's eyes followed the unnamed blonde pert posterior bounding off back towards the hotel. Rohan shrugged, with a cheeky grin.

'How many of these do you have stashed away?'

'Never enough,' Rohan winked as Aria rolled her eyes in disdain.

'You know, Aria runs too,' Shaan said, with a sly grin. 'And I don't mean how she runs away from any fun.'

'And you run off your mouth,' Aria replied archly, visibly irritated with her friend and this unwelcome addition.

'Running is actually such a good way to discover a new place, no? It just gives me this burst of energy, as soon as I land, I go out for a run,' Rohan smiled.

'I do the same, actually,' Aria found herself admitting. 'I tried to convince Shaan to come on a running tour through Madrid a few years ago . . .'

'And I decided to ditch her and divert my flight to Ibiza instead. I mean, who goes on holiday to exercise?'

Rohan laughed, picking a French fry off Shaan's plate. 'I still don't get how you two are friends?'

'So Shaan Singh, tell me. Your one best friend is getting married, your other best friend is . . .' he looked at Aria questioning, who just shot him a look. He continued. '*Tumhare kya* plans *hain*. Found some bechara yet?'

'I would have asked you the same question, but I see your harem is unending. So are you with Karishma or you aren't? Are you with Malika or are you not? Are you with Barbie 1, 2 or 3 from today?'

Rohan guffawed. 'You know me, living my best life. Until I find a sweet, homely girl I can take home to mum. And then game O.V.E.R.'

'Ugh,' Aria groaned loudly.

Shaan and Rohan looked at her curiously.

'That's so regressive. What is it with you men? Clearly, you're all about a good time, and the minute the girl has more than a pulse you . . .' She rolled her eyes. 'Why must every guy in this generation act like a serious relationship is like a noose around a neck?'

Rohan let out a whistle. 'Wow, SoBo girl, don't hold back. Tell me how you really feel.' He propped his arm around her chair, turning towards her.

Aria bristled. 'You've shown up to every event with a different girl, are too self-centred to even find out or remember their names, happily dismissed them when you found a better plan and basically treat women as disposable entities. It says a lot about you.'

'So tell me something, Aaarrria. If a woman, let's say, your best friend Shaan, who is known for sharing her dating escapades . . . she's entertaining right? But I become a regressive philanderer?' He cocked an eyebrow at Aria.

Aria was flabbergasted. 'Are you seriously using reverse sexism . . .?'

'Oh Ari, he's just teasing you. Lighten up.' Shaan winked. 'And besides, we're all young. Who wants a noose . . . I mean a ring, on your finger anyway? So boring.'

For the rest of the evening, despite their best efforts, Aria played the silent spectator while Rohan and Shaan's banter turned towards his latest role.

'God, I don't know how you tolerate him? Is he that sexist or is it just pure arrogance? Clearly, his self-worth is not lacking,' Aria commented to Shaan later as they headed to their rooms.

'I was wondering what all that was about,' Shaan said. 'That was prrettyyy judgy, even for *you*. I've never heard you go at someone like that, let alone someone you first met. And then you just sulked . . .'

'I'm not judgy and I didn't sulk,' Aria protested. 'I just can't bear self-important, egoistical . . .

'You know, they say actors and celebrities are all about themselves, and I've never experienced that until . . . it's like he expects every woman to come swooning when he's around.'

'Really, you got all of that from one conversation? And I hate to break it to you, but it kind of does happen to him, nearly all the time.'

'Well, I refuse to be one of those girls.'

Shaan laughed. 'Trust me honey, no one would ever mistake you. Come on, he's a good-looking guy, it's harmless fun and he was just trying to get a rise out of you. Which he did and how!'

Aria felt Shaan looking at her, as she fumbled in her bag for the key card.

'He's a good guy, Ari, behind that swag, he's a decent, decent guy. And you know how often I say that about men these days?' Shaan hugged her friend good night.

As Aria got into bed, she thought back to Shaan's words. Wasn't her reaction warranted? He was being piggish. Or was she acting like a prude? Was Shaan right, had she taken it too far?

What *had* prompted her to be so vocal?

What was it about Rohan Rawal that triggered her in such an unlikely way?

~

It was Tara's stubbornness and her father's deep pockets that saved the wedding ceremony from being a complete washout. When the weather alert mentioned a hint of rain, Tara, not wanting to leave anything to chance, turned on waterworks of her own, until Mohan Mehta agreed to the additional expense of tenting the location. The drizzle had turned into a full-blown storm, so it could be said that the father-of-the-bride had gotten his money's worth.

'Well, old chap,' Rusi boomed, as Mohan moaned about the additional expenditure. 'Money well spent, I'll say. It all went off splendidly,' as he watched Tara and Nakul pose for photographs in the orchid-festooned mandap, grateful that it was the last day. In a few short hours, he would be on a flight to Italy.

'I joke to my *jamai*. Now, her bills are your problem. Tomorrow, I'm sending her credit card statements in the Louis Vuitton briefcase,' Mohan laughed uproariously.

'We're up next, Rusi!' Arjun Singh said with a strange smile. 'And you have two to go.'

'Well, my girls know that they will just have to get married simply and quietly,' Rusi frowned.

'Where did our little girls go? Twenty-eight years, in the blink of an eye. We're old men now . . .' Arjun, said with a tinge of sadness.

'Well, I for one, am grateful for the wisdom of age. Especially when I see how these young ones behave,' Rusi cleared his throat.

'*Naya zamana hai*, Rusi. Now, these children have their own plans. We just follow them. *Dekho*, Tara, *abhi hi itni si thi aur abhi . . .*' Mohan gestured to his forearm, his eyes welling up, as he watched his daughter giggle at something the pandit said, with her new husband to be. '*Abhi, toh*, it's all, "Papa, I want the wedding *this* way, no Papa *you* don't understand, Papa, *nobody* does like that any more." *Haan, haan, aapke budhe Papa kya jaane?*'

For the remainder of the ceremony, the fathers stood side by side, watching the couple, in complete silence.

~

'Hello!'
'What's up, dudes?'
'*Kem Cho?*'
'*Sat Sri Akaal*'
'*Bonnnnsoirrr*'

Shaan's voice reverberated through the centre of the tent.

'Now that we've gotten all the boring niceties out of the way. I will introduce myself. You should all know me by now, but in case you've been hiding in your room during this extravaganza, my name is Shaan Singh. Standing next to me, this elegant, composed, *extremely* well-mannered young lady, is Aria Mistry, and we are as different as baturas and foie gras, or Jägerbombs and red wine, or . . . you get my point.'

She paused, as the audience tittered. Aria shifted nervously, trying not to notice the sea of faces in front of them.

'But one thing we have in common. We are the bride's oldest and dearest friends. And so, I guess, that makes us her maids of dishonour. Oh wait, that's just me. Aria, here, is too pure to be true.'

Aria shook her head at her friend, as the audience laughed.

'I hope you all are having a good time,' Shaan whooped, pumping her fists in the air. 'Now, raise your hands, honestly. How many of you came for this wedding to see Rohan Rawal rip his shirt off?' Half the ladies in the audience stood up as did a few men, to much laughter. Rohan leapt on his chair and took an exaggerated bow.

Shaan let out a wolf whistle as the chant 'Take it Off' gathered steam. Rohan just shook his head coyly. When the audience calmed down, Shaan continued.

'Boo, Rohan, be a party pooper. Anyway, back to the bride. Let me tell you about the first time we met Tara. She was a pudgy little girl, with big glasses—yes, yes, this same fashionista, who spends hours at the gym, working on her eighteen pack. You see those luscious curls? All a result of the oily plaits she used to sport. And the cleavage, well, I leave that to your imagination'

Tara covered her face, in mock embarrassment.

'But behind it all, the fake hair, the fake nose . . .' she paused for effect. 'Wait, you did know about that nose job, when she was nineteen? Oookay, OKAY, Whatt? They know I'm joking,' she said, as Aria shushed her.

'Or maybe I'm not,' Shaan winked. 'Behind this glamour and gloss is a heart of pure gold. Twenty-one-carat, not that rubbish eighteen-carat version that the jewellery aunties now try to palm off. I often wonder how the three of us got thrown together. And more importantly, what keeps us together? Now, if you ask Tara, she will say, it's because I'm a Gemini, Aria is a Capricorn and she's a Cancer, and she'll then proceed to give you all the characteristics of each and what happens when Mercury is in retrograde and Saturn is in alignment,' she rolled her eyes, pausing dramatically, lapping up the audience's laughter.

'I don't have such deep explanations, but I do know this. From the time she walked into our lives, she has been our North Star. And for that, to the universe and to the stars and *jo bhi aasman mein hain*, I am grateful.'

Tara blew a kiss to her friend, her heavily-lined eyes welling up with tears.

'Now, let's move on to the least important person at the wedding—hi Nakul,' Shaan said cheekily, as the groom, clearly unamused, raised his glass. 'No, in all seriousness, you look great. Did you lose some weight? Do something different to your hair? Are those new glasses?'

Aria elbowed her friend in the waist. 'Ouch.'

'Okay, okay. Nakul, welcome to the family. And by that, I don't mean the Mehtas. *Mubarak ho*, in marrying Tara you inherited US! So, be prepared for calls at all hours, slumber parties in your London home –WHAT– you thought distance was ever an issue? And every small little, tiny detail of your marriage and life dissected,' she smiled.

'You are a very, very, veryyyy lucky guy, *sacchi Tara mili tumhe*. In English, that translates,' she enunciated slowly for effect, 'You caught yourself a real star.' Here's wishing you all the love, happiness and beautiful children, who look exactly like your wife.'

She raised her glass.

'And know, my friend, that in every move you make, you have two more sets of eyes watching you.'

'Now, I'll let my sidekick say a few words.'

Aria took the mic, her hands shaking. 'Uh. I don't know how to even start after a speech like that,' her voice faltered. She straightened up and cleared her throat. 'But I just wanted to say that I wish you both all the love and happiness, today and always. This has been such a beautiful, magical few days, and the Mehtas and the Puris have surpassed all expectations with their kindness and generosity. Tara, we love you with all our hearts. You are kind, loving and have always been an incredible friend, daughter, sister and now I know you will be an incredible wife. My wish for you both, is to have a marriage of equanimity, one filled with all the happiness, love and respect in the world . . . Nakul, take care of our lovely Tara. You, like all of us, are lucky to have her.'

Aria put down the mic, and the two friends walked over to the bride's table, engulfing Tara in a long group hug.

~

'Not bad, SoBo girl,' Rohan stood up, as Aria walked past him to her seat.

'Really?' she turned, momentarily forgetting her ambivalence towards him. 'I get very nervous speaking in a crowd.'

Aria looked at him, not sure how to react.

'I thought so. You were yourself . . . no pretence, it's actually what I first liked about you. You know who you are . . . but hey, what do I know? I act for a living,' That smirk again.

Aria looked at him, not sure how to react to this admission.

They stood there awkwardly till they were interrupted by Tushad Mody, Aria's family friend.

'I thought you could use a glass of wine,' he handed one to Aria. 'You looked rather uncomfortable up there.'

Rohan let out a chuckle as Aria introduced them.

'Tushad, my man. Smooth, very smooth,' he slapped him on his back.

Tushad looked at him, bemused.

'Aria, we're being rather rude, the first course is being served and we're still not seated.'

As the evening continued, she couldn't help but sneak a few glances at Rohan, holding court during dinner, while she half-heartedly listened to Tushad prattling on.

Who was Rohan Rawal? Had she misjudged him? Or was she right and he was just always playing to his audience?

~

The door to the restroom was locked. Rusi knocked twice, contemplating whether it would be quicker to cross through the tent and go back into the hotel to the suite.

'Just a minute,' a high-pitched voice called out, followed by a giggle and a low moan.

Rusi waited. He knocked again, growing impatient.

About five minutes passed, just when Rusi was about to leave, he heard the door unlock.

A young woman in a gold-dusted lehenga, walked out, feigning nonchalance. Her eyes met Rusi's, and she smiled sheepishly, walking away, back towards the party as fast as her six-inch heels and voluminous skirt would allow.

Following, a few beats behind, was Rohan Rawal, tucking his shirt back into his trousers, wiping his nose with his other hand. He winked at Rusi as he sauntered past him, looking like the cat who got the cream.

~

He wasn't one for sentimentality, but the *bidaai* stirred up a well of emotions in Rusi. Seeing the genial Mohan break down, he realized that it was just a matter of time before Aria and Leah would marry and move away. He wasn't the religious sort either, but after all that he had seen the last few days, he fervently prayed that there were some gentlemen left in this generation and that his daughters would find them.

As they boarded their plane, en route a quick family holiday, his daughter too was dealing with a jumble of emotions. As the only one of the three left in Mumbai, Aria wondered what her life was going to be like now, with Shaan and Tara living miles away. She'd always been incredibly reserved, she could count those close to her on one hand, and the thought of making new friends, at this point, was somewhat unnerving.

Equally unnerving was the scrutiny on her love life, almost a given at a wedding. It wasn't just all the overbearing aunties in the room, her single status seemed to be on her parents' minds too. With an MBA under her belt and her position at the company determined, it seemed their attention had moved on to her personal life.

Last night, her father, in a move quite unlike her, had very obviously orchestrated a run-in with Tushad Mody, the son of a childhood friend, a well-known advocate. Tushad had lived away from Mumbai for most of his life—first to study at Eton and then at Cambridge. After passing the law exam, he returned to Cambridge to join the family law firm.

Throughout the meal, Aria half-heartedly listened to his long-winded stories about the cases he was working on, practising law in London versus India, his hiking trip in the Himalayas—all narrated in a rather affected Brit accent with some choice Gujarati swear words thrown in, which had driven Aria to hit the Montepulciano hard. She could feel her father's gaze on them, and she had woken up this morning, worse for wear and confused. She was not used to questioning her father's choices. But his overstepping last night had concerned her.

What exactly did he approve of when it came to this boy? Was it that he had grown up around the corner on Altamount Road? That their fathers had been boarding school buddies? Or that, on paper, he was the boy with the right kind of Parsi lineage?

Would she really be averse to meeting someone through her parents? She looked over at her parents, her mother flipping through a magazine, her head resting lightly on her father's shoulder. Theirs had been a love marriage, though their families had been friends for years; thirty years later, they seemed more in love than ever.

Maybe, in a few years, if she was still single, she could have that conversation with them. But, at the moment, as much as she loved her father, the thought of him dictating yet another aspect of her life was overwhelming; there were some boundaries she had to keep sacrosanct.

When it came to romance, Aria was ruled by practicality. She believed that there was the right life partner for her, someone who would be her equal in all respects. And she knew that when she met him, she would be rational, led by her head as much as her heart.

But despite all that, even for someone who considered romance flighty, Aria wanted those butterflies.

~

Ping! Shaan messaged on The Originals.

Good morning? How's the Tuscan holiday? And how's the Caribbean honeymoon?

Without waiting for a reply, she typed on.

So, let's play a game this morning.

Guess who asked for Ari's number today?

When Aria didn't respond, Shaan called her incessantly, till she answered.

'Are you really pretending you don't care who has a crush on you?' she demanded.

'Shaan, I've just woken up,' Aria's voice was drowsy. 'What are you on about?'

'Rohan asked for YOUR number!!!!!!!' Shaan exclaimed.

'What? Why?'

'Why do you think? Has it been that long since a guy asked for your number? What kind of question is that? God Aria, really.'

FINE. Let me spell it out. He's INTO you. COME ON, he was clearly flirting at the wedding.'

'Really? That was flirting? And isn't that his MO with every woman he meets? Does he even remember my name or am I to be brunette barbie number four?' Not waiting for a response Aria continued. 'Now, I love you, but I have thirty minutes before my alarm goes off for my morning run. Good night.'

Aria, burrowed her head under the duvet, now wide awake, her cheeks slowly turning a deeper shade of pink.

3

Nearly Seven Months Later
The Runway, Chhatrapati Shivaji International Airport

'I've just boarded the flight to Paris, but let me have a look at the reports, and I will call you as soon as I land.'

Aria hung up and settled into her seat, as the airline rep put her hand baggage into the overhead compartment.

'I won't be having dinner. I'm looking forward to a quiet flight,' she said to the flight attendant, who looked on curiously as Aria zipped open a pouch, snapped on a pair of rubber gloves, sprayed disinfectant and started wiping down the television screen and armrests. In a few minutes, she was completely engrossed in scrubbing down her seat, when a loud cheer erupted.

'What's happened?' she asked the now beaming attendant.

'We have a very special guest on the plane, Ms Mistry . . .' she breathed. 'It's the . . .' Her words were drowned out by another bout of loud cheering.

'I really hope this isn't going to go on for the next nine hours,' Aria was irritated by that possibility.

'Well, well, well, look, who it is,' a vaguely familiar voice said. Gloves in hand, Aria lowered the partition dividing the pods and looked up to see who had spoken. She could hardly believe it.

'Cleaning crew on strike?' Rohan smirked at her paraphernalia. 'I think I can see a spot you missed!'

There he was. In a red Gucci tracksuit, headphones around his neck, a Louis Vuitton backpack slung over his shoulder, minus the cigarette and the drink but with a coterie of grinning attendants trailing after him. It had been months since the wedding and their awkward interactions; and besides a friend request she'd received on Facebook, she hadn't thought about him much or seen him in person, but his beaming mug, promoting everything from real estate to underwear, courtesy billboards across the city, had been difficult to ignore.

Before Aria could react, he plopped down on the pod closest to her. 'If it isn't your lucky day,' he grinned at her startled expression. 'Of all the flights and all the seats, in all the world, she just walked into mine. Fasten your seat belts, darling, this is going to be the ride of your life . . .' he added in his best Bogart impression.

'I did not walk into YOUR flight; I was here first,' she retorted defensively, snapping off the gloves, spritzing the air with Bach's Rescue Remedy and rustling through her tote-bag for her files. 'Now, if you don't mind, some of us have work to do.'

An hour or so later, she got up to change (gloves and Dettol wipes in tow). He was at the bar, drink in hand, the attendants and unsurprisingly a few female passengers hanging on to his every word. He winked at her as she walked by.

'Have a drink with me, I promise I won't bite,' he grinned, gesturing to the stool next to him. The women with him turned, glaring somewhat suspiciously at the new target of his attention.

'I think you have enough of a crowd,' she said as sweetly as she could manage.

The rest of the flight passed by uneventfully. Rohan tried to make a few attempts at small talk but soon gave up and went back to his iPad and giggling girls. When they landed in Paris, Aria was whisked through the VIP entrance, into a waiting SUV and straight to the Georges V.

As they pulled into the hotel foyer, Aria felt the thrill of excitement that came with being in her favourite hotel and city. This time around, it was even more special.

As a newly minted executive director at Mistry & Sons, her 150-year-old family business with interests in shipping, infrastructure, technology and hospitality, Aria's purview extended to the latter. She was particularly fascinated by the changing nature of travel and hospitality, and she wanted to honour her grandfather's vision, the man responsible for building India's first chain of luxury hotels.

If this deal went through, Mistry & Sons would be the proud owners of one of the world's most iconic hotels that, over the years, had fallen out of favour. A major coup—the first time an Indian company had managed to make such inroads, in notoriously xenophobic France—and it would also position Aria as capable of leading the charge. She had worked on this project tirelessly for the last eighteen months, and now she was days away from seeing it to fruition.

She strolled into the gilded hotel lobby, past the large mirrors, Flemish tapestries, the marble statues and its much talked about lavish floral displays; today, an orchid jungle in vivid shades of purple and pink, serving as the perfect backdrop to a Chanel-clad girl, furiously directing her partner to get the perfect shot. The sight of a Louis Vuitton backpack stopped Aria in her tracks. The oversized monogrammed tracksuit was now Fendi but it was undoubtedly him, in stark and ridiculous contrast to the sophisticated surroundings, chatting away easily to the hotel manager.

This had to be some kind of joke.

'Are you following me?' she tapped him on the shoulder.

He turned around and burst out laughing. 'I think this may be what they call fate. And I was here first?' he didn't miss a beat, mimicking her.

'Bonjour, Bonjour, Ms Mistry,' the hotel manager greeted her. 'Ah, you've met our other special guest from Indiyaaa. You are both in suites, quite close to each other on the eighth floor,' he smiled, rubbing his hands together.

'You have to be kidding me,' Aria rolled her eyes. 'Surely, there must be some other rooms?'

'Unfortunately, we are all sold out. And this is your usual suite, non? Your office had especially requested it,' he smoothly guided them towards the elevators.

'Not to worry, sir, we are old pals,' Rohan added, slapping Aria hard on her back. 'It'll be fun, Ari-Poo.' He was laughing at her discomfort. 'We'll raid the minibar together!'

The trip, Aria thought, couldn't have started on a worse note.

London

#coffeedate
#coldbrewgivingmelife
#earlymornings

Tap. Tap. Tap. Whoosh.

It was 10 a.m., and Tara Mehta Puri was at the Starbucks on North Audley Street, waiting for a friend who was late. So, like every bored millennial, she was scrolling through social media.

Yesterday's #OOTD at Berners Tavern had garnered over 80 per cent engagement and nearly 2000 likes, and the sneak peek of her home had gotten 10,000 likes! She made a mental note to up her lifestyle content over the next few weeks.

Now at nearly 50,000 followers, Tara was happy to share every little detail of her shiny, newly-married life. Her wedding alone had doubled her clout. She was now a bona fide style influencer, with a profile in *Vogue*, multiple spreads on her home with star-architect Mindy Smith in *Hello*, and just this week, three brands she loved had been in touch for a collaboration. Sometimes she couldn't believe her luck, that she could get dressed up *and* make a living at the same time.

Not that she was in it only for the money, as she was known to say. She just *loved* fashion.

As the pampered daughter of Mohan Mehta, the canny businessman, Tara could afford to be flippant. A life of privilege, surrounded by money and all its trappings, was all she'd ever known. But her father, who came from simpler stock, had to work his way up to their Malabar Hill penthouse.

Growing up, Mohan's father had been the manager at an export house; and his mother, a homemaker with entrepreneurial dreams who supplemented the family income by running a Gujarati farsan business out of their one BHK home in a Mumbai suburb. They'd placed heavy emphasis on education but Mohan, the youngest son and the proverbial black sheep, had dropped out of college, much to their dismay. At his parents' insistence, he'd half-heartedly taken on several office jobs, but a restless spirit and a propensity for get-rich schemes kept him from being a steady employee.

Instead, Mohan found himself hanging around at the Irani cafes and sizzler joints in town, spending his last few rupees on bun maska or Campa Cola and paneer shashlik, watching the South Mumbai college students drive up in their fancy cars, casually nonchalant in their bell bottom jeans, their faces obscured by tinted sunglasses. He would try to emulate them, craving the easy confidence and entitlement that came with having money. 'I was just a boy from a simple middle-class family, but I always knew that I would achieve big things. In Bombay, all the old *raees* lived in Malabar Hill. So, one day, I knew I would open shops there and buy house there,' he had told a reporter in a profile for *Business Digest*.

Fortune favours the bold, and Mohan, quick on his feet and savvy enough to realize the changing needs of the growing Indian middle class, borrowed money to go into the retail business with a friend. At Tara's birth, he had four stores, and had made his way to South Mumbai, where he opened a 3500-square-foot flagship MohanSons in Worli, a precursor to the hypermart. He expanded his retail empire to include electronics, dry fruit, imported baby goods and clothing and staked his claim across cities in the state. It wasn't long before the pink sheets had anointed him 'Retail Raja' for his shrewd business decisions and his monopoly of the sector. His former partner and best friend was long edged out.

But it wasn't enough. With the stores running on autopilot, he left the day-to-day decisions to his brother-in-law, instead focusing on a loftier goal—the Mumbai skyline. Mohan knew that real money and power in the island city was only possible when it came to its expensive real estate, and he was determined to break ground. 'I want MohanSons to be the only name you see—you live in MohanSons building, you shop for food at MohanSons, you watch Amitabh Bachchan movies on TV from MohanSons and you get all that at fair price. No company in India will have the reach,' he had boasted in the same profile, explaining his decision to expand into real estate and his dream of setting up community townships for middle class families, like the one he had come from. By the time Tara was nine years old and his son Rishabh just a toddler, the Mehtas had moved into a sea-facing apartment in Walkeshwar. He enrolled both his children at Cathedral and John Connon School, the city's famed Anglo-Scottish institution that taught children from the country's leading families.

But despite hitting the big time when it came to his business, his social currency was still in the doldrums, and Mohan tried to compensate by profligate spending. The penthouse in Malabar Hill, where he now lived, famously had an M.F. Husain painting in the bathroom. Mohan had been fascinated by the artist who walked around barefoot at the members-only Willingdon Club and bid on several of his works, with the help of an overpriced art consultant. Oversized pieces of Italian furniture made up the 3000-square-foot living room, that opened up into a terrace overlooking Hanging Gardens. Crystal showpieces from Swarovski, Baccarat and Lalique lined shelves on the walls, Kashmiri and Persian carpets covered marbled floors and the pièce de résistance—a 25-kg chandelier shipped in from Austria. Every inch of the 10,000-square-foot home was over-decorated and overwrought, and every detail, down to the crown mouldings, had been overseen by Mohan himself. Including his wife Bina's walk-in wardrobe, stocked with all the right labels. 'In Bombay, only two things matter—dress and address,' he was known to say. His point and expenditure quite validated when the leading society magazines profiled the house and its inhabitants in extensive spreads.

When it came to his children, there was nothing they wanted for. Tara and Bunty, as his son was referred to, grew up dressed in designer clothes, holidayed internationally and were sent to the best schools and colleges abroad. Mohan was single-minded in his determination that his children would never struggle for acceptance or long for a better life, the same way he had.

That Tara had found a match in Nakul Puri, a boy from an old-moneyed, socially prominent family in London ('*Joona paisa. Bahu khandani manas che,*' he would boast to his social circle) made his heart fill with pride. Nakul's father had made a fortune in rice trading in London, and that was also where the couple had met as students: Nakul at the London School of Economics and she at London College of Fashion. For her, it had been love at first sight. He, however, took a lot longer to settle down. Nakul was notorious for his philandering ways, and Tara had to endure a great deal of heartache before finally convincing him to marry, much to her father's excitement. On paper, he was everything Mohan had imagined for his little girl. His biggest dream had been to get his daughter Tara married, international (as he was known to say!) and in million-dollar style. And thanks to his new *samdhans*, the Puris, he believed he would finally get his social due.

Tara took a sip of her latte and pinged her friend, Farah.
WRU??????

The past year though had been everything she had wanted.
She'd settled into her London life easily, keeping herself
busy blogging while Nakul was at work, spending time with
architects and decorators on their new Mews home, which
they would share with his parents; being the most dutiful
daughter-in-law, accompanying Nakul's mother to charity
and ladies' lunches; and making sure her husband came home
to a healthy dinner and a wife who didn't have a hair out of
place. In short, she was excelling in her role as the perfect
young society wife.

'Finally! You're only an hour late, that has to be some
kind of record,' she said to her friend Farah who strolled into
the cafe. 'And Fa, is that really what you are wearing to a
meditation class?' Tara laughed, taking in the fur vest and
over-the-knee croc boots.

As Nakul's wife, Tara's social set included his childhood
friends and their spouses, and the Mayfair Mrs—as their
WhatsApp group was called—met often for shopping and
lunch dates, Pilates and dance workouts. They all had the
same hair colourist, the same facialist and the same guru. It was
important to Nakul that she keep up these relationships and
so Tara, with her easy disposition, made sure she seamlessly
blended in with the crew.

Farah was her closest friend and they were now also
business partners. They were the 'Shopping Mafia Mrs', as
their husbands teasingly christened their venture, creating
unique pop-ups for Indian designers in London. Using Tara's
social media reach, their last one, over canapes and champagne
ice pops, had been a sell-out success and they were meeting

today to plan the next edition. Both the girls had credited their chanting and meditation for this higher life state of success they were experiencing and wanted to spend some time with their guru before embarking on their next project. They were, as Farah documented in their walk to their guru's centre on Instagram, so #grateful and #blessed.

New Delhi

Fuck my life, thought Shaan, as a loud ring pierced through the dark stillness of her bedroom.

'Huhh,' she grunted, reaching for the phone, her eyes still half-closed.

'Bitch, where the eff are you?! The party started two hours ago, and you are missing the most epic drama!' Shiv screamed into the receiver as the background pulsated with EDM.

Shaan's head was throbbing. Last night's combination of tequila and red wine was excessive even for her. The last thing she remembered was being up on the bar, teaching some white guy the steps from 'Chaiyya Chaiyya'. It wasn't her fault that in her dramatic re-enactment, he had lost his balance and broken his nose.

Anyway, that's where the night had ended. Or had it? She thought, stumbling to the bathroom, with the phone to her ear as Shiv rambled on and on. She vaguely remembered drunk dialing Abhishek. After that, it all was a blur. Ugh. Had she made a fool of herself with him once again?

She leaned against the sink, closing her eyes for a second, her head spinning. Opening them, she did a double take at her reflection—bloodshot eyes, smeared kohl, remnants of last night's lipstick, her curly hair even more matted than usual.

Shit. She put the phone on speaker, as Shiv shrieked on, and splashed water on her face.

It had been a month of non-stop partying in Delhi's high season and Shaan loved the invitations that were piling up in her inbox. She was no fool—she knew that her father's political power made her a must-have on every guest list, so why not use it to her advantage?

Last night it was the hosts, those uppity Khannas, who hung on to every word and didn't leave her side all night— they wanted approval for a new business park. And then there were the Mehras—after mining rights in Madhya Pradesh— who sent her caseloads of Louis Vuitton bags as soon as any new styles hit the store. Finally, there was Rishi Raichand, whose father had escaped a long jail sentence thanks to some manoeuvring by Singh Saab and was totally indebted to the family. It just took one call from Shaan and whatever she needed—access to his beachfront home in the Hamptons, a table at Le Baron in Paris—it was all organized. And the tab taken care of. All Shaan had to do was snap her fingers.

In this age of smartphones and viral social media videos, it was almost a miracle that Shaan's drunken antics had not made it to the mainstream media. The theory was that Singh Saab's paranoid behaviour and his wide network of informants ensured that no one in his only daughter's inner circle would have the guts to betray her. His indulgent ways cast a blind eye to her rowdy behaviour. '*Bachi hai, mauj masti karne do*,' he would tell his wife, Sheela, when she expressed her concern. But privately, even he worried that Shaan may be getting a little out of hand.

It didn't help that Shaan, a consummate Gemini, managed to play both aspects of her personality—the wild, crazy one when with her friends and the Anokhi-wearing politico's daughter when she was with her father. Dynastic politics was always a big talking point in India and Singh Saab, a man who had made it in politics on his own, was not one to ignore what the people wanted. He nurtured big dreams for his daughter, his only heir, and from the time Shaan was a young girl, he had her sit in on his meetings, with constituents, with *karyakartas*, patiently taking the time to explain, to answer questions, to show her how essential it was to have her voice heard.

He wanted her to see up close what real India was like, not the fancy car driving, farmhouse living India that she had become accustomed to. And in spite of her fiery personality, Shaan managed to forge connections with people immediately, showing patience and empathy; as a young girl, she'd helped found several initiatives in her father's constituency—reading programmes, summer cricket camps, after school skills training. The party workers loved when she was on the trail with her father. She was an asset, aiding in the projection of the image of a doting family whose only life's work was to build a new India. The weekly news magazine *The National* had put her on the cover, anointing her as one of the most promising next-gen leaders; the issue, framed, had pride of place in her father's study.

Shaan was also known to love a good time, and over the last few years, there had been a gradual shift in how she was living her days. Always bright, Shaan returned from university abroad brimming with ideas on how, as a young female member, she could help influence change in a decades-old party that was struggling to find its ground in modern India. She'd earnestly presented them to her father, one night in his study; a PowerPoint presentation that had been a part of her graduation thesis and had earned her a Dean's List spot.

'Firstly, you need to find young voices, *young* ideas. *Bas ab budhon ko retire kar do*, Papa,' she told her father, railing against the top heavy, traditional male leadership.

'*Main bhi budha hi hoon*, so will you take over my job soon too, Shaan?' her father laughed.

She ignored him and continued.

'In the future, social media will make or break an election, not only in India but across the world. And India is poised to become one of the world's most connected countries.' She insisted he strengthen the party's social media arm, to bring their message across to wider audiences.

'And WOMEN, WOMEN, WOMEN! How many women MPs and MLAs do we have, do you even know off the top of your head?' Singh Saab shrugged. 'The numbers are shit,' she shot back.

She paced the room. 'My generation and gender wants to be represented, or you'll find that we have no interest in actively participating. And, Papa, you NEED the female vote. It's predicted that in the next Lok Sabha election, female voters are going to kill it. *We* will be deciding the elections of the future,' she finished with a flourish, reeling off statistics, to emphasize her point. Her solution, to recruit female candidates and set up a women's focused cell, to help draft a robust female-focused agenda for the election manifesto.

'These are monumental changes you are expecting, Shaan,' he told her as gently as he could, not wanting to discourage her enthusiasm. 'But remember, babies need to crawl before they learn how to walk. This is a strong foundation to build your own political career on, but you will need to have patience. You have the platform, you just need to use it wisely.'

Over the next few weeks, they discussed in detail the role Shaan would play. She'd put off standing for elections, telling her father that she felt that systemic change needed to be implemented in the party first, and that's where she wanted to focus.

Her father watched with pride as his daughter passionately launched these ideas to the party's core committee; his life-long dream of the two of them working together, his legacy passing on, finally realized.

But even with Singh Saab's power, the wheels of patriarchy proved hard to turn, mired as they are in tradition and apathy. Shaan found herself battling systems and ideas that were held on to dearly; to her face, to keep Singh Saab at bay, the grey-haired brigade enthusiastically commended her ambitions. 'Young people like you, Shaan *beti*, are what our country and this party needs today!' Arvind Nath, the party secretary, thumped his hands on the table as if to emphasize his point further. 'We are but toh your humble servants, madamji, *aap jo bhi kahe . . .*' another wily old fox said. But, as soon as Singh Saab's attentions were diverted, in private, they dismissed her.

'*Haan, haan, ladki* foreign *se aake, hame dikhagi, yeh desh kaise chalega,*' was the most common refrain, as the older guard banded together to put spokes in the wheels she was attempting to put into motion. They'd scoff at her ideas, wondering if Singh Saab was losing his touch. After all, it was ludicrous to even think that a young woman, especially one wearing designer clothing and educated abroad, would ever understand the needs of this country better than them, with their decades of experience, their rise from the ground up, their knowledge of what the vote banks wanted?

4

Nearly Four Years Earlier

Shaan met Abhishek Ghosh, an ambitious young reporter for the international newsmagazine *Pulse*, when he'd been assigned to profile Singh Saab. On summer break from university in her final year, Shaan, an intern in the party's media cell, had been tasked with ensuring that Abhishek got access to her father, with certain limitations of course.

The sardonic, wiry former state footballer from Kolkata wasn't much older than her, but his hair already had salt and pepper streaks, as did his three-day-old stubble. His hazel eyes were hidden by a pair of Harry Potter-esque glasses, he smelt of a strange combination of tobacco and citrus, and his speech was measured, filled with long pauses that disoriented others, forcing them to fill the silence.

Abhishek lit a hand-rolled cigarette, exhaling slowly.

'So you're the *daughter*,' his lips curved into a half smile.

'And you're the *journalist*,' Shaan bristled. She pointed to his clothing—white kurta with sleeves rolled up, distressed jeans, kolhapuri chappals and a beaten leather case. 'And should

I say pseudo *jholawala*? Is it exhausting wearing a costume to work every day?'

He'd only raised an eyebrow in response. During the four-hour drive to the Singh ancestral home, he sat up front, smoking cigarette after cigarette, happily chatting with the driver, asking questions about his family back home, the progress in his village during this government's tenure, his thoughts on the new farming bill, all the while choosing to keep Shaan, in the backseat, out of the conversation completely. When they reached, he was taken to the guest house by another aide, while a peeved Shaan made her way to tell her father about their strange house guest.

Over the next few days, he kept his interactions with Shaan and her mother brief and to the point, choosing to only focus on Singh Saab. 'What kind of journalist is this guy?' Shaan muttered to her mother. 'Aren't you supposed to at least pretend to be gracious to family members, so you can build a detailed profile?'

'It takes all kinds, darling,' Sheela shrugged.

On the last night of his visit, he found Shaan, smoking furtively in the far corner of the garden, post dinner. He stood next to her, their backs to the main house, facing the expanse of green.

Shaan was acutely aware of how close they were standing and the peculiar tension between them.

'My father doesn't like when I smoke,' she stubbed her cigarette, carefully picking up the butt and wrapping it in a tissue paper she'd fished out of her pocket.

'Do you only do things your father approves of?'

She turned to face him. 'Is that on the record or off? Just trying to gauge your method here.'

'Ha,' he chuckled. 'This isn't a soft feature. I don't write for one of those magazines you probably read, you know?'

'And what do I read? *Bolo*. I can't wait to hear,' she crossed her arms, tapping her foot impatiently.

'All I'm saying is,' he stubbed out the cigarette with his foot. 'This is a serious profile that will identify where your father stands in the Indian political scene today. He's been hiding behind party walls, so to speak, for quite a while now.'

'It sounds to me that this "serious profile" may already be seriously lacking.'

He leaned in, so close that she could smell the tobacco on his breath. 'Is there something you want to say? Okay, let's get to it, where do YOU stand, Shaan Singh?'

She looked at him, her mouth curling.

'I have a lot to say, Abhishek Ghosh. Just not to you.' she handed him a tissue, gestured to the cigarette butt and walked back to the house.

~

At some point, they started hooking up. It was before the profile had come out; before she'd headed back to college.

'The summer fling I was not expecting,' she said to Aria.

When her father found out, as he always did, he expressed his displeasure. 'It's a very fine line, Shaan—journalists and politicians. And he's not even that impressive. Really, what is it in this fellow that you see?'

'*Kuch nahi*, Papa. We're just friends,' Shaan fibbed.

In hindsight, when Shaan looked back upon that summer, she admitted that their dynamic would probably be classified as one-sided, even though the sexual tension between them was undeniable. Shaan found herself making excuses to interact with him—inviting him to dinner at home on flimsy pretexts of setting up interviews with other party members, casually suggesting chai breaks at the cafe around the corner when he stopped in at HQ, messaging him links to stories. She made all the first moves, and Abhishek seemed to go along.

When, in passing, he'd mentioned a small gathering for his roommate Vir's birthday, she'd invited herself, (he'd murmured a half-hearted sure in response), arriving with a heavily frosted cake and a bottle of champagne. Besides Vir's girlfriend, a news anchor, who made a perfunctory attempt at conversation with Shaan before rolling a spliff and zoning out, and another writer, who spent most of the evening lip-locked with her editor boyfriend, Shaan was conspicuous in being one of only three women, and the only outsider, to this motley crew of reporters and editors, cameramen and photographers, who were sprawled out on the diwan and oversized cushions that made up the living room furniture of the rather dingy, two-bedroom flat.

They'd smoked, worked their way through several bottles of Old Monk and debated hotly about the role of the *bhadralok* in Bengal politics (Abhishek naturally leading the way), the People's Party movement that was gathering steam, the perennial issues of reservation and whether Aamir was a bigger star than Shah Rukh (Abhishek feigning disinterest in any films that were not Ray).

For the first time, Shaan felt content to nurse her drink, sit back and watch; no one had asked for her opinions, in any case. She was fascinated by the scene unfolding before her—at university, her group of friends were more likely to debate spring break in Cancun or New Orleans, or which college bar had the cheapest beer kegs or, if the conversation ever turned political, it was all insular—focused on American politics, Republicans vs Democrats; while her Delhi crew's opinions flowed with the tide of where the most money was to be made. This level of passionate discourse was exhilarating—these young men and women, from all over the country, who exercised their right to question everything and never shied away from having an opinion.

She kissed him that night. She'd lingered on as everyone left in the early hours of the morning, Vir and his girlfriend long passed out. There, on the rust-checked diwan, with the clashing yellow pillows, she'd leaned over, pushed his glasses off his nose and kissed him. He seemed surprised for a second, and then led her by her hand, into his bedroom. They had sex, and Shaan later recounted to Aria, he'd been happy to let her take the lead. 'Don't worry, I won't scar you with the details but let's just say, nothing is more of a turn-on than being in control, for me. Besides, it's been a dryyy summer,' she laughed giddily.

She began to spend more and more time at the apartment, arriving in the afternoons and leaving late at night, showing up with bunches of flowers to brighten up the space, using an empty Coke bottle as a vase, or bringing a tiffin made by her cook. They would have sex, and then she'd be content to spend hours in his bed, watching him write, or perusing the bookshelf in his room (Marx, Kafka, Tagore, Harry Potter!). She ate greasy Chinese takeout straight from the containers, drank more Rums and Cokes than she ever had in her life. She never stopped to gauge the reciprocity of Abhishek's feelings; if she had, she would have noticed that while he seemed to have accepted Shaan's presence in his space, he often seemed surprised to find her still there.

Shaan was smitten.

'Bas, bored ya of meeting the same types with their LV belts and their fancy cars, and their first-class holidays. Same stories, all the time. But Abhishek, he's really smart and has this desire to change things. I don't know how to explain . . .' she'd said to the girls, on their weekly call.

Just before she returned to university, Abhishek's story had gone live and all hell had broken loose at the party HQ.

'IS ARJUN SINGH, THE FORMER CORPORATE, MINOR ROYAL AND SITTING MP FROM SHANTIPUR STILL THE MOST POWERFUL MAN IN INDIAN POLITICS?'

The piece traced his rise from a corporate career to Shantipur MP, to his role as president of Azaad Party, a small but integral part of the coalition currently in power at the centre. It's not that it was all negative, but in his own way, Abhishek pierced the aura that surrounded Singh Saab; and depending on who you asked, the profile was at best a balanced view of his policies, and at worse, a damning point of view, of a man who was trying his best to hold on to diminishing political capital. It was the first time in many years that a journalist who had been given this level of access had written in less than exulting tones.

When she'd first read the piece, Shaan had been furious at his portrayal of her father. She'd fired off a text:

You're meant to be a journalist, to provide a balanced point of view. This piece reeks of your bullshit liberalism and your pseudo intelligent arguments. All hot air. Really thought you would do better.

He'd responded a day later:

Dissension and debate is the cornerstone of my writing. I wasn't writing this piece to make you or your father happy. I was very clear on that from the beginning.

Shaan shot back: *WTF does that even mean? Do you even know what a pretentious asshole you sound like?*

He hadn't bothered to reply.

So she'd showed up, to get her point across in person. She'd barged into Abhishek's room; he'd just emerged from the shower, a towel wrapped loosely around his waist, his cut midriff always a surprise, given how she'd yet to see him move a muscle.

Focus, Shaan, she told herself, holding on to the anger that had been simmering within her.

'What the hell were you trying to achieve with this?' she furiously blasted out all the aspects of the piece that were problematic. He listened silently, head cocked to one side, biting his lip to keep from laughing.

'What's so funny?' Shaan was now livid. She sat on the edge of the bed, as far from him as she could.

'You're sexy when angry.' Abhishek bellyflopped on to the bed, next to her. He touched a loose tendril that had escaped her tightly wound topknot. Shaan swotted his hand away. He reached up for the black butterfly clip that held her curls, her hair tumbled down over her shoulders. Shaan looked away. He turned her chin towards him. He kissed her, she put her hand on his chest, pushing him back. He kissed her again, this time longer and deeper. And despite her every instinct, she found herself kissing him back.

'Angry, pissed off sex.' Shaan later told Tara. 'And for the first time, it was all him. It's like the balance of power completely shifted.' She'd sighed. 'I'm not proud of myself, but this guy just pushes all my buttons and it is the biggest turn-on. That and the fact that he has the biggest balls . . . he's not scared to take on my father or anyone for that matter.'

'Aren't you nervous?' Shaan asked him, as they shared a post-coital cigarette. She leaned against his sticky chest, the temperamental box-like air conditioner whirring in the background, providing little relief against the arid Delhi summer.

She tried to ignore the feeling of guilt that had settled in the pit of her stomach.

'Of your father? Aren't you?' he countered.

She knew that her father would count this as a betrayal, but there was something about Abhishek that incited such curiosity in her. He was arrogant, condescending, infuriating but he was also smart and unafraid.

'You know what just happened doesn't mean that I'm not really pissed off. That piece was *bullshit*,' she stubbed the cigarette out, sitting up to face him. She raised her index finger . . .

'You say my father is aiding the corruption that's taken over the party, yet you don't have a single piece of evidence, or anyone who would go on record with these claims.

'You accuse him of pandering to the basest values of the vote bank, yet you choose to ignore the progress he's made in getting this party to where it is today. Should I remind you of the mass defections, the crumbling leadership before he came on, ya?'

When he didn't respond, she continued.

'Point number three. You say he supports big industry, ignores the environment, all to make his cronies wealthy and line his own pockets. Yet, you don't mention how many THOUSANDS of jobs came with those industries. Or, or—the villagers, who were compensated, fairly. Even your brethren, the press said so. Or wait, that despite this focus on industry, he's also fought alongside Adivasis to protect thousands of acres of forest land. He's been one of the ONLY politicians to do so.'

'You accuse him of being soft on women's issues and white-collar crimes, and fine, I'll give you that, he could take a harder stand and I'm pushing him . . .'

She coiled her hair in a knot, rooting around the covers, for the errant butterfly clip.

'But at the end of the day, this piece is severely lacking. It shows him as some kind of corrupt megalomaniac. Is he perfect? No! But then who is? And honestly, I just thought . . .'

'You thought what, Shaan? That just because we are having sex, I would make it favourable?' Abhishek shook his head, rolling another cigarette.

Shaan flushed in anger and embarrassment, taken aback. 'I, uh,' she stuttered.

He laughed. 'You did, didn't you? You are so used to everyone in your insular little world doing your bidding that you can't even imagine another reality. That I wouldn't be enthralled by you and your family. And that I wouldn't be able to see what your father is really like. But, let me tell you, I am not impressed, not by your power, or your father's power, not by your designer clothes and underwear, or your massive farmhouse.' He paused, his lip curling.

'This may not seem much to you,' he gestured around the room, 'But for me, it's fine. I grew up in a simple family in Kolkata, where education and knowledge, and books, art and culture, and music were honoured; where the values of an egalitarian society rather than an elitist quest for power were revered. I'm not into materiality, I'm about fairness, the freedom of expression, the freedom to question those who claim to have people's best interests at heart. The only power I am interested in is the power of the pen.'

'*Wah*, *kya* line *hai*. "The power of the pen",' she laughed, adding air quotes. 'Do you have any idea how cheesy that sounds? And how fucking naïve? Everyone wants power. Everyone wants to be close to power. That's just the way the world works. And this pen that's so powerful, let's use it to fight wars and droughts and . . .'

Abhishek slow-clapped sneeringly. 'Now, that's an original response. But what else could I expect from a narrow-minded, spoilt little daddy's girl?' he threw off the sheet and pulled on his boxers. 'What do you really know, Shaan Singh, about this country? About its people? About politics? Oh wait, let me guess—you and your "brethren" have all the answers, you found them while sipping some fancy latte in your million-dollar-college coffee shop? Or what you watched on *The West Wing*? Wake up. India doesn't work like that.'

Shaan clenched her jaw.

'You know what I realized about all you journo types? Pointing fingers is sooo easy,' Shaan was now inches away from his face. 'You call yourself egalitarian, but the bhadralok that you're such a proud member of is as elitist as it comes. Why don't you ask the rest of the people of Bengal how your lot really treats them?'

She saw the look on his face. 'What, you think I can't hold my own with your little crew—you so-called intellectuals

and anti-establishment activists, and all your "we'll save the
country, we are all equal" bullshit. Please.'

She laughed bitterly. 'You're not the first to underestimate
me. And my father. But we'll see who gets left behind,
hain na.'

'This is where this . . .' he gestured to the two of them,
'comes to an end.'

She'd stormed out, furious at herself for getting involved
with him. 'Bloody, pseudo crap that he kept pulling. I can't
believe I slept with him again, like some stupid, insipid girl.
What the hell was I thinking?' she vented to Aria.

'You do this, you know?' Aria told her matter-of-factly.
'You find these guys and then you keep going back to them,
for what? It's like the worse they behave . . .'

'I know, I know,' Shaan threw her hands up in the air.
'This is it. It ends here.'

~

'Are you watching this shit?' Shaan stormed into her father's
study, where the news played on loop on three screens. Her
father looked up from his book as she hit the unmute button.
'You have to do something, Papa. How can we even be
associated with people like this?' Shaan railed.

'Calm down, darling, and breathe.'

A week prior, the brutal rape and murder of two young
sisters had devastated the country. In the days that followed,
the CM, refusing to claim responsibility for the lawlessness in
his state and his dismal track record in women's safety, chose
to deflect the blame. The opposition and the media were up
in arms, calling for his resignation.

'I mean, instead of really investigating and looking for the perverts who did this, he is sitting in press conferences, blaming noodles, jeans, pop music and god knows what else. The gall of this man—he's slut-shaming these poor girls. It's DISGUSTING. I don't know how you can sit there being so calm. How can you not see that this reflects on you and the party?'

'I'm handling it, Shaan,' her father sighed, going back to his book.

'This is going to take us back years, Papa. You cannot let this go unchecked. He NEEDS to resign,' she urged.

But no resignation was forthcoming. Shaan was furious at her father's inaction and whenever she tried to question him, he snapped at her. In retaliation, Shaan ensured that she was front and centre at the candlelight vigils, protests and marches calling for the CM's resignation, making it to the papers for her vociferous support.

In Singh vs Singh, we have a formidable battle between two generations. With Arjun Singh's only daughter putting forth her very public support in calling for the CM's resignation, how much will that sway Singh Saab's opinions? On one hand, replacing the CM could cost the party the state elections in the next cycle. On the other hand, ignoring his behaviour will just emphasize how out of touch the Azaad Party really is with the country's needs. What will be interesting to see is how Shaan Singh develops her political voice going forward. And how much leeway she gets from the party's senior members.

Another columnist wrote:

> What do we know about Shaan Singh? And why is she
> suddenly causing such a stir in political circles? Singh Junior
> is a recent graduate of the famed Georgetown University
> in the other power capital—Washington DC. Like so many
> foreign returnees, Singh Junior comes back home with the
> goal of challenging the status quo. She's clearly fiercely pro-
> women, anti-corruption and, sources tell me, she is intent
> on rebuilding the party inside out, before standing for
> elections herself. All lofty and admirable goals, albeit ones
> that reflect a dreamy idealism. Sure, this is the reform we
> all need, but is Singh Junior really the one who will achieve
> it before the next election cycle? It makes this columnist
> wonder, will this millennial, Twitter-obsessed generation of
> armchair experts be able to bridge the chasm between their
> ideas of how governments should function and how they
> actually do?

'I don't know if I should be furious or proud,' Singh Saab said
with a wry grin at breakfast the next morning, as he flipped
through the newspaper.

'What is with this constant ageism? And especially from
so-called empowered women,' Shaan balled up the paper and
threw it across the room, narrowly missing a vase.

'I'm telling you Papa, this is your chance to show the
people that we are hearing them, that we represent the India
of the future, one that puts the safety of women as paramount.
Oh and that your daughter is not naïve.'

'All in good time, darling. All in good time,' her father buttered his toast. 'Shaan, I don't want you to get discouraged, but often there are no clear-cut answers.'

'What's not clear here, Papa? He's not leading. He's not doing ANYTHING.'

Her father continued buttering.

'And it's becoming quite clear what your answer is,' Shaan shot back.

In the end, much to Shaan's disdain, a compromise was reached. The CM apologized, allocated more funds to a women's safety drive, got the culprits arrested—one of whom was a prominent businessman in the state—and promised to enact stricter rape laws.

'You're gross. All gross,' Shaan railed against her father. 'What did Nehru say—evil unchecked poisons the system.'

'Shaan,' her mother shot her a warning look.

'I'm impressed that you're quoting Nehru,' her father chuckled. 'But you'll learn, darling. Everything is a compromise. Give and get, it's the age-old mantra of politics,' he sighed.

'But let's be clear about one thing, no more public dissension. I don't want there to be more news fodder. Is that understood?'

Shaan stormed out of the room. Maybe that columnist was right. Maybe the future she imagined was just a pipe dream.

5

Shaan hung up on Shiv and looked at her call history. 4.05 a.m. Abhishek's name was on her call list. At least she hadn't shown up at his apartment. Or had she? Everything was a blur.

It had been a couple of years since that profile. Shaan had gone from being an intern to a full-time party member, the head of the party's youth arm and the women's cell. *Pulse*, the magazine Abhishek wrote for, had to disband their India office; their international team believed it was retribution for Singh Saab's profile. Abhishek and his flatmate co-founded an online news startup that staked its claim on 'quality, unbiased journalism reporting from the frontlines of modern India'.

While Shaan had publicly only expressed her ire at the way he'd behaved, privately, she had been heartbroken. Despite or maybe in spite of Abhishek's cool detachment, she'd developed feelings for him, and it was weeks later that she realized that what she'd really been devastated by was not so much the piece on her father—but the fact that he'd been unable to see the real Shaan. Or at least the person that she considered herself to be. She'd deleted his number, unfollowed him on social media and gone back to her final year of university, determined to forget what had transpired.

When she'd moved to Delhi and joined the party, she'd gotten a message that could have only been him:

Congratulations! Daddy's little girl is going places.

She'd typed and retyped every kind of reply she could think of but decided against taking his bait.

And then a few months ago, he'd texted her again.

My sources tell me that the party seniors are not too happy with beti's big plans. Anytime you want to have a coffee, or a rum and coke, you know where to find me.

She'd ignored the message for weeks. Every time she picked up her phone, the unread icon served as a reminder.

And then, the horrific rapes had devastated the country. Shaan's fury had given way to a sense of frustration at the insensitivity shown by those in charge. And then there was her father. With his inaction, he was just as complicit. She reached peak disillusionment, questioning her future in politics. The misogyny, the red-tape, the apathy, the fear of change in the status quo. Did she really have what it took? Could she really action the change she wanted? And if she couldn't, was she still willing to be a part of the system? At what point would she be taken seriously? At what point could she stop running to her father for help?

Her questions remained unanswered. When she tried to talk to her father, he would just counsel patience. Tara was too engrossed in her relationship with Nakul and life in London, and Aria was just about finding her own way at Mistry & Sons.

And so, she texted Abhishek. She was curious to see him, to hear what he had to say and to see if he would apologize for the way he had behaved all those years ago.

They met at a tiny coffee shop in Hauz Khas. 'I write here most evenings, their cold coffee is decent,' he held the chair out for her. 'And plus, I don't think anyone will recognize us.'

She looked at him curiously. He'd become leaner since she'd last seen him, swapped the kurta for a mandarin collar shirt and slacks; the Harry Potter frames for sleeker metal ones.

'Arré, arré, corporate *ban gaye*. Whatever happened to "I don't believe in capitalism, I'm all for free society, blah blah", all that bullshit?' she found herself awkwardly joking, as he ordered for them both.

He'd raised his eyebrow, deflecting her question.

'So, I'm waiting?' She stirred the thick, milky drink with the plastic straw that the barista had put down in front of her.

'For?'

'Your apology is still pending.'

Abhishek just laughed, leaning back into the chair. Shaan met his gaze, unflinching.

'Okay, here's what I think, let bygones be bygones. And consider this an olive branch. Let me help you.'

Shaan looked at him for a few minutes, stopping only to take a sip of the sweet, icy drink.

'And what makes you think you can help me? Or that I need your help?'

He sighed. 'Your intentions are noble, Shaan. But in all seriousness, this country wasn't built in a day. And what led you to believe that a party that's been around since Independence was going to do a full U-turn when for so many years it's been serving the needs of its members and your father just fine?'

'I'm not here to hear criticism of my father,' she said hotly. 'And definitely not from you.'

'Then what are you here for?' he leaned back, his arm outstretched on the wooden chair next to him.

She sighed. 'I don't know.'

She faltered, 'I don't know why, but I thought you of all people may understand. To most of my friends and the people I hang out with, well . . .' she gave him a look.

'Are you really telling me that the Jor Bagh scions have no interest in how the country they are looting really works?' he mocked.

She rolled her eyes.

'So, tell me what's going on,' he prodded.

Shaan took a final sip of the now watery dregs of coffee and cleared her throat. She told Abhishek about her thesis, the three-point plan she had presented to her father, the comatose women's cell that she had revived, the corporate sponsorship she'd negotiated for pilot programmes for rural women, the focus on recruitment of more women candidates.

She sighed, 'But it's been one obstacle after the other. Why can't they see that getting more female candidates is a good thing, if for nothing else but that it will help them secure women's votes!' She shook her head. 'Anyway, here I am, only talking about women, women, women. And then, when these awful rapes happen and that asshole CM spews so much shit, my father does zilch, what does it look like? That I'm just talking through my ass. That we are a party of hypocrites—we build these great campaigns and yet when it comes to actually ensuring the safety of women, forget the basics, we're in effect slut-shaming them.'

She laughed bitterly.

'It's no wonder that all my MNCs want to pull out. I feel like I'm banging my head against a brick wall. Sometimes

I think, this country's leaders would rather get into debates about where fricking cricket is played and which Bollywood movie should be banned, rather than focusing on what really matters. Do I want to be a part of such a broken system?'

Shaan took a deep breath.

'So, in effect. I'm lost. And I don't know why I thought coming here would help.'

They sat in silence for a while as she poked the remnants of ice with the straw.

'Say something!' She nudged his foot with hers, impatient for a reaction, a response, something from him.

He removed his glasses, wiped them with a tissue and looked at her.

'I'll say that I misunderstood you, Shaan Singh. You're not the princess I thought you were,' he said with a smile. 'More like a minor royal.'

'God, I knew I . . .'

'Listen,' he said, enunciating his words. 'You know how I feel about the party and its wavering policies. In my opinion, yes, it needs a full overhaul, get rid of all the lifers. Is it naive? Is it going to happen?'—another long pause—'probably not. I'm jaded enough to know how little change actually happens.'

He paused again.

'Do I think you should stop? As a friend, and I think we are friends, hain na?' he imitated her, his teasing voice taking on a higher pitch. He paused again. 'You may not make the biggest impact immediately, but slowly, SLOWLY you'll chip away. And then, you can finally move their politics to the left, where they should be,' he laughed at his own wit.

'Uff, this is all a joke to you. I should have never come,' Shaan got up to leave.

Abhishek held on to her arm, and she felt a familiar thrill go through her. 'I'm serious when I say I'm here if you need me. What I can do, I'm not sure, but I can at least listen?'

In the weeks that followed, she took him up on that, popping into the cafe on the pretext of a cold coffee, when she knew he would be around.

'What can I say, you've gotten me addicted,' she joked, the first time she'd orchestrated a run in. They'd chatted till the owners pulled the shutters down. The times after, she hadn't even bothered coming up with an excuse. And he never seemed surprised to see her.

He'd changed, Shaan told Aria, who immediately expressed her misgivings. 'He's mellowed, matured, he's willing to listen, he's being a good friend.' And in reciprocity for this newly-established friendship, Shaan facilitated a few ministerial meetings that he needed for a story. She'd given him a heads-up on some changes in her father's committee before they had happened, allowing his website to break the news first. Her father hadn't been too pleased, but she'd been amply convincing that the website was tracking high enough numbers that all past transgressions would have to be ignored.

She started putting in more effort into how she dressed, when coffee began stretching to nachos and beers at the Irish pub, across the street.

When the women's cell completed a milestone under her leadership, expanding their membership significantly and putting in place several key campaigns in her growing network of rural villages, she'd shown up at his new apartment, around the corner from the cafe, a larger, more light-filled space with a terrace and a home office, bottle of rum in hand. 'I thought we could celebrate! Imagine, four female *sarpanches* across my home state!' she said excitedly, as he let her in, surprised. He'd poured them both a drink and settled on the couch, watching her pace the room, talking and gesticulating non-stop with one hand, her drink sploshing out of the glass in the other.

She sat down next to him. 'Finally, finally, I feel like I can breathe. I did this, I made a difference!' she leaned in and kissed him.

'Shaan,' he gently pushed her back with one hand. 'I don't . . .'

She'd put both their glasses down, put her arm around his neck, and kissed him again.

'Shaan,' he said as firmly as he could, disengaging himself from her embrace. 'I don't think this is a good idea.'

Shaan looked at him, the confusion that flitted across her face soon replaced by fury. Abhishek got up and walked to the other side of the room. With his back to her, he exhaled.

'I . . . I just don't feel that way any more.'

'Turn around and talk to my fucking face!' Shaan's voice rose. 'At least look me in the eye and tell me you used me, for all those inside tips, all that information, for your stories,' she laughed bitterly. 'I would at least respect you for that.'

'Shaan, relax. It's not that.'

'Then what is it? What were the texts, the coffees, the long conversations?'

'I was just being a friend,' he gulped down the remnants of his drink. 'I don't feel that way about you. If I'm being honest, I don't know if I ever did.' He took off his glasses, wiping them with the corner of his shirt.

She looked at him incredulously.

'So, what was it before? Just sex? You and Vir must have had such a laugh. Stupid Shaan Singh, she doesn't even know

when she's being played,' Shaan was horrified to feel tears fill
her eyes. She refused to let him see her cry, she had at least that
much dignity left.

She grabbed her bag and made her way to the front door.

'Shaan, wait,' he grabbed her arm.

'Now you'll see what Shaan Singh can do,' she shrugged
him off, her lips curling. 'I hope the articles were worth it—
because you've now made an enemy for life.'

~

The incident with Abhishek shut Shaan down completely. In
the days that followed, she feigned illness at work, ignored
calls and messages from Aria and Tara, and despite her father's
many entreaties, refused to confide in him. She spent her
days holed up in her bedroom, flipping through channels,
showering occasionally and living in a rotation of printed
kaftans, smoking cigarette after cigarette—brazenly in the
garden outside her room—and downing cups of coffee.

This continued for a few weeks, until one evening, while
her parents were having a post-dinner drink, she emerged in a
sexy mini dress and high heels, curls blow-dried straight, eyes
heavily lined with kohl.

'Shaan? Where are you going, dressed like that?' Sheela
asked, surprised.

A dinner at the Puris. The next night, it was a birthday party
at the Sahnis. Over the weekend, it was a quick trip to Jaipur
for the opening of a new bar. Then it was the Talwars' tenth
wedding anniversary in Dubai and a bachelorette in Bangkok.
Shaan's schedule was now filled, her days spent sleeping and the
nights out on the town, only to return home with the milkman.

'She's getting out of control, Arjun,' Sheela complained, after yet another one of Shaan's all-nighters, as she slithered into the house as her parents were having their morning tea. 'For how long are you going to indulge this behaviour? She's not a teenager any more. In fact, she was a lot more responsible then,' she added, pouring herself another cup.

'*Lambi rassi di ho, usse,*' Singh Saab's sister, who was visiting, concurred. '*Aur, sach kaho, ab toh shaadi keh liye* time *toh ho gaye.*' Sheela nodded in agreement.

'It all seems so pointless,' Shaan told Aria, who received a call from a worried Sheela, asking her to talk some sense into their daughter. 'I refuse to waste my youth on things that aren't going to change,' she said morosely. Then brightening up, '*Yeh Jawaani, Hai Dewaani*, baby.'

'Shaan, I was thinking,' her father brought up over dinner. 'There's this young NRI chap I met from a tech company in the US. He's been pushing us to build some kind of app and to use it to target women voters and for us to collect data. I'm not quite sure how it works, but it's similar to what you've been saying for so long. I'm thinking of getting him on board. See what you think?'

To keep her father at bay, she attended a few meetings, but was soon distracted.

'What is it, Shaan? What will it take for you to get serious?' he asked, exasperated, when she'd ditched yet another meeting. 'I know something happened with that journalist chap. Why won't you talk to us?'

Shaan had just looked down, picking at her food and refusing to meet her parents' concerned gaze.

Taking a deep breath, he said, 'Since you won't talk to us and since you feel it is okay to do everything and go everywhere except work, I'll surmise that it's something related to work and this fellow,' he sighed. 'I haven't raised you to be some silly lovestruck girl who will let a boy deviate you from your life's plans.'

'It's not only that,' she shook her head. 'I don't want to talk about it.'

Singh Saab waited expectantly but when he realized no more details were forthcoming, he continued.

'Listen, beta, if you've realized that politics isn't where you would like to be, then I will understand that. But I don't want you to waste your life like this, do something, *anything*. But you cannot continue partying all night and sleeping all day. At some point you have to grow up.'

His pleas fell on to deaf ears, and Shaan continued, taking less and less responsibility for her decisions. And so, Singh Saab, on the insistence of his wife and sister and without his daughter knowing, put out feelers for a prospective match. As liberal as he had been with her upbringing, maybe they were right, maybe once she was settled, Shaan would have to make better choices. And maybe a steady relationship would be just what she needed to move ahead.

Which is why, on that Sunday afternoon, post her escapade on the bar, he summoned her to the lunch table. 'Still in your kaftan?' he commented archly, as a visibly hungover Shaan, her face now scrubbed clean, hair tied back with a scrunchie, served herself a heaping mound of chicken curry and rice.

'*Jee* Papa, you know the Khannas, they had this dinner, and they just wouldn't let me leave,' she said, looking down at her plate with a shrug. 'They send you their best and said they are happy to help in any way with the election.'

'Hmmph. Speaking of the election, I'm going to the farmhouse with some party members to brainstorm next week, and I'd like you to come with me. You've already put in so much effort into the campaign, it seems a shame to waste it.'

Shaan didn't respond.

'Also, don't make any plans this evening. We have guests coming over. Ram Chandra Sharma and his wife and son, Pratap.'

'But Papa,' Shaan, looked up from her plate. 'I have to go to Deeya Talwar's birthday drunch.'

'Drunch. Never heard of such a thing. Cancel. Shower and change out of that kaftan, for god's sake.'

6

Like every seasoned politician, Ram Chandra Sharma was bringing his son Pratap over to get Singh Saab's blessings. Shaan was right on one front—with the political climate so untenable, it was really up to the younger generation to spread their message or the party risked being seen as out of touch with what the voters wanted. While her push focused on diversity and female candidates, for many of the self-serving senior politicos, keeping it in the family, so to speak, was the solution.

Ram Chandra Sharma, a curmudgeonly old hand if there ever was one, knew that his position was especially precarious. He hailed from a well-rooted family of zamindars-turned-politicians; his uncle still held office as the MP. He'd ensured that for decades, his political hold as an MLA from Karoli had been largely unopposed, coasting by doing minimum work and gaining maximum benefit. But in the past few years, ill-health and younger, more politically inclined activists, had put a dampener in his grand plans. So, to ensure the prodigal son got the Iron Throne—quite literally, because Karoli was a veritable mine of the metal—he was at the Singhs' well-manicured Lutyens home at 5 p.m. sharp, with son in tow and a tray of gifts.

They say the apple doesn't fall far from the tree, but in this case, it seemed the son was a whole other case of fruit. Pratap had inherited his father's thirst for power, was a lot more determined to play the game and would do whatever it took for him to get into the country's inner circle. And he knew that impressing Singh Saab was his means to get there. Their paths had never crossed, but he'd heard stories about Shaan— her partying ways, the dalliance with a left-leaning journo, her women-focused agenda, which Sharmaji had not minced his thoughts about—and Pratap had soon gathered that Singh Saab's only Achilles heel was his daughter. Like every power player, Pratap knew that you always find the weakest spot to make your mark.

'Welcome, welcome,' Singh Saab's voice reverberated as his guests were ushered on to a covered patio where a high tea was laid out. 'It's been too long since we saw you, RC. Where have you been hiding?'

'You know how it is, Singh Saab. Getting away to Delhi has become so difficult. And now my health also doesn't allow the travel,' Sharma moaned, accepting a cup of tea from the bearer. 'Too much you've done, Sheelaji! Why so much effort?' He eyed the spread, adjusting the buttons of his already too tight beige safari suit. 'My wife wanted to be here, but my daughter has just had a baby and needed her mother. You know how children are these days.'

'Mubarak, mubarak, Nanaji. We are just waiting for that part of our lives to begin,' said Sheela, as she saw Shaan quietly walk out and seat herself on the swing furthest from Pratap and his father. Shaan sneaked a quick look at their young guest.

She'd caught on to her father's game and gathered that this afternoon was some kind of set-up.

Unsurprisingly, Pratap was dressed in the uniform of every male millennial politico, that is, when they weren't in the requisite white kurta-pyjama—jeans, loafers and a navy bundi paired with a white short-sleeve shirt that accentuated his beefy arms. He'd shaved his head bald, a pre-election visit to Tirupati, she gathered later, and when he stood up to greet her, he loomed over her, more than a foot taller.

Was that a tattoo she spotted on his left wrist? Shaan narrowed her eyes, curious to ascertain the shape of the inky blue blob, hidden by a leather watch strap and puja *maulis* in varying shades of crimson.

'Shaan beti, come here.' Her father pointed to the seat next to Pratap. 'Meet Sharmaji and his son, Pratap. Pratap hopes to contest as MP in the next election.'

Shaan walked over, greeting them both with a namaste and a demure smile, and sat primly, hands folded in her lap, next to Pratap. Singh Saab was relieved that his daughter had, at least, made a little effort with her appearance. Shaan had tamed her curls and they hung naturally. She'd lined her eyes with kajal, put on a little gloss and a delicate blush salwar kameez; though her eyes gave away how hungover she really was.

When the bearer came over with the tea trolley, Shaan leaped up, grateful for the distraction, busying herself helping fill Pratap and his father's plate with piping hot bhajiyas, chutney sandwiches and the Mumbai-style sev puri their cook was famous for.

'Sugar?' she asked him, as she poured tea from the porcelain teapot.

'Do you have stevia?' he asked.

'One cube won't hurt, hain na.' She plopped it in the tea. 'You can CrossFit a little extra tomorrow,' she smirked, directing the bearer to hand him a filled plate and a steaming cup.

He laughed. A deep throaty laugh. 'Busted. How did you know I CrossFit?'

She'd googled Pratap earlier that afternoon, scrolling through his public Instagram page, which was populated with red-tilak, hand-folded, white kurta-pyjama images, news stories lauding his and his father's achievements, quotes from Mahatma Gandhi, Martin Luther King and JFK, and photos of his father with dignitaries. Just moments before Pratap and his father had arrived, she'd uncovered videos of him training, a news clipping of a broken engagement and a photo of him, standing muscle to beefy muscle with Sal Khan, at a film premiere. But she wasn't about to let on her sleuthing.

'Genius *hoon*,' she laughed lightly, taking her cup and going back to her original seat on the swing, putting enough distance that she could observe and listen.

While they ate, the conversation stayed light, with Sharmaji trying to bend Singh Saab's ear on party gossip and the recent run-in with a young MP and the British police while on holiday in London. The press in India hadn't managed to get a whiff of the whole story just yet, but when it did, the party would have to go into major damage-control mode.

'But maybe the media here should get the story. The real one!' Shaan piped up from her perch on the swing. Sharmaji turned his head, his annoyance at being interrupted evident. Shaan ignored it, barrelling on. 'It's a pure case of racial profiling. My friend Aanchal was also there. These white guys were hitting on Ravi's girlfriend at a bar, and when he went to defend her, it escalated. The witnesses supported his story, and so the police were forced to drop the case. But, of course, the more fun story is how badly behaved Indians are when they come to London.' Shaan rolled her eyes. 'The days of the British Raj are clearly not over.'

'*Meine toh suna ki* Ravi *kuch phirang ladkiyon se* misbehave *kar raha tha.*' Sharmaji looked put out at his story being hijacked. 'It is a good thing that no one took a video. I tell you, Singh Saab, this younger generation has it so much harder. So many people looking all the time, with their phones, and what is that twatting, twittering all the time? I tell Pratap, now is not the time for *mauj masti*, but to put on your head and work. And nobody is your friend.'

'*Aap theek kehte hain*, Sharmaji. You can find everything now on the internet—nothing is hidden any more and nothing goes away,' Shaan said slyly. 'Technology can be your enemy, but also your friend.' She laughed. 'Just like us, hain na.' Her father shot her a warning look.

'How is Naveenji? *Suna hain, ki aap dono mein kuch problems hai?*' Singh Saab referred to Sharma's uncle, the current CM. The family friction between the two made for gleeful headlines.

Sharmaji sighed. '*Kya bataoon*, Singh Saab. *Abhi hamara zamana kahan. Agle* generation *ka* time *aa gaya hai.*' He pointed to Pratap. 'See, Singh Saabji, his beti Poonam, she is in family way, so who will take on? *Aap se ham tassali lene aaye hain.* Pratap will win the seat, I am confident. We need young, dynamic, active leaders, Singh Saab,' he urged.

Time for the elevator pitch. Pratap, who had been quiet so far, cleared his throat, taking the opportunity to explain to Shaan, Sheela and Singh Saab what his plans were.

Infrastructure, he explained, was a big part of his campaign; he was determined to adequately utilize the MPLADS funds to finish the network of highways that the current government, that is his uncle, had left incomplete. He moved on to talking about the rights of workers in the mining industry along with his long-standing passion for fitness and nutrition that he would like to adapt in schools and in the police force. '*Maine Sal Sir se baat kiya hai*. He said he will come to the rally for me. And he will also give motivational talks on the importance of being healthy.'

Singh Saab nodded, waiting for his guest to go on.

'I will tell you frankly, Singh Saab. My uncle's campaign is on caste-based politics. That has to be left behind. Our focus has to be on development, on infrastructure, on economic reform.'

'See the work Shaan is doing.' He looked towards her, Shaan reacting in surprise to hear her name spoken. 'Giving rural women employment opportunities, making them empowered. All this, *you* have taught her, shown her. THIS is how our country moves ahead. In politics, we need more examples.'

Shaan narrowed her eyes, at him, somewhat skeptical.

Later, even Sheela, the most cynical of the three, would tell her husband how impressed she was with the way he had spoken. 'He's a politician, through and through. This may be the first time you've had someone come pitch you in this manner. If he can put his money where his mouth is, well . . .'

The high tea ended on a high note, with a peg of whisky and a fond farewell, but not before Singh Saab strongly suggested that Shaan and Pratap find some time to hang out in the near future. Never one to miss an opportunity (especially when he only stood to gain), Pratap DMed her later that very night and drinks were confirmed for Thursday night at The Oberoi.

~

PING! PING! PING!

Who's awake? Chat needed. ASAP. Shaan typed furiously on The Originals WhatsApp group.

Hello? Hello? Answer girls.

Every Sunday, the friends would usually get on to a three-way call, no matter where they were. It was their way of staying connected, but for the past two Sundays, this hadn't happened and Shaan was desperate to talk to her two confidantes.

'I mean, where the hell were you guys?' she wailed, puffing on her e-cigarette as first Tara, all red-faced and sweaty, and then Aria, poised as always, joined in.

'Sorry love, just got out of a Psycle class. Kale Me Crazy, please.' Tara spoke off screen.

'Okay, Crazy. Who goes for a run at 6 a.m. on a Sunday?' Shaan laughed, despite herself.

'That's awful, really. Lame. And it's a spin workout, and it was at 8 a.m.,' Tara rolled her eyes.

'And you, Princess Aria, where in the world are you?'

'I'm in Paris. Work.' Aria cupped her hands around her cafe au lait.

'London. Paris. The village of Delhi.' Shaan gestured dramatically to herself. 'Anyway, not that you both care about my village life and the fact that my father is acting like I'm some piece of political property, but seriously, I need an exit strategy.'

After their first meeting, Shaan and Prats, as he had told her to call him, had ended up having drinks—a relatively tame experience. A few quiet dinners followed.

'He isn't a great conversationalist. I have to drag the words out of him. And when he does talk, I want him to shut up. He's obsessed with his workouts, *yeh nahi khana*, carbs, protein blah blah, some cricket team that he is on, and oh yeah, the actor Sal Khan. I've never met such a fan. I mean, I really couldn't give a fuck what Sal Sir eats for breakfast.'

Tara burst out laughing.

'But then . . . when he starts talking about work and his campaign, even me in this current blah state can't help but listen. He's trying to look like Sal, with those big muscles, so you think, you know, that there's not much up there. But when he talks about the work he wants to do, it's impressive. I hope it isn't just talk, but he makes sense.'

'But the only thing is this, three times during our dinner last night, he jumped up to take a call. What was so urgent that he had to pick up a call during a date?'

Anyway, as she said to the girls, there hadn't been any other major red flags. Until the previous night, when he invited her over to his place for a quiet evening in. Or, at least, that's what she thought. Shaan told the girls that she wasn't sure she was ready to take it to the next level, but still ended up going, curious about his intentions. 'Also, it was Saturday night, everyone is in London, and I was bored.'

On reaching his Gurgaon penthouse, she was taken to a dark study, where Prats was nursing a scotch, surrounded by a few 'hangers on'. After offering her a drink and patting to a seat next to him on the sofa, Prats proceeded to pretty much ignore her, focusing instead on the cricket match playing on the television, breaking into a ghazal as some '*dukhi* singer' crooned in the background. At one point, one of the girls, Ira, who was playing hostess, ordering his staff around non-stop, had started massaging Pratap's shoulders and neck.

'After about an hour and a half, I'd had enough. I don't know what his deal was. First off, at our age, who the eff goes into ghazals and shayaris? I swear, if I had heard 'wah, wah' once more from his cronies, I was going to punch them.'

Tara was now shaking with laughter.

'I'm sorry Shaan,' she said, in between giggles. 'But your stories are really something.'

'Wait, it gets better. So, this snot nose, blonde bimbo Ira, who was really pissing me off . . . every time Prats would try and talk to me, she would find some way to distract him. The entire evening, her decibel level was beyond shrill, especially when she spoke to Pratap's staff. So, Madam Ira then decides to nibble, and I swear, like a little rat, on this miniscule bite of cheese and a cracker, and in a very not-ladylike manner, I have to say, spits it all out. Apparently, the imported gouda that she had bought "just like yesterday, at the new supermarket in Def Col, was disgusting".' Shaan mimicked Ira's high-pitched indignance.

'This is why like I just can't live in this country. I mean, we just can't get good quality basics. Like three weeks ago, I ordered this cream that my dermat in London says I have to use for my pigmentation and it's been stuck in Customs and it's like they refuse to release it. And then I go to take my nephew to Häagen Dazs for ice cream, and they have no flavours. I'm like what the hell. The dude behind the counter says, madam, it's all stuck in Customs for past two months. And like, Customs has all this stuff like just *rotting*. I mean, like look at Dubai, everything comes from abroad, and like the

food is just so fresh, hain na. I just don't understand why our
government can't get its act together,' Ira ranted, as the two
other girls nodded sympathetically.

'Honestly, Prats,' she turned to him, smiling sweetly.
'When you become PM, you have to make things easier,
like . . .'

'Really Prats,' Masoom nodded. 'I mean, look at our
quality of life. The pollution, like, you have to run away from
Delhi in like smog season. Luckily, the house in London is
always there, you know.'

'Then move,' Shaan snapped.

'Excuse me?' Ira said archly.

'You heard me. I said, if you have so many issues with
living in this country, move.'

All the others turned their heads.

'What do you mean?' Ira huffed.

Shaan sighed. Her voice took on a bored tone.

'Do you even vote? From this conversation, I doubt it. I
mean, you're hoping that your friend becomes PM, which let
me tell you is laughable, considering he's not even an MP yet,
but let's go with it. So, your friend becomes PM, and his most
pressing business—forget about the fact that this country has
millions of other issues that need tackling first—is that he can
ensure that you get your avocados and cheese? I mean, are you
really that stupid?'

Ira and Masoom's mouths fell open in a synchronized
motion.

'And I'm so sick of silly, entitled people like you all
moaning about quality of life. Don't like it, then do something.
And if not, then shut the fuck up and deal—or just leave.'

'Oh, Shaan,' Aria shook her head. 'You did not.'

'And how did YOU leave?' Tara asked, still giggling.

'Pratap just laughed, while the Def Col ditzes sulked in the corner. Anyway, I'd had enough, and when I'm at the door, he literally just gives me a wave, looking up for a second with this weird smile and then goes back to the match. I mean, I just don't get it. Why even call me? Was this all a play to show me how he sets the dynamic? And then this morning, my dad asks me with a big smile how my evening was. I know him, I can already see him planning the engagement. He and my mother are completely swayed by this boy, and I just . . .'

'Just, what?' Aria prodded.

Shaan took a breath. 'So, rumour is—and I really don't know how it hasn't reached my dad, because I really would like to think he hasn't ignored it—is that Pratap has been having a scene with Serena Varma for a while now. Naturally, his parents aren't happy and he's smart enough to know that politically he needs to keep it on the DL.' Serena Verma was the forty-year-old married Bollywood bombshell, who was every hot-blooded Indian male's pin-up. The fact that she had a husband and child hadn't made her any less desirable.

'No wayyyyy,' breathed Tara, always alert for juicy gossip.

'Shaan, you know your father is obsessed with you, and he's not going to want you to be unhappy,' Aria rationalized. 'Just talk to him and explain the situation. This isn't the dark ages, where he would expect you to marry a stranger!'

'Do you even like him?' Tara asked.

'I really don't know,' Shaan admitted. 'He seems like an okay guy, but then there's this Serena thing, and am I attracted to him? I don't know. And then, the thing with Abhishek really,' her voice cracked. 'I still don't know where my head is at. But with my parents, I've cried wolf too many times when it comes to this whole matchmaking thing, and on paper and in person, Pratap is like the dream son-in-law for them. Then there's Vidya Bua, she's been on my dad's case, how she thinks I'm going to end up an old spinster and the only way to settle my wild ways, according to her, is to marry me off. I don't know, I don't even know what to say . . . I don't think they'll believe me any more.'

'Is this something you even want to explore?' Aria asked.

'I'll have another espresso and the cheque, please,' a male voice rang out in the background.

'One second, hang on, whose voice was that? Who are you having coffee with?' Shaan's eyes narrowed suspiciously. 'Whose arm is that?'

'Huh, uh, what? Nobody! I'm, I'm . . . on my own,' Aria stammered, taking a second to compose herself. 'You know how these French cafes are, the tables are all crammed together. Anyway.'

'I DON'T believe you, Aria Mistry! Pleasure or business, hmm? And in the city of love of all places, where you are very conveniently stuck. Don't you DARE lie to us.'

'Read. The. News. It's a natural calamity,' Aria said as calmly as she could muster. 'Anyway, have to say bye girls, I have a meeting in ten minutes.' Before they could get a word in, Aria signed out.

'But it's Sunday!' Both Tara and Shaan screamed in unison at the now blank screen.

~

'Close call,' he whispered in Aria's ear, making her insides flip. As he drew her closer, his hand pulling her waist, she closed her eyes and breathed into his musky cologne that now enveloped her days, making it difficult for her to discern any other scents around her.

'So, when are you going to tell them about us?'

7

Paris

'What do you mean there are no flights?' Aria's usually calm voice rose an octave as she paced the hotel foyer.

It had been a frustrating few days. At the very last moment, the deal Aria had been working on for the last two years had stalled. She had spent the past week just trying to get back into the boardroom to see how to salvage the situation.

'Maybe, it's better we do a new round of meetings when Mr Mistry is present?' one of her father's executives had said, not so subtly, after a particularly frustrating discussion with their French partners.

'Mr Trivedi. Are you trying to say I cannot get these issues sorted without him?' she snapped. Though, if she was being honest, she wasn't sure she could. The last thing she wanted to do was make an SOS call to her father. He hadn't been pleased with the break in negotiations, but had rallied behind her in support. 'I know you can handle this, Aria. What are the three things I've always taught you—never concede, use your leverage and don't be hesitant to call their bluff.'

She was sick of the French. Sick of their snobbishness. Sick of men in suits treating her like some little rich girl on a whim. Sick of living out of her suitcase. Sick of constantly wondering if she was worthy of this role. Sick of wondering if she even wanted it. She just wanted to get home, crawl into her own bed and never get out.

But nature, as it always does, had other plans. Another volcano had erupted in Iceland, leading to a cloud of ash, making air travel across Europe an impossibility and causing complete chaos on the ground. Her flight back to Mumbai had been cancelled, with no rescheduling in sight. Her assistant had tried everything—checked every airline, called every private jet operator in the region and had even tried, without success, to get Aria on a train to London, but it had all come to naught. Right now, it seemed her only option was to take a boat from Normandy to Southampton, and even that was proving to be a stretch.

Her family was anything but supportive when she called them, whining.

'It's Paris, for god's sake!' her sister Leah said, with her trademark eye roll. 'Tough life, a forced holiday in such a dump. Live a little. Eat a good meal, have a drink or five, hook up with a local hottie.'

'Darling, why don't you go shopping,' her mother suggested. 'I think you could do with a new wardrobe.'

While her father, ever the workhorse, jumped into the fray, trying to get more meetings on the table.

Aria was not good with being spontaneous. Uncertainty made her uneasy and even in a large city, being stuck with no way out enhanced her claustrophobia. She was so used to scheduling every minute that the openness of her days was almost terrifying. So far, she'd been up since 6 a.m., finished her morning run, had her green juice, egg whites and avocado in her suite while fielding calls back home. It was now 11 a.m., and she was at a total loose end. The concierge, seeing her pace up and down in the lobby, kindly suggested she check out the new exhibit at the Musée d'Orsay; she was about to head in that direction when she heard a familiar voice.

'*Hum tum*, Paris *mein bandh ho jaaye, aur chabi kho jaaye . . .*' he sang out, causing several heads to turn and Aria to cringe. 'I guess we are just destined to be?' He bounced across the lobby in her direction.

There he was again—Rohan Rawal, this time dressed in a lilac tracksuit.

'What is it with the nineties hip-hop star vibe?' she thought to herself, further irritated at the sight of him.

It had been a miracle, Aria thought, that she had managed to avoid bumping into Rohan so far, though she'd gathered from the gaggle of giggling Indian teenage girls hanging out in the lobby that he was still in the city. Truth be told, it had more to do with his late-night shooting schedule and the fact that Aria's days started as his ended.

Months later, when Shaan would ask her what made her agree to coffee with a guy she'd been so ambivalent about, Aria would be stumped for an answer. Was it a longing for someone familiar, the thrill of attention or just plain boredom? Café au laits led to a walk (he'd bounced, in what she was now recognizing as his signature exaggerated step) down the Champs-Élysées, towards the Tuileries Garden, where they parked themselves in a sunny spot on the grass and nibbled on crêpes, the museum and its new exhibit long forgotten.

Surprisingly, conversation hadn't been difficult. The awkwardness they'd had at the wedding somewhat dissipated, and while Aria had been particularly conscious about not seeming hypercritical, Rohan seemed to be doing more than his part to not trigger her. She was discovering that behind the outlandish clothes, the swagger and the blusteriness—he wasn't the country's top performing actor for nothing—Rohan was unexpectedly thoughtful, with varied interests and a sense of curiosity.

She found herself slowly loosening up and relaxing after weeks as he talked about his work—a challenging new role, a script he was reading and his dream to one day direct. 'A small, indie kind of film,' he'd smiled shyly. She asked detailed questions now and then, preferring to deflect from his inquiries.

'Aria Mistry, you've haven't given me a single straight answer and here I feel like I've just done Charlie Rose!' he laughed, stretched out on his back, his face half covered by an oversized trucker cap.

'Charlie Rose? You watch him?'

He'd thrown the cap off dramatically, propping himself up on one shoulder, and turned towards her.

'You know,' he'd joked. 'You would be a nightmare to have in the interview seat. You question every question! And yes, you little townie, just because I'm from the other side of the Sea Link, doesn't mean . . .' he teased.

'Uh, no no,' Aria found herself stammering in response, a blush rising to her cheeks. 'I thought you were more the David Letterman kind,' she covered up lamely as he shot her a disbelieving look.

A few minutes later, he'd piped up.

'Admit it,' he sat up, now looking her squarely in the face. 'You thought you had me totally down. This Versova boy, who grew up dancing to Govinda tracks, who spent his college life trying to be a 'hero' hanging out at the canteen rather than in class, who only eats, sleeps and breathes films, who on screen and off fights the bad guys wearing a white VIP *banyan* . . . And, oh yeah,' he gestured to his face. 'Worships his own mugshot on a daily basis and treats women as—how did you put it?—"disposable". Tell me, am I wrong?'

He wasn't that off the mark. She wouldn't go that far, but she had totally boxed him into the popular and problematic archetype of a wannabe actor—all muscle and make-up. Aria wasn't one to admit her mistakes easily, though she did feel a wave of embarrassment at being called out.

'I'm actually quite tired, I think I'll head back now,' she abruptly stood up. She'd registered the surprise on his face, but he hadn't argued.

And that had been that. They'd headed back to the hotel in relative silence. Aria knew she was behaving childishly but, for someone who prided herself on being a great judge of character, this boy had totally unnerved her.

Ms Mistry was not used to that.

~

Granny Shelley, Meher's mother, had passed down to her eldest granddaughter a love of baking. As children, Aria and Leah were often left in the care of their beloved maternal grandmother, who used their time together to recreate the recipes she had, in turn, learned from her English mother—fluffy sponges and wobbly puddings, indulgent pies and cinnamon-dusted apple crisps. In Aria, she found a dutiful pupil, always happy to sieve, measure, roll, pour, dust, while Leah, too impatient for the precision that baking required, could be found licking batter off the spatula and scampering off to create mayhem elsewhere.

For Aria's sixteenth birthday, Granny surprised her with a trip to Paris that involved a culinary tour of the city's iconic patisseries, ending with a one-on-one masterclass with Pierre, the legendary, mononymous French chef. It was a weekend that Aria would never forget. When Granny Shelley passed, she willed to Aria her blue-recipe binder, all perfectly indexed, with Shelley's handwritten notes in the margins. It occupied pride of place on Aria's bookshelves, and every few weeks, when Aria needed a pick-me-up, she would create something Granny had taught her, always adding a little twist of her own.

And so, after a somewhat unsettled night, Aria decided to embrace her extra time in Paris by spending it in the kitchen. She'd put in a special request that the hotel's famous pastry chef allow her to shadow him and she was looking forward to the day he had chalked out.

Waiting for her in the lobby, coffee cup and umbrella in hand, was Rohan. She wasn't expecting to see him, especially after her abruptness the previous night.

'Morning, sunshine. I thought we could make it to that exhibit?'

Aria was taken aback. 'Actually, I can't today. I'm spending the day with the hotel's pastry chef. He's going to show me a few techniques.'

'Doing what? Baking?' He looked incredulous, visibly suppressing his amusement.

She stiffened. 'No, painting. Yes, he's going to show me how to make this delicious meringue dessert . . .' She trailed off. 'Is that amusing? Or am I missing some joke?'

He laughed. 'I just can't picture you slaving over a hot stove. You don't seem like that kind of girl, you know, the kind who would mess up her clothes. And besides, I thought you fancy CEO types have a kitchen full of chefs and all to do your bidding.'

'Oh, like you actors, who do all your own cooking.'

He put his hands up in mock surrender. 'Hell no. I just about make a mean spaghetti, but beyond that, my mom and Ritesh, my cook, keep me well fed.'

'You and your sexist comments . . . would you even point this out to a male CEO?'

'I guess we're both guilty of typecasting . . .' he raised his eyebrow at her.

She blushed.

'Bonjour, Ms Mistry. Are you ready?' Chef Luc walked up to them before she could come up with a fitting reply.

'Hi buddy, I'm Rohan, I'll be joining you today as well,' Rohan interjected, putting his hand out. Aria just stared at him.

'So, what are we making today?'

~

'You know, I was in London in 2010 when the last volcano erupted and Europe was grounded. It was one of my first trips abroad.'

It was a beautiful day in Paris, and Aria, who had been going stir crazy in her suite, decided to make her way down to the hotel restaurant for breakfast, only to find Rohan wrapping up a meeting. Without a second thought, he'd slid into the chair across from her and was now sipping on coffee, chatting away, seemingly oblivious to her somewhat morose silence.

He continued, 'I was living at an aunt's house and every day, I would hop on a train, go to a new place—Oxford, Windsor . . . I'd just signed my first film, so with the signing advance, I booked my mum to come with me. She was a travel agent, you know, and she would spend her days booking people's flights, tours and cruises and all that. I wanted her to finally see all the places—Buckingham Palace, Big Ben, Lake District, that she would send her clients to.' Rohan beamed.

'Anyway, I've never had that kind of time again, so in a way, it's nice to be able to really see a city.' He laughed. 'The moral of my long story is, don't look so *mareli*,' he ribbed her. 'When else would you be able to say you were locked in Paris?'

By the end of the previous day in the kitchen, while Aria worked on perfecting her meringue, Rohan had buddied up to Chef Luc and his assistants, even inviting them to come visit him on set the week after. Aria had been incredibly annoyed by his presence. She'd been trying to focus on following Chef Luc's instructions and Rohan's constant banter and the blaring French rap he'd convinced Luc to play had been an unwelcome distraction. She'd declined his invitations for dinner with as much politeness as she could muster, and finding him on her breakfast table, this morning, was not what she was in the mood for. But this story, till he had called her glum, had softened her annoyance. Just a little.

'Oh, by the way, chef and the boys sent me these sick almond croissants this morning. They were insane.' He continued, oblivious to her silence. 'Yesterday was actually a really fun day. I'm glad you invited me to join.'

'Are you kidding? I didn't invite you. You invited yourself and then proceeded to take over my entire lesson, with nonsense conversation,' Aria put down her fork, now really annoyed.

'*Ah, badi badi desho main, choti choti, baatein hootein rehti hai senorita . . .*' he grinned.

'What?'

He burst out laughing. 'Never mind, I should have known that would go above your pretty little head. But, I'm sorry, I didn't mean to ruin your day. I actually had a really great time with you. I had no idea how skilled you are with, what do you call that thing you used to make those clouds . . .'

Aria laughed despite herself.

'Let me make it up to you? Let's find *our* Paris. They say this is a city that will make sure you fall in love with yourself.' He winked. 'If not with someone else.'

The next few days were a blur—they'd made it to the Musée d'Orsay (where she could see him stifling a few yawns, though he had quite hilariously feigned a great interest in the Impressionists on display); taken numerous walks down the Seine; took a turn on the Grande Roue; and spent the day in the Marais, where he'd convinced her to wait in line and then eat a rather messy falafel sitting on the sidewalk. For Aria, a germaphobe, the idea of street food was totally unappealing. ('Why would I want to eat my meal standing?' she said incredulously in the past, when friends had made dinner dates to try out some hip new food truck.) With Rohan, she tried to play it cool; she didn't want to seem prissy and give him more ammunition to tease her. It didn't help that the woman next to her had spilt garlic sauce all over her new dress, which Rohan found rather amusing.

But despite how quickly the days passed, the fun she'd had, she still wasn't sure what to make of him. He was the opposite of what she had pegged him as—he had a rakish charm, but there was a genuineness to him; romantic, sensitive, a little self-absorbed. Though, if Rusi Mistry was right, so was every member of her generation.

She watched him interact with fans when he was recognized on the street—taking that selfie, answering their questions patiently, cracking a joke when their reactions bordered on the extreme.

'Doesn't it get to you? Having no privacy at all? You have to be constantly *on!*' she asked, after a rather long-drawn conversation with an older lady, who insisted he FaceTime with her single daughter.

He just shrugged. 'Who wants to listen to me complain? It's so lame. And this will probably make me sound soft, but the fact that two minutes of my time can make a lifetime memory for someone . . . I don't know,' he looked somewhat embarrassed.

Aria felt a sudden rush of affection for him.

'Too egoistical?' he laughed, deflecting.

'And let's just say I've found ways to blend in when I have to.' He laughed again. 'Yes, even in these clothes.'

She was slowly seeing why women found him so attractive. And reluctant as Aria was to admit it, a part of her was enjoying their time together.

He started joining her for her morning run, always followed by a pit stop at a different bakery for a treat, and she was surprised to find that she didn't mind his company.

'My trainer would make me do a hundred suicides if he saw me now. How did you even find this place?' he said one morning, as he bit into a pain au chocolat, warm from the oven. 'Mmmm . . . this is sick. The best I've ever eaten.'

'Isn't it? My grandmother brought me here when I was sixteen and I try to come at least once every time I'm in the city. George, the owner, is third generation, and it's like they have magic in their fingers, this pastry is so delicately rolled. It's heaven.' She closed her eyes, savouring the last bite.

When she opened her eyes, she found him looking at her.

He leaned towards her, wiping off a crumb from her lip with his thumb. Aria felt her breath catch.

'You are so full of surprises, SoBo girl,' he said.

~

Slowly, Aria was beginning to let her guard down. She knew he was into her—but so far, things between them had been purely platonic.

The first time he took her hand while crossing the street, a shiver of excitement had run through her. But the minute they'd made it across, he let go. Had she been single for so long that she was misreading all the cues?

Not a single complaint

Are you alive?????

Hellooo???

Remember us, your family?

Okay, I'm just going to assume you're French kissing in some corner of Paris and are not buried in a ditch somewhere. Xo

It had been less than a week since she and Rohan had begun hanging out, and Aria had barely glanced at her phone. Even Leah was surprised at the radio silence. She'd missed The Originals' weekly call, skimmed through emails and not even checked in with her family as regularly.

As she got dressed for dinner, after which Rohan had suggested they see a Truffaut film that was playing at this little art-house cinema he'd discovered on his last trip, she found herself putting a little more thought into what she was wearing. Her favourite jeans, a slinky slip that was just the right kind of sexy, a cat eye, her shoulder-skimming straight hair, blow-dried and freshly highlighted that afternoon, and a spritz of her signature Le Labo fragrance.

Not bad at all, she thought, surveying her reflection as she made her way down to the lobby.

Her look got the desired reaction. Rohan let out a low whistle as she walked into the hotel bar. 'Wow, you look amazing,' he said in a low voice, kissing her on the cheek, his day-old stubble grazing her ear. In his plain white tee, black leather jacket and trainers, he was more her speed—less LL Cool J, more Luke Perry, circa 90210.

It was still early, so he suggested they grab a glass of wine at the hotel bar, leading her to a corner table. They sat on the sofa, knees almost touching, his body angled to hers. She couldn't remember what they had spoken about, but she did remember when his hand brushed hers, when he pushed her hair away from her face, how he made her laugh.

When they left the hotel, he asked if she was okay to walk. It was one of those perfect spring nights—clear skies, a light breeze. As they strolled down the boulevard, side by side in easy silence, Aria found herself shivering slightly (more from the thrill of the evening ahead, than the cold). 'Here, take my jacket,' he slipped out of it, throwing it over her shoulders and pulling her towards him.

And then he kissed her. Just like in the movies he made, there, in the middle of Place Vendôme, Rohan Rawal, Bollywood heartthrob, kissed Aria Mistry, uptight townie, like she had never been kissed before.

Later, she replayed that moment over and over again. How he'd felt, how he'd smelt, how he didn't let her hand go all evening. At dinner, he kept leaning over to kiss her gently, and later on in the cinema, longer, deeper. She had no idea what they'd eaten or even what the movie was about but she remembered feeling electrified.

He'd walked her back to her suite, playing the perfect gentleman. They'd had quite a few glasses of wine and as he kissed her, she nestled her head against his chest and surprising herself, invited him inside. That night, they'd made love for hours. He was patient, gentle, drawing her out, and Aria found herself wanting more and more of him. She couldn't get enough, that woody fragrance, the taste of his lips, his fingers caressing her.

They found their Paris. They kissed in public on street corners, in cafes, in bars; lay on the grass in the Jardin du Luxembourg, talking till the sun went down, walked for hours, indulging in bottles of wine and rich French food. She did things she couldn't remember ever doing in her adult life—relaxing her schedule, switching off from work, her friends and her family. One morning, on a whim, they drove out to the vineyards in the Loire Valley and spent the next twenty-four hours drinking copious amounts of wine and making love; it was the first time that she'd had sex in a hot tub. Rohan lived in the moment, and Aria felt herself just letting go, of her inhibitions, of her need to control, of her obsession with order and routine.

'You never called,' she said to him suddenly, one afternoon. 'Shaan said you asked for my number . . .'

'Aha!' Rohan rubbed his hands gleefully. 'I knew it! You WERE waiting . . .' He looked at her. 'But I have to say, I didn't peg you as the girl who wouldn't ever make a first move.'

'Don't be ridiculous,' she reacted defensively. 'If I had been interested, I would have.'

'So, let me get this straight,' a smile played on his lips. 'You weren't interested, but you were still waiting for my call?'

'Come on. After all those women, all those remarks about women, why would I want to be another notch on your belt?'

'So, what I get from that, is that you thought I was hot and you wanted me?'

Aria gave him a withering look.

'I never thought we would have anything in common,' she finally admitted, as they cleared away the remnants of their picnic and walked back, hand in hand to the hotel.

'Why do you say that? We're both young, both relatively successful, both intelligent, at least, you are,' he laughed, his eyes crinkling.

'I don't know. We come from such different worlds, and our experiences are different. I'm, I guess, I'm more conventional, you may say,' she laughed, somewhat nervously. 'You're brave, you followed your dream, even at the risk of not succeeding. Because let's face it, it's a small percentage who do make it, especially in your world.'

'You know SoBo girl,' he took her face in her hands. 'Everything doesn't have to amount to numbers and percentages and calculations. Sometimes, you just have to take that leap, that risk, follow that passion, whatever it may be. When I got my first break, I had no idea if it would be the first of many or the last. But I knew that I had to see it through. I would regret it otherwise.' He kissed her. 'I know, I know. It sounds like some self-help book bullshit, but it's true. For me at least. It's what gets me out of bed every morning.'

'And at what point every morning, do you decide, which nineties rap star you are going to dress like?' Aria deflected, changing the topic. 'In all seriousness, what is this obsession? I think I may need to call Tara to give you a makeover.'

'Mon Dieu. You have so much to learn,' he said in mock horror, and the rest of the afternoon was spent delving into the finer nuances of TuPac, Snoop and Eminem's music, as they walked the streets.

Now they were on their last day together, the airspaces finally cleared. They'd delayed getting back to reality as much as they could. Rohan was off to shoot in a small village in Romania, and Aria, back home and back to work; the hotel deal again in negotiation. She'd just gotten off the phone with her closest girlfriends, but hadn't had the courage to tell them about him just yet. This safe space they'd created, anonymous in this big city of love, where all the background noise could be muted, was unravelling too fast for her to swallow and reality was slowly seeping in.

Last night in bed, she had brought it up, as gently as she could.

'So, are you trying to say that I could never mix with your Parsi blue blood?' he said with a mocking grin, but Aria could see the hurt in his eyes. She'd tried to explain to Rohan that her father belonged to another time, another way of thinking and another social order; a man of black and white, of right and wrong, of tradition and future. He would never accept this relationship. Of that, she was sure.

Rohan just shook his head.

'I know, I know, I get the dichotomy,' she said miserably. 'I'm meant to be this empowered young woman, trying to make my way in a male-dominated industry. And my father shouldn't have a say in my relationships. But, at the end of the day,' she sat up, pulling away from him. 'My parents, my father . . .' Her voice broke a little. 'His approval, his blessing, whatever you would like to call it, means a great deal to me, it always has, and I don't know how he would react to this.'

He traced the curve of her bare back with his finger. She felt her insides go weak.

'Why are you pre-empting a problem? I made you fall for me like this.' He snapped his fingers and winked. 'Didn't I, SoBo girl? So, what makes you think I can't do the same with your father? I'll win him over, don't worry. Parsi banker boy from Cambridge I may not be, but I have enough tricks up my sleeve,' He pulled her back down towards him and Aria gave in, as he kissed her.

Aria couldn't sleep that night. She lay next to Rohan, watching his bare chest move with every breath, his mouth slightly open, his arm behind his head.

Was this just a holiday fling? This was such uncharted territory for her—they'd gone from zero to hundred in a matter of a few days. And that kind of intensity doesn't really sustain in a relationship, a voice argued in her head. She let out a long exhale. It would be a few months before he was back in Mumbai, and who knew what could happen in the meanwhile? Could she trust him? Given his track record with women, wasn't it hubris on her part to believe that she would be one to change him? To get him to 'settle'? Distance makes the heart grow fonder, or does it make the heart forget?

Her heart sank at the thought.

But what if this was it? What if he was the one? What if they made it work? Would Rusi see Rohan the way Aria saw him? And if he didn't, would Aria fight him on it?

She yawned, her eyes finally heavy—and then there was this, was she really okay to be, to the world at large, just another star girlfriend?

8

Three Months Later
Mumbai

'So what? It was just chitty chitty bang bang in Paris? One hot French kiss?' Shaan asked, bursting into peals of laughter at Aria's horrified face as she ducked the fry that was thrown in her direction.

It had been a few months since Paris, and the girls were finally reunited. Just like old times, all three were sprawled out on the large couch in Aria's sea-facing bedroom—a spread of their favourite childhood snacks—cheese toast, French fries and brownies with extra fudge sauce, now accompanied by a bottle (ok, two) of Tignanello—laid out in front of them. Even gluten-free, sugar-free, everything-free Tara had succumbed to the nostalgia and was dipping her fries into chocolate sauce, her eyes widening with Aria's stories.

'I can't believe you kept this a secret from us for so long.' Shaan scowled.

'I didn't want to say anything till I knew it was something. And, it was—is—something,' Aria said softly with a smile, thinking back to Paris. 'I can't believe the speed at which things went—from finding him so abrasive and sexist and a cad to . . .'

'Boning him?' Shaan cackled.

'Must you be so crass all the time?' Aria's tone revealed her annoyance.

Aria had finally told them about Rohan—partly because she needed to get her head straight and also because she would see him the next night, and that too in a very public setting.

When they'd said goodbye in Paris, she insisted they keep things casual, in a bid to protect herself from any heartbreak and also making him swear to secrecy that he wouldn't talk publicly about what happened. And yet, despite her attempt to be standoffish, she'd gotten into the car moments later to a message that made her smile:

I miss you already.

The messages and long FaceTime calls had continued and she found herself checking her phone incessantly; at the gym, in meetings and even at dinner, causing her eagle-eyed father, who was used to her undivided attention, to caustically remark several times, 'Are we keeping you from some life-threatening issue, Aria?'

Rohan was flying back later that night and though he'd dropped several hints that Aria should meet him in the early hours of the morning at his apartment, she demurred, mustering up every last ounce of restraint. She would see him tomorrow, she'd told him breezily, at the *Style* awards, though her stomach churned at how public it would all be.

The annual *Style* awards, which honoured the country's headlining women (and one lucky man!) had become the year's most coveted event. Rohan was winning for a much-buzzed about performance and Aria had been anointed a Gen Next Business Leader. While Aria usually stayed away from social evenings, Tara had just been appointed the title's contributing editor and had arm-twisted her childhood friend into being present. Unsurprisingly, Rusi had been condescending about her decision to attend and accept—'I'm sure you must have a better way to utilize the evening darling,'—but Aria, to honour her commitment to Tara, had argued, that it actually brought into focus the Women Leaders programme that she was piloting at Mistry & Sons. 'It can only show us in a more positive light,' she'd emphasized, given the heavy criticism the company had come under recently for its lack of diversity.

Shaan, who in her current state of mind would never miss a good party, had flown in from Delhi. And so, The Originals had been reunited.

'He's so hot, though, Aria,' Tara said dreamily. 'I mean just LOOK at his latest post.' She scrolled to Rohan's bare-chested selfie that showed off every sinewy abdominal muscle. 'You guys are like the perfect power couple.'

'Exactly. He's hot. You're rich and kinda cute, at least when you're not in those *behenji*, Max *Marela* high-collared blouses and trousers. So, what's the problem, Mistryji?'

The problem was, that every way Aria tried to look at it—the very nature of his profession, the legions of women throwing themselves at him, his incredibly public, outlandish persona was the opposite of what she had ever imagined for herself. She had spent her entire life cultivating herself as a future business leader, a serious member of corporate India, a worthy heir apparent. If she showed up with an actor on her arm, one who was known as much for his sartorial histrionics as for his colourful, chequered love life, what would that signal?

Her father's inevitable disapproval notwithstanding, was such a public life really for her?

'I don't know,' Aria sighed, pulling her knees up to her chest. 'I just keep going round and round in my head. I don't want to be made a fool of. There's so much at stake here, you know? And let's face it, can you name one actor who has been in a committed relationship?'

'George and Amal. Hugh, and his wife, whatshername . . .' Tara rattled off.

Aria shot her a look. 'It was a rhetorical question, Tara!'

She'd only been in one long-term relationship so far, with a sweet schoolmate—a Parsi boy, Zahan—and they'd dated until they both left for college. Zahan was now married to an American girl and ran a ski school in Utah, but while it lasted, their relationship had been uncomplicated, steady and, for the most part, had her father's tacit approval.

'Okay, I'll tell you what.' Shaan leaned over to grab the monogrammed pad and pen that was always by Aria's bed side. 'Let's go old-school, Aria and make a list.'

ARIA + ROHAN	
PROS	CONS
Power couple	Aria is boring
Hot together	Aria keeps everyone at a distance
	Aria is scared of her father's opinion
In love	Aria's scared of EVERYONE's opinions
Adds some fun to AM	Aria overthinks
	Aria is judgyy

'Ta-da,' she pronounced with a flourish. 'Am I right or AMIRITE?'

Aria took one look at the list, made a face and crumpled the sheet, aiming for the bin in the corner.

'What!!! I worked hard on that,' Shaan grinned.

'So why aren't you seeing him tonight?' Tara asked.

'For a BOOOTYY, Boooty call,' Shaan danced around to a made-up tune, enjoying riling up her friend. 'Three months is a looong time. That is, UNLESS . . . there's been some naughty phone sex . . . come onnnn, spill. Nothing to be embarrassed about. It's hot.'

'Shaan, really. You are just so . . .' Aria shot her a warning look.

'Crass. Crude. Vulgar. I know, Miss Prudy.' Shaan reached over and tapped Aria on the nose cheekily as Aria suppressed a smile.

'Anyway, if you're not seeing him tonight, you better look smokin' tomorrow.' Tara walked over to Aria's large but surprisingly sparse walk-in wardrobe. 'What are you planning to wear?'

Not finding anything that she deemed suitable in Aria's closet, she convinced her to raid Leah and her mother's. The final two options were a vintage red Valentino one shoulder dress, which showed off Aria's lithe runner's frame or a ruffled Johanna Ortiz suit that was 'the perfect balance of power and puff', in Tara's words.

'Whatever that means,' Shaan rolled her eyes.

'By the way, Shaan, I should warn you that Serena Verma just confirmed.' Tara was alluding to the Bollywood starlet who was Pratap's rumoured fling. 'But I've asked the editor to ensure that she's not seated at the same table as the two of you.'

Shaan scrunched her face in disgust.

'What is this obsession with her? She's SO tacky. Wanna take bets on what she'll show up in? She wears La Perla lingerie to dinner. God knows what she finds to wear to bed.'

~

Aria couldn't figure out whether the butterflies in her stomach were from the excitement of seeing Rohan after so many weeks or the thought of having to give an acceptance speech to a room full of people. She said a silent prayer that she wouldn't be as awkward as she'd been at Tara's wedding.

If there was one thing she did know, it was that she looked good. She'd chosen the classic Valentino. A pair of Burmese ruby and diamond drops that had been her great-grandmother's glittered in her ears. The hair and make-up artist that Tara had sent over had been a good call—she'd swept her hair back into a loose knot and kept her face minimal with just a swipe of Mac's Ruby Woo lipstick. Even her hard-to-please sister had approved—'Siren instead of sullen. What an upgrade.'

But her nerves on this very public evening refused to settle. Rohan had been texting her non-stop, and every time her phone pinged, another thrill went through her, distracting her from the speech that she was going over, line by line, in her head. On the drive over, Shaan prattled on—the latest Delhi gossip, something about a major paternity suit and divorce, a new diet she was on, her ruminations on whether Serena Verma's husband liked being a cuckold, whether her hair looked better up or down, but Aria, only heard half of it.

'Excuse me, hello. I understand your life is going as planned, but some of us have real problems. Can you pay a little attention? I only have an item girl to deal with tonight.' Shaan snapped her fingers to get Aria to focus. With all the press present, Shaan had had to push the glitzy minis she usually preferred back into her closet, choosing instead a demure black dress, and she was currently fretting whether her outfit was too 'nun-like,' given what Serena Verma was sure to be wearing—or rather, *not* wearing.

'Sorry, Shaan. Just want to make sure I don't freeze up again. I don't have you on stage to distract,' Aria smiled.

'And for the record, you look lovely. Elegant. And the hair is perfect as is,' Aria patted her friend's hand. 'So, stop fidgeting. But let me ask you this—why are you letting this woman that you don't even know get to you? Could it be, that maybe you like Pratap more than you are letting on? We all know how competitive you can get . . .' Aria winked.

'Elegant. Hmph.' Shaan grumbled, with a shake of her head. 'You just aged me fifty years. *Budhi bana dia* in front of that sexy number.'

At the hotel, Shaan and Aria made their way through the gathered crowd, greeting friends as they waited their turn on the silver carpet. At the bottom of the grand staircase of the Palace Wing was a photographer's pit, to capture the headlining guests against the dramatic backdrop.

'There you are,' said Tara as she hurried down the stairs, ducking so as to not photobomb yet another starlet. Dressed in a slick velvet Prada suit worn with just a diamond lariat underneath, Tara had teased her hair into a high ponytail and added on a dramatic cat eye. Not that her look was a surprise. They'd already seen her #OOTD posts on Instagram while driving over, along with a very thorough video documenting

her beauty regime. The caption read, quite naturally: The
Devil Wears Prada.

'Uh, SO much chaos already.' Tara rolled her eyes
dramatically, revelling in every minute. 'Sunaina Gupta
cancelled last minute, and then Naina Mehra and Kamna Sarin
refused to sit next to each other and nearly walked out, and
then there's this whole drama with Serena Verma. I swear to
god, I need a Calmpose and some champers.'

Without missing a beat, she turned on her heel, back up
the stairs. 'We're going to start soon, so come on girls. And
let's get at least one photo together,' Tara waved to Viral, the
pap photographer, to get his attention.

Snap. Snap. Snap.

'Not a chance in hell, T,' Aria sprinted up the side of
stairs, her head down to avoid any chance of a photograph
and stepped straight on to the sweeping tulle train of current
favourite society It girl. 'Oh god, Isha, I am SO sorry.'

Isha Randhawa, she of the statuesque frame and perennially
tanned skin, could really give any of the film stars a run for their
money. A small-town girl, she had spent her twenties getting
married and divorced, with each husband a step up socially and
financially from the previous. Her third coupling was into one of
South Mumbai's oldest families, and she had quickly learned the
ropes of a whole new social world. Surprisingly though, she had
held on to her easy demeanour and Aria was quite fond of her.

Isha had quickly established herself as quite the fashion
lover, attending couture shows internationally and making
her presence felt at the right places at the right time. Her
much older husband, the portly Rishad Arora, who preferred
spending his days playing golf and betting on cricket, had
soon been relegated to her plus one, but was rumoured to be

thoroughly besotted by his new wife (his fourth). 'Rumour
has it that every time they do it, he gives her a ten-carat,'
Shaan had cackled. Isha was a bit of a flirt but she was smart
(an aspect many underestimated about her) and knew when to
hold on to a good thing. And an ageing, devoted, supremely
wealthy husband was just that.

'How are you darling? It's been just too long,' Isha
gingerly air-kissed, careful not to muss her cheek highlighter.
'I was *just* thinking about you. I've been meaning to call you
and Leah over for dinner at our new place.' Rishad and she
had just built a multi-storey tower for the two of them, and his
two young-adult children, who, much to the glee of the other
society ladies, were openly derisive of their new stepmother.
'But it's been SOO hectic, I was in New York two nights ago
for the VMA after-party, and then I leave tomorrow morning
for Venice, for a meeting for the biennale, and then finally
off to Viva, for a much-needed detox, and then it's Mira's
fortieth in Peru. It's just exhausting,' she launched straight into
her frenetic travel schedule, a burden carried heavily on the
shoulders of the world's one per cent.

A loud cheer paused Isha's soliloquy. She and Aria
both turned to look over the banister, at the scene that was
unfolding below. In what seemed like a blink of an eye, the
silver carpet was plunged into chaos. The pit started chanting
'Romeo, Romeo', a surge of guests pushed towards the stairs,
and bouncers tried their very best to cordon off the area, as
Rohan 'Romeo' Rawal, in a flashy red and gold outfit, made
his way through.

As he positioned himself to show off his best side, shoulders
back, body angled to the right, head tilted slightly, a hand on
that ridiculous gold fedora, a woman in a black suit, adjusting

his lapel, he looked towards the first floor, where Aria and Isha were standing together, mouths slightly agape.

And after three months, three days and twelve hours, as Aria Mistry locked eyes with Rohan Rawal, her heart leaped in her chest.

~

'Ms Mistry, Ms Randhawa, you're both at Table One. Let me show you.' An usher directed the two ladies over to the mirrored table that was set with glittering crystal candelabras, grey and white Hermès crockery and Baccarat glasses. The overall effect was breathtaking—towering vases of hydrangeas, lilies and jasmines gave the already majestic ballroom a heady fragrance. The entire second floor had been transformed with not a hint of colour in sight.

The magazine was known to go all out for this celebration, Tara told Aria, when convincing her to recognize the honour. The winners that evening, besides Rohan, the only male awardee and Aria, were Malika, the young ingenue who went by one name only; an erstwhile royal who had reinvented herself as a guru of hospitality, a female artist who'd had her first showing at the V&A and several other women who had headlined the year. The guest list included the usual Mumbai and Delhi suspects—entrepreneurs, philanthropists, tech gurus, arterati, society girls with pet causes, long-legged models and their photographer dates, and, of course, the country's leading designers, who air-kissed and schmoozed both the young stars and grand dames, all attending in the hope of a future cover or at least a double-spread. This was exactly the kind of scene that Aria dreaded and Shaan and Tara thrived on.

As promised, Tara seated Shaan and Aria together. Their table had quite the motley crew: Isha was a seat away, along with the magazine's editor, the young ingenue Malika, the designer Manish Malhotra, the film director Karan Johar, Divya Dalal . . . and Rohan Rawal.

'Oo, I'm going to do a little switcheroo,' cooed Isha, deftly switching Rohan's place card, so he could be close to her. 'He's SO cute and apparently SO available, now that he's done with that tarty Karishma.' She winked. Aria found herself greeting several of the guests—her mother's best friend Maya Sethna looked elegant in a black and gold Benarasi sari; the social media-obsessed Damani twins popped over to say hello, dressed in head-to-toe Dior couture, and promptly tried to pull her in for a selfie; 'Darlings, you must come see the collection at the store. You'll love our edit,' expat store-owner Alice Mehta called out, sweeping past Aria and Isha in a dramatic cape. The artist Aziz Patel, known for the giant heart sculptures that dotted major streets around the globe, one occupying pride of place in front of Mistry & Sons Ballard Estate headquarters, nodded shyly as he made his way to his seat. And Malika, the young actress, was busy barking orders at her assistant, standing at attention behind her holding a bottle of champagne.

'Well, well, well, if it isn't the triumphant return of the terrific three,' slurred a voice behind Tara. Surbhi Shukla, trashy novelist, gossip columnist and full-time opportunist, was looking a little worse for wear, precariously balancing a glass of champagne in one hand and the trail of her overly ruffled pink dress in the other. Her waist-length thick jet-black hair hung around her face, and the bright pink lipstick she'd worn to match the dress was bleeding out.

An old classmate and former friend of the three, Surbhi had been frozen out when Shaan had found her hooking up with Junaid, her then-boyfriend, at the school social. For Shaan, breaking the girl code was unacceptable. Even so, many years later, when school dramas should have been done and dusted, the wound still festered. Surbhi took every opportunity to take potshots at Shaan and, as an extension, Aria and Tara, in her columns. And Shaan always reacted aggressively.

'You know, you are giving HER all the power,' Aria cautioned Shaan for the hundredth time when Shaan sent Surbhi yet another threatening email from her lawyers. 'Ugh,' Shaan groaned heatedly. 'There's something about her, she's such a little cockroach. She feeds off us.'

Surbhi's blog, 'Bubbles, Birkins and Bimbettes', serialized, daily as Page 2 of the city's leading tabloid, was what bleary-eyed society swans read first thing in the morning, while sipping apple cider vinegar concoctions. Her not-so-secret blind items (her sources were rumoured to be embedded in the most rarefied circles around the country) had WhatsApp groups across the city dedicatedly playing guessing games.

'Oo, look at what the cat dragged in,' said Shaan, looking Surbhi up and down. 'Or should I say the mole dug up? By the way,' she whispered loudly. 'You have lipstick on your teeth,' Aria shot her friend a look, shifting nervously; she was always uncomfortable when Surbhi was around, preferring to avoid confrontation of any kind and knowing full well that Shaan always took the bait.

'My Delhi darlings tell me, Shaan, that you are soon to be packed off by daddy dearest. Clearly he hasn't been reading my column, or he would know what his new protege is really up to,' Surbhi said snidely, running her tongue over her teeth, somewhat self-consciously.

A bright red blush crept up the usually unflappable Shaan's face, but before she could retort, the cacophony of a marching band had them all covering their ears. In a look that could best be described as bandmaster meets *badshah*, Rohan Rawal danced his way into the stately ballroom, high-fiving guests and performing for the camera phones that had immediately gone live to film this dramatic entrance for digital posterity. To Aria, it was cringeworthy but the rest of the audience lapped it up.

'Ro,' purred Isha as he made his way to the table, with a woman in black, who Aria presumed was Divya Dalal. 'Guess you're stuck with me all night.' She winked.

With one eye on Aria who was doing her best to conceal her annoyance, Rohan let out a slow whistle, twirling Isha, who was in a nude tulle Giambattista Valli dress that gave off the illusion of bare skin. The photographers stepped over themselves to snap this moment. He finally let go and made his way around the table, greeting everyone before coming face to face with Aria.

'Hi,' he smiled.

'Hi,' she bit her lip awkwardly as he reached over to kiss her on the cheek.

Aria could see a photographer aiming to shoot, so she put her hand on Rohan's chest and pushed him back gently, turning her head away from him and leaving him hanging. She felt his body stiffen, but he quickly changed tack, engulfing Shaan, who was next to her, into a bear hug instead.

For the rest of the evening, Aria tried to catch his eye, but he avoided her gaze. She was cringing inwardly at the way she reacted and knew she owed him an apology.

Sorry, a reflex, she texted.

Every minute of the ceremony seemed excruciating, her emotions spanning the gamut. Excitement, to have him close. God, he looked good; even in that inane get-up. Nervousness, about speaking in front of such a large crowd. Annoyance, at seeing Rohan and Isha's heads together in conversation and hearing her flirtatious giggles. Embarrassment, at her behaviour. Anxiety, waiting for his text.

The show seemed to go on interminably and he still hadn't replied.

He had to understand that she didn't have a choice. She couldn't have a photo of them getting out there, for people to make assumptions. Not until she was sure what they were. She stared at the back of his head, willing him to turn and look at her.

She started to type out another message, but stopped. No, Aria, she scolded herself. She wouldn't be *that* girl.

When it was her turn on stage, Aria accepted the award with a brief thanks, hopeful that she sounded coherent enough. When she passed Rohan on her way back to her seat, he stood up, and for a second, she thought he was going to try and hug her again. But he ignored her, instead offering his arm to the dainty, perky Malika, who could barely walk up the stairs, thanks to a constricting mermaid skirt.

Aria was now fuming. He could play this game alone; she refused to be a part of it.

It took all her self-control and lessons in propriety to not walk out. She couldn't wait for the evening to be over. It didn't help that Shaan was getting drunker, thanks to Surbhi's dig and the very presence of Serena Verma, dressed to kill in a lace corset and sheer skirt, shooting daggers at her.

Aria crossed and uncrossed her arms, breathing in deeply and attempting to appear as unflappable as possible. She wished she'd never agreed to this damn night.

When Rohan's award finally came up and their table erupted in cheers, Aria busied herself, picking off imaginary lint from her dress. He bounded up the stage in that ludicrous outfit and she couldn't help but wonder if she had been thinking straight. How could something like this ever work out? They were complete opposites in every way.

'I've been honoured to be surrounded by incredibly strong women in my lifetime,' he began as he accepted the award. 'After my father left us, I was raised by a single mother who pretended to love watching cricket, just so I was never made to feel the absence of a male figure. Though I know she would much rather have watched *Chandni*.' He paused, clearing his throat. 'My biggest mentor in this industry,' he said, doffing a hat in Divya's direction, 'has been a woman who has guided me and been a north star. And look at me now, in a room full of such cool chicks! I'm one lucky dude. Now, I also know that I'm in a room *full* of media folk who want to know who that one special woman in my life really is. To them, I say all the women in my life are incredibly special, but one in particular has my heart. Thank you again for this.'

And with a subtle wink at Aria, he sauntered off the stage. And just like that, try as she might, Aria felt her cheeks colour and her anger slowly dissipate.

~

Aria's phone dinged as she made her way through the dispersing crowd. A wave of people were making their way to the Crystal

Room, where the afterparty promised to go into the early hours. 'DJ RJ is on decks. It's going to be *some* show,' Tara promised. Shaan, clearly in the mood to do some further damage, held Aria's hand and dragged her to the closest door, knowing full well that Aria was trying to make her usual 10 p.m. escape.

It was Rohan, finally replying:

Make it up to me. Presidential suite. Fifth floor.

Aria was exhausted. Her feet hurt. She wanted to get home, shower the night off and pretend nothing had happened. But she also *really* wanted to see him.

He'd been so infuriating tonight, with the whole get-up, flirting with Isha, ignoring her messages—he hadn't made it hard for her to question their relationship; and then he went and made a statement like that on stage. So public, and yet, like those lovesick heroines in cheesy novels, she'd been secretly thrilled. It was momentary; a majority of the people in the room had presumed the declaration had been directed towards Malika, his latest co-star, #rolika trending online almost instantaneously. Tara had surreptitiously shown her the GIFs and images doing the rounds. It was all just too much. Everything with him was just *too* much.

It had been so simple in Paris, she thought again, wistfully. Since she'd returned home, she'd found herself going back time and again to their carefree days.

'What should I do?' she asked Shaan and Tara. She may as well have been talking to herself. Shaan had worked herself up into a drunken stupor and Tara was heady from how well the evening had turned out and her role to play in its success.

'I need to pee and I just saw that slag Serenaaaaa headed for the loo,' Shaan said, now swaying. She pressed the elevator call button as they waited for the gilded doors to open.

'Uh-oh. What, all this too plebby for you? Is there some secret event only for rich, spoilt brats?' There was Surbhi again, watching them with a freshly coated pink smirk.

'You, you, you'll never make it to any of our guest lists . . . once a leech always a leech,' hissed Shaan, getting into Surbhi's face as the crowd around them stared on curiously. Much to Aria's relief, the doors finally opened and she pulled her friend into the elevator before the evening got even more out of hand.

'Why do you let her get to you so much?' Aria asked Shaan. 'You know you can't create such a scene, with so many people here.'

'Fuck everyone.' Shaan slumped against the mirrored wall. 'She deserves it. But what the fuckk do I do about Pratap. Ey-everyone knowsss?' she was now wailing.

'Firstly, you have to ask yourself, are you into him even a little? And then, you're going to talk to your parents,' Aria said firmly. 'This isn't like you, I've never seen you cower before on even the smallest things, and this, this, is your life we are talking about. You need to figure out what's best for you, not for your father, not for the election and definitely not for Pratap.' Even as the words came out of her mouth, Aria wished that she would follow her own advice.

She steadied her emotional friend as they made their way down the carpeted hallway, which was empty save for two navy safari suit clad guards standing at attention in front of the double doors to the suite. They were clearly expected, as the men opened the doors wordlessly.

'Presumptuous,' Aria muttered to herself as Rohan walked out of the bedroom, wet hair slicked back, in black sweats and a grey tee. Before she could say a word, he pulled her towards him and in that one gesture, as he nestled his face in her hair, Aria felt her frustration with him and the night give way.

'Uh . . . I'm just going to, to . . .' said Shaan, pointing to the direction of the bathroom. Not that any attention was being paid to her presence, given how oblivious Aria and Rohan were to their surroundings.

'You look beautiful.' Rohan pushed a stray wisp of hair away from Aria's face as he leaned in to kiss her gently. 'I've been waiting to do this for such a long time.' He kissed her again, slowly, biting her bottom lip. 'Even tonight, when I first saw you, all I could think of was . . .'

'Isha? Malika? Or should I say #Rolika?' Aria disentangled herself from his embrace, making her way to the couch, just to get some distance between their bodies; her mind needed to be clear. She was Aria Mistry, not just some fangirl thrilled at the idea of a superstar calling her up to his suite. She refused to let him off the hook. That's what the voice in her head kept saying. She knew how this night would end, but she couldn't give in that easily.

'Ah. Do I detect a hint of jealousy?' Rohan smirked, making his way to her. 'You know you are the only girl for me.'

'In this empty room, you mean,' Aria moved away from him to the edge of the couch, sitting ramrod straight, smoothening the imaginary creases in her dress. 'What was with that spectacle anyway?'

'It's an act, come on, you know that. It's all part of the game, it's not who I really am—not with you at least,' he said, scooting next to her, his mouth inches away from her ear and his fingers running up and down her bare arm.

'And who are you? That's what I keep asking myself,' Aria turned towards him.

'A guy, who has been counting down the minutes till he could see you. I swear, Aria, I'm falling more in love with you every damn day.'

Crash. A shattering glass led them both to turn towards the corner, where Shaan, in her inebriated state, was trying to pour herself another drink from the bar cart.

'Whoops,' she shrugged her shoulders, blissfully unaware of the moment she had interrupted.

'So, wherefore art thou, Romeo,' she said, unsteadily making her way to a stuffed armchair, spilling some tequila on the way. 'Oh man . . . you'll are sooo cuteeee. Romeo and Juliettt,' she slurred. 'Wowww, first time I'm seeing you with my girl . . . my girl, my girl, is something so here . . .' She couldn't even finish her sentence and collapsed in a heap on the carpet, missing the sofa almost entirely.

Later that night, after Shaan had eaten a club sandwich and sobered up slightly with a coffee, she finally left the lovebirds to make her way back home. As she slipped out of the suite in the early hours of the morning, heels in hand, Rohan's arm on her elbow to keep her from falling, a high-pitched giggle caused them both to stop in their tracks.

Turning the corner was Serena Verma riding astraddle Pratap Sharma, both clearly high as kites and not expecting to bump into anyone they knew at such a late hour. On spotting Shaan, Pratap stopped suddenly, nearly throwing Serena off his shoulders in the process.

'Uh, uh, heyyyyyy,' he recovered his composure first seeing Shaan and then doing a double take spotting Rohan.

She would give him that, Shaan would later tell the girls, he had a poker face through and through. 'And that *bechari* Serena, she just stood there awkwardly, in her skimpy outfit, while he acted like she wasn't there!'

'Shaan, *meri* Shaan. After partyyyy, in 501! Come on, there's a whole bunch of us.'

Serena shot him an annoyed look, as she hugged Rohan in greeting, refusing to even acknowledge Shaan.

An awkward silence ensued, with Pratap trying to lamely break the ice.

'Big night, big night for you man,' he fist-bumped Rohan, who looked bemused. 'Respect, bro . . . you killed it man, in that last film, killed it . . .' he simpered.

'Ugh, you're gross,' said Shaan, pushing past him and straight into the waiting elevator.

~

'Wow, these have to be the most lethal shoes,' Tara thought to herself as she hobbled into her parents' Malabar Hill penthouse in spiky stilettos. But then again, no pain, no gain, was her fashion motto, and she knew she'd aced the look.

It was 4 a.m., and she was exhausted, exhilarated. It had been a night! At some point, she'd lost her friends, but had spent the remainder of the evening dancing to the eighties' and nineties' hits the DJ kept spinning, and finally with the rest of the *Style* team, continuing up to the publisher's suite for an after after-party that involved way too many shots. She grimaced, the spa day tomorrow at the Four Seasons was a smart plan and much deserved, she thought.

As she headed up the stairs to her old bedroom, she was surprised to find the door to her father's study ajar. Pushing it open, she saw all the lights on and her father crumpled over his desk, head in hand, sifting through files, a glass of whisky next to him.

'Papa,' she called out. 'What's wrong? Why are you up so late?'

Mohan looked startled to see his only daughter, standing at the door.

'You surprised me, beta. No, no, just catching up on some foreign calls.'

'*Saru che*? All ok? You've been looking stressed the last few days. Have you been taking your sugar? Are you eating properly? Is everything okay at work?'

This was Tara's most extended visit post her wedding and she'd noticed how much time her father and brother had been spending post work in his study, in closed-door meetings. Her father had seemed uncharacteristically stressed and snappy, but when she'd asked her mother about it, she'd dismissed Tara's concerns, vaguely citing some important deal and changing the topic to her latest obsession—when Tara was going to give them all 'good news'. Her brother, the prodigal son, Bunty was equally unresponsive, but that wasn't a surprise, he was too involved with his new yacht and string of flighty girlfriends to ever even have a real conversation with his sister.

'*Reva de*. I said it was nothing, Tara. Just some pending work matters. You will not understand,' her father said harshly.

Tara bristled at her father's tone and insinuation.

'That's not fair, Papa. I'm a smart girl, you educated me abroad, I run my own business, I'm not five years old that you have to keep me in some glass box.'

'Tara, this is not the time,' her father, raised his voice and held up his hand in warning. '*Bas, keh diya*, don't ask again. This is not a job for ladies. And please don't go filling your mother's head with all these questions—*mera sar kha jayegi*.'

She couldn't remember the last time he'd spoken to her that way. But she knew him well enough to know, he wasn't in a state that could be reasoned with.

'Now tell me *bitiya*, party *kaisa tha*? *Kis kis seh mile*? Selfie *liya*?' he softened slightly, seeing the crestfallen look on her face.

They chatted for a few minutes, Tara half-heartedly sharing stories from the night, still smarting from her father's words. When she left to go upstairs, she cleared away his whisky glass exhorting him to go to bed. As she got under the covers that night, having taken off those five pounds of hair extensions and finished her twelve-step nightly beauty regimen, she couldn't help shake off the niggling feeling that something was terribly wrong. She made a mental note to sit her brother down the next day for a serious chat.

9

'I don't mean to be disrespectful, but if you don't include more women-focused agenda points, *baat hi khatam*,' Shaan spoke up as the party secretary finished outlining the manifesto. 'I've said before, for this party to become more relevant, we have to get women to vote, to stand for elections.' Shaan slapped on a smile and rattled off the same lines that she felt she had said a hundred times before, to seemingly deaf ears. 'And *uske liye*, you have to do what matters to us.'

She sighed at the disinterested faces staring back at her. '*Acha*, Sudiptaji,' she said, turning to one of the senior karyakartas. '*Main toh sirf* foreign-returned *hoon. Main kya jaanu?*' Shaan arched an eyebrow to a smattering of nervous laughter. '*Aap bataein, jab woh aurat pehli sarpanch bani, aapke gharwale ne kya kaha?*'

They broke for lunch soon after Sudiptaji recounted how impressed the women in their circle had been at the news of a first woman sarpanch being elected in another village. Chaya, the twenty-five-year-old daughter of another karyakarta, who worked with Shaan on educating local villagers on health issues, spoke about how, for her generation, seeing women in this position was aspirational, to which a male voice from the back heckled, much to the amusement of the male members. '*Desh* Indira Gandhi *ke baad itne saal chal gayi, abhi bhi chal jayegi.*'

Shaan walked out on to the lawns, the sweet fragrance of her mother's roses filling the air. She closed her eyes, exhausted from the futility of these meetings.

The original Singh farmhouse was built in the haveli style with open courtyards and surrounded by acres of farmland on the banks of the Ganga. Calling it a house now was somewhat of a misnomer, because thanks to Singh Saab's growing good fortune, it had expanded to include the neighbouring acreage and the several single-storey outhouses, all in varying styles. The result was a little compound (his desi version of Kennedys' Hyannis Port) that, despite its disparate architecture, still had a great deal of charm and provided the family with both a necessary escape from Delhi's vicious politics and a strong power base.

Everyone who was anyone in the capital had a house in the hills, but Singh Saab used this ancestral home as a power base to further strengthen his ties in the constituency. As Singh Saab was building his career in politics, Sheela cultivated a love for farming, bringing in new concepts and technology and creating a robust organic farming ecosystem, that ensured that the land brought livelihood to the community. The home was an *adda*, especially during the lead-up to elections, for brainstorming with his core team and furthering his connections—it wasn't just a coincidence that most of Singh Saab's relatives occupied powerful positions in local politics.

Network, for the most part, was poor, and he could get his advisers to focus on the task at hand.

'No distractions,' he would tell his wife and daughter. In most political dynasties, patriarchy reigns supreme, with sons groomed for office at an early age, but for Singh Saab, Shaan, his only child, was both a son and daughter, and from the time she was a young girl, in the hope that it may incite a political calling, Shaan had been summoned to sit through the meetings.

This is where she had headed post the run-in with Pratap and Serena at the *Style* awards, and she was hoping to get some alone time with her father to discuss the situation. He was a reasonable man, she told herself; he loved her and wouldn't want her to be unhappy. Even if her feelings for Pratap were to develop, what would the point be, if he was screwing someone else? She was slowly building up the courage to have a heart to heart; a few tears here and there in the past had gotten the trick done and gotten her out of several escapades before, and she was hoping she could swing him in her favour this time too.

Shaan sighed, as she walked barefoot on the cool grass. She was dreading the conversation. She knew it was going to lead to a lecture on her lack of responsibility and her overall disinterest. Lately, she didn't know how to answer her father's constant questions about the future. Or give him the answers she knew he wanted to hear. Did she want a life in politics? At one point she had, but so much had happened since she'd returned from America. Her naivete back then was laughable; had they even moved forward an inch?

Did she want another career? Possibly, but she really hadn't found anything else that sparked her interest as such. Choosing a path that was already chalked out seemed easier sometimes. But then, she'd get frustrated at the slow pace, at the circular arguments, at the archaic mindsets. She felt stuck, in perpetual limbo, and rather than turn inward and recalibrate, she chose to barrel on.

For the last forty-eight hours, in a bid to appease her parents, she had played the perfect daughter, showing the calmer, more rational Shaan; the one who had been missing in action the past few months. She switched into her wardrobe of block-printed cotton salwar kameezes, sat through every session from public relations to retuning the campaign manifesto, helped her mother and staff organize the constant flow of tea, snacks and food, spent a few hours in the local village talking to women and interacted with the karyakartas. Most were fond of Shaan, or at least pretended to be, according respect, knowing full well that Singh Saab expected that his daughter's opinion be heard, especially when it came to the youth vote. In the past, as the campaign moved to social media, she had become an invaluable asset, for no reason other than her generation's obsession with technology. That was, until recently, when she'd been too distracted to focus on the tasks at hand.

She made sure she was never out of her father's sight but, despite her best intentions, Singh Saab's rip-roaringly bad mood prevented any personal discussions. Thanks to some key party defections, Singh was tackling the possibility of a major political crisis, which could sound a death knell for victory so late in the game. The bloodthirsty media was camping at the gates hoping for some tasty morsels.

She was biding the days, hoping to find the perfect moment, when her father announced at dinner that evening that they were extending their stay and to expect a new crop of visitors, including Pratap and his father, who were joining them the following afternoon.

'What?' Shaan spat out her nimbu pani. 'No, Papa. He can't come here. You can't do this to me.'

'What exactly am I doing, dear girl? The last time I checked, it was my name on the gate, so I can invite whoever I damn well please.'

'B-b-but, Papa . . .' stammered Shaan 'I've been wanting to talk to you about this whole Pratap thing. You should know . . .'

Her father raised his hand in warning. 'Not the time.'

'But Papa, he's a complete . . . '

'ENOUGH, SHAAN!' Her father slammed his fist on the table, upturning the crystal vase full of hydrangeas from his wife's garden and soaking the floral tablecloth. 'Bas. All I know is that I don't have time for your spoilt brat drama. This is not the time or place for inane society gossip. This is important for me politically. I really shouldn't have to tell you how essential it is that we retain all the talent in the party now? He raised his eyebrows at her. 'And they are important personally, as well. You will treat them like the family they are. Please do not cross me on this.'

'Sheela,' he turned to his wife, who was watching this exchange in silence. 'You will make sure that the second-floor bedrooms are ready for them. They will stay in the main house with us and tell the cook to make those kebabs he likes for dinner tomorrow and keep the good Scotch out.'

With that, Singh Saab threw his napkin on the floor and stalked out of the room, seemingly impervious to the tears that were now rolling down his daughter's cheeks.

'Mom, talk to him, please . . .' pleaded Shaan the next morning. Shaan, who wasn't used to not having her voice heard, decided to try and play on her mother's sympathies—a stretch, given that her mother and she hadn't seen eye to eye on many things in the past few years. But Shaan figured it was worth a shot.

While mother-daughter were often at odds when it came to their personalities and opinions—Shaan was messy, impulsive in the way she lived life; Sheela measured, a perfectionist—their physicality was in complete sync. Anyone who met them marvelled at how looking at Sheela was akin to imagining Shaan, three decades later.

That morning, Shaan found her mother in her favourite spot, in her gardening uniform—a pair of khaki slacks and a cream linen shirt that were pristine, despite the mulch she had been digging up a few minutes ago. Hidden under a wide-brimmed straw hat were the same thick curls, hers a mercurial silver, worn in a close crop. Sheela's freckled, make-up free face broke into a frown, as her daughter interrupted her quiet time to plead her case.

They had just gotten word that Pratap's mother would also be joining, making Shaan even more anxious and Sheela keen to get back to clipping roses for the fresh flower arrangements for the guest rooms.

'*Abhi nahin*, Shaan,' her mother said, exasperated. 'You see, Papa, he is under a lot of pressure. Please don't add to it,' she turned around to face her daughter, putting a hand gently on her shoulder.

Shaan shrugged it off. 'What about the pressure you are putting on me? What did he mean by *personally*? Are you guys really thinking of something happening between me and Pratap? Because let me tell you, NO way,' Shaan answered defensively, not willing to back down and trailing her mother, who had turned back to inspect her handiwork.

'And why not? Do you know better than your parents? Have we not managed to raise you just fine for the last nearly thirty years?' Her mother turned back towards her. 'Come on, Shaan, you have to stop behaving so irrationally—you're not getting any younger and I don't see a line of men waiting outside the door.'

'So what, you just marry me off to the first one? As if my whole life I've been waiting for this Prince Charming that only you can present to me. Here, beta, birthday *ke liye pati le lo, aur papa keh liye* vote *bhi la do*?' Shaan retorted, her eyes filling fast with tears.

'You make it sound like we are primitive people who would marry you off as part of some deal. Don't be ridiculous. If you'd brought home a decent man you were in love with, we would have happily embraced him. But so far, I've only seen you ridicule all the boys you meet.'

She paused, filling the basket with the cut flowers.

'So what if we introduce you to someone who could be your future husband? Don't we know you best? And so what if it also helps Papa? My parents made these decisions for me, and look how happy I've been.'

'But Ma, you don't know the truth about him,' Shaan choked back the sobs. 'He's got such a reputation. *Sab bolte hai* he's a creep. *Uske pata nahin kitne* affairs *chal rahe hai.*'

'You're not some *sati-savitri* yourself, Shaan. Just because your father turns a blind eye doesn't mean I don't know what you get up to. *Sab kahaani maine suni hai.* Now, if I was to listen to what everyone said about you . . .' she exhaled. 'Trust me, we wouldn't expect you to marry, if it even comes to that, some, what did you call him, creep? But the way you've been behaving and the reputation you are building, you should be grateful that a boy like Pratap is even willing to overlook all the stories he's probably heard about you. He's from a good family, and if he wants to marry you, frankly, I don't see an issue with that.'

A few hours later, when the Sharma family drove up the hill, Singh Saab sent an aide to look for Shaan. He came back perplexed, saying that her room was empty and she hadn't been seen by anyone on the staff since breakfast that morning.

'Sheela, call her NOW,' he bellowed to his wife, who turned on her heels and headed straight to the house.

This time, Shaan had gone one step too far, Singh Saab thought to himself as he readied himself to welcome his guests. She had to face the consequences.

~

'Morning, gorgeous. Coffee?'

Shaan propped herself up on an elbow and gratefully accepted the steaming hot cup from Matt's outstretched hand. Seeing him shirtless in his chrome and glass thirty-third floor apartment overlooking Manhattan's Battery Park, a familiar frisson of excitement ran through her, until she remembered just what had brought her here, 12,000 km away.

'UGHHH, how are you even alive?' she groaned, falling back into the pillows, nearly spilling the inky brew all over his striped sheets.

'Hey, careful there, train wreck. I don't really have maids and servants to clean up after me, ya know? Ya wanna finally tell me what this drama is all about? Or did you just miss me?' Matt winked at her, while making his way to the sink in his open bathroom to brush his teeth, but not before pausing to admire his gun show in the mirror.

It had been over a week since Shaan had fled the scene back home. That morning, seething at her mother's remarks in the garden, she convinced one of the many party workers hanging around that she had to get to Delhi on some urgent work for her father and had made her way back to the capital in record time. Back in the city, she fled to her friend Shiv's house, planning to hide out there till she was discovered, only to find Shiv packing his bags for a trip to Frieze in New York.

When her mother had quite easily tracked her down and demanded that she make her way back to the farmhouse immediately, she'd realized the extent of her parents' displeasure and that salvation wasn't going to come so easily this time. So, blame it on hubris or a fit of pique, she boarded the plane with Shiv later that evening, texting her parents to let them know that she loved them, but she needed time to think. Sixteen hours later, she landed up unannounced on Matt's doorstep in New York.

Since she'd arrived, it had been a blur of late nights at the city's hotspots (she knew she'd overdone it; the bouncer at Le Bain now followed her on Instagram), alcohol-fuelled sex, uppers and the general madness that seemed to surround her whenever she was with Matt. It had been the same cycle since she'd met him after the summer fling with Abhishek. Though they had never officially dated, they kept coming back to each other, or, if she was being honest with herself, Shaan kept coming back to him, every time she needed an escape.

He was a bad habit she couldn't, or rather, wouldn't break. With them together, it was too much of everything— too much partying, too much booze and a couple of times, too many drugs. There was no middle ground. They were combustible.

Initially, every few months, a bender with him would then sober her up for a little while and she'd go back to normal life—dating, her classes, hanging out with friends—until she felt off-kilter. And then boredom, monotony, or a need to rebel against the norm would kick in and the cycle would begin again.

It had been a while since she had seen him, though they sexted regularly. She'd told herself she had grown out of it. He was working as a trader in Manhattan, had an on-off girlfriend from what she gathered. 'Nothing really serious,' he told her as they hooked up the first night. But he still managed to party as hard as he had in college, while making it to his desk in time the next day.

'I'm headed to brunch with my parents. Wanna join?' he pulled on a clean T-shirt, spritzing cologne liberally.

'Uh, parents and me . . . not a good combo right now, ya,' she said, half-teasing. 'Besides, what would your 'girlfriend' say? You know, she's kept all her Victoria Secret shopping in your top drawer. She's marked her territory,' Shaan winked at him.

'Why don't you mark yours?' Matt added, sitting next to her on the bed and running his fingers up her bare legs. 'Why did you stay away so long? Aren't you done playing Miss India back home? Move to New York.'

If only it was so easy, thought Shaan. She was tempted— to not have parents interfering, to not always be worried about 'party *log kya kahenge*', to walk down the streets with a cigarette in her hand, to not have to be married off to someone for political gain but just be able to keep her options open, just like guys like Matt were allowed to do.

Here was Matt, offering her an easy way out. But his attention span was worse than hers. He'd be bored of her in a few weeks once reality had set in. They could never have a life together—there's not enough room in front of the mirror, Aria had once said in her annoyingly perceptive way (Shaan had taken umbrage with being pegged, but she knew Aria was right) and that thought had always stayed with Shaan.

And Shaan was smart enough to know all she would be throwing away. She loved the power that came with being Arjun Singh's daughter. She would be bored of the anonymity in no time; if she was being honest, isn't that why she had gravitated towards the Indian crew at her college where she could play Queen Bee? And then there was the question of lifestyle. She'd never worked a full day in her life, she wasn't disciplined enough to hold on to a nine-to-five, nor was she willing to live in some hole in Queens if and when her father cut her off. She shuddered at the thought.

Her mother, she knew, hadn't taken her side in a long time, but her father, the man she idolized . . . 'How dare he think it is okay to marry me off as a political pawn?' she'd asked Aria facetiming her as she absentmindedly went through the racks at Bergdorf Goodman. She would play his game and hold her ground.

And then, a voice that she would have liked to keep buried, surfaced, asking the questions she didn't want to answer. Was the issue with being set up with Pratap more because her parents had initiated it? Would she have been more open if she'd met him at, say, a bar? There had been an initial fascination with Pratap, and wasn't that because of the power dynamic that he brought with him? The new blue-eyed boy of politics and Singh Saab's daughter—they could make for a formidable duo. His policies and agenda, for the most part, she agreed with. And wasn't it her ego that was hurt, that even after meeting her and going on a few dates, he still hadn't ended it with Serena? And the fact that everyone around them knew and kept throwing it in her face?

For the last week, she'd been wallowing in anger, in pity, furious at how her parents had spoken to her, that she'd been cornered into this position where she had little control over her life, that Pratap hadn't been enamoured enough to end his affair. After Abhishek, she had sworn that she wouldn't let anyone else have an upper hand in her relationships.

But now, the partying was starting to wear thin, and she was realizing that this move could have major repercussions. Her bluster and bravado were crashing. Directly disobeying her father and humiliating him in front of his guests—jumping on a plane to New York and, that too, into an old lover's arms—was quite the stunt, even for her. Had she gone too far?

She knew her parents were worried. They had been sending her frantic messages, and when she hadn't replied, they had gotten word to her through Shiv. Her father's patience had probably been worn thin. And her mother and Bua filling his ears about how he had spoiled her would probably get to him at some point.

She grabbed her phone from the nightstand, readying herself to suck it up and grovel for forgiveness. She would make him understand—she was his little girl, his favourite person in the world, he would say that to her every night when he tucked her into bed as a child. It's not that she was completely against marrying Pratap, she would tell him, right now, she just didn't know if she wanted to get married, period. She was still young and she wanted to see what was out there. She needed time to find what she was looking for. He could understand that, right?

After what seemed like an hour of typing and deleting, she finally sent him a long message:

Papaji . . . I know you must be so angry, disappointed and upset. I know I was wrong to run away and worry you, especially at such an important time. I can't explain, except that I was scared. I'm lost, Papa, I need some time. I don't know if Pratap is the right person for me or if I am for him. I'm in New York with my friends but I'm coming home in a few days. I promise to be more responsible from now on, and I will do everything else you ask of me. Please forgive me. Love you, Shaan.

~

Five hours later, her phone pinged with a message from her mother.

Papaji is very busy and stressed. Your ticket has been booked for Monday. Be on the flight.

That's when Shaan knew the proverbial shit was going to hit the fan.

~

'We'll be landing at New Delhi's Indira Gandhi International Airport shortly. The outside temperature . . .' as the flight attendant's voice droned on, Shaan felt the anxiousness in the pit of her stomach growing. For all her bluster, she thought to herself, when it came down to it, her father had summoned her back, and, tail between her legs, she was heading back to his domain. It hadn't helped matters that his aide had followed up her mother's message with a call with her flight information. He had also let her know, not so subtly, that if she failed to board, her credit cards would be cancelled and her father would also have her visa revoked, leaving her little choice. Shaan wasn't about to call his bluff.

As the doors opened, she half expected to see her father there, but was greeted instead by the usual special handling team, who whisked her through immigration and straight to a waiting car.

At home, there was no welcoming party. Even though it wasn't yet midnight, her parents were asleep, their room door shut and the lights all turned off. Only Kanta didi, her childhood nanny, had stayed up for her, with a plateful of her favourite chicken biryani and raita, which Shaan gratefully scarfed down.

It was nearly afternoon when she woke the next day, and the house was a hive of activity. In the formal dining room, she found her mother in the throes of dinner prep.

'*Aa gayi?*' her mother looked up at her with a seemingly blank expression on her face and then proceeded to fire off instructions on polishing silver, sending the white-liveried staff scurrying.

'Means? You sent me my flight details. Where's Papaji?'

'He's at a meeting. He can't be disturbed. Also, Papa is having a big party tonight for the senior leaders. He wants no distractions. Kanta didi will bring you dinner on a tray to your room.'

'So, I'm being locked in my room like a six-year-old? That's just absurd. I want to talk to Papa.'

'We have wanted to talk to you for weeks too, Shaan,' Sheela replied pointedly. 'It's about time you realize that actions have consequences and to be honest, I really don't have time for your drama today.' Sheela walked around the oval-shaped, teakwood table, adjusting the silver thalis that had been set. 'For once, you can just listen and not argue. Babu, *woh maali ko bula do, yeh phool ka kya halat hai.*'

~

'So, it's been the silent treatment for days. My father has pretty much been MIA or locked in his study and my mother, well, she's been . . . my mother. Like a loser, I've eaten every meal in this room alone and I must have watched every episode of *Sex and the City* again,' Shaan complained to the girls on their weekly Sunday call. She was lying in bed, puffing on her e-cigarette, her unbrushed curls in a jumble on top of her head. She blinked back tears which these days were coming on pretty easy.

Finally, last night, she recounted, her father summoned her into the living room, where he and her mother were having their after-dinner cognacs. In no uncertain terms, the guidelines for her continuing to live under their roof were put forth. She would never pull a stunt like she had again, her international travel was now curbed till the election and only after her father's permission, she had to be careful about the social perception around her, and she had to get back to taking her duties at the party seriously or find herself another job. When it had come to Pratap, she told the girls, she tried to explain to her father all the issues—the stories with Serena and Ira, his disinterest in her when they had been on their own, the weird mind games he seemed to be playing.

'Shaan, answer this. Is Pratap mean to you? Is he violent? Does he treat you badly whenever you meet?'

Shaan shook her head.

'So, it seems your problem with Pratap is that he had some affair with Serena, correct?' her father asked.

'It's still going on, Papa . . .' Shaan whined.

'Have you asked him? I've never heard you not speak your mind. What's stopping you?'

Shaan shrugged.

'Everyone needs to grow up, Shaan, and it's about time for you. And when it comes to past affairs, we all have them. You were involved with that reporter, what's his name, Abhishek. And that's just recently ended.' Shaan's mouth fell open. 'What?' Her father laughed. 'I know what's going on in every political circle in this country, and you thought I won't know what's going on in my daughter's life?'

'To me, Shaan, it appears that you don't want to take on the responsibility of marriage,' Sheela said, her tone patronizing.

'Maybe you are right, but I didn't realize we'd flashed back to the 1950s where your parents control your life . . .' Shaan bristled.

Her father held up his hand. 'Shaan, right now, YOU are out of control. I don't think that's difficult to see. We've tried to talk to you, to reason with you, to help you. But it seems every option we present is problematic for you. On one hand, you tell me I'm disinterested and lackadaisical about your ideas for progress in the party; on the other hand, I'm controlling your life. Which is it? Anyway, I would like for you to give this boy a chance. This is your future. Let's not argue about it any more.'

'It's like a switch is just off in my father's head. No matter how much I try to talk to him, he's blocked me out,' Shaan said dejectedly. What she wasn't telling her friends was the extent—she had sobbed, she had screamed, she'd even thrown his cognac tumbler against the wall, shattering the glass into hundreds of pieces but he had sat unmoved.

'Ohh love.' Aria couldn't remember a time before when she had seen her friend in such a state. 'What happens next?'

'What happens next is that I'll be shipped off to Gurgaon, where I'll be expected to play some desperate housewife while he's dancing around trees with that slut. He'll then want to knock me up, so I'll be changing diapers for the rest of my life, while he and my father rule the country. The END,' Shaan let out a morbid laugh.

'Shaan, can I say something without you completely losing it?' Aria began tentatively. Shaan rolled her eyes.

'I caught this interview with Pratap the other night on television. It was one of those segments where the reporter follows the subject around. And I have to say, he spoke well; I was impressed. And yes, yes. I get that he's a politician,' she said, pre-empting Shaan. 'The way you described him, I thought he would be uncouth, but he was articulate, he outlined his agenda. I can see why your dad is impressed.'

'I don't think you need to be with a guy who won't commit. But, in my experience, men can change, look at Nakul. He had his fun, now he's . . .' Tara continued. 'If he gives up Serena and is willing to try and work things with you. Who knows where it can lead to? And if it makes your parents happy, it's a win, right?'

Shaan shrugged, the tears now filling fast.

'Gosh, guys, can I be such a cliché? Marry the first guy my parents like?'

'But if you like him, even a little, then how is that so bad?'

Pratap and Shaan were going to meet the following night. Apparently, her parents had covered up for her, explaining her absence at the farmhouse as a long-committed college reunion in New York and some date confusion on their part ('If only they knew how close that was to the truth!' she laughed wryly to the girls, thinking of Matt).

Pratap, she told them, had messaged her, inviting her for dinner that evening.

'I'm just going to be honest with him. *Aur kya baaki hai,*' Shaan said, dejectedly. 'I'm going to ask him point blank about Serena and about that Ira. Oh, and I'm also taking a *mannat*— I'm giving up tequila. Every night, I've been praying that the more he gets to know me, the less he likes me and that will be the end of that. Any suggestions on how else I can make that happen?' She attempted a laugh, to lighten the mood.

Aria just shook her head. The irony of this conversation wasn't lost on her, she'd been annoyed at the set-up with Tushad, and here she was on tenterhooks about her father's reaction to Rohan. No matter how happy he made her, her father was the elephant in the room, looming larger and larger, as they got more and more into each other.

'Anyway, you girls give me the scoop, na? I'm so bored I could scream. Tara, what was the scene like at Tramps last night? I heard all of Bollywood was there? Sakshi was facetiming me nonstop, she nearly hooked up with Kunal again! They are so up-down, it makes my head spin.'

'Huh? Sorry,' Tara said, distracted. 'It was the usual scene . . . hey girls, I'm sorry, I really have to go. Nakul needs something. Chat later, love you . . .'

10

'Tara, let's get one of you smelling the flowers,' Amy the photographer suggested. Tara clutched a fistful of peonies, handed to her by the make-up artist, drawing in their sweet scent. The team was on location at Columbia Flower Market, documenting a series of looks that Tara had styled for a popular high street label. It was one of her biggest collaborations till date, and she was determined that it would all go as planned. It had been a gruelling forty-eight hours of hair, make-up and 5 a.m. call times, but the images had a vitality that Tara knew would go down well with the label.

Since her return, Tara's days in London had passed in the usual routine of shoots, workouts, meditation, lunches with the Mayfair Mrs and appointments with her mother-in-law. But, for the first time, her mind and energy were elsewhere. In Mumbai, to be precise. She couldn't shake off the feeling that things were more serious than her father was letting on.

She'd tried to talk to Bunty several times; the day after she found her father in the study, she'd woken up and headed straight to her brother's room.

'No office today? Do you even work any more?' Tara gingerly stepped over the clothes littered on the floor. She was tired, hungover and irritable and her brother's slovenly state annoyed her further. It was 12.30 p.m. and he was still in his boxers and tee.

He yawned. 'Late meetings, what's your problem?' he rubbed a hand over his unshaven face. 'Call for a coffee, na,' he gestured to the intercom near her.

Tara ignored him, standing in front of him, her arms crossed. 'Listen, Bunts, I'm really worried about Papa. He's looking so stressed, he's drinking so much, you both are in these hush-hush meetings. Tell me what's happening.'

'Just chill, ya, it's regular work stuff,' he grabbed a ball lying next to him, bouncing it on the wall opposite, the thwack, thwack, sound aggravating Tara's already fried nerves.

'Call na, for that coffee,' he yawned again.

'Focus, Bunty,' she said firmly. She pushed him over on the leather couch, prodding him further. He shot the basketball through the hoop in his room.

'Don't worry, Princess. Your life and your darling husband won't be affected *at all*. So, go on, go shopping and meet your friends, take those silly photos, nothing for you to worry.'

'What the hell is wrong with you?! Why are you such an asshole? What will it take to have a normal conversation?'

He grabbed his phone, grunting vaguely in response to her additional questions, until she finally gave up and left his room in a huff.

His dismissiveness wasn't surprising, the siblings hadn't been close in years, growing further apart due to the competitive, constant one-upmanship that characterized the relationship between Bunty and Nakul.

Even though in front of Nakul, she stood up for her brother, privately, she was finding lesser and lesser ground for commonality with him. Bunty seemed to be running with a hard-partying crowd, and even her parents seemed to be struggling to connect with their son. Though her father would never admit it, she'd surmised that Bunty had made some poor decisions at work, bringing in friends and contacts that, like Bunty, overpromised and under-delivered.

'Are you cleaning up his mess, Papa? Tell me, is Bunty responsible for all this stress?' asked Tara, concerned, as she FaceTimed her father who was back at his desk, whisky tumbler in hand, looking even more haggard than a few weeks ago.

Her father demurred, reiterating that they were minor issues that he was sorting out, and changed the topic. Bina seemed clueless, though Tara's questioning sent her down a rabbit hole, bemoaning Bunty's irritability with her, his constant partying, his lack of responsibility when it came to his parents and his refusal to settle down. She brightened up after a few minutes. 'Acha, Tara, tell me, have you thought about planning? It's high time now.'

'Babe, can I ask you a favour please?' Tara turned to Nakul, handing over his morning tea. They were having breakfast on their terrace, a rarity with London's grey weather, and she'd finally gathered up the courage to broach this conversation. She knew how Nakul and Bunty felt about each other and her brother would be livid at Nakul's involvement. But she'd hit a wall with her parents and a niggling suspicion prevented her from letting it go. 'Would you just call my father? I feel something is so wrong and I know he would talk to you. You know how protective he is of involving me with the business . . .' she pleaded.

'Darling, is it really my place though? I don't want to overstep in his dealings. And for whatever it's worth, which I'm not sure is much, he has Bunty. I'm sure between them they have it sorted,' he sipped his tea. 'There's a reason he's asked you to stay out of it, and I think you should respect that. And I don't think Bunty would want me snooping around,' he said in his clipped tone.

'It's not snooping! You ARE his son-in-law, and if my father's in trouble, don't you think we ought to know? Bunty can think whatever he wants, but maybe we could actually be of help?'

'Hmm,' he said absentmindedly, replying to a text on his phone. 'I doubt that, darling. We're very different kinds of businessmen. What your father and Bunty do . . . anyway, I really need to get to the office now. Let's chat later, maybe?' he headed inside to grab his briefcase.

A few minutes later, he appeared at the cream French doors that led from the living room on to the terrace.

'Darling, don't forget about the gala dinner tomorrow. What are you going to wear? I just got off the phone with Mum and she told me to tell you that she's taken out one of the diamond sets,' he looked at her expectantly.

'The duke and duchess will be there and we're seated on one of the major tables, so please make sure my tuxedo is back from the dry-cleaner's and that you're wearing something new but not *too* sexy. And for god's sake not anything too elaborate and Indian and you know . . .' he rattled off instructions, blowing her a goodbye kiss.

Later that day, Tara headed to the standing weekly lunch date with her mother-in-law at Selfridges. Even though they lived in the same house (on different floors, thankfully),

Anjali Puri insisted on this one-on-one 'quality time' as being non-negotiable. If you knew the sharp-tongued Mrs Puri, who hailed from one of Nigeria's wealthiest Sindhi families, even by reputation alone, you knew that declining any of her much-coveted invitations was tantamount to social suicide. Naturally, as her daughter-in-law, the pressure was on Tara to always be available to her mother-in-law's whims and fancies.

It was hardly a secret that the Puris hadn't really been thrilled about the match. What Mohan Mehta made up for in wealth, he lacked in culture, Anjali was often known to say within the four walls of their home. She had long set her sights on an old family friend's daughter for Nakul who fit all the right boxes—Sindhi, educated at Seven Oaks and then at Bristol, an art gallerist and a bona fide member of the Sloane Square set.

But when Nakul insisted, the Puris caved. Truth be told, his father Ajay had been quite indifferent, but was smart enough to know when he shouldn't go against his wife's wishes.

At five-feet-one (though you could never tell thanks to her trusty Sergio Rossi wedges), Mrs Puri packed a punch, ruling her home and husband with a diamond-encrusted fist. She looked on the right side of fifty, courtesy a few strategic nips and tucks, and an extensive maintenance regimen, and her instantly recognizable signature silver-grey streak in an otherwise jet-black bob had earned her the nickname Cruella de MIL, courtesy Shaan, given just how much Tara seemed to be terrified of displeasing her exacting mother-in-law.

The differences between Anjali Puri and Bina Mehta, in fashion terms, were as vast as Loro Piana and Versace. And Mrs Puri was determined to bring Tara over to her side of the taste spectrum and, in an Eliza Doolittle-esque transformation, create a social swan worthy of the Puri name. She was a sweet girl, just a little insipid, but she could work with that, Anjali confided to her sister in Lagos at the time of the betrothal.

Weekly lunches were set, often followed by a spot of shopping with Anjali's long-time Selfridges personal shopper to make sure that Tara's wardrobe was replaced with more polished pieces from Prada and Celine. An art appreciation course was signed up for and Anjali had her favourite sommelier conduct a private session with Tara. Every six weeks, a hair colour refresh and trim were scheduled, and monthly facials with Dr Kapur were added to the calendar. All this was important, Anjali had explained to her diligent, eager-to-please protégé, because, as the new Mrs Puri, she would be taking on the mantle—not only as a partner to Nakul, supporting him, but also as a patron of the charities that the Puris had long been involved in, and she had to always look and act in a manner befitting.

Today, in her usual daily uniform of a cashmere twinset and pearls, a tan Hermès Kelly bag on the seat next to her, Anjali nibbled on a chopped chicken salad (no cheese) in between sermonizing the importance of the upcoming gala dinner. Ajay Puri was winning an award for his contribution to the British-Indian community in the presence of the duke and duchess and Anjali was determined that the family put their best foot forward. She was displeased with Tara's choice of outfit, something she had clearly already discussed with her son Nakul, given his comment at breakfast, and was now suggesting they peruse the new evening wear salon on the fifth floor for some appropriate options. Tara, who normally would have immediately acquiesced to her mother-in-law's often irrational demands, was in no mood to deal with her interference today.

'The dress is couture, it fits beautifully. Why don't you like it?' she asked somewhat irritably, stabbing at the few remaining lettuce leaves on her plate. 'I have a busy afternoon of meetings. So shopping is a little difficult for me today. And besides, it's what I would like to wear.'

Never one to miss a beat, Anjali wiped the edges of her mouth delicately with her napkin. She turned up her surgically sculpted pert nose, narrowing her eyes. Her disdain did not register on the rest of her unlined face.

'What you want is irrelevant. In this family, we have a certain image and on such an important night, I will not have that ruined in any way,' she hissed, her mouth set in a firm line. 'I refuse to let you embarrass me.'

And with a gesture for the bill, she effectively signalled the end of lunch and the conversation.

'Since when is couture a source of embarrassment?' Tara grumbled later to her friend Farah, over a glass of wine. 'It's a beautiful dress with an embroidered *gota*-work jacket. You would have thought by her reaction that I was planning to attend in sweats!'

After her mother-in-law stormed off, Tara, unsettled, had wrapped up her meetings and called Farah (she knew better than to call Nakul when it came to his mother) and begged to meet her for a glass of wine. In the few years of being married, this was the first time she had actually vented to a friend, other than Aria and Shaan, about Anjali's constant need to control. Aria and Shaan were too far away, and she just needed someone to talk to.

'It is the first time that I really held my ground. You know, she can't pinpoint one thing wrong with the dress. It's just her ego, that I didn't consult her on it,' Tara leaned back in the chair, pouring herself another glass. 'I swear, she wants to control everything. She's picked out everything in our house, even the plates we eat on. When we go on family holidays, she plans every little detail according to her interests, and last week, I'm not even kidding, but I even heard her tell Nakul that Guruji said that 2020 was a good year to have a baby and definitely not before that. So effectively, she's even planning our sex life!'

'Haha, at least it's designer clothes. Beat this, mine has become so miserly, the other day she fired the housekeeper for buying blueberries at Waitrose because they are 25p more expensive than the ones at Tesco. I mean, you live in a five-million-pound home, and you're moaning about 25p.'

Two glasses of wine and a good mother-in-law bitch session later, Tara made her way home. Her husband was sitting on the terrace, smoking a cigarette and nursing a drink. In the evening light, he looked handsome in a navy jumper and jeans. Even so many years later, she still felt the same attraction, as she had when they'd first met at the nightclub Mahiki. The single deep-set dimple, the wire-framed glasses, the preppy wardrobe, even the cockiness, it was all such a turn-on. She breathed deeply. She was willing to tolerate all the nonsense with his mother, just to be with him.

'Hi baby,' she purred, a little buzzed, leaning in for a kiss.

'Where have you been?' he demanded, giving her a half-hearted peck. 'I got home half an hour ago and texted you.'

'Oh, sorry, love, I haven't looked at my phone. I was with Farah.'

He looked at her, an annoyed expression on his face.

'Getting drunk in the middle of the afternoon? Really, Tara. What's going on with you? First you are rude to mum and then you come home sozzled. And what happened to your very *busy* afternoon of meetings?' he asked sarcastically.

'Firstly, it's 6 p.m., and I'm hardly drunk. I had two glasses of wine. It's not an everyday thing. I just needed to take the edge off.'

'Well, I've had an exhausting day at work. And I come home starving, expecting that my wife will be eagerly waiting for me, preferably with a hot meal, if that's not too much to ask, but instead I find you are out and about,' he snapped.

'We never eat before 7. What's going on with you?' Tara asked. 'Is there something else behind this mood?'

'I'm hungry. I'm tired. And I have enough going on at work without worrying about my wife fighting with my mother.'

'Ah. So, that's what this is all about. Your mother called you to complain and without even hearing my side of it, you've presumed it's all my fault?' Tara was close to tears by this point, but whether it was the alcohol or just the mood she was in, she refused to back down.

'All I know is mum feels disrespected and is incredibly upset. I expected more from you. You knew the kind of family we were when you got married.'

'And what kind of family is that? One where every step I make needs to be authorized?' Tara felt the blood rush to her face. 'Do you realize how ridiculous this argument is, Nakul? It's about a DRESS. I work in fashion and yet—the fact that we are sitting here screaming at each other about an outfit is just nuts!'

He stayed silent, unmoved, fiddling with his phone and refusing to look at her. Tara sat on the chair next to him, waiting for some reaction. When she realized none was forthcoming, she took a deep breath and headed towards the kitchen, to get dinner ready.

'Fine, if it's such an issue, I'll go downstairs and apologize to her, but this is really not a big deal. And you're being so ridiculous.'

'No, don't. She's taken a sleeping pill and gone to bed. Dad said her blood pressure had shot up.'

Tara rolled her eyes, plating the salmon that the housekeeper had prepared.

'And if it's *just* an outfit, I'm sure you can find something else that will make Mum happy. This is a very big night for us and everything has to be perfect. Mum and Dad have worked too hard for any missteps to happen now. So, please, do as she says.'

That night, Tara and Nakul ate dinner in silence. And the next morning, after having to apologize profusely, she was on her way back to Selfridges with Anjali, to find a dress that had Mrs Puri's seal of approval.

~

'You are a natural-born leader. You are intelligent and dependable, though a teensy bit too stubborn. You are loyal to your friends but turn to very few for help. Take a break from the books and head to the mall with your crew. Go on, have a little fun.'

Shaan doubled up laughing, seeing the look on Aria's face. 'Bingo!'

It was just another after-school hangout in Aria's bedroom. Aria, Shaan and Tara were poring over magazines, filling in those multiple-choice, magazine quizzes—what kind of BFF are you? How to tell if he is your soulmate? What's your future career? Which Spice Girl are you most like? (Aria, Posh. Tara, Baby. Shaan, Scary).

And every time, no matter how much Aria tried to change her answers, she was pegged into a box, all variations on the same: dependable; decisive; dedicated . . .

'Du-ulll' Shaan sung out, teasing her mercilessly, as Tara patted her friend's shoulder in solidarity, stifling a giggle.

'You could never be boring, Aria,' her mother said, smiling kindly, when Aria wandered into her parents' bedroom after her friends had left, flopping down on their four-poster bed, magazine in hand. Meher looked at her older, far too serious and sensitive daughter, with a touch of concern. Aria had suddenly shot up, a jangle of limbs. Her long legs were now developing defined muscle, a result of an arduous tennis-swimming-gymnastics routine; her face was dotted with bursts of acne, and she was meandering through her early teen years with a self-consciousness guiding every thought and behaviour.

'She is, a 150 million per cent!' her younger sister Leah, who had followed her in, shouted.

'Let me see that,' said her father, who had been sitting on the sofa by the window. He took the magazine from Aria's hands and put on his reading glasses. 'All hogwash, filling girls' heads. Really, darling, you cannot . . .' he started, changing tack when Meher shot him a look.

'But, let me tell you. These character traits: dependability, loyalty, intelligence . . . It's what separates the men from the boys and, in your case, the women from silly little girls who insist on believing such rubbish.' Rusi rolled up the magazine, swatting Aria's shoulder playfully and trying to get her into a bear hug, which she squirmed out of awkwardly.

She was becoming a young lady, Rusi found himself telling Meher, reminiscing about Aria as a little girl who loved nothing more than to sit on her father's lap while he played the piano, who cried every time she watched *The Sound of Music* ('Why is the Papa so mean? Does he not like his children?'), who at the age of six, when she couldn't write the lowercase 'w' correctly, spent hours practising till she'd gotten the little flicks just right. She worked hard on every aspect of her life, but made it look effortless; she took perceived slights to heart, she held those she loved close, and from the beginning, her father would say proudly, just like him, she put a premium on doing things the right way.

And Aria plodded along, graduating from teen magazines to inspirational self-help books, working hard in school, making it home by her deadline, acing her SATs, getting into Harvard (though critics would have pointed to the campus building bearing the family name as her admissions ticket) and then interning at various companies in the States, to round out her experience before heading back home for the role she'd been groomed for. Under her father's wing, she was learning the ropes at their family's 150-year-old company, working her way up and slowly gaining the respect of employees and the board alike with her dedication and work ethic.

Fifteen years after taking those quizzes, she was learning to let go, just a little. There was a lightness to Aria, now, that had never been there before. Leah had commented on it, in her own inimitable way. She scrutinized Aria at breakfast one morning. 'Your face seems stuck in a perma-grin and you're looking almost . . . luminous.'

For the next few days, her sister sized her up considerably, following her around, examining every little expression, much to Aria's amusement, and reporting back to her mother that there was definitely something going on—Aria was in a state of constant conviviality. So, she, Leah, had come to the consensus that either Aria was on Xanax—and could Leah also get a prescription?—or that her older, boring sister was crazy in love.

Only Aria, holding her cards close to her chest, as was her way, knew how in deep she was. It was safe to say that she'd never felt like this before. Rohan, who was workshopping his next film, had been in Mumbai for the last few weeks, and Aria and he had been spending all their free time together. Quiet dinners at home, long nights on his couch, talking and watching old movies, Sunday brunches that stretched to Sunday dinners. They'd fallen into a comfortable rhythm, and given the constraints they both lived within, it almost made their relationship normal.

On weekends, she would join him for early-morning runs on Juhu beach when it was still deserted and before sneaking home to breakfast with the family. That Saturday morning, she headed, flushed and exhilarated, to the glass-fronted patio overlooking the swimming pool, to find Leah at the table reading the papers. 'You're up rather early? Where are Mum and Dad?' she said, as she poured herself a glass of chilled orange juice from the crystal carafe on the table.

'I'm catching a flight to London in a few hours, and I thought I would get in some quality time with my sister,' said Leah rather sweetly, tossing the paper she was reading in Aria's direction. 'Anything you'd like to tell me, darling, big sister? If I didn't know better, I would say this is sounding suspiciously like you.'

Today's column by Surbhi had a blind item Leah had so kindly highlighted:

> Which billionaire, SoBo heiress has been spotted entering and exiting a Versova high-rise at all hours of the day? Crossing the sea link (and sleeping on the other side of the tracks so as to speak) has become a daily task to see her paramour—a studly hero whose list of female acquisitions is as long as his box office hits. Whispers tell us that this time, he's telling friends it's serious. At an award's show recently, he even dedicated an award to his notoriously uptight new love. Tsk, tsk, now what would Sir Daddy Big Bucks say? Stay tuned.

Aria could feel the colour drain from her face but before she could say anything to Leah, her father's booming voice sounded, causing her to fold the page and shove it into the pocket of her sports jacket.

'Well, there must be something wrong with the world,' her father said, seeing the two of them eating in relative silence. 'If my daughters are having a civilized breakfast together with absolutely no bickering.'

Who did you tell about us???

We never discussed going public . . .

I don't think you realize what's at stake for me . . .

She sent a photo of the piece to him.

Out of all days, her father had been in a rather loquacious mood, taking his time over breakfast and then insisting Aria join him on a conference call in the study with a potential partner. He was now suggesting they go visit a new site together, but she'd managed to wangle out of that with the feeblest of excuses.

When she finally got to the privacy of her bedroom to call Rohan, he of course hadn't answered, so she'd typed out a series of frantic WhatsApp messages.

Would it be such a bad thing for it to come out? Clearly, he was committed, and she, despite her misgivings, knew he made her happy.

One part of her was furious and the other part somewhat relieved that they wouldn't have to hide any more. But what about her father? Everything about Rohan's life was antithetical to his core belief system. Would he really even see Rohan for who he was? Would he put her happiness over his obsession with propriety, with legacy, with his antiquated way of doing things?

Ping.

Relax, baby. Take a breath. This is just nonsense.

Relax. He wanted her to relax. Aria was now livid. Nothing infuriated her more than being told to relax. But then, of course, he would be relaxed. With his need for attention this was all in a day's work. Who knew? Maybe he'd even planted it himself, she thought rather darkly.

She remembered a conversation several weeks ago, when she'd told him how, from the time they were young girls, her father had ingrained into both her and Leah, that unless it was for specific professional achievements, the only times your name should make it to the papers was at the time of birth and then at death. How he had derided the crop of girls whose social antics and wardrobes, magazines and even newspapers devoted valuable column space to. ('How is that newsworthy, how many rows of shoes a person has?') Rohan laughed, telling her that social media had obliterated all that. 'Where's the line between public and private any more? And let me tell you, it's only going to get more intimate. And then, there's the world I come from—where if you're not written about, you're pretty much written off.'

She scowled. How could she expect any other reaction?

She volleyed back a series of messages not mincing her words at his cavalier attitude.

I think you're overreacting, you're not the only SoBo heiress. ☺

But I'm at an event, with twenty-five people listening to my every word. Let's discuss tonight. Still on for dinner at 9?

Okay, baby, seriously, what did you expect . . . that we'd hide out forever in this flat and that no one would find out?

When she'd arrived at his penthouse half an hour ago, in what she thought was her best disguise—oversized sweatpants and a hoodie, her hair swept under a New York Yankees baseball cap—he'd burst out laughing, much to her chagrin.

'Now, even the liftman will know that Surbhi's blind items are true and the SoBo heiress is you!'

Aria had built herself up to a state of serious annoyance but even she had to crack a smile and admit that she looked absurd. Her resolve to stay angry weakened. It didn't help matters that he was freshly showered, the familiarity of his cologne quickening her pulse. She shook her head, trying to get her mind and the body in the same place. What was it about this boy? The allure of the forbidden? Could it be that she was actually enjoying this cat and mouse game?

Almost reading her mind, he teasingly asked her that very question pulling her up against his chest on the couch.

'But in all seriousness, Aria,' he took her by the shoulders, turning her to face him. 'Gossip or not, there was a lot of truth to that piece. I am IN this. But I need to know how much you are. Are you willing to talk to your parents?'

He continued, searching her face for answers. 'I don't want to hide any more. I want to take you out for a meal in this city, I want to take you to a party with my friends, I want you to come to watch a movie with me. Yes, we'll be photographed, yes, there will be stories, but we can deal with it. I just need to know where you stand.'

And Aria Mistry, Harvard MBA, future CEO of Mistry & Sons, who had known from the age of seven what direction her life would take, was suddenly left unmoored.

11

Nearly Six Months Later
New Delhi, Singh Home

There had to be few things more grating than the *shehnai*, Shaan thought irritably, as the high-pitch sounds from the instrument wafted through her open bedroom window, alternating with an even more annoying deep-throated 'Testing. Mic One, Two, Three. Testing. Check'.

'I'll shove that mic up your . . .' she yelled at the empty room, burrowing her head further under the duvet cover.

Just as she was about to drift off again, there was a loud banging on the door.

'Go away!'

'Morninggg, sunshine. It's time to get up, Up, UP.' Scratch that. Tara's cheery voice was even more irritating, besting the shehnai, Shaan thought to herself as her friend sashayed into the room. Even in her bleary state, Shaan could make out her friend, perky as ever, coffee cup in hand, dressed in a white blouse and high-waisted trousers, her shiny hair perfectly blow-dried. Behind her, stood Shaan's beloved Kanta didi with her breakfast tray.

'Scoot, sleepyhead,' Tara sang out, kicking off her cork wedges and peeling back Shaan's duvet. 'We have a hectic day ahead. Here's the plan.'

A few hours later, after Shaan had reluctantly showered, thrown her curly hair, unbrushed, back into a top knot and, in defiance, dressed in her oldest sweatpants, she found herself standing in front of a three-way mirror, swathed in a delicate, blush-pink lehenga, flanked by Tara and Aria.

'My god, can the world have more beauty?' boomed TT's voice as he walked into his bridal studio, appraising Shaan. 'Well, maybe if you'd washed your hair and put on a little make-up, it could,' he teased.

One of the country's leading designers, TT, as he was known, was also Shaan's mother Sheela's childhood friend, and she'd enlisted his help in making sure her daughter looked every inch the radiant bride on her big day. It was out of affection for his friend that TT was enduring Shaan's brattiness, which had been in full swing. Her almost catatonic behaviour while shopping, her refusal to arrive to fittings on time, let alone commit to a look, not to mention her constantly shrinking waistline (that could hardly be attributed to a bridal glow diet but more to a steady subsistence on cigarettes and tequila), had exhausted every last bit of his paternal feelings towards this petulant bride-to-be.

'For god's sake, Shaan, chin up. This has to be my most stunning work yet, and you, my dear, are being a bore with that sour face. Let's pop some champagne, will that cheer you up?' He made minor adjustments to the lehenga while cracking jokes with Tara and Aria, as Shaan stonily smoked cigarette after cigarette, flicking ash all over the place.

Even with TT, who she was incredibly fond of, Shaan couldn't muster up much enthusiasm. She couldn't believe how life had changed in the last few months. After that trip to New York and her father's newly unforgiving attitude, she sat down with Pratap to have it out. She hoped that by being honest and calling him out on his game, he would be completely deterred from pursuing any kind of relationship with her.

But the opposite had happened. They'd actually had a good conversation. She'd been surprised at his candour—he'd told her about his relationship with Serena, promising that he was ending it, he'd talked openly about his political dreams and all they could achieve together, how he believed that Shaan and he were more similar than it appeared and the clincher—'Listen, Shaan, *shayad yeh tumhare plan mein nahi tha.* But let's give it a shot? I think we could be a force together.'

'What the hell,' she recounted to the girls about agreeing to a trial dating period. 'Not like I have, anything or *anyone* better to do. And let's be honest, my judgement was so off-base with Abhishek, so maybe Pratap will prove me wrong, hain na?'

And so, over the past few months, they'd dated, spent time with the families at the Singh farmhouse, Shaan visited his sister and baby, and took his mother out to lunch and shopping when they happened to both be in Mumbai. There were moments when she could imagine their lives together and others when she felt completely stifled at the thought. But seeing the resulting ceasefire in the Singh home, and still smarting from the entire Abhishek episode, she'd let the relationship take its own course.

'What does your gut tell you?'

'My gut is too filled with alcohol these days to be trusted,' Shaan joked. 'I guess I could do worse? He could be a psycho but he actually just seems . . . so boring sometimes. Maybe you should date him, Ari?'

'But what's he really like, Shaan?' Tara asked. 'Now that you've spent more time with him?'

Shaan didn't know what to make of Pratap. He vacillated between being aloof and attentive. He came alive when talking about three things—workouts, cricket and, of course, politics; when it came to talking about himself, he held back. His curiosity in Shaan's life and her interests seemed almost perfunctory, but then there were times when he'd make an offhand remark that would reveal that he either knew more than he was letting on or was in fact listening to what she said. Their dates were unlike any Shaan had been on, yet as their relationship progressed, she realized that despite all her talking, they both circumvented any in-depth conversations about what the future held.

Many evenings after they'd hung out, back home in bed, Shaan would try to imagine their life together. She'd picture herself in the Gurgaon penthouse, as his wife, at the dinner table, just the two of them, the silence only broken by him chomping on a protein-rich meal. She'd think of them in bed having sex, or on holiday together (did he like the beach or the mountains?) and she'd struggle to find visuals that would fit her idea of a happy marriage. And there were scenarios where she could imagine their lives coming together quite seamlessly, on the campaign trail, with their families, at party meets presenting a united front, and their relationship, or courting, as her father referred to it, seemed to have possibility.

She found herself questioning if besides their politics, there was enough in common. Her concerns were compounded by Pratap's seeming lack of interest in her physically. He was keeping their relations relatively chaste. After a few drinks one night, she found herself taking the initiative and leaning over to kiss him. That evening, they went as far as they had, until Pratap slammed the brakes. He'd pulled away from her, put his fingers through her hair, held her face with his palms, kissed her in finality and then walked himself to the bar to get a drink, leaving Shaan open-mouthed on the couch, confused at what had just happened.

'What the fuck is wrong with you?' She was furious at herself, at being left hanging, again. When no answer was forthcoming, she stormed out.

'He's hot, then he's cold. I really don't know what goes on in his head,' Shaan railed to her friends. 'It's not like I want to jump him. But does he even find me attractive? Or am I just a means to an end for him? Gaaahhh . . . what kind of guy doesn't even try to make a move? Can he not get it up? Or is it that he is still boning Serena?' she wailed, finally pausing for breath.

'God, what if this becomes a *bhai-behen rishta*.'

After every evening with Pratap, she would find her parents waiting expectantly at the breakfast table the next morning, keen for updates. Her father would very casually ask, while not looking away from his newspaper, 'So how is Pratap? How was your evening together?'

'I really don't need all this pressure,' she grumbled to her mother, the day after she'd stormed out of Pratap's home. She was still smarting and the fact that she hadn't heard from him was only rubbing salt in her wounds. 'It is getting annoying. Things are *not* great, and I honestly don't even think *usse* interest *hain*,' she said, trying to convey the issue to her mother in as roundabout a way as possible.

But Sheela waved her off. 'That all comes later, Shaan, with companionship and love. Let me ask you this, is he good to you?'

'I mean, he's not bad to me but . . .' Shaan struggled to enunciate her concerns without getting into yet another heated argument.

'You don't have to be scared of commitment, Shaan. It is good to have someone in your life that you can count on. When I first met your father'—Sheela smiled—'it wasn't all love at first sight, like you see in the movies. But he was a good man and he accepted me for who I am, and I did the same. Our marriage blossomed.' She patted Shaan on the shoulder. 'It will happen beti, give it time.'

'Stop treating me like I'm a fucking rose in your garden,' Shaan sniped at Sheela, unable to restrain herself any more. 'You are my mother, you should be on *my* side.'

Pratap finally did call to apologize, even sending flowers. He'd feigned feeling unwell and when Shaan tried to press him, on his inability to be forthcoming both physically and emotionally, he'd just said, 'Shaan, this is new for me too, but it doesn't mean I'm not interested, it's just, we are both different people, with different ways of . . . reacting. *Ab chor na*. Please.' Shaan wasn't convinced, but later, whenever they'd met, he'd been incredibly attentive and they'd actually had a decent time together, though Shaan hadn't made any moves, and Pratap seemed to be satisfied with leaving her with a few goodnight kisses.

And then, a few weeks later, Pratap's sister Anuja and her mother dropped by for tea at the Singh home, Anuja's toddler in tow. Shaan and Anuja had developed a friendship of sorts; only a few years older than Shaan, she was easy-going and loquacious, the opposite of her brother. And Anuja's doe-eyed toddler had taken quite a shine to Shaan. When Singh Saab, arrived home, to the women sitting on the lawns, chatting, while the nanny chased after the little fellow, he insisted that they stay for dinner and drinks, immediately dialing Pratap and Sharmaji to join the merry party.

Bottles of wine were opened and consumed, whiskies poured neat, martinis shaken and tray after tray of hot steaming food appeared in front of the group, who chatted and laughed till the late hours of the night. Even Shaan found herself having a good time. At some point in the evening, Sharmaji broke out into ghazals, crooning in a rich baritone, and Shaan found, to her surprise, Pratap, who was sitting next to her on the swing, taking her hand, lacing his long fingers through hers, as he joined his father in song.

'*Thoo, thoo.*' Anuja swayed over to the couple after her father had finished, circling a crumpled Rs 1000 note over their heads. 'Look at you, match made in heaven,' she cooed. '*Abhi baat pakki kar do. Kyun hamhe wait karva rahe hon*? I'm toh waitinggg to dance at my brother's wedding!'

'*Haan, haan, main yeh hi* Pratap *ko keh rahi thi*,' his mother, Meenu, piped in, looking at Sheela. 'Now you both know each other. Romantic dinner dates *shaadi keh baad bhi ho sakti hain.*'

Her parents beamed, almost in sync. 'We are in agreement, but let's ask the couple,' Singh Saab said, turning to them. 'Shaan? Pratap?'

Shaan blinked rapidly. She had to have missed something—had they just jumped from drinks and shammi kebabs to designing a mandap? She looked at her father, at her mother, their faces zooming in and out of focus, their wide, toothy grins obscuring all their features. Someone was giggling in the background, her father, she thought (or was it her father-in-law?). More laughter. She blinked again, turning her head, Pratap was nodding, a strange, shy smile on his face. She tried to get his attention. Was he really okay to take this step? Her parents' excitement she could understand—this was their mission, their bright, brash, unpredictable daughter settling down with a man they approved of. Someone who ticked all the right boxes—stability, a steady home, a good partnership personally, professionally; a union of two families. It was all she had heard for months. But Pratap? She thought . . . why had she thought they would be in sync? On most days, she didn't even know if he liked being with her. And what about Serena?

She heard her father call out. She looked at him, eyes blinking again, like a newly developed facial tic. He was smiling, his eyes crinkling behind his glasses, the garden lights reflecting on his newly shorn head. She silently willed him to not rush her, to let her find alternatives, to not be so convinced that marriage, and marriage to Pratap, was the only solution. But Singh Saab only saw what he wanted to. He saw Shaan, his opinionated, bold, unafraid daughter, unable to put into words her feelings, overcome with emotion, the appropriate sense of coyness; considered de rigueur for a blushing bride-to-be.

'For the first time, it must be said that my daughter is speechless,' she heard Sheela say.

If you asked Shaan later how it happened; how she agreed to marry a man she was so unsure of, she would just shake her head, trying to clear the cloudiness, trying to remember. She remembered her father calling out to her. She remembered looking at him. She remembered her mother making a glib comment. She remembered blinking constantly. She remembered seeing all their faces, way too close, looking at her expectantly. She remembered seeing a flash of fabric as Anuja shouted 'Mubarak Mubarak,' and draped Shaan in the maroon dupatta she was wearing, hugging her and whispering in her ear. 'I've always wanted a sister.' She remembered hearing her father call out for champagne and cigars. She remembered seeing him and Sharmaji embrace, one long, backslapping *jhappi*. She remembered the 'pop pop pop' of the bottles being opened. She remembered being hugged, by her mother, like she hadn't been in years, Sheela's arms tight around her ribs. She remembered being fed gulab jamuns, the thick, sweet liquid coating the roof of her dry mouth. She remembered her father kissing her forehead. She remembered Pratap reaching for her hand, the same hand that his fingers had been laced through a few minutes ago, so they could bow before both sets of parents, accepting their blessings. She remembered that night, in bits and flashes, like you remember scenes from a movie.

But she didn't remember saying yes.

~

It took Shaan three days to tell Aria and Tara that she was now engaged.

'I just froze. I don't know how else to describe it,' Shaan's voice was flat. 'I felt like I was watching this movie unfold, and even I wanted to know how it would end.'

'I don't understand it, how can you not know? You either said yes or . . .?' Aria pressed on. 'This is a big deal, Shaan. You've never not spoken your mind. What's changed?'

Shaan's indecisiveness when it came to minor issues had always been a running joke amongst the three of them, but this wasn't deciding whether she felt like pizza or sushi. This was a decision she would have to live with for the rest of her life and Aria just couldn't understand her ambivalence.

'You know what Aria, everything is not always so black and white,' Shaan snapped. 'Thank you for telling me it's a big deal. I would not have known otherwise.'

'I, I'm just trying to understand.'

'I can't do this. I can't fucking do this. I don't need my friends to constantly question me. I don't have the answers, okay?! I don't KNOW!' Shaan was now shouting. 'I have to go.'

'No, no, wait, Shaan,' Tara spoke up, after watching her two friends volley back and forth on screen. 'We are here for you. Whatever you may need. Honestly, this could be good. People get married like this all the time, you know, when it's an arranged set-up. And a lot of them are really happy.'

Aria shook her head at Tara. 'Arranged marriages happen, but not when the bride has amnesia about saying yes. This is sounding like a bad film plot.'

'Are you jealous, Aria? That I'm also going to be married, that you'll be the only one left behind. Is that it?' Shaan taunted.

'That's absurd, Shaan, and you know it.' Aria held her hands up in surrender. 'If that's your attitude, then all I have to say is . . .'

'So, what would you like me to do? Since you have all the answers. Tell me, what should I do? It's not like I hate him. It's just that, I'm not sure.'

Aria took a deep breath, simultaneously annoyed and worried for her friend. 'This isn't the time, Shaan, to be confused. You either know or you don't. I will ALWAYS support you, but are you sure you want to go through with this? This is the rest of your life we are talking about. You're only engaged yet.'

But the ball had been set in motion. At warp speed. Before Shaan could wrap her head around the situation, rings were exchanged, locations decided, invitations printed, a photo of the couple and their families sent out to the press, announcing their happy union. As the days to the wedding drew closer, Shaan woke up with a sinking feeling every morning, promising herself that today would be the day that she would speak her mind with her parents, with Pratap. She would convince them to maybe put a pause on things. Not an end, just a pause. Just so she could organize her thoughts. But every time she gathered the courage to have the conversation, she faltered. She knew the argument would go around in circles and she was exhausted at the thought.

Was this marriage really such a bad thing? she caught herself wondering. Things with Pratap had actually been relatively good post the engagement. He seemed more relaxed, and though their meetings had been infrequent, thanks in part to him being back in his constituency, they'd managed to spend a few evenings together, without any drama. It helped that they both, for different reasons, had a complete lack of interest in the actual planning, leaving it up to their mothers and Anuja to take on the heavy lifting. Was it possible that they could actually work? Even at home, with her parents, there was a sense of calm that hadn't been there for months, her mother engrossed in the wedding and her father back to doting on his only daughter.

'Could I be wrong?' Shaan asked Aria one night. 'Everyone around me seems to think this is the right decision. And god knows I've made some poor judgments when it comes to men and relationships.'

Aria, wary after their last argument that had led to them not speaking for several days, said diplomatically, 'I think Shaan, that's a question only you can answer. In any relationship, there are moments of doubt, but only you both know the reality. What does Pratap say?'

Shaan laughed. 'Pratap doesn't say much at all. He's not really a talker.'

In the week leading up to the big day, her best friends moved into the guest bedroom next to hers, in full support. Sheela ensured that every inch of the house was covered in fresh flowers, twinkling lights that came on at dusk and music that played non-stop. A steady stream of family and friends added to the air of merriment.

Sheela was frustrated with her daughter's lack of enthusiasm but determined to host a wedding where no detail was left unattended. Shaan, however, had put her foot down at the idea of a sangeet with family and friends' performances ('It's a merger, not a marriage. And I refuse to have my friends participating in this fakeness,' Shaan had let off to Sheela, in a moment of unbridled candour, who though taken aback, in her customary way, chose not to delve further). And so, notching it up to political propriety, it was decided that a small day wedding at home would be followed by a larger, more public reception. For all intents and purposes, it was just another heavyweight Delhi wedding, but as they say, things are not always as they seem.

~

'Shaan is WHAT?' Sheela hissed to Aria and Tara, as they frantically dialled their friend's phone. The *baraat* had nearly reached the gates of the sprawling Chattarpur farmhouse, but the bride was nowhere in sight.

It was the perfect day for an early winter wedding—sunny, crisp, not a cloud in the sky and Shaan's aunt's farmhouse had never looked more beautiful. Sheela had outdone herself, though clearly her definition of a simple backyard wedding differed vastly from her daughter's. Lush green topiaries lined the walk up to the main lawns, where white-suited bearers wearing pink pagris welcomed guests with silver trays of fresh juices. The circular mandap, nestled in the shade of the property's 150-year-old banyan tree, had been created out of a rose-pink fabric canopy covered in white and green flowers. Shimmering silver *kaliras*, hanging from the branches, caught the sunlight.

Near the swimming pool, covered in pink rose petals, a bar and a dance floor had been set up. And on the main lawns, tables for the post-ceremony luncheon, envisioned by Sheela as a traditional Indian affair, were set with beaten silver thalis and mogras with the most intoxicating scent. Given the 500-strong guest list ('*Sirf bilkul kareebwale,*' Sheela had told friends), which included cabinet and state ministers, the country's wealthiest industrialists and even some Bollywood stars (including of course Rohan Rawal), security was incredibly tight. Two days later was the bigger, more public reception for over 3000 people and a special VIP enclosure for their more high-profile guests.

Earlier that morning, Aria and Tara had driven with a rather sombre Shaan from her home to the farm and set up camp in the pool house while the hair and make-up artists set to work on the bride. Both the girls had tried to keep the mood as light as possible and after she was nearly dressed, Shaan had shooed them all away, citing a need for a quiet moment. What her friends didn't know was that Shaan hadn't been able to sleep a wink the previous night. She couldn't come to terms with the fact that in just a few hours, she would be a married woman. A marriage where she knew the odds were not stacked in her favour.

At 4 a.m., her hands shaking, she had lit another cigarette, and called Pratap. They had to call this off. Together. Be a united front. He could go back to Serena—if he'd even left her. And she could just *breathe*. It was better than them being miserable together.

But Pratap hadn't answered.

Till light broke, Shaan, paced her room, smoking cigarette after cigarette, going through scenarios maniacally. If she left him at the altar, would her parents disown her? What would she do? Where would she go? If they got married, was she okay to play the role of Mrs Sharma? And what would that entail? A political Stepford wife or a real partner? Then there was Serena. Did she trust Pratap? Or would they be those couples who lived their own lives? The thought of that was exhausting. It was not the first time Shaan Singh was dithering, but the stakes now were monumentally higher.

By the time Pratap had returned her call, she'd missed it because of a cadre of people fussing over her hair, make-up and drape.

What was holding her back? What was preventing her from just coming clean to her parents? Or from being a runaway bride, leaving it all behind? Was it fear? Uncertainty?

A future of regret? Love? She didn't think she was in love with Pratap. Was he in love with her? Not a passion-filled love, for sure.

If she could just have more time, if she could just go away from all this wedding talk, get some clarity on what she wanted, out of her life, out of her relationships. Why did it have to be so final, be married or not married? Why couldn't they both have more time?

Half an hour later, when Aria and Tara returned, there was no sign of Shaan and her phone was switched off. With the help of Shaan's younger cousins, they formed a search party, but forty-five minutes later, with the baraat nearly at the gate, they had to sheepishly break the news to Shaan's parents, that the bride in fact had gone missing.

Sheela had immediately gone into action mode, summoning a few security guards, dispatching family members to try and delay the groom's arrival. As she continued to bark orders, like a general leading the troops, albeit one in a cream sari with flowers in her platinum hair and professionally done make-up, Dhruv, Shaan's sixteen-year-old cousin rushed in panting. 'Found her!!'

And that's how, dressed in all their wedding finery, Aria, Tara, Sheela and Singh Saab followed Dhruv, through the pool house, past the staff quarters and the kitchen garden to the periphery of the ten-acre property. It was there, up in the tree house, Shaan's favourite spot as a child, that her youngest cousin had found the bride-to-be, smoking a joint.

'How did she even get up there in that outfit?' Tara whispered to Aria.

It was almost like a scene out of a bad romantic comedy but it was also heartbreaking, Aria would tell Rohan later that night. She couldn't believe that Shaan had actually gone through with the wedding and Shaan's behaviour only confirmed Aria's misgivings, that her friend had compromised such a big part of her life.

It was a while before her parents finally cajoled Shaan down from her perch, her lehenga now wrinkled and her make-up smudged. She was clearly stoned and refused to look any of them in the eye or answer any of their questions as she made her way through the kitchen garden back to the pool house to freshen up.

As they made their way to the ceremony a short while later, Singh Saab took his daughter's arm. Refusing to meet his gaze, Shaan shrugged him off. '*Main itni bhi filmi nahi hoon* that you have to drag me to the mandap, Papa. But remember this always, *kanyadaan mein*, you've not only given your only daughter away, but you've also taken away so much from her.'

With that last salvo, Shaan, head held high and back ramrod straight, walked straight into a marriage that was not of her choosing, leaving a crestfallen Arjun Singh behind.

~

The first time Aria met Pratap, it was over sushi.

It had been a couple of weeks since he and Shaan had decided on their trial dating period, but Shaan was still breezily assuming things wouldn't work out. After much cajoling ('What's the point? I'm asking Tara to chant that he will go back to Serena'), she'd finally caved. And so, when Rohan was shooting in Delhi, Aria had flown in and orchestrated a double date.

Meeting your friends' significant others for the first time can be somewhat daunting, but this dinner was further heightened by how different they all really were.

It had been downhill from the beginning, when Pratap had put up a fuss, insisting on a plate of tandoori chicken from the hotel's Indian restaurant and summoning the manager till he got his way, much to Aria's chagrin. Shaan had rolled her eyes in irritation. Even several bottles of sake couldn't quell the strange dynamics and Aria had breathed a sigh of relief when they were finally headed back to her hotel.

Awkwardddddd, Shaan texted on The Originals.

Wait, what happened? How was it? Why didn't y'all FaceTime? Tara pinged.

No, no, it was sweet. He seems like a good guy, Shaan, a little reserved, but then, you need the balance. Ha ha. :P

Ever tactful, Aria knew that Shaan had been embarrassed by Pratap's standoffishness. His entire attention had been focused on Rohan, talking up his politics, trying to pin him down for a rally ('Chal, you girls do your *gupshup*, Rohan and I have important matters to discuss'). He'd barely exchanged a few words with Aria. Every time, Rohan or Shaan steered the conversation back to neutral ground, Pratap would turn it back to Rohan.

'So, bro. I'm doing this campaign event with the youth arm and I really want you to be there. '

'So, bro, you know that scene where you jumped off the Burj. There had to be a stunt double, right?'

'So bro, the other day, I was talking to Sal, and he was telling me about his sick new pad in Dubai. Let's plan a boys' trip . . .'

And so on. Shaan had rolled her eyes throughout, finally interjecting.

'Bro, the romance is meant to be on this side,' she said, gesturing to herself.

Taking it as an affront, Pratap had become decidedly quiet and dinner had come to an end.

Rohan had laughed Pratap's behaviour off.

'He's not so bad, harmless, babe. Though I give this a month. Shaan will be bored of him in no time.'

His prophecy had been wrong.

The next time Aria met Pratap was at the intimate *roka* ceremony. Aria had flown solo to Delhi and was walking eggshells around Shaan since their last heated conversation. Pratap had been perfectly polite, but kept their interactions minimal. Tara, who'd also flown in at Shaan's request, put out at Pratap's lack of warmth, had commented, 'He should make a little more effort, no? I mean, we are her best friends.' Aria couldn't help but agree.

But nothing was ordinary with this entire arrangement. To Aria, it could hardly be called a relationship. Shaan and Pratap seemed as indifferent to each other, as they were to the guests present. Post the engagement ceremony, Shaan was on one end of the lawn with her close girlfriends and Pratap in the study with his father-in-law to be.

'Even when they stand together—they don't really seem to fit. She's petite and curvy, and he's so brawny and like big—I don't know . . .' Tara shrugged.

'You know what I've realized with relationships? Sometimes the oddest couples just work. Maybe Shaan is taking her bets?' Rohan said to Aria when she'd questioned her friend's decision for the umpteenth time. 'You would know better, but from what I can tell, she's always been impulsive.'

'Hmm, that's rather wise of you, Mr Rawal,' Aria teased. 'And yes, Shaan is impulsive, but there's a time to be an adult and make thoughtful decisions. I should think this is one of those times. This is a big, big gamble and I'm worried for her.'

'I know better than to argue with you, boss lady.' Rohan nuzzled her neck.

That the couple had made it to the wedding was a feat in itself. Though, given this morning's incident, it had been touch-and-go till the very last minute.

Aria made her way to the bar. It had been an exhausting few days; she felt incredibly sad for Shaan's predicament and to see her friend so subdued on what was meant to be such a joyous occasion. She still couldn't understand why Shaan had put herself in such a situation. It seemed so archaic that in today's world, a young, independent woman would just go along with a marriage that she didn't want. In the last ten days, Tara and Aria hadn't left Shaan's side, constantly trying to find ways to manage her vacillating moods. She had to admit, somewhat ruefully, that she was looking forward to getting back home to normal, everyday life.

'Hi baby,' a voice whispered in her ear. With his hand on her waist, Rohan spun her around. From her vantage point behind Shaan on the mandap, she'd spotted him earlier taking his seat as the *pheras* had begun. For once, Aria thought with a smile, he had been dressed appropriately, blending into the crowd.

'Stop it. What are you doing? Everyone's here,' her eyes widened, as she pushed him away, albeit somewhat half-heartedly. While it had been nearly a year since Paris, their schedules rarely had them in the same city for more than a few days, letting their relationship remain under the radar for the most part. In public, Aria kept her distance from him as much as she could. But it had been two weeks since she'd last seen him and a familiar frisson of excitement passed through her. She couldn't wait for them to have some alone time later that night. As they waited for their drinks, they chatted easily, with him teasing her, touching her arm, her waist, tucking a stray strand of hair behind her ear; Aria trying to move away, but with minimal effort. She was so grateful to see him and too tired to keep up any more pretences.

They made their way over to a canopied daybed, glasses in hand, to where Tara and Nakul were waiting. As Aria settled her sari, her face to the winter sun, she leaned against Rohan, his arm casually draped around her shoulders. It really was a beautiful day for a wedding.

When music signalling the arrival of the bride and the groom started up, she snapped out of her reverie, to find her father standing a few feet away, staring at them both, an inscrutable expression on his face.

12

After the blind item in the newspaper and her conversation with Rohan, Aria knew she had a decision to make. He'd left the timelines up to her, but he had been unequivocal about his desire to make the relationship official. Aria knew she was testing his patience.

He was particularly irritable when she cancelled yet another plan, her third in a matter of weeks, citing a family obligation.

'Let's be clear about one thing, Aria,' Rohan said. 'I don't want to be screwed around with. I'm not sitting around waiting for your call.'

'It's . . . it's not that,' she stammered. 'It's just, Dad has this dinner that he now wants me to attend.'

'Tell him you have other plans. I have one night off before I start shooting again. You're not five, that you can't stand up to him.'

She'd argued back, but even her defences were getting weaker and weaker.

'Isn't it fucking time you come clean to them?'

Months passed this way, but Aria couldn't seem to build up the courage to tell her parents. She'd sworn Leah to secrecy and had managed to orchestrate an evening together in New York when their schedules had matched. Rohan and Leah had immediately hit it off, even if it was over finding common ground in making fun of Aria's many idiosyncrasies.

'Leah's cool and all. But let's call this evening what it was—a consolation prize,' he'd joked, clearly hurt. 'Do I embarrass you?'

The fact that her parents were in New York too and she still hadn't introduced them, had not escaped his notice.

Aria was torn between what she wanted and what was expected. The subterfuge from her parents, the constant arguments with Rohan, the indecisiveness—her stomach was perpetually in knots. She was barely sleeping, snapping at everyone at work and at home, frustrated by a lack of clarity. After yet another argument with Rohan, surprising herself, she set up a session with a therapist who had helped her cousin Rishad through a particularly difficult time. Dr Shroff had listened to Aria hemming and hawing, and posed one question at the end:

'If at this very moment, you had to decide whether to stay with him or break up? What's the first thought that comes to your mind?'

And so, Aria had taken baby steps to try to be more a part of his life. She'd hung out with a few of his buddies—Kunal, Adi and Saif—and their girlfriends Priya and Hina over dinner at home. Adi and Kunal were both ADs with different production houses, so the conversation focused on industry gossip, box office turnovers and dissecting the latest indie films they had seen.

Throughout the evening, a smile plastered on her face, she'd felt on the periphery. The girls had tried to make her feel included, but Aria's reserve coupled with her inability to really participate meaningfully in this conversation had her withdraw further into her shell.

'So, Aria, which one of Rohan's films are your favourite?' Hina asked.

'Uhh . . .' Aria licked her lips nervously, feeling put on the spot.

She caught Rohan looking at her curiously.

'I, uh, to be honest, I don't really watch movies,' she'd said. 'I'm more of a book girl!' she added brightly, not missing the look that passed between Hina and Priya.

Later that evening, when his friends had left, Rohan asked quietly.

'You've never watched a *single* film of mine?'

He'd withdrawn a little after that. And Aria found herself overcompensating. She'd spent the following weekend in the home theatre, emerging bleary eyed, post a marathon of his films.

At dinner, she'd spent an hour rattling off details of every role, like a diligent student looking to dazzle her professor. Far from impressed, Rohan seemed even more irritated by her misguided efforts.

She'd pressed on. She'd agreed quite easily to his half-hearted invite for a dinner at his director's home, though she'd ensured they weren't photographed together, leaving separately. She'd taken to calling his mother, spending an afternoon with her in his apartment, and she'd even made another plan with Priya, Hina and the boys, this time inviting them to dinner in the private dining room of her favourite Chinese restaurant. Surprisingly, the press hadn't found out, and Aria let herself breathe. Rohan slowly came around again, though the elephant in the room remained larger than life. 'This could work,' she told Leah, contemplating bringing her mother into the fold.

But after the last few days, she had realized that she had to be in control of her future. Not her father. She knew Rusi wouldn't be thrilled at the prospect but was there a chance he could be persuaded? And if it came to a head, how far was she willing to go—would she choose Rohan over her family, the only world she knew, and the legacy that she stood to inherit?

~

The incessant vibrating of her phone stirred Tara from her sleep.

The wedding brunch had wound up in the early hours of the morning. The ceremony and the morning's drama done and dusted, Shaan decided that she wasn't about to let her ambivalence about her wedding day ruin a good party. 'I have a reputation to protect after all,' she told her friends, as she changed out of her cumbersome lehenga into a dress and a pair of sneakers, and bid a drunken adieu to 'Shaan ki Jawani', as she kept yelling out, requesting the DJ to play the song on repeat. And most of Delhi had been only too happy to comply. The night ended with the five of them, the groom MIA, a tureen of butter chicken and straight-from-the tandoor butter naans, to wash down the alcohol they'd all been drinking.

It was nearly 3 a.m. when Nakul and Tara stumbled back to their suite, both a little drunk, but also deliriously happy.

Tara loved weddings, even ones with their share of drama, and this one made her even more grateful that she was married to a man she truly loved.

8.58 a.m., the clock on her phone read, as it continued to vibrate.

Her mouth dry, she grabbed a bottle of water from the bedside table and tiptoed into the bathroom, so as to not wake Nakul.

Tara sat down at the edge of the bathtub and unlocked her phone.

Five missed calls from Surbhi Shukla; 200 notifications on WhatsApp—from her editor at *Style*, Surbhi, and an assortment of friends and acquaintances. What the hell was going on?

The phone vibrated again, an incoming call from a number she didn't recognize.

'Tara?' an unfamiliar male voice asked. He did not wait for an answer. 'It's Rahul Bhattacharya, from *Financial Post*. I wanted to get your comment on . . .'

'I think you have the wrong Tara. I have no matter to comment on,' Tara's voice was reed thin.

She hung up, turning back to her WhatsApp.

Babe, are you okay? Call me.

What's going on, Tara? You need anything?

Multiple messages in the same vein continued as Tara scrolled through her phone, bewildered.

Care to comment?????

The last message from Surbhi shared a link to an article from the Mumbai-based paper she wrote for. Tara clicked on it.

EOW INVESTIGATING BUILDER AND RETAIL KING MOHAN MEHTA

Sources reveal exclusively to *Mumbai Daily*, that the city's Retail Raja Mohan Mehta is under investigation by the Economic Offences Wing

Jaideep Arora Mohan Mehta, the founder and chairman of famed MohanSons stores across the state and the upcoming MohanCity, is now a person of interest for the EOW. Sources reveal exclusively to *Mumbai Daily*, that Mehta, known as the Retail Raja, for founding and expanding the first hypermart across the state, is being investigated after several irregularities in dealings with regards to MohanCity have come to light. Over the past six months, authorities have been looking into accusations of banking fraud, title fraud, delays in construction and more.

On September 15, as Mumbai recorded its highest rainfall in a decade, six storeys of an unoccupied building in the Mohan City township collapsed in the early hours of the morning. While there were no injuries, the collapse raised several questions as to why so many of the towers had not been handed over to residents . . .

The article went on for several paragraphs to list how her father had been coasting on his relationships with the local corporators to keep the story buried, but a whistle-blower had brought into focus the irregularities in loan repayments, the lack of cash flow and the pending environmental clearances, that had made a dream township resemble a ghost town. While the agencies refused to comment on record, it was obvious, even to Tara, whose knowledge in these matters was rather limited, that her father was in trouble.

Tara felt the bile rise in her throat. She dialled her father, but his number was constantly busy. She called her brother Bunty; his phone was switched off. She tried her father's assistant, again with no luck. Her mother was on a flight to Delhi from Tokyo, where she had gone for her annual bonsai convention, but she tried her too.

Is this why her father had been so stressed recently? How much money did he owe? What would happen to them? Thoughts and questions swirled in her head as she redialled her father. She thought about waking Nakul, but what would she tell him? She needed to hear from her father that all this was a mistake. It had to be.

She kept hitting redial. And after what seemed like hours, the call finally went through.

'Papa? Papa? Can you hear me?' Mohan's voice came through faintly. 'What is going on? Where are you? I need to see you.'

'I am finishing some meetings and coming to Delhi for the reception.'

'You're still coming? But, Papa, what is this in the newspaper? What is happening? And where is Bunty?' Tara's voice was breaking, hot tears sliding down her cheeks.

'All is fine, all is fine. Nothing to worry. Press *gando che*. Don't worry, beta. Now, have other call incoming.' He hung up before Tara could even get a word in.

She sat down on the cold marble floor, phone in hand. It was there that Nakul found her, hours later.

'This is bad . . . really bad. What has your father gone and done, Tara?' Nakul asked angrily, as she wordlessly handed over her phone, and he read through the piece.

For the rest of the day, Tara's stomach was tied in knots, her head buried in scrolling through news sites. Under any other circumstances, her husband and friends would have risen to the occasion, cracking jokes about Tara reading the financial section instead of the gossip pages, but Shaan and Aria had either not read the news or just didn't know what to say to her and Nakul was in a foul mood.

'But, Nakul,' Tara tried to reason with him as well as the voice in her head. 'Don't you see, he's coming for the reception, so that must mean this is just . . . I don't know, some kind of error. Maybe, maybe, someone is trying to ruin his reputation?'

'You can't be that stupid, Tara. The government, even in this country, doesn't work on gossip. There's no smoke without fire.'

For the rest of the afternoon, he'd given her the cold shoulder. He'd spent most of the time on the phone, talking in hushed tones, to his parents from what she could gather.

As the hours passed, Tara kept waiting for some news, from her father, from her brother, that all this was just some sort of mistake.

At 4 p.m., Nakul marched into the room, and seeing Tara under the covers, her lunch laying untouched on the room service cart, he barked:

'What? Why the hell aren't you ready?'

Tara looked at him, confused.

The tea with his uncle and aunt. Why hadn't he cancelled?

'Because it's rude. They are expecting us. In our family, we don't cancel at the last minute.'

Tara scrambled to get dressed, taking her husband's attempt at normalcy as a good sign. 'So far it only seems to be in the Bombay newspapers. I really hope the news hasn't reached Bade Chacha. It will be mortifying,' he'd muttered on the ride over.

She'd been distracted through the afternoon, finding it difficult to partake in the social chit-chat and the inquisitive questioning ('Bitiya, not yet in the family way . . .?') posed by her husband's relatives.

Thankfully for Tara, the tea had gone off with no mention of her father or the news. She slipped away twice to the restroom, her hands shaking, to scroll through her phone for any updates, bursting into tears, both out of relief and fear, that so far it had only been that one newspaper report.

On the car ride back to the hotel, Nakul had snapped at her for being absent and they'd gotten into another argument, with him doing most of the berating. If the news report wasn't stressful enough, lack of sleep, endless cups of black coffee, very little food and Nakul's aggressiveness had her stretched thin.

She finally snapped when she saw him emerge from the bedroom, hair gelled back, doused in cologne, dressed for a night out.

'You're going out?'

'Yes.'

'I don't believe you,' she said, her voice rising. 'I have had the worst day of my life. My father is obviously in trouble, as you keep reminding me. My brother has gone missing. You haven't said one word in support.'

She was now sobbing, tears flowing down her cheeks.

'I didn't realize that it was only about the good times for you. You are not the guy I married. That guy, that guy, he wouldn't behave like this, he wouldn't be so cold, he would give me a hug, he would be there to support, to stand by me . . .'

He'd stared at her unflinchingly. 'Do you even understand the ramifications this has on my family? Being in the press like this, it's so . . . so tawdry.'

She stared at him, unbelieving at what she was hearing.

'You are such an asshole. How have you made this about YOU?'

'How is it not about me, Tara? Stop being your ditzy self and use your brain for a minute. Our family has decade-old ties to the British royal family, my father is the head of the British Indian Society, Dad is in the running for an OBE. We've made our money the right way, without bribes, theft and murky dealings. This could ruin everything we've worked for. So, yes, news like this, family associations like this, become about me.'

The room was silent.

'So, you're calling my father a thief?' Tara's voice dropped to a whisper.

Her husband just shrugged. He opened the door to their suite and walked out.

~

Desperate for some answers, Tara waited up for her mother's flight to land, but exhaustion finally overcame her. She'd woken with a start at dawn when Nakul had come back to the suite drunk, bumping into the furniture and reeking of whisky and cigars. Without a word, he flopped over on the bed, fully clothed and was soon passed out.

Tara couldn't go back to sleep, so she spent the next couple hours refreshing her feed, scrolling through the headlines, gritting her teeth in anticipation of more bad news. By 6.30 a.m., she couldn't wait any longer and in pyjamas and hotel slippers, she made her way to Bina Mehta's suite.

In a shiny floral kaftan, her hair in overnight curlers, Bina seemed surprised to find her daughter at the door. Her helper, Savita, was already in the kitchenette, brewing masala chai in the travel cooker that was packed in her madam's luggage for every trip.

Tara collapsed into her mother's arms, not holding back her tears.

'Taru, taru, what it is? You and Nakul had a fight?' Bina stroked her daughter's limp hair.

'Savu, Tara *la chai, biskoot ani ghatiya,*' she rattled off.

'You have reduced *too* much. You need to eat little,' her mother chided.

Tara pulled back and stared at her mother in shock.

'You think this is about Nakul? Have you not read the papers? You're sitting here feeding me ghatiya, when Papa . . .'

'What, what happened to Papa?' Bina's voice rose an octave in panic.

'The newspaper, Mummy. They say that Papa is being investigated. That, that, he's done some fraud . . .' Tara choked back a sob.

Bina looked at her, the panic turning to realization.

'Haan, that . . . Papa, told me few days ago, it may come out,' she said dismissively, waving her pink fingernails. 'Oh, Taru, I got you something from Tokyo.' She reached for her oversized Louis Vuitton tote, digging through it.

Tara closed her eyes for a second, willing herself to be patient with her mother, who seemed to be behaving absurdly obtuse.

'You knew a few days ago, and you didn't think to tell me?'

'Haan, here it is,' she removed a grey box with a flourish, handing it over to Tara. 'Papa said nothing to worry, beta. So what I would tell? Now open.' She looked at her daughter in anticipation, as Savita left the tea and snacks on the table.

'Papa said that the Patels are jealous, and they are spreading all these rumours to spoil our name,' she continued, taking a sip of the tea. 'You know, ever since Papa got the Andheri plot, they have been making trouble. In business these things happen.'

Tara looked at the box in her hand and then back at her mother, who was dipping the Parle G biscuit into her chai.

'I don't understand why you aren't taking this seriously. There must be something you both are not telling me, otherwise why would the press care? These are not minor charges, Mummy. They are saying Papa could go to jail.'

'Patel *ni dikri*, her bhabhi's brother, owns the paper, Taru. It is all to scare us,' her mother sighed, picking up another biscuit from the plate. 'Tomorrow, it will be forgotten. Papa is meeting with lawyers and Surveji, they will sort out, that is why he is coming late. Now,' she changed the subject. 'Tell me you liked the pearls.' She gestured to the unopened box. 'Special Akoya pearls, from Japan. Papa told me especially to buy them for you. Nearly 7000 dollars, you know. I went with Bijal Ben to store and you aren't even looking,' she pouted.

Tara pushed aside the box. 'Mummy!' she yelled. 'I can feel something is wrong. I have been telling you for so long, Papa has been looking stressed. Is he telling you the truth? And where is Bunty? His phone is constantly off.'

'Tara,' her mother sighed. 'What you want me to say? Papa is coming tomorrow, you ask him yourself. And Bunty, he was in Dubai, with friends and then is going to South America, for some business.'

'What business do we have in South America?'

Bina sighed again. 'I don't know, some chocolate business he wants to start now. But you know Bunty, I ask him any questions—"Bunty, are you going on holiday? Bunty, dinner mein what you will eat? Bunty, high time you got engaged now?" Any question, he only shouts at his mummy.'

'Now, Taru, no more worrying,' she pulled her daughter close. 'If you worry, it will happen. Think positive. And pray to god that all will be fine.'

Tara lay there, head in her mother's lap, feeling as unsettled as before, as Bina chatted on, scrolling through photos of her prizewinning bonsai. Either her mother was in denial, or she was completely oblivious to her father's dealings. Or, was there any way—Tara felt a little hope flare up—that maybe she was overreacting; when it came to her parents, her anxiety level was always at its peak—her father teasingly called her *dramebaaz*.

'Taru, come na, to Manish Malhotra store in afternoon? I have blouse fitting.'

It was nearly 6 p.m. when Tara got back to the hotel. Her mother's blouse fitting had trumped the other alternative, spending the day with her hungover and pissy husband. She'd avoided both Shaan and Aria's calls earlier and their upbeat messages of support had only embarrassed her further. When she got back to the room, Nakul was sprawled across the couch, beer in hand, watching a football game.

'You went shopping?' he cocked his head. Before she could even answer, he added. 'Do you think that is wise, given the circumstances?'

They'd wordlessly had a room service dinner, Tara having bailed on their plans with Aria and Rohan, feigning a headache, and they'd both gone to bed early. Tomorrow was the reception, but more importantly, tomorrow, Mohan Mehta was arriving in Delhi, and Tara was determined to get some answers.

~

MUMBAI DAILY

With Friends Like These . . .

While Delhi's power politicos get ready for Arjun Singh's daughter Shaan's mega reception tonight, all eyes are going to be not only on the bride but also on her bestie Tara Mehta Puri. The social media 'influencer' is used to being the centre of attention but methinks the spotlight may be a little too bright. Reports say that her Retail Raja Papa is on the radar of all the government agencies, and a little birdie tells me that he's relying on his daughter to help lobby the bride's very powerful father to get him out of this mess. Meanwhile, darling daughter seems unperturbed by this bad publicity (or is any publicity good?) posting selfies of her #ootds during the functions. Ah, if only we could all have BFFs to make SOS (save our sins) calls like these.

Tara, call me.

Listen, I've said it before, that Surbhi is an effing cow.

Tara, please call. Aria and I have been trying to reach you.

Tara, I'm coming to your room. You're worrying me.

Tara stared at the phone, as The Originals chat kept pinging in the darkened room. What was she supposed to say? Tears streamed down her face and she wiped them away furiously, as her emotions spun the spectrum from anger to disillusionment. She was furious with Surbhi, with her father, with her insensitive husband.

She was embarrassed, embarrassed that she was in this situation, that she had become an object of pity. How could she face the crowd tonight? How could she face Aria and Shaan? And Sheela Aunty and Arjun Uncle? Every word, every action she took, would be questioned, maybe not vocally, but in their minds.

And then there was her father. Was he this opportunistic? Would he really use her friendship in such a way? Is this why he had been untruthful to her, so he could come to Delhi for the wedding and plead his case to Arjun Singh?

~

As grand Indian wedding receptions go, Shaan Singh and Pratap Sharma's wedding reception, barring the high-profile guest list, wasn't all that out of the ordinary. The stage was set, quite literally, on the vast lawns of a five-star hotel, where a specially-built platform, covered in 50,000 pink and white roses, twinkling electric diyas and gilded chairs, awaited the newly-crowned bride and groom. The chairs were superfluous; the couple would stand at attention, smiling politely as 3000 guests, waiting for their turn in snaking lines across the lawn, would come up on stage, to shake hands, pose for photos and pay respects to Arjun Singh, Ram Chandra Sharma and their newly-merged families.

It was only thirty minutes into what was going to be a long evening, and Shaan, with her straightened hair frizzing with the heat of the lights and the glare of eight different cameras, was already on edge. Despite the heels, Shaan's diminutive frame only made Pratap seem bigger, his biceps straining against the black fabric of his *bandhgala*. Every few minutes, he would mop his brow with a handkerchief, shifting nervously back and forth from one leg to another, and stepping on Shaan's long diamanté-encrusted trail. 'Ouch,' she cried out, as he yanked her lehenga sari for the umpteenth time.

'Sorry, sorry,' he mouthed back. She shot him another dirty look. 'One more hour, tops,' she hissed back at him. 'I don't care if the Queen arrives. I'm getting off this fucking stage.'

As the couple squabbled through the tedium that characterizes these receptions, the real action was taking place offstage, in a specially-built VVIP tent constructed for the honourable Prime Minister, honourable Home Minister and close friends and family. The tent, with its rich velvet drapes and ornate furnishings, also had a custom ice bar housing over twenty-five different kinds of whiskies (the honourable Home Minister was quite the connoisseur) and a plated dinner by one of the country's leading chefs. Security was tightly controlled, the area had been cordoned off and was being manned by sniffer dogs and the SPG unit. It was to this tent that Mohan Mehta was desperately trying to get access. His daughter Tara and Nakul had gone inside earlier but for some reason the guards were refusing to let him in.

'*Aap jante ho main kaun hoon?*' he threatened, getting as close as he could to the six-foot guard, who looked away, unperturbed. Mohan took a swig of his drink and tried another tactic—'*Meri beti andar hai,* phone *nahi lag raha hai aur pass mein bhool gaya . . .*'—while Bina tried to reason with her husband to not create a scene. Mehta shrugged off her arm and continued to berate the guards for several minutes. When that didn't work, he paced around outside, looking frantically for someone who could get him access to this social Narnia.

'Mohan Uncle, why are you here?' Shaan quizzed, over an hour or so later, when the bride, as promised, had ditched the reception stage and was headed to the tent in search of some food and, more importantly, a large drink.

'Clearance *nahin hain,*' a guard stopped Mohan again at the entrance.

'*Meri shaadi hai, main* clearance *doongi.*' Shaan shot back, daring the guard to challenge her and escorting a mortified Bina and a suddenly smug Mohan into the tented area.

'You should fire those security guards! *Badtameez!*' he told Shaan, now quite a few drinks down and sweating profusely despite the wintry evening.

'I'm so sorry, Mohan Uncle. Please forget it happened, you just enjoy the evening,' Shaan smiled, as guests came up to congratulate them.

But Mohan Uncle wasn't listening. He was headed in the direction of the chief minister of Maharashtra, an old acquaintance, appearing soon at his elbow. 'Ministerji, Ministerji, *tu kasa ahis, mala vichara . . .*' he started, in broken Marathi. When he saw who had spoken, the bespectacled, slight CM nodded briefly and turned back to his conversation while Mohan stood awkwardly by his side. Over the course of the next few minutes, he tried to get the CM's attention several times by attempting to angle his way into the conversation but was rebuffed again. A little later, without even a backward glance, the CM strode off, a phalanx of guards in tow, leaving a bewildered Mohan standing alone.

Before anyone could notice what had played out, he quickly gathered his wits and made his way to a table on which were seated several ministers, two of whom he'd had long-term dealings with. 'Shastriji, Alamji . . .' he called out to them, pulling up a chair to join them. But Messrs Shastri and Alam, though not as obvious as the Chief Minister, kept their exchanges with Mohan rather brief and excused themselves as quickly as they could. For the next hour, as Mohan worked his way around the tent, he found himself rebuffed, ignored and frozen out by most of the politicians he knew and even by some business colleagues. He had worked his way up to quite a state of inebriation by the time Tara and Bina found him, slumped over, alone on a corner settee.

'Papa, Papa, get up,' Tara shook her father's shoulder. Her father woke with a start and looked at his daughter blankly. Before she knew it, tears had filled his eyes.

'Bitiya, *meri* bitiya, don't worry. We'll show them all. Your Papa is thee BEST,' he took another swig from his nearly empty glass. He struggled to get to his feet, and Tara took an arm to steady him, keenly aware that guests around them were starting to stare. Despite his state, it didn't escape Mohan either.

He stood up shakily. '*Dekhte raho, dekhte raho* . . .' he gestured wildly. 'I'll show you all.' He threw the empty crystal glass on the carpeted floor, its shattered pieces glistening against the gold fibres.

A loud gasp went through the collected crowd and before he could make more of a scene, Tara with the help of a guard quickly ushered her father through the closest exit, past Nakul, who was watching this scene unfold with his mouth set in a hard line.

~

While Tara Mehta Puri was watching her father's every move that evening, Aria Mistry was trying her best to avoid hers. After Rusi Mistry had spotted her and Rohan together at the wedding lunch, she knew a conversation was imminent and she was doing everything in her power to delay the inevitable. It had helped that he'd been caught up in meetings in their Delhi office over the last two days, but she'd been dreading coming face to face with him at the reception. She thanked her lucky stars that Rohan had flown out for a shoot, so there would be no uncomfortable, public encounters between the two.

When her mother had called the day after the wedding, to join her for tea, Aria had finally told Meher everything— the Paris days, her doubts about her relationship with a film star, the fear of her father's reaction and also the extent of her feelings for Rohan. She told her about the constant yo-yoing in her mind, how hurt he had been when she hadn't introduced them in New York, how he and Leah had gotten along so well and how fond Aria was of his mother.

After a long pause, her mother had, much to Aria's relief, said quite simply, 'You know darling, all my life, I've only wanted you and Leah to be happy. I wish you had felt that you could have come to me sooner, but if this boy makes you happy, then I will do my best to support you both.'

She had warned her that Rusi wouldn't come around so easily, something Aria was acutely aware of.

'You know that when it comes to you, your father has exceptionally high standards,' Meher sipped her tea. 'And we both know that this boy stands for everything he is so vociferously against. But Aria, if this is something you really want, I will speak to him and convince him to at least meet Rohan. I can't promise more. But before we even get to that stage, you need to know in your heart and in your mind that this is what you want.'

Her mother had then added, 'Rohan is in the prime of his career, and in an industry like this, there are bound to be . . . how do I say . . . many distractions. It's not enough that you are committed, you need to trust that he is too,' she echoed a worry that had been plaguing Aria from the beginning of their relationship.

She'd replayed the conversation to Rohan later that evening.

'This is a big step for me, Ro,' she said, her voice shaking. 'My father is not an easy man to convince and I am not used to going against him.'

She continued, 'I need to ask you this. And I need you to be honest. I know you've said you are in this, but are you really willing to give up this lifestyle for this relationship? I need to know that I never need to worry. I don't want to open the papers and read about some random hook-ups. Can you make me that promise?'

'Aria,' he'd taken her face in his hands and looked her in the eye. 'Trust me, okay?'

And so, armed with assurances from Rohan, for the first time in her life, Aria was ready to take on Rusi Mistry. But she just didn't want it to happen in such a public venue, so besides an awkward hello and some rather stilted small talk, she'd chosen to stick to her friends, including a devastated Tara, who'd only come to the reception after Aria had shown up at her room and helped her get dressed.

The evening had passed off relatively smoothly. Just when Aria thought she could finally breathe, there had been that incident with Mohan Mehta, which had caused quite the scene. When the melee had settled down a little, guests started heading home, and Shaan and Pratap were heading back to their suite, Aria, finally done with bridesmaid duties, went upstairs to check on Tara.

As she crossed the lobby, she caught her parents leaving for the airport. On seeing his daughter alone, Rusi Mistry didn't miss a beat. 'Young lady, I know exactly what you are up to,' he said sternly, towering over his older daughter. 'I'll be back from London in two days. Please make sure you are home on Thursday evening. We need to have a serious talk.'

13

Five Weeks Later

10.30 a.m., Mumbai

Aria was just cooling down from her run when her phone lit up. 'Oh my god,' she exclaimed, jumping off the treadmill, and clicking on the breaking news alert, her mouth open as she scrolled through the developing story.

10 a.m., Maldives

'It's never too early for a Bloody Mary,' Shaan said with a cackle to the butler, enjoying the disapproving look on her new husband's face. She put on her sunglasses, turned her face to the sun and sipped on her cool drink, dangling her legs over the edge of their private infinity pool. Bliss. Now, if only it was Matt instead of Prat . . . she thought.

'Fuck, Shaan, you have to see this . . .' Pratap whistled, making his way to her from the deck chair, phone in hand.

5.30 a.m., London

The shrill ring of their landline jolted Tara and Nakul. They'd just gone to sleep after a sit-down dinner at his parents, followed by an argument that seemed the course these days. Tara, exhausted over the last few weeks, had turned her ringer off and taken some NyQuil to help sleep. 'It's your aunt,' Nakul handed the receiver to his wife. 'Maasi, what happened?' Tara said with a note of panic in her voice. 'Mama, Papa????' Her aunt's voice came through sobbing. 'Taari, I don't know. I think you should turn on the news.'

~

BREAKING NEWS: RETAIL RAJA ON THE RUN.
EOW APPREHENDS MOHAN MEHTA AT THE
AIRPORT LATE LAST NIGHT . . .

'I WAS JUST GOING TO VISIT MY DAUGHTER IN
LONDON,' MOHAN MEHTA TELLS COURT.

MOHAN MEHTA EVADED EOW SUMMONS.
APPREHENDED AT MUMBAI AIRPORT ENROUTE
LONDON

DEVELOPING STORY: RETAIL RAJA IN RS
5000-CRORE LOAN SCAM. INDIA CO-OP BANK
MANAGER ALSO ARRESTED

MOHAN MEHTA DENIED BAIL. THE PRIME
ACCUSED IN THE RS 5000-CRORE BANKING
SCAM IS REMANDED TO JUDICIAL CUSTODY

MOHAN MEHTA BREAKS DOWN IN COURT:

- The sixty-five-year-old is prime accused in a Rs 5000-crore banking and construction scam
- Authorities say that he defrauded property buyers at his MohanCity township
- Advocate says he's being made a scapegoat

BREAKING DOWN THE SCAM: HOW MUMBAI'S RETAIL RAJA WENT ROGUE

Jaideep Arora It's the case that has the upper echelons of Mumbai and Delhi society transfixed. Mohan Mehta, the founder of the MohanSons chain of retail stores and the real-estate tycoon behind MohanCity, was arrested by the EOW at the Mumbai airport ten days ago. Mehta, who had been evading the summons of the agency, has been remanded to police custody, while the investigation continues.

Sources tell us that Mehta is now fully cooperating with officials on charges of cheating and fraud under the Indian Penal Code, 1860. Sources tell us he is also under the scanner of the Income Tax Department, and the ED is filing an Enforcement Case Information Report (ECIR) under the Prevention of Money Laundering Act, 2002 (PMLA), looking into dealings that Mehta and his son Rishabh alias Bunty have abroad.

But how does a seller of grey market goods allegedly pull off one of the country's biggest scams?

By the early 1990s, Mehta's chain of MohanSons, the precursor to the hypermart, had expanded across the state. It became a flourishing business, dealing in imported electronics, food, clothes, dry fruits and more, and he was anointed Retail Raja, as he slowly bought over kirana stores and consolidated his brand.

Behind the scenes, it was another story altogether. Mehta, now sitting on large reserves of unaccounted cash, wasn't content with being just a glorified store owner. Sources close to the family tell us that Mehta, in a bid to garner the respect of the old moneyed elite of Mumbai society, set his goals on conquering the city skyline.

With the help of his childhood friend, former Ghatkopar MLA Sunil Desai, a silent partner in MohanCity and also an accused in this case, Mehta began bidding on large parcels of land and gaining contracts to plum construction projects.

In 2010, they broke ground on their most ambitious venture yet—a township called MohanCity, eight residential towers with amenities including a four-floor MohanSons branch, a school and a hospital that would give middle-income families like the ones he grew up with their dream home.

But sources tell us that's when the problems started. To bankroll the project, Mehta's finances were stretched, leaving him highly leveraged. When the project got stuck over an environmental clearance mid-way, Mehta, in a scramble for additional funds, managed to secure additional funding from the India Co-Op bank, despite missing previous interest payments.

Though the project suffered delays, Mehta continued his jet-set lifestyle. Authorities allege that he apportioned a part of the loans to enrich himself personally. In the last decade, Mehta has invested in a two million-pound townhouse in Mayfair, a million-dollar apartment in New York, a

Rs 5-crore beach house in Alibaug and has also thrown his daughter a multi-million-euro wedding in Monaco, which was attended by some of the country's most influential men, including Rusi Mistry and Arjun Singh.

'Ultimately, it is the common man who suffers,' says Gopal Krishan, senior officer. 'Mehta was not only using depositors' money to finance his lifestyle but we have also found instances of him selling the same flat to multiple buyers. For these first-time homeowners, every last bit of their hard-earned savings has been invested with Mehta. And now their dreams may all come to nothing.'

With additional reporting from Surbhi Shukla in Mumbai.

For more updates and developments on this story, visit our website.

THE FABULOUS LIFE OF THE MUMBAI MEHTAS:

- SON BUNTY'S CAR COLLECTION INCLUDED A MASERATI, PORSCHE
- INFLUENCER DAUGHTER: 50K FOLLOWERS ON INSTAGRAM, LIVES IN POSH LONDON HOME, WARDROBE WORTH MILLIONS
- HOUSES IN NEW YORK, ALIBAUG AND LONDON
- MALABAR HILL PENTHOUSE SEALED; ARTWORK WORTH RS 150 CRORE CONFISCATED
- BANK GOES BUST: 5000 DEPOSITORS LEFT STRANDED WITHOUT ACCESS TO FUNDS

ED ATTACHES MOHAN MEHTA'S RS 25-CRORE
MAYFAIR APARTMENT, STUDIO IN NEW YORK.

MOHAN & SONS. SON BUNTY ABSCONDING,
MOHAN MEHTA REMANDED TO ED CUSTODY
TILL APRIL 20.

MOHAN MEHTA SPENT MILLIONS ON
DAUGHTER'S WEDDING; SANJAY BHOIR,
ACCOUNT HOLDER AT INDIA CO-OP BANK, HAD
TO CANCEL HIS.

'I PUT EVERY PENNY OF MY SAVINGS FOR 2BHK
IN MOHANCITY. WHERE IS MY HOME?' ANGUISH
OF HOMEOWNERS, AS MOHAN MEHTA IS
ARRESTED.

A GHOST TOWN: WITH ONLY 20 PER CENT
OCCUPANCY, THE UNFINISHED TOWERS OF
MOHANCITY REPRESENT A BROKEN DREAM.

THE RISE AND FALL OF MOHAN MEHTA, HIS
INFLUENCER DAUGHTER TARA MEHTA PURI
AND PLAYBOY SON.

SEVENTY-FIVE-YEAR-OLD PENSIONER, INDIA
CO-OP DEPOSITOR ANAND PATEL DIES OF
HEART ATTACK. SON SAYS HE WAS IN SHOCK AT
LOSING ALL HIS SAVINGS, FILES CRIMINAL CASE
AGAINST MEHTA.

'I KNEW THERE WAS SOMETHING DODGY ALL ALONG . . .' MUMBAI DAILY COLUMNIST SURBHI SHUKLA TALKS ABOUT GROWING UP WITH TARA MEHTA PURI.

WILL HIS CLOSE FRIENDSHIP WITH ARJUN SINGH SAVE MOHAN MEHTA?

Surbhi Shukla By now, the entire country has seen the photo of the *jaadu ki jhappi*, or shall we call it jailbird *ki jhappi*? The now viral image of scam accused Mohan Mehta hugging power politico Arjun Singh at his daughter's recent wedding, just a few days before he was arrested, is the biggest proof that Mehta coasted by all these years thanks to his friendships with all the right people. A skill inherited by his daughter, Tara, who as this diarist has noted before, is besties with Singh's daughter Shaan and Mistry & Sons heiress Aria, who have both been giving Tara a shoulder to cry on. But when it comes down to the wire, can and will her BFFs save her father from a lifetime in jail? That's what methinks Tara is praying for. Wait and watch this space for more . . .

~

@taramehtapuri #ootd should be #LOOTED.
@taramehtapuri let's see how you would look in a prison jumpsuit. #orangeisthenewblack
@taramehtapuri kapda bech do, hamara paisa wapas do
@taramehtapuri shame on you! We can't pay my father's medical bills while you continue to prance around in designer frocks.

@taramehtapuri cockroaches. worst kind of people, you get rich by stealing.

@taramehtapuri UNFOLLOW. I don't have time for thieves and liars.

@taramehtapuri What did your father do with our money? Our home is gone. Help us please.

@taramehtapuri such criminals. You should all rot in jail.

@taramehtapuri this is the problem with this country today. Spoilt brats like you are considered 'influencers.' Well Daddy can't buy himself out of jail now. So we'll see what happens to the likes of you.

@taramehtapuri IT girl, more like THE PITS Girl. How does it feel to have blood on those manicured hands?

~

'I am standing outside Mohan Mehta's palatial penthouse home in Mumbai's Malabar Hill,' the female reporter breathed excitedly into her microphone, gesturing to the steel grey gate to her right that had policemen milling around.

'Mohan Mehta is the prime accused in the MohanCity and India Co-Op Bank construction scam. His 15,000-square-feet penthouse has been covered in magazines and has hosted many lavish parties with the rich and the famous. But today, his visitors are of a different kind,' she smirked, visibly impressed with her wit. 'Officers from the ED and EOW are searching the apartment and sources reveal that they have already found incriminating black money, gold bars and loose diamonds.'

She steps further to the right. 'Only on Khabar 24/7, we bring to you an insider look into what Mohan Mehta is really like. What went on in the mind of the man? What goes on behind these steel grey gates? Only one person can tell us. Baburam, namaskar.' The camera shakily pans on to a short, portly man, with a head full of hair and a stomach straining against the light blue collared shirt of his uniform. The reporter enthusiastically shoves the mike into his face. 'Baburam has been a security guard at this building for over ten years and knows the Mehta family. *Bataein hamare* viewers *ko*, Baburamji, Mohan Mehta *ke baare mein.*'

Baburam, smiles, revealing large gaps in his front teeth. '*Bahut bade aadmi thein, bade bade log aate jaate thein. Istaar bhi,*' he shakes his head. '*Par hamare* Mohan Sir *na, woh ghamandi nahi thein, bade dilwale thein,* party *ke baad, hamein biryani, khana, aur bakshish bhi dete the,*' he beams, licking his lips as if conjuring up the taste of the meaty dish. '*Bitiya bhi acchi hai, itna kuch bolti nahi.*' His expression changes. '*Par beta toh baap jaisa bilkul nahin hai. Bahut bigada hua, aur kya gaadi ko* speed *karta.*' He widened his eyes.

'You heard it first, a powerful Mohan Mehta, entertaining the creme de la creme of Bollywood and powerful industrialists. And his son, Bunty, spoilt and badly behaved. Over to you, Prashanth.'

~

Tonight on NewsNight, the shocking story of how Mumbai's Retail Raja Mohan Mehta scammed tens and thousands of crores to live a high-flying lifestyle. Houses in London, New York! Artwork worth crores! A coterie of the rich, powerful and connected! And yet, it was not enough. He stole from the poor to make himself richer.

BUT how did he escape getting caught for so many years? WHO is protecting Mohan Mehta? And WHAT will happen to the thousands who have lost their life-savings because of his greed?

The   REAL   story   only   on   NewsNight. #RAJABANGAYACHOR

~

Shaan: *BABE! This news. Just keeps getting worse. And it's everywhere—in the papers, on television, the radio. They are out for his blood. This is BAD, so BAD.*

Aria: *I'm in shock. I can't believe Mohan Uncle would do this. My heart is breaking for all these victims.*

Shaan: *Have you seen the comments on Tara's Instagram post? Fucking trolls. As if she's not going through enough. Bas, I tell you.*

Aria: *I just . . . I just . . . can't imagine. That visual of that old man on the news, sobbing, his hands folded. I just can't get that out of my head.*

Shaan: *Listen, I think we should go to London. Whatever we may think, we don't know the real story, she doesn't either, I'm guessing, and she's our friend. She needs us.*

Shaan: *Ari?*

~

'In India, YET another millionaire scamster was caught trying to flee to Britain. When arrested, MAW HEN MEY-TA, the man who scummed—I mean, scammed—his way to the top, says that he was just planning on visiting his daughter, who lives in London.'

The blonde host paused, his expression sceptical, while the audience tittered, in anticipation.

'These buggers seem to be confusing our tourism slogan, you know, the famous OMGB—Home of Amazing Moments, that we spent millions of taxpayer pounds on? Home of the Greedy Bastards, it's not, innit? We have enough of our own rich, thieving wankers here. Stay at HOME.'

The audience cheered loudly.

The screen went blank.

'Fuck this shit. I can't even relax and watch the telly any more,' Nakul threw the remote at the screen. Tara looked up from the pasta she was half-heartedly tossing.

'Seriously, Tara, it's too much. It's everywhere. It's just too fucking much.' His eyes glistened.

'Imagine how I feel Nakul. It's . . .' Tara put down the spatula and walked over to her husband. She put her hand on his chest, but he shrugged her off.

'I'm going for a run. I need to clear my head.'

14

From the time Tara was a young girl, Mohan Mehta had spoilt her silly. As his fortunes rose, so did his indulgences. When Tara wanted a doll house, he shipped the most elaborate one he could find in from the United States; when she learned how to drive, he bought her a pink Mercedes convertible, the first of its kind in the city; when she went to college in London, he bought her a plush apartment in Mayfair and hired a housekeeper; when she wanted to get married, he spared no thought, showering both Tara, her new in-laws and her husband Nakul with the finest watches, jewellery and gifts and giving them a wedding that most couples could only dream of. 'Nothing but theee best for my bitiya,' he would tell everyone. His old friends cautioned him, advising restraint, especially when it came to his children. 'You spoil Tara too much . . . children don't need all this,' Tara remembered Tony Uncle saying, after the elaborate twenty-first birthday celebrations that Mohan had hosted, flying out fifty of her friends for a weekend in Goa.

But you know what they say, new money brings new friends. Swept away in his success, Mohan had forgotten those like Tony Uncle, his childhood neighbour, choosing instead relationships that were mutually beneficial, socially or financially.

'And where are they all now?' Tara thought to herself as she sat in the conference room overlooking the city, for yet another meeting with lawyers. As the news cycle around her father had increased in frequency, not to mention the vitriol, the calls from their 'friends' had abated.

She was living in a unique kind of hell. She couldn't believe it had been only fourteen days since the call from her aunt. Fourteen days since her father had been in prison. Fourteen days since her world had collapsed. Fourteen days since her life had become filled with anger and a new-to-her bitterness.

On the day her father was arrested, Tara and Nakul, across the world, sat in silence, in the darkness of their bedroom, both too shell-shocked to speak. It wasn't long after that Nakul's parents appeared, in matching monogram dressing gowns. Her father-in-law had patted her hand briefly, shooting glances of sympathy, while her mother-in-law had launched into a tirade almost immediately, the gold under eye-masks and her Christmas socks an incongruous contrast to her tone, which went from harsh to despairing.

Tara tried to block Anjali Puri's words out, as she watched the news, almost catatonically. The ticker announcing the breaking news kept flashing against a carousel of images of her father with various celebrities and politicians; images of MohanSons stores; images of Tara taken from her Instagram account; from the wedding, her back to the camera, Nakul's arm around her waist, as they watched the spectacular firework display; Tara with Aria and Shaan, at the *Style* Awards, chatting

with Rohan Rawal and Isha Randhawa; images of a ribbon-
cutting ceremony at the township, done by Singh Saab as a
personal favour. Tara remembered that day so clearly; her
father, post the groundbreaking, had chartered a flight to
the Maldives as a thank you, and the Mehtas and the Singhs
had spent a weekend in a private, luxury beach villa, eating,
drinking and laughing. These photos, they defined the only
life she knew. Had it all been just a sham? How long had her
father been living with his lies? How had she not been able
to tell?

She touched her face absent-mindedly. Her cheeks were
wet.

Her attention diverted from the screen as she heard her
name. Her husband was hunched over his phone, as his
mother and father argued over the best course of action—a
pre-emptive statement, to distance themselves and their
company from her father and his deeds. Nakul looked up and
caught her gaze for a brief moment before he looked back at
his phone again.

Tara swallowed a lump wedged in her throat and
wrapped the duvet around her, her legs shaking. She dialled
her mother's number mechanically. Pick up, pick up, she
chanted in her mind. She knew she couldn't. Her mother,
her Maasi had informed her, had been detained, along with
her father.

Where were they now? Were they scared? Were they
together? She tried to picture the room they were being held
in. Was it like in the movies? She shivered, wrapping the duvet
around her closer, imagining a windowless, hot, paan-stained,
sparse room, her parents huddled on the floor together. Or
were they being questioned individually? One of those setups

where the police officer sits across from the suspect, a notepad in front of them, while other cops watch through a two-way mirror.

Those were the only references she had. She'd never had to enter a police station before. Even after that accident. She remembered the evening so clearly. She'd just gotten her licence, and driving to a friend's house, she'd hit the cart of a fruit wallah at Breach Candy, causing the cart to topple and pin the fruit seller flat underneath. An angry crowd had gathered around her pink convertible as the poor man writhed in pain. One hysterical call to her father and he'd taken care of the matter in minutes. Soon, the ACP of the local police station and a few *lal batti* jeeps arrived on the scene, their tires squelching the oranges, mousambis, watermelons, bananas, that now covered the road. The crowd had soon been dispersed, the fruit wallah taken to hospital, fortuitously, just a few doors down and the police accompanied her home, where they'd taken her statement over tea and nashta. The fruit seller had been handsomely compensated and the matter had been closed.

Now it was her father in trouble. Who would he call for help?

She tried her brother again. Where the fuck was Bunty? After their conversation in Mumbai, post the *Style* awards, she'd taken to checking in on him every few days, trying to get some information about what was going on at work, much to her brother's irritation. He'd started avoiding her calls, sometimes sending her messages to fuck off, or otherwise just not responding.

When the news about the EOW investigation had first come out, Bunty had apparently been in Dubai. He'd finally answered her calls, only to dismiss her concerns. 'It's all politics, *yaar*. Papa has it sorted.'

Had she missed all the telling signs? The fact that he'd skipped Shaan's wedding citing work? The fact that he hadn't taken the first flight back when the article had come out? The fact that her father had also insisted that Bunty stay abroad till the matter was sorted and Bunty had agreed.

Was Nakul right? Had she just been plain stupid, refusing to see what had been right in front of her eyes?

What she'd thought was her brother's callousness was actually plain cowardice. What she'd thought was just her father's indulgence was just his paternal instinct to shield her from the truth. But it still didn't take away from the fact that her brother had fled to protect himself, to let their father, a sixty-five-year-old man, with diabetes and an existing heart condition, bear the brunt. Who did that?

Her in-laws, argued out and exhausted, finally headed back to their room, without as much as a second glance to Tara, whose eyes were still glued to the TV screen.

'Did you know they were coming to London?' she suddenly heard Nakul say, from the couch, looking towards the television and avoiding her gaze.

'No,' she whispered, her voice raw with pain.

He just sighed, leaning back on the armchair, his eyes closed.

At 10 a.m., the entire Puri clan, Tara included, made their way to the family solicitor's firm where, amongst much hand-wringing, it was decided that they would, through the solicitors, put out a statement distancing themselves from the Mehtas and sympathizing with the victims of this terrible crime.

'Is that really necessary?' Tara asked. 'You don't even know the entire story yet . . . I mean . . . They are still my parents. I don't feel okay about this.'

Anjali Puri just ignored her, asking the junior solicitor present to read out the final language for her approval.

It was also decided that if summons were to come Tara's way, and the lawyers predicted they would, a statement, excusing her from flying back to India, would be communicated by the team. Tara, who had naively thought she would be on the afternoon flight to Mumbai, had tried to argue but had quickly been shot down by her mother-in-law.

'We are here protecting YOU. This is for your benefit,' she jabbed her lacquered index finger at Tara to emphasize her point. 'Do you even realize what this means for us? Years of our reputation and hard work, all down the drain. Everyone is going to be talking,' she'd hissed at her, narrowing her eyes. 'If you want to stay Mrs Puri, you will do as we and the solicitors say,' she'd added as an uncomfortable silence settled upon the boardroom.

Through it all, Nakul had stayed silent, letting his parents do all the talking. When they'd gotten home, Tara had broken down, and for the first time, Nakul had taken her in his arms. 'I just want to go home,' she sobbed. 'I just want to see them . . . I just, they have to be okay . . . I just.'

As he stroked her head, her body heaving with sobs, he asked quietly, 'Did you know?'

She'd pulled back from him, her face now contorted in disgust.

'It's okay. You can tell me,' he'd continued, softly.

'You're a fucking asshole,' she stormed out of the room.

Bina Mehta was released forty-eight hours later. When they'd finally spoken, it had been a good hour of sobbing, neither mother nor daughter getting a word out, their exhaustion and fear finally finding a release.

Tara's solicitors had warned her that her mother's calls were most likely being monitored and to avoid discussing the case or sharing any information that may be used against them, and so Tara, wary of giving the authorities any more ammunition against her father, when she managed to finally speak, just kept repeating, 'I should have known. I should have pushed Papa to get help. I should have asked more questions.'

'It's all in god's hands, Tari. Papa will come home. This is all a mistake.'

'How did this happen, Mummy? How did this happen to us? Why is this happening?

Did her mother really believe her father was innocent? Was he a scapegoat, a political pawn? The media had already sent him to the guillotine, he'd been pronounced guilty the minute he'd been arrested. And in Tara's brief conversations with the lawyers, it was clear that the case against him was strong. Tara hadn't had the heart to tell her mother that her father being exonerated and leaving all this behind would quite literally take an act of god.

In the days that followed, as Tara walked through her home in a daze, her in-laws continued to speak about her and her family as if she wasn't present.

Anjali Puri wailed to her sister (knowing Tara was within hearing distance) about having to cancel their annual Easter luncheon.

'What will I say to people? What are they all saying about us—that we have such nefarious relatives . . .'

'I'm telling you, she conned my poor son into this marriage. Even the wedding, you saw how they took over? Making it so flashy and over the top. She demanded that we do it all her way, and my Nakul, he's got such a big heart. She's no better than the father,' she'd said, another day, another conversation.

'My BP is through the roof. I'm getting palpitations, I can't eat, I can't sleep' she complained to the doctor Nakul had called after she'd refused to get out of bed. 'There's nothing wrong with HER!' Tara wanted to scream. Nakul sat by his mother for the rest of the evening, patting her arm in reassurance as she bemoaned this plague that had befallen their principled family.

Tara was too numb to even let her mother-in-law's jibes get to her. She was living in a state of isolation, her despair compounded by the unending news cycle. What Mohan Mehta had done had impacted thousands of families, denying many their basic right of a roof over their heads. The laundry list of allegations against him including selling multiple flats to the same buyers, using poor and substandard quality of materials resulting in the building collapse, triple mortgaging the parcel of land and the buildings and using depositor funds for personal expenses. Every day seemed to bring new developments—commentary from so-called insiders on their family's private life, more photos from her childhood, pictures of their homes, protests by bank depositors and property buyers demanding justice. And the videos. They played on loop—the seventy-five-year-old man sobbing over his life savings; the young girl, with her parents, who couldn't get her married; the son who could no longer pay for his mother's medical treatment; the family living in a four-by-five room with a leaky roof, unable to pay rent any longer, the interest on the loan for their dream home cutting into all their savings. They played on the news, on social media and through her leaked number, on WhatsApp messages to her, through all hours of the night. Her phone pinged constantly with alerts, hate comments flooding her Instagram, reporters calling her incessantly. Tara knew she should turn it off, delete her social media, but in a convoluted, masochistic way, seeing them, hearing them, made her feel that this was a small atonement for the sins of her father.

Nakul, whenever he was home, was distant, and when he did speak, he would keep prodding her for information.

'For the last fricking time, Nakul. I DID NOT KNOW ANYTHING!' she screamed, after another persistent round of questioning. 'You were the one who said not to interfere when I felt something was wrong. And now you want to find me guilty?'

He'd moved into the guest bedroom shortly after.

A few of the Mayfair Mrs had sent messages, varying from polite platitudes to shamelessly prying for information:

Thinking of you!

Big hug, sweetie!

Chin up! Remember what guruji says. Manifest your father's release!

OMG babe, you must be shattered. This is crazyyy. So, what's the update right now?

With the camera crew parked outside her home, visitors were few and far in between; her friend Farah ventured as far as the street outside and then skittered away.

I'm sorry, darling, she texted later. *I wanted to see you, but I didn't think my in-laws would be too pleased if my face was plastered across the news. But know I am thinking of you. Xo.*

On his way to work one morning, Nakul ended up having an altercation with the cameramen, leading to the police showing up and only adding to the storm that was raging inside the Puri household.

'Maybe you should go back to Bombay,' he said, furious, after the officers left. 'Thanks to your father, this house has become our prison.'

She'd shrugged, too exhausted to even get into another argument she knew she wouldn't win.

The day she heard that her father's bail had been denied again; seeing him transported to the courthouse, she had broken down. He was shrunken, his jet-black hair streaked with grey, a beard covering his now gaunt face. He shuffled, his forearms gripped by policemen on either side, as the cameramen hunted him down, shoving their mics and lenses in his face. She watched those videos, of that short walk between the police van and the entrance of the courthouse, over and over again, unable to connect this frail man with her jovial, bustling Papa. The look on his face behind the barred window, as the van made its way through the crush of cameramen, his eyes watery and bloodshot, would haunt her for years to come.

She'd called Shaan that night, still in hysterics. Since the news had broken, she'd only had a few stilted conversations with Aria and Shaan. It wasn't lost on Tara that her best friends hadn't flown to be with her in London. They'd always been there for each other and the absence of this gesture, especially given the magnitude of the situation, was telling in more ways than one.

Tara was slowly coming to the realization that she was, thanks to what her father may have done, in many ways now a social pariah.

But would Aria and Shaan not stand by her?

~

The phone call lasted over half an hour and while most of what Tara had been saying had been incoherent, the conversation rattled Shaan. Given the intense scrutiny on this case and the probability that calls were being monitored, they'd only exchanged a few messages so far. This had been different. In between hysterical sobs, Tara had come out and literally begged Shaan to help.

'Only you,' she'd hiccupped, 'can convince your dad. He has to do something. Please Shaan, I will do anything, I beg you . . . He's not a bad man, you know him, Shaan. He's made mistakes but I know, I know, he'll find a way to make sure it's all okay.' Shaan heard her blow her nose through the receiver.

There was a long pause before Tara spoke again, clearing her throat.

'During your wedding, when the first piece came out . . . he'd mentioned that it was a business vendetta. Could he,' her voice faltered. 'Could he be framed? I know my father, Shaan. He is not all the horrible things they are saying he is.'

She'd started crying again, for several more minutes, and Shaan, at a loss for words, tried to offer up some weak platitudes.

Tara said softly, 'I feel so helpless. He's done everything for me and the only way I can help is to ask you. I know, this is such a big thing. But wouldn't you do the same? I really don't have anyone else to turn to,' her voice broke, and Shaan found herself choking up.

Tara cleared her throat and composed herself. 'You are my oldest friend. We've been through so much together, and now I beg you, please, help my father, help my family, help me. Promise me, promise me, you'll help. He won't make it otherwise . . .'

Shaan stared at the receiver in her hand, tears rolling down her cheeks. What could she say? Shaan thought miserably. How did you make a person feel hopeful, in a situation that was so far gone?

How could she come out and tell her oldest friend that there was nothing, in anyone's power, that could help her father now? And even if Shaan could ask her father to intervene, it would be political suicide.

In her years with Singh Saab on the campaign trail and even at his home office, Shaan had encountered some of the most heartbreaking stories—of missing children, financial ruin, families facing acute hunger, caste and communal violence destroying lives and homes. She'd grown more and more aware of her privilege, waking up in her plush bed in her air-conditioned room and looking out at throngs of people waiting to meet her father, outside the gate, for hours, in the heat. She'd seen grown men and women, children, lying prostrate at his feet, begging for help and mercy.

And for days after Shaan would not be able to get those images and stories out of her mind.

'How can you sleep, Papaji? Hearing all these stories . . . and not being able to help?' a younger Shaan asked dejectedly, looking down at her plate, pushing the grains of rice with her spoon, many years ago.

'I sleep just fine,' her father bristled and continued eating his dinner. A few minutes later, he added, somewhat tiredly, 'Shaan, beti, I love that you have so much empathy. But you will learn in time that you cannot help everyone. The world's problems are not ours to solve.'

And he'd been right. As she'd grown older, a part of her had become desensitized to all that was occurring around her. As her father's power had grown, everyone had seemed to want or need something. It wasn't just the average man in his constituency, it was their old neighbour from Mumbai, it was their mother's college classmate's husband, it was the Khannas, a few doors down, it was the Gupta's son-in-law in America. Everyone had a problem that needed to be solved, a string that needed to be pulled, a favour that needed to be called in. That was how this country ran, her father had been known to say, in a matter-of-fact tone.

But this time, it was different. It hit home again, harder than it ever had before. It was Mohan Uncle. Her best friend's father. The Uncle who always gave them an extra scoop of ice cream when no one was looking, who would always also buy Aria and Shaan gifts when he travelled, who had always been so kind and affectionate to his daughter's friends.

It wasn't lost on her that helping Mohan Uncle would be tantamount to absolving him of all that he'd done. Could she live with the hypocrisy? Could she ignore the stories of hundreds of lives, to save one of her own?

She wouldn't be the first. She'd boasted enough about her father coming to the rescue every time one of his friends had bent laws and been caught with the proverbial pants around their ankles.

This time, though, she knew that help from her father wasn't forthcoming.

Shaan threw her phone across the room, hearing it thud against the floor and put her head in her hands, the tears now flowing copiously. And that's how Pratap found her.

~

When it came to the whole sex before marriage debate, Shaan was known to say, 'How can you not try it before you buy it?' Well, the joke's on me, she thought to herself, as she dove into the turquoise waters that surrounded their lavish villa.

After the wedding ceremony and the all-night party, Shaan, both drunk and stoned, had passed out on what would have been the much anticipated ('Or dreaded, depending on who you were asking,' Shaan in a previous avatar may have quipped) 'wedding night.'

She'd woken up the next morning, to find Pratap awake next to her.

'Hey,' he'd smiled, turning to face her and lacing his fingers through hers. He'd pulled her closer and kissed her gently.

'Uh, I haven't brushed,' she turned her face away, self-consciously.

'I don't mind,' he said, softly, kissing her harder. Despite her surprise, she found herself reacting. He pulled back to remove his T-shirt, and she traced his well-defined abs with a finger as he bent down to kiss her again, taking a fistful of hair in his hands. In one swift move, Shaan found herself underneath him. Shaan had to choke back a laugh as Pratap, catching sight of his bare upper body in the mirror across the bed, sucked his stomach in and flexed his biceps.

But that's where the smooth moves and Shaan's laughter ended. From then on it was an almost comical series of fumbling, him on top, her on top, a drawstring that wouldn't untie, unwieldy duvets that got in the way, polite apologies and more fumbling. Shaan had wanted to scream in annoyance and frustration. She couldn't wait for it to be over, so she could forget it had ever happened this way.

Finally done, Pratap had leaned back on the pillow, one hand behind his head and winked at Shaan, who was lying next to him, '*Now* we're married.' Shaan, in response, had gotten out of bed, furious, dragging the duvet with her and leaving him lying on the bed naked.

'What?? What did I do?!' he yelled, as she slammed the bathroom door shut.

Married people sex sucks. I couldn't wait for the finish line, Shaan texted Aria. *How could I not do a test run!*

Oh gosh, Shaan. TMI.

Who would have ever thought that Aria Mistry would be having hot, steamy, can't get my hands off you fucking sex, and I would end up with a guy, who . . . I can't even talk about it.

Tell me, na Ari, she typed, imagining her friend's discomfort. *Tell me about the hot sex you and Romeo are having. Maybe that will get me somewhere?*

BYE, Shaan.

In hindsight, maybe a honeymoon on a deserted island wasn't the best idea. Pratap and she had spent the first two days continuing to behave like polite strangers both in and out of bed, exhausting all small talk and leading to Shaan drinking copious amounts of alcohol to keep up pretences.

Their days differed and they spent more time apart—Pratap, diving, paddleboarding, jet skiing, while Shaan was content laying around the pool, a cold drink in hand, her phone in the other. She'd taken to passing out drunk every night to avoid any more awkwardness and she'd find, most mornings, Pratap gone by the time she woke up, or asleep on the daybed.

The days post the wedding in Delhi had passed in a flurry of smaller functions with her in-laws and the big reception, giving them no time for their new reality to set in. Pratap and she had seen each other briefly in between, walking eggshells around each other. Not even one month, and I'm already in one of those pathetic, stale marriages, Shaan thought to herself for the hundredth time, as she wandered through the rooms of his Gurgaon apartment (she still couldn't get herself to use the possessive pronoun that characterized a union), in a permanent sense of ennui.

'Things will get better, you will find an equilibrium,' the ever-rational Aria counselled, though Shaan couldn't help but wonder if her friend felt vindicated in her concerns. But she was grateful to Aria, that she never brought up that conversation again.

So she willed that a change of scenery, a neutral environment, would help propel them forward. The Maldives is the most romantic place in the world, maybe that's what we need. But, when they got there, it was more of the same. And Shaan knew she was as much to blame. By day three, she had decided enough was enough, and she had to talk to Pratap about their dysfunctionality.

But something changed the day the news about Mohan Mehta broke. Sitting shoulder to shoulder with Pratap on the deck, their legs dangling in the water, Shaan had watched in shock and horror as the news had developed.

She'd dialled her father, furious at his duplicitous silence.

'You HAD to know. You know *everything* that is going on, so don't even try and deny. How could you not tell me?' she said, the stillness of their villa shattered by her shouting. She'd been unwilling to listen to any reasoning on her father's part and had hung up on him, pacing the deck. Pratap sat there, watching her.

'You know, I asked him. I asked him,' she gestured angrily. 'The day after the reception and the article and that whole scene. And he just avoided the question. I should have guessed then.'

'What would you have done if you had known?'

Her eyes flashed. 'She's my best friend, Pratap. Maybe loyalty doesn't mean anything to you—'

He laughed softly.

'Are you fucking kidding me right now?'

He held his hands up in surrender. 'Be realistic, Shaan. You're not naive enough to believe that it would have changed anything. It's not like you could have warned her and, to be honest, chances are he already knew this was coming, *isliye bhaag rahe the.*'

He took a breath and continued. 'And if you think your dad can be even within ten feet of this, you are being seriously . . . they are waiting for him to slip up, haan. It's every man for himself now, Shaan. You better wake up to that.'

She'd gone to bed, irritated. With her father, with the situation, with Pratap pretending to know it all.

The next morning, she'd woken up to find him already in the pool.

'So, maybe, just maybe, you have a point,' she alluded to the conversation the night before. 'But I still think Papa can help, he's done it before, he has his ways,' she dipped her toes tentatively into the water, the morning breeze ruffling her sarong.

He'd scoffed.

'It's a different time, Shaan. We are a year out of the election, the other side is gaining ground, and this case,' he whistled. 'This case has everything the media wants—the rich getting richer on the poor man's back. They are going to be ALL over it. It's fucking TRP gold.'

When she'd finally gotten through to Tara, her friend just kept repeating, 'It's not true, Shaan, It's not true. It's a mistake. It's a mistake, no?' It broke Shaan's heart. Pratap sat next to her, wordlessly, holding her hand for the rest of the evening.

Over the next forty-eight hours, they monitored the news together, their mealtimes no longer consumed by silence, but filled with debates and arguments. The ramifications on Tara and her mother, Bunty's involvement, how it affected the Singhs and the party, given the Mehtas' closeness to them and other politicos; the media coverage, and without even realizing it, they organically segued into other conversations. In those two days, she learned more about Pratap than she had in all the months she'd known him. And when they had sex again, this time it was Shaan who initiated, catching Pratap off-guard, and guiding him to what she liked. It was far from perfect, not even close to what she'd imagined her honeymoon to be like, but with them, she was realizing, it was baby steps.

In someone else's tragedy, two relative strangers had found some synchronicity.

Landing in Delhi, they'd gone straight to Shaan's home at her insistence. She was still angry at her father about the wedding, frustrated by his lack of clarity when it came to this situation, but she just wanted to be home. Seeing images of Mohan Uncle pushed and shoved, handcuffed into a van, had caused a visceral reaction in Shaan. She was hardly one to philosophize, but the ephemerality of success and power was not lost on her. Differences with her parents aside, she just wanted to go home and hug them both.

'Don't think I've forgotten my anger.' She shot her father a half grin, before curling into his arms.

He'd just laughed, hugging her even harder.

Singh Saab knew that when the headlines were accusatory, the only real solution was keeping a low profile, at least until the next story broke and the public moved on. And despite the cameramen at his gate, that was exactly what he planned to do.

'Before you even ask, Shaan,' he shot her a warning look, as he poured Pratap a drink. 'I cannot be involved. You've seen the news; my name is in every frame. I'm too closely associated with this as it is.'

Pratap mouthed, behind her father's back, 'Told ya.'

Singh Saab shrugged. '*Bachi hai*, and I am very fond of her,' his voice softened. 'But my hands are tied. It's best she stays in London. This mess Mohan has created is not going to go away soon.'

The three of them had gone on to discuss the case in detail. Mohan Uncle had just appointed one of the country's most formidable advocates, but even then, from the news that was developing, his position was looking weak.

'And I know you don't want to hear this, Shaan,' her father said. 'But you don't know how much Tara knows. Bunty, toh, they are saying, has been the cause of the mess. Now, whether Mohan is just protecting his son, or the son is being blamed, we don't know. We'll never know the truth . . . and that's why we have to be especially careful to not get more involved in this.'

'Let this be a lesson to you both,' he continued to Shaan and Pratap, as Sheela called them to the dinner table. 'Everyone is your friend, until no one is your friend.'

'Papa, you had to see her,' Shaan shivered involuntarily. 'I get goosebumps even thinking about what she's going through. And that asshole of her husband is no support.'

'I know it's difficult, but what have I always taught you? It's every man for himself. You have to be careful, Shaan,' he said sternly.

He'd strongly shot down her idea of going to London. 'There's only that much I can do to protect you both. Once the press finds out, and the other side will ensure they find out, that you've flown there to meet her . . . I know how important Tara is to you, but you have to think of your family—even if you don't want to think of me, you have both your position and your husband's to think of now. Pratap still has his elections to win. And any wrong move could ruin his chances and yours in the future. The public is angry at the moment and they want to find a scapegoat.'

When it came down to it, Shaan knew her father was right. Her whole life, she'd had a front row view to the high stakes power brought. If it was anyone else, she would not have even entertained the idea, but this was Tara—ditsy, fun-loving Tara, who loved nothing more than a good gossip session with both her girlfriends. Tara, who loved her society it girl persona, but when it came down to it, was a solid good person. Tara, who had not left Shaan's side during the drama surrounding her wedding. Without judgement, without any fuss, she had come through for her. Could Shaan really just forget all that in just a few weeks?

And that was what plagued her as she, along with the rest of the country, watched the details of the scam come out. As new properties were uncovered in different parts of the world; as hapless bank depositors appeared on national television, appealing for access to their funds; as news anchors and talking figureheads bayed for his blood; as snapshots of Tara's mother and her aunts, leaving the ED offices after questioning, designer handbags covering their faces showed up on smartphones and screens, as did a video of an irate Nakul, pushing a cameraman outside their London home.

And the cry for help from Tara had only made things worse.

~

She lifted her head and turned to Pratap. 'It was Tara,' she said, gesturing to her phone. 'I know what my father says is right, but Pratap, how can I do nothing? She's broken, I'm so worried about her . . . what if she . . .'

Pratap sat on the armchair across from her and let out a whistle as she recounted the conversation.

'It's *Tara,* Pratap. You don't know the history. But she's been such a solid solid friend. Even when things with us . . .'

He looked at her quizzically, but she looked away.

After several minutes of them sitting in silence, Pratap spoke up.

'It's "burn the rich" time. *Sunne ko aa raha hain* that this is just the tip of the iceberg. News *aur nikalne wali hai* Shaan, too many powerful figures involved. *Ab use koi nahi bacha sakta.* Not his daughter, and not her friends.'

'But if you really want to go see her in London, I can try and figure something out so the trip doesn't raise any red flags. Let me speak to a few people and I'll handle your dad . . .'

Shaan stared at him in disbelief, 'You would do that? Why?'

He laughed at her expression, his eyes crinkling. 'Isn't that what husbands are for?'

15

In the Mistry house, an alternate reality was slowly settling in. Even routine family meals were fraught with tension, characterized by frigid silences. Aria and Rusi both held their ground, while Meher and Leah were playing peacemaker. Meher tried to reason with husband and daughter, but to no avail. 'Both cut from the same cloth—stubborn as ox,' she told Leah exasperatedly.

The tension had been mounting since their return from Shaan's wedding. As expected, Rusi had summoned Aria, and the conversation had evolved into an epic showdown, unlike anything their household had ever witnessed before. The angrier Rusi got, the more defiant Aria became, surprising both Leah and her mother by refusing to back down. That Aria, a self-confessed daddy's girl, who thrived on Rusi's approval, was going against her father, was enough of a shock, but the fact that she was willing to open her private life to such public scrutiny, made Leah and Meher both realize that this relationship was far more serious than they'd thought.

'I'm just done with him talking AT me. He never talks TO me,' Aria railed to Leah, pacing in her bedroom, her fists clenched by her side, after Rusi had categorically demanded that she stop seeing Rohan. 'Whatever is going on between you and that, *that* boy,' Rusi said, his ruddy complexion now even more flushed, the deep tomato shade spreading across his cheeks and his bulbous nose, 'it ends, here and now, Aria. Do you hear me? I will not have our family's lives become common, tawdry gossip.' The rich baritone that landed him a coveted spot on the choir at his alma mater Eton's College, was now at an almost deafening volume.

In an effort to calm him, Meher put her hand over his, but Rusi glared at her, pulling it away. He narrowed his eyes at Aria, who sat at the table stone-faced, arms crossed across her chest. With his towering stature, both physical and social, Rusi was used to being heard; he had a quick temper, with zero tolerance for disrespect, and his daughter's defiance was testing his limits.

He spoke slowly, enunciating. 'Aria, you are on the right path. Don't let some juvenile boy distract your focus. You may not see it now, but you will thank me. ONE day, you will. Before this goes any further . . .' he paused, 'I have implicit faith, that *you* will do the right thing.' Having said his piece, Rusi pushed the chair back and strode out of the room, effectively signalling the end of the discussion.

'He's controlled every minute of my life—where I went to school, what I studied, what department I started in at Mistry & Sons. Not once, not ONCE, has he ever asked me what I wanted. Did you hear him? This ends NOW,' she imitated her father's posh public schoolboy accent, that became even more pronounced when he was angry. 'Am I to be given no choice in the matter?'

Leah had listened silently.

'Can I ask you something, Ari?'

'Umm, are you really, really sure about this? Forget Dad, this is a big, *very* public move for you,' Leah prodded.

'I love him, Leah. I really do.'

And so, after days of this cold war, Leah decided to take matters into her own hands and sat them both down in her father's study.

'Now, you will listen to what I have to say . . . ah, ah,' she said, as her father tried to interrupt.

'I'm just done with eating alone, done with this constant ice between you two, and I'm even more done with the raised voices when you do deign to speak. We've never been a family that shouts, so why has that changed? Mum is hanging out here being Switzerland, but I'm DONE with this bullshit.'

'Language, Leah,' her mother cautioned, trying not to show her amusement at her younger, more laid-back daughter taking control.

'Jeez! Mum!'

'Anyway, here's how it's going to go. Aria, you are going to invite Rohan to dinner, and Dad, you will welcome him to our home and get to know him. He's a decent guy, you know? Just give him a chance, please?'

Her father had tried to argue. But Leah refused to let him get a word in.

'ONE dinner will not kill you.' Meher nodded in agreement.

'Rusi, it's very normal for a young man to be brought home. And Rohan deserves as much a chance.'

'Over my dead body,' is what he wanted to say, but he knew when he was outnumbered. 'Fine,' Rusi muttered, wanting to end this conversation and get back to his crossword. 'I'll meet the actor boy, But more than that . . .'

And so a detente was reached and after months of dating, Rohan was on his way to the majestic, seaside Windsor Villa, a home that had welcomed heads of states, international royalty and leading industrialists. Yet the arrival of a young Bollywood star was causing 'quite the tizzy', as Meher confided to her brother.

Aria warned Rohan ahead of time—no outlandish clothing, no smoking, no more than two drinks and no politics. 'Political affiliations, like dirty laundry, should not be aired in public,' Rusi had preached, time and again. The comment was then almost always followed by a quote from Socrates, his personal favourite, that both the girls could now recite from memory—'Strong minds discuss ideas, average minds discuss events, weak minds discuss people.'

'No breathing?' Rohan ribbed Aria.

And so, when their long-time house manager led Rohan to the poolside gazebo where Meher had set up cocktails, even Aria did a double-take at the clean-shaven, neatly gelled hair, white shirt and slim navy trouser look Rohan was sporting. Walking behind Rohan were his bodyguard and spot boy lugging a Louis Vuitton trunk.

Oh god, Aria groaned inwardly, as Rohan's staff presented the trunk to Meher, revealing twelve shiny gold bottles of Armand de Brignac champagne.

'Aria mentioned that you love bellinis,' Rohan said, somewhat nervously, as a way of explanation, to Meher. 'This is considered the world's best champagne.'

'That's too generous, Rohan,' Meher smiled. 'Please, be comfortable, we're happy to finally meet you.'

'Very nice to meet you too, and you, Uncle.' Rohan offered his hand to Rusi.

'Young man, I am not your Uncle,' Rusi scowled.

'And we've met before, but I'm sure you wouldn't remember.'

Rohan looked at him, momentarily confused.

'I'm curious, were you expecting an onslaught of fans?' Rusi interjected, bypassing all niceties and gesturing to the presence of his spot boy and bodyguard, who were now standing at the edge of the gazebo. 'I assure you, neither my family nor my staff will be harassing you. You are quite safe here.' His tone dripped with condescension.

Visibly embarrassed, Rohan quietly asked them to leave.

And that's all it took for the dominoes to fall. Aria could see that Rohan felt slighted, even though Meher was at her solicitous best. And through the dinner, she could see her father flexing his best intimidation tactics; but whether it was Rohan's acting skills or a genuine refusal to cower, they didn't seem to have Rusi's usual desired effect.

'You have a beautiful home,' Rohan said. It was one of the last cool nights; a slight nip in the air that characterized the city's brief winters, before the hot humid summer set in. The view from where they were sitting was spectacular. Beyond the cerulean blue of the Olympic-size pool with its intricate mosaic was the twinkling lights of the Queen's Necklace and the Arabian Sea, the waves lapping the stone walls that lined the property. The lush green lawns were intertwined with walking paths. Behind them was the main house, built in the style of a stately manor home. Soft yellow spotlights highlighted its neoclassical details—the marble columns, the fifteen-foot-high French windows that showcased the 1000-

bulb Murano chandelier that greeted guests in the foyer and a large terrace, edged by a balustrade, on which rested two magnificent lionhead statues on each corner.

'It was built by my great-grandfather Sir Rusi Pestonji Mistry over a century ago, he was knighted by King George,' Rusi puffed his chest. 'This was all wild, undeveloped land,' he gestured around them. 'But he was smart, he trusted his instincts. As soon as he made his fortune, he built this for his wife, Persis, who also came from an illustrious Parsi family.'

'Wow. That's cool. Really cool. To go back so many generations.' Rohan put his arm around Aria as he spoke. Aria could see Rusi visibly stiffen at the gesture. As gently as she possibly could, she angled her body out of Rohan's reach.

'It's more than *coooool*,' Rusi drew out the word. 'It's imperative. This house has seen generations of Mistrys and if the walls could speak . . . Aria and Leah know that these are stories and values that they will pass on,' his booming voice reverberated through the gazebo.

'Tell us about your childhood.' Meher took advantage of the pause in her husband's monologue, to turn to Rohan.

'There's not much to tell, quite honestly. It was just Ma and me. My dad left when I was very young . . .' Rohan recounted his mother's struggle to make ends meet and her dedication to ensuring that Rohan had a good childhood. He laughed as he spoke, his dimple flashing, 'She would have loved for me to be a doctor or an accountant, but I wasn't exactly the best student. And then I was offered my first movie in the first year of junior college and that was that.'

'So, you dropped out of college?' The disdain was evident on Rusi's face.

'You know what they say, school and college don't teach you everything, Sir,' Rohan had said. 'I think I learned more on the set of my first movie than I did in all those classes. I'm lucky that way, I'm living my dream,' his smile tightened.

'Spoken like those "hippies". The dream is in the work, that's what I always say. When I was in college, my friends were taking gap years to backpack around the world. I could have joined them, you know, to "live the dream", but, I knew that would be remiss . . . look at Aria, she has an MBA from Harvard.' Aria shifted in her seat awkwardly. ''To run a company like ours, which she will one day, Aria has a responsibility. She couldn't just drop out of school to follow a "dream".'

He gestured to the bearer for another pour of the single malt. '"If a man neglects education, he walks lame to the end of his life," Plato, the ancient Greek philosopher,' Rusi ended with a flourish, raising his eyebrow at Rohan.

'I'm surprised to hear you say that, Sir. I thought a man like you would be more open-minded to the idea that reading textbooks and learning by rote doesn't necessarily prepare you for the real world . . . Wasn't it also Plato or one of those Greek guys, who said knowledge is the food of the soul? Knowledge isn't only through schools, I think enough people have proved that. Look at Steve Jobs, Bill Gates . . .'

'Young man,' Rusi, leaned forward in his seat, looking squarely at Rohan. 'If you had to get a job in the real world, what would be your qualifications? What are you going to put on your resume—playing dress up? Dancing around trees?'

'With all due respect, that's a rather outdated view of Indian cinema. Every profession has its dignity, Sir. I'm proud of the work I do, and I do a lot more than you give credit for.'

'Dad . . .' Aria spoke out, shooting her father a warning look. 'This is really going a little too far.'

'No, Aria,' Rusi said, putting his hand up. 'You wanted us to meet this boy, to get to know him. Well, that's what I'm doing. I would like to know his intentions. I'm curious to know how he plans to live when all this actor business comes to an end. And it will come to an end, acting has an expiration date. So, what will he do? Or will you go to work and he live off you?'

'DAD!'

'RUSI!'

'I don't need your daughter's money, SIR,' Rohan clenched his jaw.

'Dinner is served!' Meher clapped loudly, ushering everyone to their feet. As they walked up to the house, her father leading the way with his long looping strides, Aria put her hand through Rohan's, but he shrugged it off, walking ahead of her.

In the formal dining room, the Burma teak table, with three-foot silver candelabras, interspersed with white calla lilies, running down its length, was groaning with the Mistry home specialities—a beautiful roast chicken with baby potatoes, steamed fish in lemon butter sauce, baked crabs in their gleaming red shells, a smattering of salads, spaghetti with freshly shaved truffles, a leg of ham flown in from London, all laid out on Meher's favourite blue and white Wedgwood dinnerware.

They'd eaten the soup course in relative silence, with Leah trying to indulge in some mindless chatter, but giving up halfway. 'Tough crowd,' she'd muttered.

Throughout the course, Aria kept looking over at Rohan, sitting across from her, but refusing to meet her eye.

'Rohan, you have to try the fish. It's Rusi's grandmother's recipe, a family secret.' Meher gestured to the liveried bearer to serve their guest.

'Everything in this house is passed down, even the recipes. The past guides the future—the very foundation of who we are, our family, our company,' Rusi droned.

'So, Rohan, what are you working on right now?' Leah asked, when her father paused to take a bite, trying to bring Rohan back into the conversation. Rohan gave her a somewhat forced smile, as he told them about his latest film and the script he had just started writing. From the corner of her eye, Aria could see her father pretending very hard not to listen.

'It's the coming of age of three young friends from a small town in India, whose dreams take them all around the world. It's still a work in progress but, fingers crossed, one day, it will make it to the big screen.' He took a bite of his fish.

'Hmm, you're right, Aunty, this is just insane, I'm going to have to work out twice as hard tomorrow!'

'I will never understand the obsession young men in your line of work have with pumping all that iron. Whatever happened to a good game of tennis to keep fit?' Rusi wiped the corners of his mouth. 'Now, its all bulging muscles and those ridiculous tight T-shirts and even tighter jeans. So unseemly. What was that cartoon you girls liked when you were young?' he asked Leah and Aria, who ignored the question.

'Ah!' He banged his palm on the table. 'Popeye!' He cocked his head in Rohan's direction, alluding to his slim-fit, slightly opaque white shirt that only highlighted his broad shoulders and taut top half, 'You've watched it, I take it?'

At long last, when dessert and coffee were served, Leah turned to her sister. 'Aria, I've been meaning to ask you. How is Tara?'

'Hmm, yes,' said Aria, her head reeling from the disastrous dinner and Rohan's standoffishness. He hadn't looked at her once during the entire meal.

'She's not in a good place . . . she's devastated . . .'

'Of course, she would be,' Rusi shook his head. 'Her father has turned out to be nothing but a common thief. Stealing from millions to fund a flashy lifestyle . . . and ruining his daughter's life. At least he had the common sense to keep Bina and her out of his shady dealings.'

He took a bite of the strawberry dacquoise.

'That wedding alone, what did I say to you about it then, Meher? Everything that went on there was just disgraceful,' he said, looking pointedly at Rohan.

~

'He's a cad, Meher,' Rusi said angrily. 'He's got a drug habit, he's, he's not respectful to women. Not to mention that he is a college dropout, with NO family history and a terrible attitude. Is this the kind of man you would like our daughter to end up with?' he railed.

'Those are very serious allegations, Rusi. A drug habit, really? How do you know?'

Rusi paused for a moment, finally saying, his tone firm, 'I know young men like him, living life in the fast lane. They come into wealth and fame at a young age, women throwing themselves at them, they begin to think they are invincible, until it all implodes.'

'There are always exceptions to every rule. I don't know, Rusi, I quite liked him.' Meher rubbed lotion on to her hands and feet. 'He doesn't come off as entitled or disrespectful. He is clearly hardworking, he's made his own life and he really does seem to care about Aria. Isn't that the most important?'

'What's important to me is upbringing and a sense of respect. Especially towards women. Trust me, Meher, when I say that you don't know anything about him. I've seen hundreds like him come and go.'

Meher's tone was gentle. 'Well, that's exactly what tonight was for. I'm surprised at how you behaved—he was a guest in your home and he was trying so hard, poor boy.'

'He's an actor!' he scoffed, 'This is his biggest audition. Of course, he was going to be on his best behaviour!'

'Oh Rus. All I know is that Aria is serious about him. And I think we owe it to our daughter to give him a chance. She's an intelligent girl, you willingly trust her with other decisions. You need to trust her when it comes to this.'

Meher removed her dressing gown, got into bed next to her husband and turned to him. 'Our girls are growing up. I know sometimes that's a bitter pill to swallow, but you cannot control their every move.'

'Well, if it's a ridiculous move that will derail her entire life and all she's worked for, I will damn well try . . .' her husband muttered, pulling up the duvet and turning off his bedside lamp.

~

A floor away, Leah crept into her sister's room, just like she used to when they were little.

'You okay?' she padded over to the bed.

Aria shrugged, gesturing for Leah to get in under the covers next to her. They lay side by side in the darkness in silence for several minutes.

'By the way, what was Dad saying about having met Rohan before? I didn't realize he had. Has Rohan mentioned it?'

Aria just shook her head. If Rohan ever spoke to her again, she would have to ask him.

As soon as dessert was cleared, Rohan, who couldn't seem to get out of their house fast enough, excused himself, citing an early morning shoot, politely declining Meher's offer for a nightcap.

Aria walked him out, an uncomfortable silence and an arm's length between them. As they stood in the driveway, waiting for his car, she reached out to touch his arm.

'Ro . . .' she reached out to touch his arm.

He'd just shaken his head and shrugged off her gesture. When his car was finally brought around, he'd gotten in wordlessly and driven away.

He hadn't answered her calls or messages since.

'I know in the scheme of things this is far from the most important, but who's going to break it to mum that the chicken was SO undercooked?'

And despite herself, Aria laughed.

~

MOHANCITY CFO SAYS MOHAN MEHTA BOASTED ABOUT HIS SOCIAL AND POLITICAL CONNECTIONS TO INVESTORS

Sources reveal to us that Mehul Bhatt, the Chief Financial Officer of MohanCity, turned approver, admitted to the authorities that Mohan Mehta knowingly defrauded both bank officials and potential investors. In a startling admission, Bhatt says that in a bid to fund the stalled MohanCity project, Mehta often boasted about his social and political connections to potential investors. Mehta promised investors right of first refusal on a high-profile project that he would soon be breaking ground with Rusi Mistry, of Mistry & Sons.

The project would be its first-of-a-kind development, one that Mumbai had never seen . . .

MISTRY & SONS INVOLVEMENT IN MOHANCITY: ED/EOW INVESTIGATES THESE STARTLING CLAIMS.

MISTRY & SONS SPOKESPERSON RUBBISHES ALLEGATIONS. 'WE HAVE NO BUSINESS DEALINGS WITH ANY INDIVIDUALS BY THE NAME OF MOHAN MEHTA OR ANY CONNECTIONS TO MOHANCITY.'

RUSI MISTRY UNDER SCRUTINY: MISTRY & SONS BOARD DELVES INTO MOHANCITY ALLEGATIONS.

~

'He needs time, and I need a time *out*,' Aria told Dr Shroff.

It had been a fraught two weeks. There was the fallout from *that* dinner, as it was now referred to in the Mistry household and now, Mistry & Sons was being dragged into the MohanCity scam. The timing couldn't have been worse, and Rusi Mistry was walking around in a constant state of fury. Unsurprisingly, his ire had been directed towards Aria and her personal life choices, which in his opinion were besmirching the family's pristine reputation.

'You were incredibly rude to him,' Aria had said to her father the next morning at breakfast. 'Whatever you may think of him, he was still my guest, and you are the one who has always told us to treat guests in our home with respect.'

'Young lady,' her father had peered over the newspaper. 'You will not lecture me on respect. Especially not when that actor boy of yours has no idea what the word means, let alone how to spell it.'

'God, Dad, why won't you even give him a chance? You keep on with this innuendo, when it's really about your snobbery . . . He's a good guy, I promise.'

'Because, Aria,' her father, stood up, drawing himself to his full height. 'I know what young men like him are really like. I've seen hundreds of them come and go in my lifetime. I'm surprised you've fallen for his well-practiced routine, given his many, how do I say it, uh . . . conquests. I'd like to believe I taught you better.' He'd left the room in a huff yet again.

'I'm just done with him, Mum. He is being so unreasonable.' Aria cheeks burned at her father's comments. 'It's a lose-lose for me,' she continued, dragging a spoon through her oatmeal. 'Rohan is understandably upset. I'm caught between both these men who are accustomed to always being lauded, to have people fall over themselves to please them.

Meher looked at her daughter sympathetically.

'I don't know, darling,' she sighed. 'We'll just have to play it out. Give your father time . . .'

'And what about Rohan?'

Despite her misgivings that seemed to lie under the surface of her relationship with Rohan, she'd never doubted his feelings for her. But something had changed.

Rohan had, and rightly so, been furious after that dinner, making no bones about the fact that he thought Aria hadn't stood up for him.

'You just sat there. You . . . you didn't object, when your father called your boyfriend uneducated, a gold digger and who remembers what else. What does that say about you, Aria, huh?'

And he was right. If there was one thing Aria Mistry always prided herself on—it was doing the right thing. When a classmate was being bullied, she stood up for her; when friends experienced loss and heartbreak, she was there to visit, armed with reinforcements (ice cream! cheesy movies! a shoulder to cry on!); she attended family functions, checked in on older relatives. She even personally funded the city's biggest animal shelter.

But first with her oldest friend and now her boyfriend, Aria had failed miserably.

'It's funny—or not really funny for me—but every argument revolves around respect. Rohan thinks my father and I disrespected him and his profession and his life, and my father thinks, by dating Rohan, I'm disrespecting him and some archaic codes of Mistry legacy,' she told Dr Shroff, exhaling tiredly.

'And what do you think?'

Aria looked around the doctor's cozy office while she pondered the question. Below the air conditioner there was now a little wet patch forming. Had it been there all this while? If she squinted, she could see the droplets, ready to fall.

She looked back at her hands. She removed a sanitizing wipe from her bag and wiped them for possibly the tenth time that afternoon. She looked at the antique clock that sat on the desk, the session already twenty minutes in. She looked back at Dr Shroff, waiting expectantly for a response.

'I think,' she let out the breath that she'd been unconsciously holding. 'I think . . .' she changed tack. 'Do you think, I don't know . . . maybe my father is right?'

Aria crossed her legs, sitting up straighter. She took another deep breath, her stomach curving outwards visibly, through her silk shirt.

'Yes, my father can be a righteous snob. But, some of his concerns are well, I mean . . . My family is old school, they value certain things, such as education and propriety, it's how I've been brought up, it's my value system too, and sometimes with Rohan and his public . . .'

'These are several different thoughts you are bringing up, Aria. Are you worried that he is not your intellectual equal, the fact that he is a college dropout or that he has this public persona that doesn't fit with your family's?

'Education is very important to us . . .' Aria began, huffily.

'I'm asking specifically about you?'

Her session ended soon after and Aria had flown off to London a few days later.

Now, after two days in London, she was feeling no less conflicted. This business trip was one she had been looking forward to. Mistry & Sons had acquired one of Aria's favourite hotel properties in Scotland, one her family had spent many happy summers at; it had been Aria's pet project, and after the Paris deal had gone south, she'd been focused on ensuring that this contract reached fruition.

But her excitement had been tempered by a conflicting emotional state. Between meetings, she would put on earphones and walk the streets in an attempt to clear her head. It wasn't only the issues with her father and Rohan that were plaguing her; it was also Tara. She'd been in London for forty-eight hours and she was yet to call her beleaguered friend.

When the news about Mohan Mehta first broke, Aria checked in on her friend often, trying to approach this unprecedented situation as sensitively as she knew how.

'What solace can we, anyone really, offer at a time like this?' she'd wondered to Meher. 'To have your father in jail. To have the world casting such aspersions on you. To know that the life you lived was pretty much a lie . . .'

'Just let her know that you are there if she needs you,' her mother had advised.

But as the story developed and the extent of Mohan Mehta's shady dealings had come through, Aria felt a shift— no doubt compounded in part by her father's vociferous condemnations and the heartbreaking stories of the people Mohan Mehta had scammed. She found herself at a complete lack of words to comfort her friend.

If she was *brutally* honest, her sympathy had moved to doubt. How could Tara not know? How could she not question her brother's sudden disappearance? Was she so enamoured by the spoils that she really didn't care where the money had come from?

And then, there had been the latest development that had put Mistry & Sons in the spotlight and cast aspersions on the integrity of the company that her father and his forefathers had built so assiduously. It was Aria who had the privilege of carrying that torch forward. She had a responsibility, a duty to her shareholders, to her employees, to her family, that she do everything to protect the company's name.

How could she in her right conscience then sympathize with Tara?

The only person she'd admitted these thoughts to was Rohan and that led to the massive argument, just before she'd flown out to London. He'd called her judgemental, citing the idealism she and her father held on to as delusional.

'Get off your high horse, Aria. The world is not so black and white.'

'So, you're defending what he did?' Aria shot back angrily.

'Don't be ridiculous. This isn't about him. And the news—god, Aria. You should know better. They'll report anything. How do you even know all of it is true? She's your oldest friend, going through something that's so unimaginable . . . and in a minute, you're worried about how it looks for *you*? What does that say about *you*?'

'What does it say about you? That you're willing to overlook all the lives he's ruined, just to make a quick buck. Bribery, cheating, robbing people of their savings, he thought he'd outsmarted everyone,' inflections of Rusi's condescending tone creeping in. She was stung by Rohan's accusatory tone. How dare he call her judgemental?

'Maybe my father's right. Maybe our moral compasses don't point in the same direction.'

And that had set him off completely.

Aria let out a long sigh, replaying the things they had both said to each other.

'What is he right about, Aria? That I come from a family that isn't wealthy? That my mother didn't have tea with the Queen? He called me a gold-digger . . . Let me tell you, your money is of no interest to me, honey.'

He glared at her. 'Or wait, is it that he's threatened? That when we walk into a room, the attention is not only on you or your family or your "legacy?" he mimicked Rusi's posh English accent. 'But that everyone wants to talk to me, be around me . . .? Can you and your father's egos not handle that?'

'Or is it that, in this new India, privilege doesn't only beget success. That a young upstart like me can carve his own place, without a formal education, without memberships to the country's elite institutions, but just by talent and hard fuckin' work alone. I earned every little bit of my money. Nothing, nothing, was given to me.'

'That's ridiculous,' Aria shot back. 'How dare you talk about my father in that way?'

He'd taken a long chug of his beer, while Aria's eyes filled up.

'And let me tell you, WE are the future. Not you silver-spoon types, who have no idea what struggle is.

You walk around thinking you are IT—your family, your legacy, your SoBo blah blah blah. But you know what I think.' He came up to her; she could smell the alcohol on his breath.

'I think you are this prissy little girl who is too whipped by her father to even realize it. I think you are selfish, you, you, cannot think beyond your money, your wealth, your image. You care so much about what people will say, you can shroud it all you want in responsibility or duty to your legacy and all that bullshit, but what it boils down to is . . . you don't know how to fucking live . . . YOU . . .'

He wiped his mouth with the back of his hand. 'You don't even know how to,' he smirked. 'Let's just say, without me, you would have stayed the ice-queen that you were.'

'If that is the case,' said Aria, voice breaking, 'then why are you with me? You should have ended this long ago, since you have so many issues with me and my father.'

'Your right, I should have. I don't need you. This was the biggest mistake. So go, go meet a posh Parsi boy that the Supreme Lord Rusi Mistry finds for you,' his words were now slurring and his gestures were getting even wilder.

Aria didn't move.

'I really don't give a fuck any more. Get out of my house and out of my life.' He walked into his bedroom, slamming the door behind him hard.

Aria cried all the way to the airport.

Ever since that dinner, it had been this never-ending cycle of fight, kiss and make-up. Repeat. It was exhausting. But this time, Rohan had said things that she didn't think she could ever unhear.

When she'd landed in London, her phone was filled with messages and calls from Rohan. Apology flowers were arriving daily in her suite at The Claridge's hotel, but she refused to respond. She needed to clear her head and never before had she so desperately wanted to disappear.

Adding to the emotional whiplash of her disapproving father and her newly aggressive boyfriend was also a strong measure of guilt—she didn't have the bandwidth to be the kind of friend she knew Tara needed. What would she even say to her? How could she look beyond her father dragging Aria's family's name through the mud? How could she pretend she was okay with everything that had gone on?

With these thoughts swirling in her head, Aria ducked into Joe & The Juice for a smoothie. She was waiting in line, deleting messages from Rohan that kept pinging her phone, when she heard a familiar voice call out.

She turned around, her heart sinking, as she saw Tara, in a baggy sweatshirt and baseball cap.

'Uh, hii . . . What are you doing here?' the words tumbled out as they hugged each other somewhat awkwardly.

'I've been walking around for the last few hours and realized I hadn't eaten anything.' Tara's tone was flat. 'But I should be asking you the same question . . . you're in London and you haven't even called?' Her eyes narrowed.

'It's been crazy with work. We have this massive deal going on . . . I was just going to call you,' Aria said cringing at how lame the excuse sounded, even to her own ears.

'Oh.' Tara twirled her hair, as their orders came up. They grabbed a window table in silence, staring at the busy street outside.

'This is a long way for you,' Aria said with a nervous laugh.

'Honestly, I don't even know what direction I was going in. I just needed to clear my head.' Tara picked at her sandwich, taking it apart. Tara was gaunt—by the looks of it, she clearly wasn't eating or sleeping. The dark circles under her eyes were prominent, her cheekbones protruding, her hair, under the cap, knotted and unkempt. Despite all her misgivings, seeing

Tara, Aria felt her throat catch. They sat together, Tara, hunched over her sandwich, Aria, taking delicate sips of her smoothie, unsure of where to begin, of what to say.

'Ari,' Tara said suddenly. There was an expectant look on her face.

'Do you think your dad can help?' 'I mean, he knows people—ministers, the police commissioner, the prime minister . . .' she mumbled. 'And everyone respects him. Maybe he can say something about my dad, you know, vouch for him in court, in an affidavit or he could . . .'

She took a sip of her coffee, her hands shaking.

'Papa's going to fix this, I know he is. He just needs help.' Her voice had a pleading edge to it. 'I feel so helpless, Ari . . . I don't know who to turn to. He needs to get bail, he won't . . .' she couldn't even complete the sentence.

Aria felt herself stiffen. She couldn't believe that Tara was putting her in this spot. She chose her words carefully, 'How can he do that, T?' she said, as gently as she could muster, her tone betraying her annoyance. 'Even if he could have in the past . . .and I don't even know how that would have worked. But even if he could have, this new development puts us in a really, really bad position.'

'To the world . . .' she searched for the right words.

'It's seeming like your father was coasting off our'— she gestured to the both of them—'our relationship, he was trying to legitimize, and now my family has gotten involved.'

'We have a board, a responsibility to our employees, we have our reputation. We have to think of all that.'

Tara looked at her, confused. 'What are you talking about?'

'It's been all over the news. Your CFO says your father claimed he had a secret project with Mistry & Sons, to bring more investors in.'

'I, I haven't seen this. Which newspaper? Which CFO? Mehul?' Tara appeared flummoxed, grabbing her phone to Google the news.

'I don't know his name. We've been put under scrutiny. We've had to put out a statement. I am sure you can understand the pressure we are now facing?'

Tara scrolled through her phone for a few minutes as Aria took a few more sips of the smoothie, then put it aside, the melting ice rendering it flavourless. Aria looked at her watch. She still had another thirty minutes before her next meeting; she was tempted to use work as an excuse to extract herself from this conversation.

Before she could say anything, Tara exclaimed. 'It IS Mehul. That asshole. You know he was fired? He behaved inappropriately with someone in the office!'

'What an asshole. I can't believe HIM! This is PURE vendetta,' she turned to Aria. 'No one will believe him. See?' She showed Aria the phone. 'No one has really picked it up. That's why I hadn't seen it. I'm sorry that he brought you all into this, but this is clearly all bullshit.'

Aria shook her head, dumbfounded. Was Tara really this naive?

'So, Ari, do you think there's anything, anything for Uncle Rusi to help?' Tara was pleading again.

Aria, was silent, unable to find a response befitting an ask, that in her mind, was beyond the pale.

Tara finally understood. Her voice hardened. 'So you won't help. You and Shaan, when you ask me what you can do, it's all just for the sake of it. You don't really mean it.'

Aria clenched her jaw. 'I don't think that's fair.'

Tara's voice grew bitter. 'REALLY? YOU don't think it's fair. You come to London and you don't even call. Who does that? Shaan gets on an international flight like most people get on the tube, and yet, it's been weeks since my dad's been in prison and where is she? Both your fathers are some of the most powerful men in the country and still you won't do anything to help.' The tears were now rolling down furiously.

'My FATHER IS IN PRISON! I can't leave this country to go to him . . . And yet, YOU want to talk about fair.'

'We didn't put him there, you know, T.' Aria felt anger bubble to the surface. 'What about those whose lives he's irrevocably changed? You want to talk about fairness, let's talk about them. They've lost EVERYTHING, EVERYTHING . . . and your father did that so he could live this sham life, to spend money that was not yours, to buy THINGS!' Her voice rose, the words tumbling out before Aria could stop herself. 'And then, your father drags my family's name into this whole mess, and now WE are in this impossible position. How can you even ask that of me? How can you put all that on me? It's beyond me. You really cannot be so naïve.'

Tara stared at her best friend wordlessly, before grabbing her jacket and storming out of the cafe.

Oh fuck. Aria cursed under her breath, trying desperately to ignore the stares from the other tables.

~

'I just snapped, Shaan. I shouldn't have, but with everything going on, it's too much,' Aria burst into tears as she recounted the episode with Tara. After walking out of the coffee shop, Aria called Shaan incessantly until she answered, horrified with what had just occurred. In the last few weeks, Aria, who avoided confrontation at all costs, had found herself in one volatile situation after another. She was reeling from the altercation with Tara; she'd never fought with a friend like that before. The guilt, the anger and the shame, oh, the *shame*, at the things that she'd said, it was overwhelming and it had all come out before Shaan in that one tearful phone call.

'What is going on?' Shaan asked herself, when they hung up. In less than a few days both her best friends had broken down.

What she couldn't wrap her head around was why Aria hadn't mentioned her trip to London.

And why had Rohan messaged Shaan out of the blue, wanting to know if she'd heard from Aria? He'd been as vague, but clearly there was something major going on between the two of them, '*Dal meh zaroor kuch kala hai,*' she said out loud as she jumped in the shower to get ready before Shiv arrived for their weekly dinner.

In Gurgaon, Shaan was settling into her marriage, her days spent back at work. Pratap had been good on his word for the women's outreach in his constituency, and after a long time, Shaan found herself excited, spending her days in training, creating campaigns for social media, pinpointing new projects the Women's Cell could embark on and garnering funds. She would deny it to her grave, but crazy party girl Shaan was now on a much-needed hiatus; she was content to spend her evenings at home.

Not that either of her friends had asked about her life, given all that had happened over the past few weeks, but if they had, Shaan would have told them that things with Pratap were moving forward. They seemed to be building some sort of foundation. It was yet to be determined how stable it would be, she noted wryly to Shiv. 'But *chalo*, slowly, building *toh nahi*, bungalow *toh* build *ho rahi hai*.'

Shaan found herself actively seeking out Pratap's opinions. He was making an effort, his willingness to help her see Tara, his insistence that she get to work, found Shaan letting down her guard slowly, enjoying having someone on her side. It wasn't all smooth sailing—physically, their relationship left a lot to be, well . . . desired; Pratap, was constantly frustrated by Shaan's drinking, and she by his inconsistent moods—but they'd come a long, bump-filled way from their wedding day.

They'd fallen into a routine. Pratap, an early riser, would spend an hour with his trainer in the building gym, and by the time he'd downed his protein shake and showered, Shaan would surface and join him for breakfast. They'd both head out on work or meetings; some days, they'd end up at her parents for lunch, the Singhs' happiness at seeing their daughter and new son-in-law settled unbridled. Most evenings and weekends were with friends in the city or away at the farmhouse.

They kept their circle relatively small and private; Shaan ensuring that none of the Def Col ditzes from the early days were now welcome, but instead including her childhood friends, the young political leaders that Pratap often hung out with, and his boarding school buddies. In just a few weeks, thanks in part to some public appearances, and the city's obsession with the next big thing, they'd been anointed a power couple, and Shaan wasn't altogether averse to the reputation they were cultivating.

On the days when Pratap was in his constituency, Shaan found herself, much to her surprise, enjoying her own company or a relaxed drink with a friend.

'Is this adulting?' Shaan asked Shiv, laughing. 'Quiet evenings with you were never part of the schedule. Have I become that boring?'

'Just don't you go popping out babies on me soon, you hear? Then I'll know you've really gone over to the dark side.'

'Not a chance. Anyway, I think I may have figured the solution to marriage—spend part of the month apart.'

'Or, the solution is not to get married and to be a slutty man like me.'

'Or, do you think the solution is to have a girl on the side?' Shaan emptied the wine into her glass, biting her lip nervously.

Shaan's relationship history was chequered. In the past, when romantic dalliances had turned serious, she was known to jump ship.

'It's too messy, *kahaan yeh* boyfriend-girlfriend *lafda mein phas jaenge*, we're young, so let's enjoy,' she would say, ending the chapter on a hook-up, before moving on to the next, but not before complaining to Aria and Tara. '*Pehle se* I say I don't want anything serious. But no one listens! And then, it's like, that whole "I'm so shocked, I thought things were going well" conversation. When did these boys become so needy?'

'What do we do with you, Miss India? You're the first girl I've been with who is more like every college guy I know— no strings sex and zero commitment. You just show up, hook me back in and then, whoosh, vanish without a trace,' Matt would say to her, when she'd appear again, after ghosting him for a few weeks.

She'd laugh, pulling him back to bed. 'What can I tell ya, you hit the lottery. So stop talking.'

But with Pratap, every rule she'd ever made had been thrown out of the window. And she was finding herself in completely uncharted territory. In her cynical mind, things were going a little too smoothly. It seemed almost unbelievable that they were finding common ground, given the drama that was their wedding not too long ago.

And she found herself wondering, not for the first time, if Pratap was being entirely honest with her.

She hadn't asked Pratap if he was still talking to Serena, though as she admitted to Shiv, she was 'dying to know'. She had taken a surreptitious look through his phone when he was in the shower one day, but so far, her sleuthing hadn't found anything suspicious.

'Desperate housewife,' she cackled to Shiv. 'Either he's really good at hiding things . . . he wouldn't be the first politician.' She raised her eyebrows, popping a kebab into her mouth.

'Or, Shaan, maybe, he's just *that* into you.'

But despite any evidence to the contrary, Shaan couldn't help anticipate the ball dropping. It just seemed too neat, that a man she had been so unsure of, a relationship that had been characterized by such vacillating on both their parts, could now actually not be as awful as she had envisioned. So, when Pratap came to her with a plan to go to London, she was sceptical, questioning his motives. He'd been invited to attend a highly publicized fundraiser for an NGO, and as his wife, she could be in the city without raising eyebrows and also without antagonizing her father, he told her.

She narrowed her eyes at him. 'But why would you do that? What's in it for you?'

'Huh? *Pagal ho gayi ho kya*? I thought you wanted to go see Tara. I'm helping you, bas.'

She'd been unconvinced.

'Chalo, you caught me,' he said with a laugh. 'I'll look good supporting an NGO, I'll meet some NRI donors, you'll meet Tara, we'll go to the casino one-two times, go shopping on Bond Street. It's London, yaar.' He walked towards Shaan, putting his hands on her shoulder.

'Everything doesn't have to have a double meaning. And *kaha na*, what are husbands for if they don't take their wives to London to meet their friends?' he laughed. 'Not that you need my permission.' He looked at her, eyes widening in clarification.

Shaan couldn't help but smile, relaxing a little. 'As if I would even ask.'

Now all Shaan had to do was tell Tara. But given the recent altercation between Aria and her, and the words that had been exchanged, would Tara see her London trip as a guilty reaction? Or would she be relieved to see her friend?

In the end, all the questions went to naught, as Tara was on a flight back to India. The one thing Mohan Mehta had done right was keep his wife and daughter out of the company books; once the authorities had realized that both Tara and Bina had no working knowledge of the business, they had in agreement with the lawyers offered Tara safe passage to India. And so, Tara was allowed to come back home to her distraught mother without any fear of prosecution.

16

It had been only two weeks since Tara had returned to India but it felt like a lifetime. On the flight back, her stomach was in knots; she hadn't been able to sleep, eat or drink, her mind half expecting a cadre of police waiting at the airplane door. But nothing that dramatic happened, and she'd made it through immigration and was home relatively unscathed.

Home. Where was that now? They'd been kicked out of their Malabar Hill penthouse, the fifteen-foot-high lacquered wooden door sealed and plastered with government notices. Her mother had moved into her sister's spare two-bedroom apartment in Lower Parel. Tara was so grateful to see her mother that even the strange, cramped quarters didn't bother her; every night, like she had as a little girl, she crawled into bed next to Bina, mother and daughter clinging to each other.

London was seeming less and less like home too. It definitely didn't seem like it was with Nakul any more. In an unsurprising development, her husband had chosen to not accompany her to India. When the lawyers had orchestrated her return, Tara couldn't help but notice the visible relief on

271

her mother-in-law's face; it was almost as if she had felt that with Tara being away, she was no longer their problem.

When Tara had asked Nakul privately if he would come with her, he'd made some lame excuse, citing work commitments. A few months ago, Tara would have been heartbroken at her husband's lack of empathy, but now, she didn't even have the strength to argue—her mind too filled with worry for her family; the state of her marriage would just have to wait.

It had been an emotional few days with her mother. They'd cried more than they had ever had in their lifetimes, unable to comprehend how things had come to such a precarious state. Her brother was still missing in action, though her mother had finally come out with the truth. With Bunty being an active part of the MohanCity project, Mohan had presciently ensured that he stayed abroad.

'Why didn't you tell me? How could you not tell me all this . . . No one, not you, not Bunty, not Papa, thought to tell me. Am I not a member of this family?' she'd screamed at her mother.

'Tari, baby, please. I didn't know also,' her mother pleaded. 'Papa . . . Papa . . . I think he wanted us to be out of it. In business, when would he tell us anything? Only before coming to London, he told me that it is better, safer for us all to be out of the country. That there are powerful people who are making him the *bakra*. And that if anything happens, he's made *bandobast* . . .'

She'd cried herself to sleep that night, furious with her family. The next morning, she'd found her mother in the kitchen. Bina smiled in greeting. 'I've made your favourite poha for breakfast.'

Tara just looked at her.

'What is wrong with you? Your husband is in jail. He's been lying to us for god knows how long. Your son is a coward. Aren't you angry? Why aren't you angry? Why aren't you screaming and shouting instead of sitting here, cooking breakfast like nothing is the matter?'

Bina turned off the flame, ladled some of the fluffy hot poha into a bowl and led Tara gently by the hand to the dining table.

Tara shrugged her off.

'Sit, Tari. Sit.' her mother said, when her daughter resisted.

'Let me tell you a story about Papa and me. Your Papa and his big dreams.'

'Just after you were born, Papa surprised me with dinner at Supper Club, the best restaurant in Bombay those days. He bought me a new salwar kurta and only told me where we were going in the car.

'But I didn't want to go, I was not comfortable, it was too costly, it was throwing money. Business was good, but it was still out of budget then,' she smiled.

'But you know Papa, he would not take no for an answer. So, we fought about money as we always did those days, and I cried the entire way and refused to get out of the car. I was angry, Papa was angry. So he tells me, I'll drop you home, and I will go have dinner alone, if you are being so stubborn. But I refused to go home, so he, even though he was angry, he drove to Liberty Cinema, bought two tickets for the new Amitabh Bachchan movie, some popcorn and samosa. When we came out of the movie, he said to me, "See Bina, I know how to make you smile again." He knew that was what would make me happy. But he also said, "One day, we will go to any restaurant in the world, and you'll never worry about budget. That I promise you."'

'He always wanted this big life, to live like raees, to go to a five-star hotel and restaurant, and he wanted you and Bunty and me, and even Kaka, Kaki, all to enjoy. To have all comfort. When I would say to him, "Mohan, don't spend too much, save, for rainy day, don't buy such costly things, you know what he would say to me?"'

She smiled sadly. 'He would say to me, "Bina, if I can't do the best for you, for my family, what is point of all this? Seeing you all smile, and your happiness, and knowing you never have to ask for anything, that's enough for me." But somewhere,' her eyes clouded over, 'his dreams got too big and got him into trouble. So how can I be angry? He was just dreaming and doing.'

Through conversations with her mother and the family advocates, she slowly started to piece together the details. She felt blindsided by the depth of subterfuge that had gone on in her family—Bunty had gotten a foreign citizenship, some money had quietly been left with other family members to make sure her mother and she were taken care of, and all assets had been transferred out of Tara and Bina's names. What had prompted her father to make these decisions? Why had he kept all this from Tara and her mother? For how long had he known that what he was doing was illegal? Was everything he had told her been a lie?

She hadn't been able to see her father yet, so these questions remained unanswered, constantly swirling through her mind, as she and her mother adjusted to a new reality. And adjusting was something Bina was struggling with.

For nearly forty years, Bina's entire day had revolved around Mohan and their two children. Their marriage may have been arranged by their families but as Mohan would always proudly say, 'It was love from day one.' They doted on each other. Every morning, his first cup of chai was made and brought to him in bed by Bina; when Mohan hired a fancy chef to take over the kitchen, Bina continued to pack his office tiffin and insisted on making his favourite foods herself; when he travelled, she personally packed his suitcases. Without her mother, Tara joked, her father wouldn't be able to find the front door. Bina thrived on being indispensable to her family.

Suddenly, she found herself alone, in a house that wasn't hers. With no one to look after and no way to fill her day except with worry. She worried incessantly about her husband; How was he doing? Were they feeding him okay? Was he taking his diabetes medicines? Mohan did not want either his wife or daughter to come visit him while in prison, and so they had to make do with brief phone calls that seemed to end before they even began. She worried about Bunty—how he was managing in a new city? How scared he must be alone? Her son, who didn't even know how the stove turned on, how was he eating? She would ask Tara these questions over and over again.

With Tara's return, Bina found a renewed sense of purpose, channelling her fear and anxiety into feeding her daughter. She would spend hours in the kitchen, cooking Tara's favourite snacks. 'Your face looking too pulled down, eat Tari,' she said, putting a bowl of peeled, skinless orange slices or a plate of dhokla or some piping hot idlis or a cold coffee, in front of her. She would sit across from her on the sofa, a printed *rajai* on her feet, reliving their childhood memories, asking Tara to tell her stories about life in London, her friends, Nakul, her work. And Tara would humour her, grateful to see her mother's despondency lift even briefly.

'You were always *meri chand ki tara*,' she smiled at her daughter. 'Even when you were small, you were always dancing, laughing, wanting to wear pretty-pretty clothes. I remember, when we took you to Disneyland, four days you wore the same fairy dress. You only wanted to meet all the princesses, and Bunty, he wanted to go on those bang bang cars,' her eyes misted.

'*Socha nahi, kis musibat* . . . How much I told Papa, *nazar utari ja*. Such big houses, such fancy-fancy cars and see what happened,' she said, a bitter edge to her voice. 'I'm telling you Tari, at heart, I am still same middle-class girl from Matunga. *Paisa haath ka mel hai*.'

She paused, looking down at her floral kaftan. 'I will be happy even here . . .' she gestured around the room, with its heavy curtains, brown sofas, the iron window guards casting a shadow against the walls. 'I just want Papa and Bunty to come home.' Her eyes filled with tears.

At night, the fear and anxiety would return, magnified. 'What is the point, Tari, if, if Papa doesn't get bail. If Bunty can't come back. What is the point for me? My life . . .' she cried, the tears rolling down her cheeks. 'No point.'

'You can't talk like that, Mama,' Tara said, hugging her mother. 'You have to be strong, for Papa, for Bunty, I only have you, you can't think like this . . .' she was sobbing too.

With Bunty missing and her mother's emotional fragility, it was left to Tara to become the de facto head of the family. She found herself buried under mounds of paperwork, trying to detangle the complicated workings of the Indian legal system and her father's case. Furious at her father and brother's duplicity, she was now determined to be as informed as she possibly could. And so, she spent days sequestered in a corner conference room at the advocate's office, working through boxes of dusty files, trying to wrap her head around the legalese, with the help of a kind-hearted junior advocate, who answered her many questions. But even Tara knew that understanding her father's case was only just beginning to scratch the surface; in the Indian legal system, the wheels turned behind closed doors. And so, she attempted to tap her father's rapidly shrinking network, reaching out to the old associates and friends she knew, greeted always with a circumlocutory politesse that ended every conversation before it even began. No doors were willing to open for such a high profile, emotionally volatile case, and slowly, Tara began to realize just how isolated as a family they were.

When not at the lawyers' offices, Tara was home, but when Shaan had flown into Mumbai, refusing to take no for an answer, Tara had agreed to meet for lunch.

'Go, Tari, go meet Shaan. She's come all the way, go beti, have some fun,' her mother encouraged.

And so, after nearly three weeks, Tara left her mother's side. For the first time in her life, Tara was looking far from her coiffed self. She'd let even the most basic maintenance routine slide—her usually blow-dried hair was lank and greasy, her gel nails half broken and chipped, her eyebrows overgrown . . . who am I, she wondered, when she caught sight of her reflection. So, right before meeting her friend, Tara decided to step into her usual salon for a little pick-me-up. It was a Tuesday morning, she was sure she could do a quick visit without being seen. She was entitled to at least that, she reasoned.

Amongst the women of a certain social set in Mumbai, visits to Michelle were an indispensable part of the day. The forty-year-old from Mazgaon had fast become the city's go-to-stylist for her famous outcurl and her staff's efficiency. The tiny, no-frills salon in a building car garage famously had a waiting list for new clients but managed to fit in their regulars at any time. Tara and her mother had been loyalists for years (so much so that they had a running tab that they would settle every month). It was there she headed in search of a little maintenance and a chance to decompress with her long-time beautician Ina.

It was still early in the day, and she was thankful to find that she'd been right, the salon was relatively empty. She walked through the tiny space, having requested the private area in the back, trying her best to not catch the eye of the few early birds. Just when she thought she was in the clear, a reedy voice piped up. 'Tara, Tara Mehta. Is that really you? I never thought I would bump into you . . . and at the parlour of all places!'

Shweta Mahtani, her brassy locks peppered with foil and her face covered in some sort of green mask, swivelled her chair to face Tara. In an earlier life, Shweta and Tara had been friends, catching up for the occasional lunch in London or Mumbai. But since her father's news had broken, Shweta, like many other girls who used to make up Tara's social circle, had gone radio silent. Tara wished her briefly, not wanting to engage in any conversation, polite or otherwise.

'But really, tell me, darling,' she continued, adopting a sympathetic tone and grabbing Tara's hand. 'How ARE you? What ARE you doing here?' The woman in the chair next to her, who Tara didn't recognize, looked on curiously at this conversation.

'Uh, it's a salon,' Tara found herself retorting. 'What do you think I'm doing?'

Shweta put her hands up in surrender, her pillow lips pouting at Tara's tone.

'SORRY . . . I just thought you'd be busy with, you know, lawyers and stuff . . . are you back from London for good? How IS Uncle? Where are you staying now? My aunt said your house is now on sale? Or was it auctioned? Oh my, so many questions!' a high-pitched giggle escaped her.

Tara felt her face redden with embarrassment. She mumbled some vague responses and headed straight to the corner. She heard Shweta whisper to her friend, 'I can't believe she's come out to the parlour at a time like this. You know, na, who she is? Mohan Mehta's daughter, yeah, yeah, that one only. Crazyyy.'

Tara didn't want to give her the satisfaction of leaving the salon but she couldn't believe she had been stupid enough to think that she could have a little bit of normalcy. She squared her shoulders and put on her headphones, turning up the volume and trying to block out any sound as Ina worked on the knots in her neck and a manicurist filed her nails. An hour and a half later, Tara felt more like herself than she had in weeks.

Later, when Tara was at the cash register (having ignored Shweta and her cohort, who were still in the throes of their beautification rituals), Michelle walked in, clearly surprised to see her old client. As Ina prepared to add Tara's services for the day to her long-standing tab, she saw Michelle gesture frantically from the corner of her eye. When Tara turned towards her, she said smoothly, 'We'll prefer cash from now on, Tara. And maybe you could clear all your mother's dues too.'

~

Tara got out of her Uber at the same time as Shaan's black Audi pulled up to the building lobby.

'Oh my god, hiii.' Shaan enveloped her best friend in a long hug.

'I didn't realize that was you,' she said, gesturing to the car. 'I would have sent my driver to have you picked up!'

Shaan hugged her again. 'Goddd, I've been waiting to do that,' she said, as Tara felt her eyes dampen. She pulled back, appraising Tara. She was in jeans and flats, her fitted white T-shirt accentuating her hollowed out belly. 'Too thin Tari . . . Are you keeping okay?' she said, as they walked into the building together, taking the elevator to Shaan's parents' fifteenth floor apartment that had a view of the city's lush green racecourse.

Lunch was waiting for them—'It's all your favourites, T,' said Shaan. Tara had to choke back tears. After that horrible incident at the salon, Shaan's warmth was a salve.

'Where's Aria?'

'She had a meeting. Uh, I'm sure she'll join us later.'

Shaan heaped some biryani on to Tara's plate. As they ate, a comfortable silence descended over the table. Tara, who had barely been able to stomach food for weeks, savoured the nostalgic flavours—the tanginess of the corn curry, the richness of the biryani, the crunchiness of the fried bhindi, all brought back a flood of memories. Even after Shaan had moved away, whenever she was back in the city, the girls would come together, often having slumber parties that lasted the weekend, baking, fighting over board games, having movie marathons. Simple times, simple pleasures.

'*Itni soch mein*, T?'

'I was just thinking about all the midnight feasts we used to have in this house—creeping into the kitchen at all hours—. do you remember that time your mum found us making brownies at 2 a.m. when she came home slightly tipsy?'

'Ha, yeah. She literally inhaled the entire pan after telling us ten times about the margaritas she'd drunk at Shah Rukh's movie premiere!'

'Oh, and let's not forget the hours of Dreamphone and Girl Talk? I wonder if those games even exist now,' both girls laughed, reliving their teenage obsessions.

The girls continued to eat their lunch, lost in happy memories, chatting casually and easily. Tara was quieter than usual but was feeling more relaxed than she had in a while, happy to slip into old habits and momentarily forget all that was going on. Seeing her like this made Shaan, who had been particularly nervous about this lunch, unclench her shoulders a little.

Shaan waited till they were seated in the study, Tara eating seconds of dessert (another favourite—home-made caramel custard), to turn to her.

'So, T, how have you been really?'

Tara paused and shrugged. 'Everyone keeps asking me how I am. My aunts, that cow Shweta in the parlour, you . . . but I don't know how to answer. How am I supposed to be? Am I meant to tell you that I'm shattered thinking of my father wasting away in a jail? That I can't stop thinking of the people that he's done this to? That I'm angry for what my life has become? That in every minute of every day I'm reminded of what he's done—no one wants me to ever forget,' she said with a sharp laugh.

'And then there's my mother. Who is literally,' she wiped away the tears that had fallen. 'She's literally . . . Shaan . . . I mean, she's barely hanging on. She's cooking and dusting and cleaning, just to keep herself busy. She's stopped playing cards, her bonsai plants are all at home, she's stopped her drawing classes. And Bunty, who knows where Bunty is?'

'Oh, and that the people I thought would be there for me are the ones who've . . .' she stopped, the anger rising in her, thinking of her in-laws, Nakul and the state of their marriage, her fight with Aria, and all the people she'd thought were friends, who had turned their back on her the minute the news had come out.

'I have never, ever felt so alone and scared and angry in my life.'

Shaan moved next to Tara, taking her friend's hands in hers. They sat silently for a few minutes.

'Let's face it, even Aria has been a Class A bitch. I mean, the things she said in London.' Tara ran her fingers through her hair. 'And she couldn't even be bothered to be here for lunch. Out of everyone in this world, I never thought YOU both would be so unsupportive.'

Shaan puffed on her e-cigarette. 'Tara. It's not that we haven't wanted to be there for you but you have to understand that it's a difficult situation. Tara, what you're going through, we understand it's tough.'

'Do you, do you both really understand? Are your fathers in jail? Are you shunned by your friends? Are you worried that you or your mother may be hauled off next? Are you worried that your family may not survive this? Are you being trolled and called all sorts of names online? Does your name come up in Google searches with the word scam in big fat letters next to it? Are you worried that at the end of this, you may not have a marriage? If your answer is no to any of the above, then no, you don't friggin' understand!'

'The thing is, what just amazes me,' she said after a few moments, having caught her breath, 'is how Aria could just sit there in judgement. She was so fucking condescending and self-righteous—and where has she gotten all her information from? The news! Has she once even asked me what's the truth?'

'I'm not saying my father hasn't screwed up. He has, and big time. And I wish I knew what had led to this. But he's still my father. And you both are still my friends. Friends who may have the power to make things happen. I'm not asking you to absolve him of everything, I'm not asking you to get him off scot-free, I am asking for you to help in any way you can. Because I don't know what else to do . . . because I don't know who else to turn to. Every single door has been closed in my face. You two are my best friends, can't I ask? Isn't that what friendship is?' she said, her body now shaking from anger, from fatigue, from anxiety.

'Of course it is. And we both want to help in any way we can. But Tara it's so, so complicated.' Shaan took Tara's hands in hers and looked at her friend. She started softly. 'The fact is that Tara, what your father did, the repercussions are just hugeeeee.'

Tara shot her friend an incredulous look.

'I know you know that,' Shaan backtracked. 'But this is also a time when, because of social media and the 24/7 news coverage, it's everywhere, he's everywhere, the stories are everywhere, and these journalists are digging, they are digging deep. It's not only your dad, I mean, it's all these guys who've been caught recently, and it's difficult for us to be near this.'

She exhaled, mentally bracing herself for Tara's reaction to what she was going to say next. 'And it didn't help that Uncle Rusi has also been dragged into this. I know that's been stressful for Aria, she has her responsibilities towards the company too. And I'm not excusing her behaviour, but you have to understand the uncomfortable position you are putting us in.'

'*Hum kyun na madat kartein*, otherwise?' she asked. 'But it puts our families under scrutiny too.'

Tara just shook her head in disbelief. 'Shaan, as long as I've known you, you've only boasted about how many people your father has single-handedly saved. That boy, what's his name, Rishi Raichand, "*woh toh mere* pocket *mein hai*",' Tara said, imitating Shaan. 'All because your dad kept his father out of jail. Every time we'd meet him, you'd remind us . . . and yet, for your oldest friend's father, who's literally seen you grow up, it's "uncomfortable",' she air quoted. 'That's bullshit.'

'I may not understand the legal implications, I may not understand the details of how my father's actions came to take place, but trust me when I say that I'm trying to learn as much as I can. I may not understand the political angle to all this, but I can understand *this*. When it came down to it, my friends, my best, best friends, in the hardest moment of my life, were not there to help.'

A couple of hours later, a teary Tara let herself into the apartment she now shared with her mother. She had no fight left. What was the point? she thought to herself miserably. If her best friends couldn't find a way to support her, who

would? Grateful that her mother was napping and didn't have
to see her in this state, Tara locked herself into her room and
sobbed herself to sleep.

~

Just a few kilometres away, back at Windsor Villa, Aria had
been looking forward to an evening reformer Pilates session, a
glass of red and an early night in, but she'd come home instead
to party preparations in full swing. In the foyer, a line of liveried
staff were getting their instructions from the house manager,
the florist nitpicking with her team about the positions of the
towering arrangements and in the formal dining room, her
mother was supervising the seating arrangements for the three-
course dinner she planned to serve. She paused to look up
when Aria walked in. 'The dinner for the Ambassador,' Meher
said, looking at Aria's quizzical expression. 'You forgot? It's on
your calendar.'

'Oh god, that's all I need. May I skip? I'm not feeling up
to dealing with people.' She'd been pissy all day at work too
and she knew that it was her guilt at skipping lunch with Tara.
She'd been wrong not to be there, and nothing rankled Aria
more than the thought that she wasn't excelling in every area
of her life.

Meher frowned, adjusting the plates, and turned to her
daughter.

'This is becoming quite a common refrain from you, Aria.
Would you like to tell me what's going on?'

'Nothing's going on,' Aria said, fidgeting with the cutlery.
'I just need some time to myself and I don't seem to ever get
that,' she whined.

'Don't touch that,' Meher lightly rapped Aria's hand. 'Well,' her mother said. 'You'll have all the time tomorrow. Tonight, you will be at dinner at 8 p.m., with a smile on your face, please.'

And so, a couple of hours later, 'trussed like turkeys', as Leah put it, adjusting the neckline of her cocktail dress, both sisters mingled with their parents' guests over drinks and overly elaborate hors d'oeuvres. 'Is this new chef on speed? Why is there foam and smoke coming out of everything?' Leah muttered. Rusi had just hired a rather eccentric Italian chef who had moved from Dubai to work full-time at the Mistry home. 'Incoming,' she continued to her sister.

Walking towards the two sisters was Sunita Mehrotra, the archetype of an aunty you would avoid at a party. The wife of Rajiv Mehrotra, Rusi's school squash buddy and now the CEO of his family's automotive conglomerate, she had met her husband on an Air India flight, where she was the chief stewardess. Mrs Mehrotra had many redeeming qualities (or so their mother, Meher, kept reminding Rusi, who barely tolerated her), but minding her own business was just not one of them.

The girls used to call her CNN—Children's News Network, for her obsession with sharing every achievement of her kids' lives, who in her eyes were far ahead of their peers in every possible way. Her daughter, Anisha, who had married an American ('But just like us, so family-minded'), lived in New York and her son, Aditya, an MBA from Cornell, as she reminded everyone, would soon take over from his father. She'd long harboured ambitions of Aditya and Aria coming together and despite her best efforts, neither party had demonstrated any interest. Aditya had recently gotten engaged to a girl he met at university, so Sunita had grudgingly backed off.

'Hi sweeties,' she sang out, engulfing the sisters in a cloud of Chanel No 5.

'Nice look, Aunty S,' Leah commented on her new feathery, blonde-streaked do that grazed the shoulders of a pleated Issey Miyake jacket.

'You like it?' she touched her hair self-consciously. 'I was in New York with my Anisha, and she took me to her hairdresser, he's this famous fellow, who even Julia Roberts goes to, and they convinced me . . .'

She sighed, still fingering the ends of her hair, and began a detailed update about her daughter's career and the ins and outs of daily life in Manhattan, which both Aria and Leah immediately tuned out.

'So, what about you, Aria, it's about time now . . .'

'Sorry, Aunty, could you repeat that please?' Aria refocused her attention.

'I said, my Anisha has been married for nearly two years now. And now even my Aditya is engaged. The clock's ticking,' she winked. Just as Aria was going to respond, Rajiv and Rusi joined the group, the former greeting the girls with bear hugs.

'I was just telling Aria, Rusi, now it's about time she settle down. See my Anisha, she's going to start family planning soon . . . it's the right time, I told her, don't wait too long.'

She continued, oblivious to the annoyance that passed over Rusi's face. Discussing his daughters' personal lives was another on Rusi's rather long list of social don'ts. 'Now, darling, tell your favourite aunty,' she patted Aria's cheek. 'I'm hearing strong rumours about you and that actor Rohan,' she winked again.

'My Anisha said she bumped into the two of you in New York at Barneys, such a good-looking boy, *chalo, pakka kar do*. See sweet pea, you don't want him to find someone else and there's a line for him . . .'

'So, Rusi, old boy. Father-in-law to a Bollywood star! Who would have thought?' Rajiv slapped his buddy on the back. 'We'll have to start practising your Hindi, so you can watch your future son-in-law's movies,' he guffawed.

Aria's heart sank as she saw her father's thunderous expression, his face turning crimson. But the gods seemed to be in her favour that evening. Before Rusi could explode, the house manager sounded the dinner bell, signalling for the guests to be seated.

'Saved by the bell,' Leah let out a long whistle as their father headed to dinner. Locking arms, the sisters made their way to one end of the long dinner table, which today had been set with an abundance of fruit and flowers, Aria praying fervently that no more awkward conversations awaited them.

~

That was a day and a half, Aria thought to herself, as she finally slid into bed. The dinner seemed interminable and halfway through the meal, Aria could see her father getting antsy. She hoped that the elaborate courses and the endless chatter from the Ambassador's wife would be enough of a distraction for him to forget the incident with Aunty Sunita earlier. At least temporarily.

She shook her head at the thought of that busybody, wondering how many other people now knew about her and Rohan. Given Aunty S's love for gossip, chances were the card room at the Willingdon Club and most of her parents' circle were all aware. It was probably only due to a fear of Rusi and his exacting sense of decorum that Rohan hadn't been brought up at her parents' dinners so far.

She massaged her temples. If only Aunty S knew what a limbo they were in—forget talking about marriage, these days if they even spoke without fighting, it was an achievement.

When she'd returned from London, after ignoring his many messages and calls, she'd been surprised to find Rohan waiting for her at the airport. He'd sneakily gotten her flight details from her assistant and insisted that he drive her home so they could talk. They'd driven in silence for the most part, and when they reached the Sea Link, he'd finally spoken up.

'I called you so many times. Did you get the flowers?'

She'd just nodded.

'What I said that day, I didn't mean, Aria.' His hands clenched the wheel. 'I was angry, frustrated, humiliated by that dinner . . . but being with you isn't a mistake.'

He'd said that he was in love with her and wanted to make this work but what was really driving him crazy was the fact that it wasn't only her father who seemed to find everything about his life problematic but at some level, Aria too.

'Where am I on your list of priorities, Aria? At the end of the day, do you choose me? It's not like I expect constant validation, but you've never . . .'

'I don't know if I can give you what you need,' she'd responded, looking out of the window as they sped past the darkened city. 'I don't know if I'm okay to be a star girlfriend, wife, whatever. I don't know how to do that.'

'But why can't you be both yourself and my wife?' he asked. 'I'm not asking you to become somebody else, so why do you constantly feel that this is an either/or situation?'

Aria didn't know how to answer. She couldn't articulate what she was feeling. Over the last few days, she'd replayed their conversations in her head. Was Rohan right? Was she a snob like her father? Was her snobbishness just wrapped in a prettier, more palatable box? She'd never admit it to him, but he was right that a part of it was just a matter of ego, that she couldn't wrap her head around the thought of her identity of being subsumed by another.

'I don't know, Ro, maybe, before this goes too far, we just . . .' her voice trailed off, breaking slightly, as she looked away from him.

They'd talked for a while longer, Rohan driving around in circles. It was the calmest conversation they'd had in weeks but at the end of it, when Rohan dropped her home, Aria was not any clearer where things stood between them. She let him kiss her goodnight, that familiar thrill going through her.

Now, a few weeks later, they were still in some sort of in-between stage that was causing major arguments. The balance kept shifting—there were days when Aria felt that this was it, he was it, and she couldn't imagine life without him, and then when her father would make some off-the-cuff, snide comment, she'd immediately pull away.

Last night, he'd given her an ultimatum—'Either you're with me or we need to move on, this see-saw is driving me crazy. I get nothing from you, and it's tough to sustain any relationship that way.' When he'd said that, she'd burst into tears, and the next thing she knew they were in bed together, and everything had felt as it should be. But this morning, when she'd woken up, that pit in her stomach had returned, and she'd slipped out soundlessly, while he was asleep.

Maybe he was right, she thought to herself, as she scrolled through his many messages that she had left unanswered, but at this point, she just seemed to be justifying her position constantly—to him, to her father, to Tara, and it was just getting exhausting.

She couldn't imagine her days without him. On a purely physical level, she craved the intimacy, the attraction between them was magnetic, and she'd drunkenly admitted to Leah once, much to both their surprise, that he was the best sex she'd ever had. With him, she was less restrained, less inhibited, and when they were together, things were good, there was an ease to her life that hadn't existed earlier. When he, for the first time, suggested that maybe they should go their own ways, she had felt her chest close up. When it came down to it, the thought of her days and nights without him was overwhelming. Even now, just thinking about it, made her feel hollow.

She dialled his number. He picked up on the third ring with a rather curt, 'Yeah.'

'I'm sorry.'

Silence.

The words came rushing out. 'I'm sorry for the last few weeks, I'm sorry for how my father behaved, I'm sorry for how I behaved. I've been cold. I've been distant. I've been so concerned with myself that I've not stopped to think of you. And I know it's wrong, and I know I've hurt you by the things I've said and the things I've not said. And the things I've done and the things I've not done, and I don't have a good enough reason why,' she paused for a breath.

'But I know last night, when we were together, it felt too much like a farewell. And I don't want to say goodbye to us just yet.'

For the next few minutes, she'd talked and talked and he'd listened silently. He'd caved finally, making her promise that this time, her commitment was a 100 per cent.

She'd asked him to stay on the phone till she fell asleep, and as she drifted off, a sleepy smile on her face, after weeks, she finally felt a sense of peace engulf her.

17

T, I know this is long overdue. I've been wanting to talk to you but I am struggling to find the words. I am sorry for all that's happened and I'm sorry I missed lunch. I would really like to see you. I'm out of town for a few days, but can we meet when I'm back? Come over, for old time's sake? Hope you are doing okay. Miss you.

Aria hit send and exhaled, pulling her shoulders back. 'There. Done. Now, officially off the grid,' she put her phone in the desk drawer and turned around. 'I'm all yours.'

'Who else's would you be?' Rohan pulled her towards him, for a long, deep kiss. 'I love you, Aria Mistry.'

With Leah's help, Rohan had surreptitiously planned a romantic getaway to Tuscany, picking up a dumbfounded Aria on the pretext of dinner, and driving straight to the private airport, where a jet had been waiting to take them to Florence. Aria would spend a few days tucked away with Rohan before heading to Rome for a friend's wedding, from where he would go on to shoot in New York.

Not usually one for surprises, Aria had been floored— Rohan had taken care of every little detail. He'd made sure they would have complete privacy, booking a luxurious heritage villa with a large estate and discreet staff on the outskirts of the city, and he'd invited Leah and her current fling, Marcus, to join them later on in the week.

It was all perfect, but something kept niggling her. Tara. She hadn't reached out to her, she'd been a no-show at lunch, and now she'd be away from the city for days, at a time when her friend needed her: could she even expect Tara to understand? Aria knew that she'd been terribly absent, but she'd struggled with the entire situation, spending countless hours in therapy dissecting the conversation they'd had, why she'd felt so personally betrayed, and the guilt she was carrying about their friendship. She knew, with a clear conscience, that she couldn't just throw away a friendship of so many years, and so she'd sent the message, hoping that Tara would be willing to repair things and also, if she was honest, trying to absolve herself of the guilt that engulfed her. She would try her best to fix the situation, and she would do that the minute she was back, but now, it was about her and Rohan, about rebuilding their relationship, she rationalized.

And she'd done just that. It had been glorious. They'd skipped sightseeing, opting to stay in bed most mornings, unable to take their hands off each other. She'd never felt so drawn to a person the way she did to Rohan. When he kissed her, undressed her, pleased her, Aria found herself owning her sexuality in a way she'd never known before.

They'd lain out by the pool, dipping in and out, when it got too hot, finding their way back to each other; Aria oblivious to who was around. They walked around the neighbouring village as the sun set, hand in hand, enjoying the icy sweetness of their daily gelatos, stopping at local bars for aperitivos, before coming back to the villa for dinner under the Italian sky, feasting on fresh spaghetti with the juiciest tomatoes, full bodied wines, light-as-air tiramisu, until heady from the day and the alcohol, they found themselves back in bed.

'Why can't it always be like this?' Aria asked him on their third night together, as he nuzzled her neck. They'd spent another amazing day, swimming, at the spa, playing a game of tennis, drinking their weight in spritzes.

He'd propped himself up on one shoulder, pushing a stray strand of hair behind her ears.

'I don't want it to be like this, Aria. This isn't . . .'

She looked at him quizzically.

'The real romance is not when you're hidden away from the world. It's in the everyday, waking up to coffee just the way you like it, seeing the person you love across the room at a party, that shared joke when you're out for dinner with friends. And as incredible as this is, as you are, especially right now,'—he caressed her slightly sunburnt cheeks—'I want that with you. The real deal, messy, complicated . . . I'll take the daddy drama and all,' he chuckled.

'This, this entire thing, is like how you build a movie set— real but not real, you know? Everything is perfect, everything is in place, it's impossible not to fall in love here. Trust me, I know,' he smiled. 'But out there, that's what true, authentic love stories are made of.'

~

Out of the three, it was Shaan who was the most territorial about their friendship; she was fiercely protective of their status as a trio, often irrationally so, and over the years, interlopers (read: new friends), as she saw them, had been denied entry.

It was Shaan who had christened their chat group The Originals, a virtual, constant reminder that they were friends first, everyone else who came later, other friends, boyfriends, husbands were, well, pretty much irrelevant. In their decade plus of knowing each other, they'd weathered Shaan moving to Delhi, dealt with the death of grandparents, lived through heartbreaks and counselled each other on life crises that with the dramatic flair of youth seemed, at the time, all consuming.

But they'd never experienced this—the arrest and the very public downfall of one of their own.

And for the first time in their friendship, which had gone from passing chits, to communicating over all the three-letter messaging apps, ICQ, AIM, BBM—Shaan could feel the strain.

'Aria is where?' Shaan quizzed, convinced she'd heard wrong.

'Idk,' Tara replied, 'She just messaged saying she's out of town.'

'Fucking Aria,' Shaan thought to herself for the hundredth time that week, before firing off another round of expletive laden messages to her friend.

She'd been furious at Aria missing lunch. She'd called and texted her multiple times, not mincing her words, but Aria hadn't responded. And now Tara was telling her that Aria had just taken off, without an apology to Shaan, without any kind of contrition towards Tara, without the courtesy of a single message, she'd just packed up and gone.

'She never wants to be the bad cop,' she complained to Pratap. 'She left me at lunch to clean up the mess of *her* argument with Tara and now she's off frolicking somewhere in the world.

After seeing Tara the other day, Shaan had decided to stay in the city longer. 'But this, this is so . . .,' she'd shaken her head. 'How can Aria with a clear conscience just bounce like that?'

'I could be wrong but I think she and Rohan are having issues, but I mean, come on, this is your best friend needing you. Put your little love spat on the side and just focus on her. I mean, what Tara is going through, none of us can even imagine, and all she's been to Tara is a judgmental bitch. I don't know, Pratap, I just don't know, how can a friendship come back from that?'

She made a face. 'And I'm done being stuck between them.'

Could this be a turning point for the three of them? So far, they'd manage to be there for each other; she wouldn't have survived her wedding without them by her side every step of the way. But this was quite a curveball.

'I'm not saying I've handled this situation well. I mean, there isn't a manual, but I just hope that Tara can see I'm doing my best.'

But she knew that was expecting too much. What Tara was asking of them for was so improbable. Not that Shaan blamed her—she probably would do the same in her position. But would they be able to bounce back from this when Tara realized that no help was forthcoming?

When she'd tried to empathize with Tara's predicament, Aria had taken a much harder stance. She kept going back to culpability and how Tara had to have known. Shaan wasn't convinced. She knew her friend, and she knew Tara was in many ways the most guileless of them all.

'Let's face it, Aria, we're three relatively independent girls and yet look at our relationships with our fathers—they are, in their own ways, control freaks and for the most part we've let them have that hold over us, despite the impression we may give. So how can you be sure that it couldn't have been you or me in Tara's situation?'

Naturally, Aria had debated hotly, throwing out words like transparency, fiscal responsibility and ethics.

'I'm really not looking for a lesson on morality or economics, Aria. I'm surprised at your lack of sympathy. You may not agree but how can you not feel for what she's going through?'

'That's empathy,' Aria corrected.

'Whatever, feel something ya. You're really being kind of a cold-hearted bitch. Are you going to come to lunch and if not apologize, at least hear her out?'

'Also, what could she have done if she had known? Do you think her father would have changed the way he ran his business at Tara's say so?' Shaan scoffed. 'I mean, been there, done that, not made a difference. I would love to think I had that much influence, but in reality, let's be honest, our fathers are pig-headed men who have always thought their way is the only way.'

There was silence from Aria.

'Ari, you've seen what I've gone through with my father, so how come you don't blame me then for every regressive and dodgy move the party makes?'

'It's different.' Aria insisted. 'I don't know why,' she admitted. 'I feel bad for Tara. I really, really do, but at the end of the day, her father crossed every boundary and now it's my family reputation at stake. I feel guilty, Shaan, that it's because of me, and my friendship with her, that my father's integrity is being called into question. Which to him is paramount.

And, really, if we support her, it looks like we are condoning everything that's happened. And I don't.'

'Aria, come on. It's not the first time that your family's name has been dropped, you know? I get that this association is not ideal, but when they find nothing to it, the press will move on. This is lunch, at my home, just us three. It's a chance for you to apologize and for us to just be there for our friend.'

'I don't know, Shaan. I can't keep getting into these confrontations. I can't handle another scene. Right now, it's been too much, with Rohan, with this . . . There's just too many. I know I owe her an apology for London, and I will . . . I just need to do it in my way.'

'I don't promise, but I'll try,' she'd hung up.

But she hadn't come.

Shaan chatted with Pratap a little longer, hearing about his day and his plans to have his school buddies over for drinks.

'Ask Manu to fry up the kebabs, they are in the freezer,' she found herself instructing.

'By the way, Prat, did you see that request from *The Times* magazine? They want to do a feature on you and shoot you on the campaign trail. I think it could be good, but I think you need to be careful about the kind of photographs they choose . . .'

She hung up with Pratap and poured herself a stiff drink, standing by the balcony, with its views of the Arabian Sea, the salty breeze, creating havoc with her already unruly curls. The last time she'd been in this house was over a year ago, before her wedding to Pratap. And now, look at her. Calling her husband to vent had almost been a reflex. Who would have thought that Pratap, the guy she had put down as arrogant, sycophantic and just weird, would turn out to be the person she confided in the most?

Was this what growing up was about? Was it about finding a compromise in a situation that may not be ideal? Could Shaan Singh have a marriage that wasn't filled with crazy passion, but with mutual respect? In Pratap, could she find a friend and a confidante, and had her mother been right, could that turn into love? Was this what love was really all about—not the *Dilwale* kind of love, but a more practical kind?

~

'Mr Mistry, I have to ask. You are known for being rather reclusive. If I'm not wrong, this is the second interview you've given in a decade. I would know, I think I've spent countless hours chasing an opportunity. What made you agree now?'

'Well, Vickram.' Rusi chuckled lightly. 'What can I say? Persistence pays, old chap.'

Vickram Gupta laughed, settling back into the wing-backed leather armchair. His CEO Conversations series was one of the most respected shows in the country, providing an insight into the minds of the country's business leaders. The format of the show lent itself to an intimate, in-depth interaction, with Gupta and his camera crew spending time touring factories, hitting balls on the golf course and dining at their interviewees' homes. Rusi had allowed access to his private office at their Ballard Estate headquarters, a wood-panelled room with floor-to-ceiling bookcases, glass encased models of some of their most prolific developments and busts of his ancestors, for the first time.

'At Mistry & Sons, we have a healthy relationship with the media. When we have something important to say, we are happy to share. And today, we wanted to share the news of our acquisition of the Smith Group of Hotels, a project very close to my family's heart and one that will solidify Mistry & Sons' position as global leaders in hospitality.'

'A project I believe that has been masterminded and seen to completion by your daughter, Aria?'

Rusi beamed proudly. 'That is correct. Aria joined the company after getting her MBA at Harvard. She trained in several departments until she decided her focus would be on hospitality. Which, interestingly, is a vertical, her grandfather, my father, started, changing India's hotels forever. This deal is her baby.'

For the next forty-five minutes, Vickram peppered Rusi with questions on this hospitality deal, on new developments in their infrastructure arm, on their new tech-focused mandate, on their latest merger in the telecom space, all while delving into Rusi's management style.

'For so many foreign companies, there is still this uncertainty of doing business in India. You've read the reports when it comes to investor hesitation. Why do you think that is?'

Rusi sighed. 'See here, Vickram. I can give you the routine response.' He listed off his fingers—'Political uncertainty, lack of clarity in vision, oppressive taxation, laws on ownership and management, all incredibly valid roadblocks to foreign investment, and all that need to be fundamentally addressed.'

He paused. 'But what's ignored and which unfortunately is becoming far too widespread, is the image of the unscrupulous Indian businessman, and the rotten apples that seem to be emerging are not helping the matter. Quite frankly,' he turned his nose up. 'We're becoming the financial Wild West.'

Vickram looked at his guest curiously. 'Am I right in assuming that you are referring to the recent slew of high-profile frauds? The most recent being the India Co-Op and MohanCity scam case that's come to light. Mohan Mehta, if I'm not mistaken, is a close associate of yours, correct?'

Rusi bristled. 'That's incorrect. In fact, I think this is the best time to clarify the ridiculous news report that is making the rounds. Mr Mehta's daughter and mine were in school together many years ago. That's the only association we have had. At no point have I personally or has any employee of Mistry & Sons had any dealings with their organization.'

'But Mr Mistry, surely we're not the only country where financial frauds take place?'

Rusi added forcefully. 'Yes, but only in India are the perpetrators not brought to justice swiftly. Frankly, it's ludicrous that many are still living off their spoils around the world!'

He leaned towards the camera behind Vickram, looking directly into the blinking red light.

'I will not comment on an individual basis, but yes, Vickram, since you asked for my opinion, I will say this. I strongly believe that to restore our image and give our foreign investors a sense of security, transparency in doing business on an individual and collective level is imperative. The government needs to take the strongest and strictest action possible to deter any and all future offenders.'

~

During the course of the afternoon she spent with Shaan, in between the tears and the anger, Tara had expressed her frustration at not having been able to see her father. Mohan Mehta had been adamant that neither Tara nor her mother would visit him in jail, leaving them at the mercy of the lawyers to relay messages. For Tara, whose time in India was limited, this inability to communicate was adding to her frustration, as was the knowledge that there was a chance that she would have to go back to London without seeing him.

This was something Shaan could do. She could at least help reunite the family, even if briefly. And Pratap, she had to give it to him, had really come through.

So, at 9 p.m., under the cover of darkness, Shaan sent a car to take Tara and her mother to see Mohan Mehta at a government office.

'I can't promise big things at the moment, T, but Pratap has helped organize a conference room where the three of you can meet. You will be monitored, of course, but for the most part, you'll be able to speak to your dad and give him that hug,' she said, as Tara burst into tears, furthering Shaan's guilt.

Bina immediately got busy organizing her husband's favourite snacks, some clothes and books. In the hours leading up to the meeting, Tara was on edge, pacing the floors, her stomach in knots—would Shaan really come through? What state would her father be in? Would the family get to actually speak to him?

True to Shaan's word, mother and daughter, holding hands in the backseat, were driven through the empty streets of Ballard Estate, the beautiful heritage area, a ghost town post 6 p.m., when office-goers signed out for the day.

And in a windowless, tube-lit room, with drab green walls, a government office prerequisite, the paint peeling in places, a lone fan kicking up dust from the files that lined the shelves, and the Prime Minister's portrait sternly watching over them, Tara was reunited with her father, after months.

He was a frail shadow of the man he'd once been; his shoulders hunched, their burdens seemingly too heavy to bear; his gait altered; his hair completely grey; the lines in his forehead deeper and more pronounced. In just a few months, he'd aged decades.

On seeing his little girl, Mohan Mehta broke down completely. Father and daughter held each other tightly as Bina watched them from a distance, silent sobs racking her body, her yellow cotton dupatta covering her mouth.

'*Mari dikri*. Sorry, Sorry, baby. Forgive me,' Mohan kept whispering into Tara's ear as she hugged him tighter. There was so much she wanted to ask her father: how had they come to this? How was Bunty involved? Why hadn't he told her the truth? What *was* the truth? What would happen to their family?

But all the questions vapourized the minute she'd seen him and hugged him.

She deserved answers. She *needed* them. But, right now, she just wanted to be a source of strength to her father.

When they'd all calmed down, father and daughter reluctantly let go, and they sat around a wooden table, as Bina brought out Mohan's favourite treats—khaman dhokla, ghatiya and kadak chai, which he wolfed down, shooting his wife a grateful look. Not knowing what to do with herself, Bina kept fussing over him, filling his plate, offering him more tea, all the while wiping tears from her eyes with the ends of her dupatta.

Tara watched him quietly as he ate, swallowing hard when she saw how much his hands shook, how his shirt hung off his previously robust frame. How could they keep such an old, frail man in jail for so many months?

'You're okay, Papa? They are treating you okay?' Tara's voice broke, asking the question, that she didn't really know she could stomach the answer to.

He nodded, deflecting. 'You, beta? Where is Nakul?'

'He's fine, he's fine,' she lied. 'He's going to come soon.' So far, she hadn't even told her mother the extent of her in-laws' displeasure or that Nakul had pretty much switched off from their marriage. Since she'd been in Mumbai, they'd barely spoken a handful of times, all perfunctory calls. For the first time, she had no idea where, how or with whom he was spending his days.

'So, you going back to London soon.' He took her hand in his, his words more a statement than a question. 'Bas, now you've seen me, you go back to your family.'

Tara looked at him incredulously. 'YOU are my family. I don't care . . .' her voice caught and she steadied herself. 'Right now, my focus is you and getting you home. But yes, there's a chance that if my paperwork doesn't come through, I may have to go back for a little while.'

Mohan smiled sadly.

'By the grace of god, next time you are here, I will be at home. We will be back in our home,' he said, looking at Bina. 'I have told lawyers, do the needful, but Bina must have our home back.'

Her mother had stayed silent.

'What do you think will happen now, Papa?' Tara shot a glance at the plain-clothes officer sitting listlessly in the corner, scrolling through his phone.

He scooted over to Tara, pulling her chair closer and taking her hands in his. The table wobbled slightly.

'I tried beta, I've tried my best to make sure that nothing will happen to you or Mummy, that much I know,' his eyes welled up with tears. 'I've made mistakes, I've made many mistakes, but I never meant for you . . .' he couldn't finish the sentence.

He took a deep breath and continued. 'Today, the advocates told me the bail appeal is fixed for Friday now. I've told them my plan on how I will start paying back the money, but beyond that I don't know.'

He turned his hands, translucent and spotted with age, the tremor more pronounced. 'I built this business with my own two hands, and it was a good business, but somewhere along the way, people I thought were my friends . . .' he lifted those hands up. '*Kya batau*, Tara. *Ek din* I will explain everything.'

'Papa,' Tara held both his hands in hers. 'I have so many things to ask you, and I know now is not the time . . .' she licked her lips nervously, looking again at the guard, who now had headphones on, seemingly engrossed in something playing on his screen. 'But, Papa. Bunty? Where is he? Did he do this?' her voice hardened.

'Shh. *Abhi nahi*, Tari. One day, I promise, soon. I will tell you everything that happened. And it's my mistake, mine alone. Bunty *abhi tak bachcha hai*. You cannot blame him, what does he know? But I told you, I have a plan.'

He gave her a wan smile. '*Dekh beta*, Sanjay Dutt went to jail. He came back and became a bigger hero. So Mohan Mehta *mein bhi jaadoo hai na*?'

He hugged his daughter again, his arms around her, and Tara, just like when she was a young girl, buried her face in her father's chest. His shirt smelt faintly of a nostalgic mix of sweat and Old Spice. She started crying again.

'Don't, baby,' he pulled back, took a long look at her and wiped her cheeks with his trembling hands. 'You don't cry any more. I want you to live *befikar*. I am an old man, my life *pati gai*, but you, you . . . you have so much, good husband, good family and you are too young to live with sadness,' he took her face in his hands.

'From the moment you were born,' his eyes were moist again. 'I did everything to make you happy . . . I misfired . . . badly,' he swallowed back a sob.

'But you just remember. Whatever happens, I love you, and I'm your same Papa always.'

~

By next morning, the news of Mohan Mehta's bail hearing had made its way into the press, bumping his story back to the front page.

One of the basic tenets of Tara's London-based guru Swami Ranji, was the idea of mindful manifestation—what you think will become, he would drone to his captivated listeners. It was a lesson Tara had taken to heart; she manifested thoughts of marriage to Nakul, a successful career doing what she loved, a sense of contentment, she would often proselytize to her friends.

Today, she realized how the concept could work inversely. The family lawyer had asked them for a quick meeting at the Oberoi Hotel coffee shop, before her father's bail hearing and the entire ride there, Tara fretted about running into someone from their 'past' life, as she now referred to it. The idea of

more humiliation by people they formerly considered friends
was paralysing, and given her mother's fragile state, Tara was
especially anxious.

In Mumbai, though a city of fifteen million, amongst a
certain set, six degrees of social separation is actually considered
expansive; avoiding people they knew was somewhat impossible.

Two hours later, as she and her mother walked towards
the entrance, Tara finally let herself breathe. But as luck would
have it, just when she thought they were in the clear, they
crossed paths with several of her mother's former kitty party
aunties, striding in, a blur of highlighted hair, too-tight clothes
and equally small minds.

'Bina?' Chaand Mehra said, spotting them. 'Hi,' she added
loudly.

'Darling, how are you?' she walked over, diamonds
gleaming on her wrists and in her ears, behind the flicks of
honey blonde highlights.

Tara sighed, inwardly bracing herself.

'We've been thinking about you. *Pata hai, woh din hi
meine Anju ko boli, bechari Bina*,' she looked to Anju Raheja
on her right, before turning back to Bina. '*Ghar bhi nahi, pati
bhi nahi, beta bhi nahi. Ek minute mein, sab kho gaya.* Life is so
unpredictable, no?' she sighed dramatically, while her equally
Botoxed cronies, standing behind her, their bags nestled in the
crooks of their elbows, monogram logo outwards, nodded in
sympathy.

'*Boli thee na*, Anju. I *must* call Bina, but you know how it
is, every day something or other,' she tittered.

'We're fine, thank you,' her mother added firmly, trying
not to rise to their bait, and removing her hands from Chaand's
vice-like grasp.

'We have all been thinking about you soo much,' Anju Raheja simpered, patting her bouffant.

'How is Mohan? He must . . .' Geeta Mittal asked, her forehead furrowed.

'At least Tara is with you,' Anju drowned out her friend, her breasts threatening to spill over from her trademark low-cut blouse. 'What a relief.'

'But Tara, darling, *itni dubli ho gayi ho*. Stress, na. Now, I hope no dieting.'

'No dieting, Anju Aunty. You know . . . times are so tough,' Tara said with an overdramatic sigh. The ladies looked at each other, eyes wide and mouths open.

'Really?' Chaand pressed her crimson-tipped fingers to her mouth, thirsty for more information that she could pass on to the rest of the gang.

'We are living day to day, minute to minute, hand to mouth,' Tara's tone was caustic, despite her mother's warning looks.

'But it's okay, Aunty, we're managing, one meal a day is enough for Mama and me.'

'Beta,' Chaand said, 'Let me send you some food. You know my cook makes the best conti, you used to eat it when you would come to meet Akash. You must be missing London also.' She beamed, mentally lapping up the accolades that were sure to come when others heard of her magnanimity. 'Now tell me Bina, what is your new address, you are in Upper Worli now, someone told me?'

'Arré, Chaand, only the builders call it Upper Worli. *Woh,* jail *ke paas* area. These new developments, *bahar se* fancy *lagte hain*, but approach is terrible. And boxes they are, so many flats, *ek ke upar ek*, I tell you,' the ever-tactful Anju interrupted.

Tara could feel her mother tense up.

'Look at us Mama, so rude. We are only talking about ourselves.'

'How is Akash, Chaand Aunty? I haven't seen him in years—he's still in New York? Speaking of cooking, his boyfriend Alex is a chef right, he must have so many recipes to share with you all!' Tara said innocently, as the colour drained from Chaand's face and her friends looked on curiously, wondering if the rumours about Akash Mehra were actually true.

'Anju Aunty, our home is just fine, thank you for asking. But what about uncle's situation at the factory? I hear his brother has completely taken over and thrown him out of the business. How is he spending his days *ab*? And I hear you'll have to take shifts in using the kitchen, tch, tch, so sad.' Anju squirmed.

'Oh, and before I forget. Geeta Aunty,' she addressed the third, 'Please tell Smita I'm so sorry I just couldn't accommodate her in the last exhibition. You know . . . after that problem with the embroidery all coming off,' she said. Geeta Mittal's designer daughter, Smita, counted on her mother's society friends to keep her rather lacklustre clothing business running. 'In London, they are just SO particular about quality,' she added, as Geeta glared at her and Bina.

Satisfied with the can of worms she'd opened, Tara turned to her mother, who was trying her best to suppress a grin. 'Come on Mama, we'll be late for all the cooking, *jhadu pocha* we have to do.'

~

'I swear, Shaan, I haven't felt this good in months,' Tara giggled on the phone later. 'You had to see their faces! I feel bad about throwing poor Akash under the bus, but his mother was being such a cow.'

'Well, they wanted gossip,' Shaan laughed, happy to have her friend sounding less despondent.

'I'm just done with all these busybodies, seriously. How did we ever think they were our friends?'

18

'So THIS is the kind of company you choose to keep?' a red-faced Rusi Mistry stormed into the sunlit breakfast room and flung the papers across the table at Aria. She looked up startled from her Kindle, wondering what had ticked her father off so early in the day.

'It's embarrassing. Downright humiliating. Your grandfather must be turning in his *grave*, seeing the Mistry name dragged through the mud,' he continued, his tone rising, shooing the bearer away as he waited for Aria to respond.

'I have no idea what you are talking about, Dad,' Aria reached for the folded paper, as Leah and her mother walked into the room.

Above the fold in the day's newspaper was a photo of Mohan Mehta, handcuffed, surrounded by the cops. Inset, Tara and her mother, pictured leaving the court post the hearing.

ACCUSED IN THE MOHANCITY AND INDIA CO-OP BANK SCAM, MOHAN MEHTA DENIED BAIL

Yesterday, the Mumbai Sessions Court denied bail to the prime accused in the India Co-Op bank scam, Mohan Mehta. Mehta, who has been charged in the Rs 5000-crore scam, approached the magistrate for bail, citing ill health.

Mehta has been held at Mumbai's Arthur Road jail since his arrest in March, along with India Co-Op Bank Chairman and the Kalbadevi branch manager. All three were further remanded to judicial custody, as the ED and EOW sought more time for ongoing inquiries. Mehta's advocate told the press that his client planned to appeal this decision with the High Court. 'These are unfair tactics to keep an elderly, sickly man in custody. He is not a terrorist, he poses no harm to national security. He is cooperating, so continue investigations, but let him be home, where he can be cared for.'

Mehta, who was a part of the high-flying Malabar Hill set, built his fortune with Mohan & Sons before branching out into real estate with his now infamous MohanCity project, and is now under investigation on various counts including money laundering, cheating and fraud. A warrant for his son Rishabh Mehta, aka Bunty, who is absconding has also been issued.

In a new update, the EOW revealed that they will also be questioning Mistry & Sons chairman Rusi Mistry on his dealings with Mohan Mehta. A spokesperson for the company maintained, 'Neither Mr Mistry or anyone at Mistry & Sons has ever had any professional relationship with Mr Mehta.'

Aria looked up at her father, concerned, 'Are you really being questioned? What have the lawyers said?'

'Look at the bottom half of the paper, Aria,' Rusi thundered, surprising even Meher with his anger.

Aria flipped the paper over, her mother and sister, reading over her shoulder. Her stomach lurched.

In technicolour, taking up prime print real estate, were two photos laid out side by side. On the left hand of the page were a series of photos of Rohan and Aria in a passionate embrace, his arms around her waist, him nuzzling her neck. It was from Tuscany, a few steps away from their favourite gelateria. She hadn't even realized that Rohan had been recognized, let alone that they'd been photographed. She looked to the other image—Malika, sitting on Rohan's lap, his arm around her waist, her head thrown back in laughter. They were seated at what seemed like a patio of a restaurant, on a table filled with people.

Aria's cheeks burned. She read the caption accompanying the image:

Part Time Lover

Exclusive!!! It seems Romeo Rawal has struck again. The heartthrob has been spotted canoodling with two different women, just a few days apart. Romeo, who is currently in New York with Malika, shooting their latest film, a Karan Johar romance, seem to be taking a cue from their characters. Sources tell us that they have great chemistry and have been enjoying spending their time together, hitting the local clubs and bars. But the question is—is this a publicity stunt or is Romeo Rawal playing the field? The last we heard, his heart was with heiress Aria Mistry, who he'd whisked off on a romantic Tuscan holiday, where they were seen enjoying Italian treats—and each other from the looks of it . . .

'It's online too,' Leah said tentatively, as she scanned her phone.

'So, what do you have to say? Is this how you want to appear to the world? Your private life . . . this, this intimate photo, OUR family name, twice on the front page, and look at the reputation we've gained, that we only hang out with cheats and liars. 100 years of propriety, all lost . . .' Rusi paced the room.

'Calm down, Rusi. Give the girl a minute,' Meher shot her husband a look.

'Calm, Meher? You'd like me to be calm?' Rusi was now shouting again, his booming voice reverberating through the glass-walled patio.

'I've told her time and time again, be careful who you associate with. It's bad enough that every article about Mohan Mehta mentions Aria, that we are now facing investigation. And this . . . this . . . scoundrel. Who professed his love! Who you told me was so devoted! Who YOU insisted I welcome into my home! Is making a fool of her again and again!'

'And it seems apparent to me, my dear Aria, that lying is now part of your repertoire too. How is it that I had no inkling of this romantic jaunt? You live under my roof, and you choose to hide things from me? I did NOT raise you that way.'

Aria sat there frozen.

'I told all of you. I told you, this boy is nothing but surface decoration. There's NO depth to him. There's NO substance. It's all just one grand performance. But NO, don't listen to me, don't listen to your father! Who has experience, who knows these types of people, who has seen what this boy is really about. NO, I'm the tyrant, I'm the snob, I'm . . . of course.' he slammed his palms down on the table, spilling the carafe of orange juice all over the cream tablecloth.

Without a word, Aria left the room, fighting back tears. She refused to cry in front of her father. She could hear her mother admonishing Rusi, as she ran to the elevator that would take her to her second-floor bedroom.

She couldn't breathe. She opened the windows to the terrace and took a few deep breaths to steady herself. Later, when she would describe the scene to her therapist, she would realize that she had been in the throes of a full-blown panic attack, the first of many to come, her hands clammy, her heart racing, her entire body trembling.

Had the last few weeks all been a lie?

Just before he'd left for New York, they'd been in bed, and he'd turned, pushed her hair back from her face and said softly, 'I feel like you're finally mine.'

'Where do you get these lines from, Mr Rawal? Is this why they call you Romeo or do you have some cheeseball writer on your payroll sending you these?' she'd teased.

'What can I say?' He'd lobbied back. 'You make me work hard for some honey.'

She should have known then. She wiped away the tears that wouldn't stop, as she looked out on to the calm Arabian Sea, taking long, deep breaths, the briny air mixing with the salt on her upper lip.

How could she have not seen that he was the guy for whom it was all about the chase? It was such a cliché. SHE was such a cliché. All these months, he thought she was out of reach and then, the moment she gave in, POOF! He'd moved on to the next thing.

It was pure delusion that made her believe that she could tame his ways. She'd gone against her instinct, against her father and what did she have to show for it? Her name and photograph in the paper, and the humiliation of being *that* girl, dumped via a grainy paparazzi photo.

The internal monologue continued along with the tears. She didn't hear Leah come in and put a hand on her shoulder. She turned and collapsed into her sister's arms, sobbing.

'But Aria, you should speak to him,' Leah said to her sister a little later, when she'd calmed down. 'Maybe there's an explanation,' she offered, somewhat lamely.

'Like what, she just fell into his lap? Oops!' Aria retorted.

'Uff . . . I dunno. But can I say something? And don't shoot the messenger.'

'I'm just saying, he seemed really devoted. He took all of yours and Dad's bullshit in his stride and still seemed to want to be with you. I don't think he would just give it all up for a hook-up. I just think there's more to this photo and that you owe it to yourself to get the truth from him.'

'He's an actor, Leah. That's what he does. Pretends, for a living. And who knows, maybe it's more than just a hook-up.' The tears threatened to spill over again. 'I am SO angry. Not just at him, but at myself . . . I did what I'd sworn I would never do. I fell for the wrong guy and let myself be made a fool of.'

The sisters sat in silence; Aria's phone vibrated incessantly, nearly falling off the bedside table, but she ignored it.

'I thought . . . I thought this was IT, Leah,' Aria, sniffled. 'I thought he was *the* guy. I was ready to fight Dad, ready to risk everything,' she laughed bitterly. 'That's the first time I've actually admitted that out aloud.'

The phone vibrated again. Leah turned over and grabbed it.

'It's Rohan again. It's the middle of the night in New York and he's calling non-stop. Just speak to him, Ari.'

~

'So, what did he say, Ari?' Leah prodded, taking a forkful of mashed potatoes.

Aria had been hiding out in her room all day, so Leah had their chef make up a tray of all her sister's favourite comfort food. Creamy mashed potatoes, a steaming bowl of garlicky pasta, rich dark chocolate cake with berries, hoping something would catch her fancy.

So far Aria's plate had remained untouched, though she had nearly finished half the bottle of red wine Leah had raided from their father's cellar.

'Eat,' she admonished, as Aria helped herself to another generous pour.

It was the perfect evening out on the terrace, the sound of the waves forming an uninterrupted backdrop and a cool sea breeze blowing. Aria burrowed further into the cream cashmere blanket.

'What could he say? He denied it, of course.'

'The thing that just gets me, Leah, is that over the last few weeks, things were GREAT between us. We'd finally gotten to a good place, and then this, this comes out of nowhere,' she paused to take a sip.

'Or has this been going on all this while and I was just too stupid and love-struck to notice?'

She replayed the conversation with Rohan back in her head. For the most part of their call, she hadn't even been able to look at him—it hurt too much. The thought of him with another woman, let alone that Malika, made her feel physically sick.

He cried. She cried. She'd never seen him cry before. He pleaded. She remained stoic. He tried to explain. She remained silent. He got defensive. She snapped. And it had continued that way for hours, in an interminable loop, till she'd finally hung up, spent. It was only when she'd walked out to the terrace, taking long, greedy gulps of air, that she realized that the sun was setting. She'd missed work, she'd missed lunch, she'd even missed the special performance by the cellist YoYo Ma at the NCPA that she'd been looking forward to all week.

'It's not what you think,' Rohan had told her when she finally answered his video call. 'I know what it looks like, and it doesn't look good,' he sat up straighter in bed, his bare torso visible on the small screen. 'But it's not what it's made out to be.' He was speaking fast and nervously.

'That's like a line in every crappy movie where the guy is caught cheating.'

'No, Ari, there's no cheating. I promise you, there's *nothing* going on between me and Malika.'

'So, explain the picture then,' she demanded.

He sighed, ran his fingers through his hair, and despite herself, she felt her heart skip a beat, seeing that familiar gesture.

'Yeah, so she has a thing for me. But it's not reciprocal any more. I don't have any feelings for her, it's only you for me.'

'Do you remember, in Paris, when you asked me why I hadn't called you, despite asking Shaan for your number?'

When Aria didn't respond, he continued.

'It's because . . .' he exhaled. 'We had a thing, Malika and me. It was meant to be casual, but then it got complicated. And you probably won't believe this, but Ari, when I met you, I felt something I had not felt in a long time, ever if I'm being really honest. I knew, this, us . . . that it was something I wanted to explore. But for that, I wanted no baggage, and that's why I didn't call right away. I wanted to be fair to her, and also, I wanted to get to know you, without any drama, on a clean slate.'

He exhaled again. 'I don't have an explanation for the photo, it was just some stupidity, and I was drunker than I should have been, and I let it happen, but it went no further, I swear on our relationship. Malika is in the past for me.'

'What relationship, Rohan? The one where I went against my father to be with you and yet you humiliate me so publicly? The front fucking page of the paper. Really.'

'Why is it always about your father? You always bring everything back to that,' he bristled visibly 'Everything I say or do boils down to what your father thinks.'

'Are you seriously getting annoyed with me right now? After what you've done, YOU have the gall to put this on me?' Aria could feel the anger building.

'YOU, YOU promised, you promised me, that you would never let something like this happen.' She grit her teeth.

'I screwed up, baby. I know, I'm sorry,' he said. 'You HAVE to forgive me, you have to.'

She shook her head.

'But why do I feel that this is your way out? You are going to hold this against me, and on this, this minor thing, you will throw everything away.'

'Rohan, it may be minor to you, but to me, you've broken my trust.'

'Ari, I am sorry. I am sorry that I've put you in this position. But it was nothing, nothing, I SWEAR. And I get you want to be perfect, but you've fucked up too. Please, let's move past this . . .'

And they'd gone around in circles till they'd both cried themselves hoarse.

'How did you guys end the conversation?' Leah asked.

'We ended it. The conversation and the relationship.'

'Can I ask you something?' she asked him. 'Did you really mean it when you said that this was *it* for you?

'How can you even ask me that?'

She fell silent. Aria couldn't look at him any more.

'I wish I could see you just now . . . I have a break in the schedule this week for two days, I'm going to come home and . . .

'We're done,' she said, her voice barely above a whisper.

'No, Ari, baby, please. Look at me, please. Let's, let's work through this. We can. I know we can. I love you. I want to spend the rest of my life with you. Let's discuss this when I come home, please. Don't make a rash decision . . .'

'I don't think you know what you want, Rohan. You've said it about me all this time, but have you really asked yourself—are you ready to give up being Romeo Rawal?'

'That's bullshit and you know it, Ari. I've never EVER given you a chance to doubt me.'

'You've never been caught, you mean. Until now. You say it was nothing and it was a mistake. Even if that's true . . .' she said flatly.

'It is, you have to believe me,' he interrupted, tears running down his cheeks.

'Even if it is,' she continued, trying to get the words out, before her voice broke. 'The next time it will be something else. Someone else. There will always be another movie, another set, another actress.'

She shook her head.

'That's not a life I want to live.'

~

Aria's phone vibrated on the marble counter. Her hands dusted with flour and butter, she gestured to their in-house chef, who she'd relegated to sous, to answer it for her.

Shaan's face popped up on the screen.

'Are you seriously baking again? Did you swap lives with Pooja Dhingra and just not tell us?' she teased. 'And how the hell do you bake with no mess?'

It had been three weeks since Aria had broken up with Rohan. Week one had seen her catatonic, staring out into the sea, wrapped in blankets on the terrace, or buried under a duvet, surfing the net endlessly. Week two had seen her on the move with no time to pause, packing her days from the moment she got up, till the time she crawled back into bed. And in week three, she'd taken to baking. Her emotional pendulum oscillated—fury, humiliation, sadness, pain, embarrassment—the various stages of a break-up, hers compounded by a very public fallout.

Rohan called incessantly, he'd flown home to try and work things out, but still furious and heartbroken she refused to acknowledge his gestures. The photo of Malika and him had gone viral, #Rolika trending again, blogs and papers in fevered speculation. Photo editors got crafty, creating triangles with images of the three of them or laying out photos of Aria and Rohan, with a jagged lightning strike through the centre. She tried to block him out, but as much as she tried, he was everywhere. On television! On billboards lining Marine Drive, on her way to work! The internet was a particularly toxic rabbit hole, where rabid fans dissected the three individuals from the confines of their homes. She deleted her social media, muted her WhatsApp, and besides speaking to Shaan, decided to go completely incommunicado.

But she found that she couldn't stop missing him. She missed the way his eyes crinkled when he laughed; how he always stole the first sip of morning coffee from her cup; she missed how they lay together, their legs intertwined in bed at night, Aria rubbing her feet against his for warmth; she missed the way he smelt; she missed the slow burn of his stubble against her skin when he kissed her neck.

She missed him. At every point of her day.

'Baking, I can control. It's an exact science. It needs accuracy, precision and perfection, and the best part, if you follow the rules, you are guaranteed a good result!' she said in all seriousness to her friend, who just rolled her eyes, laughing.

'Yeah, one that will stay a lifetime on your hips,' Shaan cackled. 'So, what's today's special?'

The friends chatted while Aria measured, poured, sieved and strained. Aria's asceticism in her daily routine—regular 10k runs, clean eating, fixed bedtimes—was in complete contradiction to her baking. Lush creme caramels, fluffy meringues, vibrant lemon pies, velvety chocolate cakes—her friends and family were all happy to be recipients of these experiments; Aria herself refrained from sugar during the week.

'So, Ari, you look good. How are you?'

Aria gave her friend a half-hearted smile and shrugged, folding the egg whites into the lush chocolate.

'Are you ever going to talk about him? What happened?'

Shaan checked in on her friend daily, but Aria was reticent when it came to discussing Rohan. In typical Aria style, she'd closed off completely, blocking the situation as best as she could. Out of sight, out of mind, was how Shaan described Aria's philosophy of not dealing with complications that threatened the order she liked to live with. She'd done it with Tara and now Rohan.

On today's call, Shaan was going to broach the topic of Tara. She had let Aria off too easily, given the developments with Rohan that followed after, but Aria needed to know what was going on with their friend.

'Babe, have you talked to Tara recently?'

Aria busied herself dusting icing sugar over the Bundt cake, avoiding Shaan's question.

'Come on, babe, you can do better than that. I've really been trying to not say much, but you've been a pretty shitty friend to her, and I think that she deserves better.'

Aria put her spatula down and pursed her lips.

'It's not that I don't get it Shaan, or I don't feel guilty.

'At the crux of it, yeah I know, I messed up with Tara, but we've also reached a point where I don't know if we can return to how things were.'

She paused, wiping her hands on her apron and taking her phone out to the kitchen garden.

'I do want to talk to her, and yes, in a way, I do owe her an apology. But at the same time, I'm still struggling to wrap my head around how many people have been impacted by what her father's done. I mean, someone died! People lost everything. I get that it's not her fault . . . but did she know and ignore it so she could lead this life? You know she's enjoyed every minute of it . . .'

Shaan stared at her friend in disbelief.

Aria continued, 'And then, there's bringing my family and my father into it. How can I not be protective? It is now our reputation at stake, for god's sake, Shaan. I wish you would understand!'

'Let me ask you this: Are you not enjoying the spoils of being your father's daughter? I am. I have no qualms in saying that. And those 'spoils'—do you know everything your dad does at Mistry & Sons, Aria? Are you involved in every business decision he makes? Do you know every deal he has done? I definitely have no idea about half the things my father does. And while I am sure a part of him is protecting me because sometimes, business dealings, especially where we live are not so clear cut.'

'My father wouldn't do something like this . . .' Aria said stubbornly, sticking her chin out.

'Exactly what Tara probably thought, Aria. Why are you being so hard on her? Why are you so judgemental about someone you've known never to harm a fly?'

Aria frowned at her friend's tone.

'You make it out like I'm some monster. It's annoying that both you and Rohan keep saying that. And honestly, Shaan, right now I don't need this. I have enough to deal with.'

'Come on, Ari. I get that you are heartbroken and it sucks what happened with you and Rohan. But have some compassion. I swear, sometimes I feel like you have had more of it for the stray dogs you feed than your own friend.'

'That's really uncalled for.'

Shaan gritted her teeth. 'What Tara's gone through, I wouldn't wish on anyone—her marriage is breaking, do you know that? Nakul is being such an asshole. And, and . . .'

'And what?'

'You should speak to her, Aria. You should. I don't want to say more. But it's time you got off this high horse and time you looked beyond yourself. At the rate you're going, none of us will live up to your standards. Call Tara, for fuck's sake.'

And with that, Shaan ended the call, leaving Aria dumbfounded.

~

Aria had just got out of the shower when her phone pinged. She wrapped herself in a bathrobe, towel-drying her hair with one hand, and clicked on the email that Sunanda Nath, their Corporate Communications director, had just sent to the family.

Subject: CEO Conversations: Mr Mistry.

PFB Mr Mistry's interview on CEO Conversations that aired last night. On the show, Mr Mistry shares news about the Smith Group merger and his ten-year plan for Mistry & Sons. The interview has already garnered substantial social media impressions in a few hours! We are tracking and will have concrete numbers to you soon.

An hour later, a furious Aria, dressed hastily in jeans and a t-shirt, barged into her father's study, where he was reading the Sunday newspapers.

'How could you, Dad? How could you?' Aria's voice was two notches higher than normal.

'Good morning to you too, Aria. Please do specify what you are now referring to,'Rusi folded the paper he was reading.

Aria gave him a withering look.

'You know exactly what I am talking about. Why did you have to throw the poor man under the bus? His bail hearing is soon and you may have destroyed any chance of him coming home.'

'He is still my best friend's father, Dad. *You* were at Tara's wedding. *You've* met him so many times. How could you be so cruel?' Aria paced the room, her wet hair sticking to the back of her t-shirt.

'Tara will never forgive me, and how can I blame her? I get what he did was awful but did you even think about the impact your words can have on his life, on his family? How could you Dad?' she asked again.

Rusi cleared his throat, leaning back against the mahogany leather sofas.

'Let me make one thing clear, Aria. I do not answer to you, not now, not ever. I am the head of this family and this company, let's not forget that.' His voice, though calm, had a threatening undertone.

Aria looked at her father slack-jawed, as he continued.

'I will decide what is best for our family and for our future. I will not have my intentions questioned by a young lady with, let's face it . . . limited experience. I said what I believe is the truth, what needed to be said. And that's how I've raised both you and Leah.'

He got up, stretched his legs and strode over to the window, his hands folded behind his back.

'Over the past few weeks, I have seen what your poor judgement has resulted in. I do not appreciate what our world has been reduced to. I did not raise you both to battle and question your parents. We are not in some awful American film where the children and parents are at constant loggerheads. That is not the upbringing I had and I will be damned if that's what we become.'

He turned around to face Aria.

'Let's be very clear what our relationship is. You are the child and I am the parent. I will end this conversation here and now before I say something that we'll both eventually regret. But I hope I have made myself abundantly clear.'

Aria nodded her head. 'What is clear, Dad,' she said, slowly, 'is that I cannot live my life on your terms. I'm sorry that you seem to think so little of me.' She clenched her jaw. 'But what does it say about you, as a parent, that the children YOU have raised, have such *limited* views?'

Rusi started at her tone, but Aria refused to cower down. She was shaking.

'What you seem to want around you are puppies that will do your bidding, not individuals with opinions of their own. My entire life, I've been that—an eager little thing who only wanted to please you. Heck, that's been my goal— to make dad PROUD. Today I've realized that in making you proud, I've forgotten to ask myself who I really am. What do I stand for?'

~

Two hours later, a subdued Aria found herself being hugged tightly by Bina Mehta.

'Aria, what a surprise,' Bina smiled. 'So nice to see you, beta. This Tara na, she didn't even tell me you were coming,' she ushered her in. 'Sit, sit. Tara!' she hollered. 'See, who's come?'

Aria placed the hamper that their chef had hastily put together on the dining table and sat tentatively at the edge of the beige sofa.

'Aria, I'm making you cold coffee. You used to love it when you were little,' Bina bustled into the kitchen, as Tara appeared at the doorway. 'You never told me Aria was coming,' she admonished her daughter.

'These days, I don't know much about what Aria is doing,' Tara said tartly, leaning against the door.

'Hi . . .' Aria hesitated. 'Sorry, I would have called first, but I didn't know if you would see me.' She smiled nervously.

Tara shot her a look.

'Can you sit, please? I just want to talk.'

Arms and legs crossed, Tara sat, back upright, on the seat opposite Aria's.

'How are you?'

Tara laughed dryly. 'You know what I've realized? Those three words carry such little weight—because honestly, no one really wants to know how you are doing. They want to hear you say, fine, okay, great, not bad, at the most. Beyond that, no one fucking cares.'

'I care, T. I'm really asking.'

'A bit late in the day,' Tara muttered. 'Why are you here?' she arched an eyebrow at her.

Bina walked in, setting the cold coffee in front of Aria. 'I put extra elaichi powder, just how you like it,' she beamed.

'Thank you, Bina Aunty. I can't believe you still remember,' Aria took a long sip. 'This brings back the best memories.'

'Now, you girls talk, and if you're hungry, Tara, ask Usha *tai* to make some bhel.'

'No, no thank you,' Aria hugged Bina.

'Come again soon, Aria beta. Tara misses you.'

When Bina left the room, Tara stated flatly, 'She hasn't seen the interview. That's why you're here right?'

'I, I am . . . Gosh,' Aria stuttered. 'Gosh, Tara, I am so sorry. I am all kinds of sorry.'

'What exactly are you sorry for?'

'Where do I start?' Aria began lightly, but Tara remained expressionless. 'For everything. For what I said in London. I wasn't being fair. I wasn't looking at your point of view. And while, let's just say that we have different perspectives, you are my friend, and I shouldn't have said what I did.'

When Tara didn't react, she continued. 'And I want to apologize for the fact that I really haven't been there for you. I don't know if you know,' she took a long deep breath, 'but there's been a lot going on with me too.'

'That's not what's important now,' she added dismissively as Tara rolled her eyes. 'And it's not an excuse. I know I haven't been there for you as a friend, and I am so sorry for that.'

After a few moments, Tara spoke up.

'So, let me get this straight. What you are saying is that you are sorry, but I have to understand that you have a different perspective and that you have a lot going on in your life, but you're still sorry? Is that the gist of it?' Tara's tone was scathing. 'Way to make it about you, Aria.'

'No, Tara. It's not like that . . . when you put it like that . . .'

Tara remained unmoved.

'I *am* sorry, that's all I came here to say. And I am especially sorry for the interview, but you have to know that I didn't know my father was doing that. I would have never, never, never, let it happen. He shouldn't have said anything and I am furious with him. I was as surprised, I promise you.'

A strange smile spread across Tara's face.

'So, what you are telling me, is that you had no idea what your father was doing? And that if you'd known, you would have tried to stop him?'

'Yes, yes. Exactly. I would have tried my best to never let this happen. I really had no idea, Tara.'

'Hmm . . . Yet, I knew *eeeeverythinggg my* father was doing, right? I mean you said that yourself on numerous occasions . . . you said it to Shaan, you said it to me. "How could Tara not know? How could Tara not know what her father was really like? Did she not care where the money was coming from?" And when I told you that I had no idea, you didn't believe me. When I told you that the rumours of my father using connections at Mistry & Sons were just rumours from a disgruntled employee, you didn't believe me then either. So why should I believe you now? Why should I believe that you care more about me than about your hi-fi values of truth, and justice, and moral integrity, and fiscal responsibility, and all that shit you keep spouting? Why should I believe that you wouldn't throw me and my family under the bus, just to prove that you and your family are morally superior to everyone?'

Aria sat, dazed at the ferocity of her friend's tone.

'Why should I believe anything you say any more, Aria?'

19

'Every time someone said Rohan, I decided to take a shot. I lost count after the fifth one,' Aria massaged her temples ruefully as Leah burst out laughing.

'Ouch, volume.'

It was the morning after Isha Randhawa's Decadence and Diamonds party, and Aria couldn't remember the last time she'd ever been this hungover. Probably never.

Like with everything in her life, Aria usually had a handle on her liquor—she was a two-glasses-of-red-at-dinner-kind-of-girl—unless it was a very special vintage. Then she allowed herself another pour. But last night was absolutely unlike her. In fact, the whole month had been like she was living someone else's life.

For a while, baking sufficed to keep her busy post break-up. Between work, workouts and a dedication to achieving the perfect glaze, she'd manage to keep herself occupied enough to not respond to Rohan's numerous calls and texts. And then there'd been that awful conversation with Tara.

For the last few weeks, Aria had felt unsteady, her world spinning out of control. She would wake up in the middle of the night, feeling the walls closing in.

In a city known for its boxy apartments and sky-high real estate, it was hard to miss Windsor Villa, the imposing Mistry family home, in the heart of South Mumbai. The black iron gates with golden arrow tips gave outsiders only a glimpse of the stately columns of the impeccably maintained, neoclassical facade at the end of a perfectly manicured driveway, lined with verdant trees and marble statues.

The Mistrys were notoriously private, which only encouraged the widespread rumours about this mythical home. 'They have three swimming pools!' I hear the Louvre wanted to borrow their Monets! They have 300 staff, all trained at the Taj!' (Only two of those three were true). It was a select few who had a chance to experience the majestic beauty of the early 20th century-built Windsor Villa. Visitors would recall the tiered, beautifully manicured lawns with the Greco-Roman statues, inspired by the gardens of Hampton Court; the sparkling cerulean blue of the swimming pool with a mosaic sunburst motif, which, in a feat of architectural magic, merged into the horizon on a clear day; the expansive terraces that looked over the Queen's Necklace.

The interiors were no less awe-inducing. An imposing foyer greeted visitors with forty-foot-high frescoed ceilings and a Murano glass chandelier with more than 100 bulbs; an imperial marble staircase split off into the two separate wings of the home, its impeccably polished bannisters the perfect slide for a younger Aria, Leah and their friends, when out of Rusi's sight. On the ground floor, to the left of the staircase, were the family rooms—the sunlit glass patio where they preferred to eat breakfast; the day room, with its chintzy drapes and cozy, oversized couches dressed with throws, that

Leah and Aria could be found sprawled on when home from school; and Rusi's mahogany-panelled, two-storey study, with its double height custom-built shelves, filled with antiquarian and modern books, lining the oval-shaped room, a Regency desk, Louis XV armchairs and velvet love seats, holding court in the centre.

On the right was where the family hosted celebrations, robin-egg-blue walls held gilded frames with artworks from Indian and international masters (Raza! Husain! The legendary Monets! A Van Gogh!), stuffed sofas in rich damask and brocades, glass-fronted cabinets showcased ancient Chinese artifacts, oversize Japanese Satsuma vases and crystal and porcelain figurines from Meissen and Royal Nymphenburg, that Sotheby's would kill their hands to get on. The marble floors were covered with Persian and Kashmiri carpets. The ballroom had hosted many society balls in the days of the British, and now, Meher, opened the doors and the terrace to private recitals, by local and international musicians. The football field formal dining room was covered in a hand painted Chinoiserie wallpaper, three-foot-tall silver candelabras running down the length of its Burma teak table, providing a rather dramatic setting for formal dinners.

The overall effect of the home was almost dizzying; it was a cornucopia of treasures, history and tradition. Rohan, had teased Aria after his first visit, that he had felt like he'd walked straight into *Downton Abbey*.

The family lived on the upper floors and while as children Leah and Aria shared a room in close proximity to their parents, as they grew older, they spread into the other wings, creating mini apartments of their own, where they could have the illusion of independence while living under their father's very watchful gaze. Through the years, Rusi had preferred to maintain the classic style (though he had caved and allowed his two very insistent girls to repaint their room pink and put up a few posters of Leonardo Di Caprio and Brad Pitt, though the Liberty print furnishings and Princess beds remained).

This was one of the country's last stately homes and Rusi was adamant it not become some 'modern monochrome monstrosity'.

But his daughter, it seemed, had other plans. Post break-up and pre-baking, Aria, on the recommendation of one of her Harvard friends, paid an obscene sum of money to consult online with a renowned colour therapist. The result of the one-hour session was a recommendation to strip bare her surroundings of any clutter and adopt a soothing colour palette as a surefire way to mellow her frazzled mind and balance her aura, a suggestion that Aria, in any other scenario would have scoffed at the absurdity of.

And so, in a quest for calm, Aria commissioned interior designer Roman Shaw, whose self-described 'monastic minimalism' was in high demand and whose contrasting persona made him the preferred favourite of society girls. Getting Aria on his roster was only going to propel him to greater heights and Roman, armed with plans for what he promised would be a masterpiece, began work breaking down the chintz and mouldings that dated back decades.

Naturally, Rusi nearly burst a blood vessel when he'd flown home and discovered that the second floor had become a construction site. Not wanting to inconvenience herself, Aria had checked into the Four Seasons Hotel, deciding to skip the step of informing her parents of her new plans.

'What is this hogwash?' Rusi bellowed at his wife. 'A colour therapist! Who the hell is this quack?'

'She feels suffocated, she says,' he continued, fuming. 'Look at the size of this house.'

'Get these workers out of here,' he screamed at Roman, who, though used to the whims and moods of his wealthy, powerful clients, was thoroughly intimidated by Rusi's towering presence.

But Aria refused to back down and the next day the workers and Roman were back. Once her mind was fixated, there was no turning back.

'Let this one go, Rusi,' Meher said, exhausted by the idea of another clash between father and daughter.

And just like that, in a matter of a few weeks, Aria Mistry painted over the history of a corner of Windsor Villa.

But even that didn't seem to make things better. Aria's obsession with cleanliness was in overdrive and the shaggy furnishings along with the stark white palette of the room were throwing up more issues for the germaphobe, highlighting every speck of dust that the damp city air brought. No matter how hard the housekeeping staff tried, they couldn't keep it as clean as Aria wanted. And so, many nights, unable to sleep, Aria could be found mop and gloves in hand, scrubbing floors or walls while contemplating whether a colour change may be in order already.

And that's exactly where Leah found her, late one Thursday, crouching on the floor, Dyson vacuum in hand.

'You know what you need?' Leah asked, red-faced from a workout, chomping on a chocolate chip cookie and scattering crumbs all over the place.

'Leah!' Aria yelled. 'No food in my room!'

Leah inhaled another chunk and laughed. 'So I was saying, you know what you need? And besides an intervention? You need a good, old-fashioned one-night stand.'

'What??' Aria yelled over the sound of the vacuum.

'Turn that thing off. I said, you need a good lay.'

'Can you not be so crude?'

'I'm serious. Isha Randhawa is having a party this weekend. It's going to be pretty EPIC! She said she texted you too, and you never replied, which is SO rude. Anyway, I think we should go. Plus, Freya has this super cute cousin, Mikhail, and he's in town from New York, and she's bringing him. So maybe . . .?'

'If he's so cute, why don't you hook up with him?'

'Ugh, because you know I've sworn off boys for a while. I'm ready to become a hermit,' Leah, in sweaty workout wear, flopped over dramatically on Aria's duvet, further irritating her sister, who she knew was already itching to change the sheets.

Ever since Leah had broken up with Jeh, her boyfriend of many years, she'd had several flings (her latest, Marcus, who she had brought to Tuscany and promptly lost interest in while there) but nothing had lasted longer than a quick weekend sojourn.

She'd met Jeh, now a successful tech entrepreneur, while at university and he'd been devoted to Leah. He even had Rusi's tacit approval. But Jeh's biggest failing—he kept asking Leah to marry him. The final nail in the relationship's coffin was when he'd flown her to Paris, to propose at the Eiffel Tower. Leah had booked her return flight an hour later. Solo.

'Ugh, so cheesy. There were roses and an orchestra. Does he NOT know me? And who wants to get married, anyway? Ruined a good thing,' she told Aria, on her return. And in typical Leah style, there had been no moping around. Within a few days, it was as if nothing had ever happened, and she'd happily adopted the life of the young and single . . .

'I'm not going to Isha's. Rohan will definitely be there and so will Malika. I'm not a masochist.'

'I knew you would say that.' Leah jumped off the bed. 'I've done some sleuthing and Rohan is out of town on an ad shoot. So there, that's settled. We're going.'

'And wear something hot.'

And that's how Aria found herself at Isha's 'Decadence and Diamonds' party. When Aria and Leah got there shortly before midnight ('Seriously, Leah, how can we walk in so late?' Aria complained), the party was just about getting started. Isha's new ten-storey building was covered in a million sparkles in some kind of computer-generated lighting effect, and the road outside was jammed with cars trying to gain entry and photographers trying to get their party shots.

The sisters made their way up to the ninth floor, to the party boudoir that Isha had designed. They walked past the pool skirting the room ('No night of debauchery is complete without a skinny dip,' Isha was known to say). The red velvet walls of the room, thumping courtesy Mia and Tia, the twin DJ duo Isha had flown in from London.

As the girls greeted friends on their way to the bar, their hostess appeared, almost blinding them. Not one for subtlety, Isha's shimmering mini dress showed off her Pilates worked posterior to perfection, while the gumball-size stacks around her wrists and neck, showed off her husband's devotion.

'Girlsssss,' she shrieked. 'I'm sooooo happy you made it . . .' she air-kissed, adjusting the diamanté-dusted veil that framed half her face. 'But where are your looks?' She looked askance at Aria's off-shoulder black dress, that may have been Celine but to Isha's eye was as decadent as a nun's habit. She was soon distracted by more guests, and another round of air-kissing.

'Drinks, drinks! Everyone needs drinks,' she waved the waiter over and poured shots down the throats of anyone in her vicinity. And then the night had begun. Roman was there and he'd hung on to Aria's arm, whispering juicy tidbits, that Aria, despite herself, was thoroughly entertained by.

'And that one, in the chiffon and pearls. That's Princess Priyashri. She may dress like Gayatri Devi, but when it comes to the bedroom, she's all Mata Hari.'

'Don't even get me started on that one,' he said, pointing to Sonam Chabra, the reed-thin art gallerist from Delhi. 'She'll have tried to sell you works by a master by the time you've left this party, and if even one is an original, well . . .'

For the few eligible men in the room, he'd remarked. 'You know it's a graph, hotness versus richness. Take Rajveer over there, he's on every bachelor list, but governments have come and gone, and he's still not married!'

'Do you even know how graphs work?' she asked him, laughing, feeling lighter than she had in days, happy with this inane conversation as distraction.

'Who are they?' she pointed to a couple who were indulging in some major PDA on the dance floor.

'Oh them, their whole life is lived in hashtags. You know #soulmate #blessed #loveofmylife #blahblahblah. When it actually should be #battingonthewrongteam. By the end of the evening, he'll have pinched every guy's ass in this room!'

'I definitely need to get out more,' she thought to herself as her old school friend Shaina dragged her away from Roman's one-man show and on to the dance floor.

At some point, Aria found herself hanging out with Mikhail, who was, in all actuality, quite cute. Loosened up by the tequila she'd downed, Aria found herself flirting. He was easy to talk to and they had quite a lot in common.

'Let's find a quiet corner where we can actually chat,' he said into her ear. 'I can't hear myself think.'

He took Aria's hand, guiding her towards the elevator that would take them to the terrace.

As the doors opened, she found herself face to face with Rohan.

He'd taken one look at Mikhail's hand in Aria's and his face had hardened.

'Wh-what are you doing here?' she stammered.

It had been two months to the day that she'd last kissed him in Florence, before he'd flown to New York, and forty-eight days since that photo had appeared.

Before he could answer, their hostess, now high as a kite from all her trips to the powder room, barrelled her way into their conversation.

'Ro . . . you made it darling. I thought you were shooting.'

Aria heard Rohan mumble something about an early pack-up and late flight, as he continued to stare at her. After a few minutes of them standing around awkwardly, Rohan's gaze firmly on Aria, the dynamics finally dawned on Isha.

'Ooh, lovers now fighters . . . why can't you two lovebirds just kiss and make-up?' she cooed, as Mikhail stared on, confused. 'Now come, on, let's drink to the two of you,' she dragged Rohan and Aria to the bar.

For the rest of the evening, she'd felt him looking at her. Every time she caught his gaze, she overdid it with Mikhail, sidling closer, whispering in his ear, touching his arm, laughing loudly, doing another shot. She wanted to show him that she was fine, that she had moved on, that she was capable of having a good time without him, that she was not as puritanical as he'd accused her of being. She'd gotten progressively more drunk and proceeded to lose interest in Mikhail, who seemed perplexed by her mixed signals.

By 4 a.m., Leah, seeing the state her sister had worked herself up to, decided that it was time to head home, despite Aria's protestations. They'd been waylaid by Rohan on the way out.

'Ari,' he came up behind her. She breathed in his familiar scent as he reached for her.

She'd turned towards him, his hand reaching for her hair.

And at just that moment, she'd pulled her head back, her eyes widening, and her hand reaching out to cover her mouth.

She was going to be sick.

~

MOHAN MEHTA RELEASED ON BAIL, SURRENDERS PASSPORT

Jaideep Arora, Mumbai The Mumbai High Court granted bail to Mohan Mehta, on grounds of ill health. The sixty-three-year-old Mehta is suffering from diabetes and a serious heart condition, and has been released, while investigations into allegations of financial fraud continue.

Mehta has been asked to surrender his passport and check in weekly with the EOW office every Monday to cooperate with the investigation, until further orders of the Hon'ble Court. Mehta, who has been booked under various charges which also include charges of Cheating (Section 415 read with Sections 417 and 420 of the IPC), Criminal Breach of Trust (Section 405 read with Section 406 of the IPC) and Criminal Conspiracy (Section 120A read with Section 120B of the IPC and the offences under the Prevention of Money Laundering Act, 2002 ('PMLA') is also being investigated by the Income Tax Department, under the Black Money (Undisclosed Foreign Income and Assets) and Imposition of Tax Act, 2015 ('BMA').

Mehta is under investigation for the Rs 5000-crore MohanCity scam.

~

Any child psychologist would extrapolate that Tara's obsession with fitting a physical ideal started early on. 'People would stop me on the road,' Bina loved to tell everyone. 'And they'd say, wow, she looks like *ekdum* "American baby".' It was that very cherubic appeal that led Tara to be chosen from thousands as the face of Johnson & Johnson's babycare range, her cute little mug streaming on televisions and billboards across the country.

As she grew older, both the senior Mehtas, dedicated in a quest for the world to experience their daughter's beauty, sent her to intensive courses on dance and diction and signed her up for the Miss India pageant. When Tara placed out of the contest in the last round and Bollywood casting agents failed to call, they channelled their energy to another glamorous field for their princess—fashion.

Through all this, Tara, with her easy demeanour, meandered, happy to let her parents define a path and never too bereft when one door closed. If she expressed any remorse, it was more from the disappointment her parents faced rather than from any personal ambition. But what did have a lasting impact was a continued focus on her physicality. As a young girl, she'd been athletic, making it to the cross country and throwball teams at school. Any awkwardness of her teenage years was minimized by visits to the city's leading experts, who cleansed and hydrated, waxed and tweezed, toned and moisturized every inch of her.

But in college, Tara went through some fluctuations in body weight, par for the course for an average college student whose daily lifestyle consists of junk food and alcohol. All it took was an offhand, negative comment from an acquaintance back in Mumbai on the 'freshman fifteen' she had gained, to spiral into an obsession with weight and food. Her parents, alarmed by their daughter's shrinking frame, scheduled her an appointment with a London-based holistic practitioner, who had helped Tara adapt her approach.

Over the years, she had relaxed the restrictive eating and punishing workout regime, though she still continued to experiment with all the latest food fads (Vegan! Dairy-free! Sugar-free! The Zone! Keto! Paleo!) that she came across in magazines and found an outlet in high-energy spinning classes. But in the last few weeks, the stress of her father's case and her marriage imploding had led Tara back to earlier habits and she was now back to being the thinnest she'd been in years.

Which made the slight curve of her belly even more noticeable. Tara sighed as she took in her naked frame, rubbing the little bump that was beginning to harden.

Tara was pregnant.

She hadn't told her husband yet. For that matter, she hadn't told *anyone* yet.

In all the stress that the last few weeks brought, Tara hadn't even realized when she had missed her period. But when she'd started experiencing extreme tiredness and nausea, instinct made her take a test. She and Nakul had been trying for months, making sure all factors were conducive, and then one night, after her father's arrest, when Tara had in vulnerability turned to her husband, it had just happened.

She wasn't sure how she was meant to feel. This baby, their baby, that she had been wanting for so long . . . months of monitoring ovulation cycles, months of failed attempts, months of stress between her and Nakul . . . had come at a time when husband and wife were barely speaking to each other.

After his bail had been approved, Mohan, Bina and Tara had spent an emotional few days at home, their relief compounded by the anxiety that at any moment, another governmental agency could barge through their front doors, issuing a fresh arrest warrant for Mohan. They waited on tenterhooks, each doorbell and each ring of the telephone, sending a current of fear through them. There was so much she wanted to ask her father, but seeing him so anxious and fearful gave her pause.

He called Tara to him one morning, as he was having his morning chai in bed. He was still a ghost of the man he once was, his white kurta pyjama and unshaven face adding to his pallor, but Tara was heartened to see that he'd put on a little weight since his return. Whether it was the lack of Nakul's presence in Mumbai or Tara's demeanour, Mohan had surmised that all was not well in his daughter's marriage.

'I spoke to Nakul last night, bitiya.'

'He called you?'

Mohan nodded. 'It's time now bitiya, you go home. Go back to your husband.' Tara opened her mouth to argue, but he hushed her.

'What is the point of you staying here? You know Indian courts, this matter will go on for years. How long can you stay? Be practical.'

'In a few days, I will, Papa,' Tara took his hand in hers. 'I'm just enjoying our family time,' she said, her eyes moist.

'Bitiya, whatever happens to me, remember I'm an old man. I've led a good life. But you, yours is just starting.'

'Right now, I cannot give you anything but I ask you one promise. Promise me you'll be a good wife. You have a good husband, a good home. Make a family. Forget about me, my problems. I will be okay if you, my Tara, are happy.'

So Tara flew back to London. She knew that it would devastate her father if things didn't work out between her and Nakul, and as she walked towards the baggage carousel, she wondered if she had the strength to make this marriage work. Did she really even want to any more? At the airport, she half hoped, despite all her misgivings, that Nakul would come to receive her. She was disappointed and, admittedly, a little relieved to find their chauffeur James waiting to drive her home. She thought grimly that she should probably be grateful that the Puris hadn't relegated her to taking the tube.

On the ride home, she braced herself for a frosty welcome, and the Puris didn't disappoint. But this time around, Tara was too weary to fight them or Nakul, and she chose to keep to herself. A part of her had not wanted to return to London; in her heart, she knew that her marriage to Nakul would never be the same again. When she'd walked through the front door, he'd been waiting, but the reunion had been awkward, the chasm between them seeming even wider.

Her days felt unending. She walked around the city for hours, listening to music; she'd cook for Nakul, though she barely ate herself, she found herself taking art classes again, finding the painting and sketching somewhat restorative. The rest of the time she hung around the house, flipping channels and magazines, nothing holding her attention for very long. She woke up in the mornings looking at his back turned away from her, feeling like she was living with a stranger. Despite so many years together, she no longer knew how he would react to anything.

A week or so post her return, Nakul surprised Tara by suggesting a post-dinner walk to get some ice cream. It was something they used to do, early on in their relationship, strolling through the city, hand in hand, stealing kisses on the corners.

'Tara, what happened before . . . before you left, with us, I mean,' he added hastily. 'It just came as such a shock and I just . . .' he said, as they'd walked back home. They'd eaten their ice cream in relative silence; Tara nibbling on her now dripping cone. 'You have to understand, it's taken our family donkeys' years to get here, to gain this respect, and I was worried for my parents. You know how sensitive Mum is.'

'I'm sorry, Tara,' he continued. 'I should have been there for you. I should have been more supportive. I should have come to India with you, but to be honest, the lawyers felt it was better . . .' He stopped and held her by the shoulders,

'Look at what you've been through, darling, and you're still here. YOU are made of steel,' his said, his tone patronizing.

'And now, hopefully the worst is behind you, and us. And we can move on with our lives as we should.'

'It's that easy? You expect me to just forgive and move on?'

'Come on, darling,' he attempted to hug her. 'Why rehash everything? We'll just go around in circles. I said I was sorry. And I am. You can't really blame me. This was such a jolt from the blue.'

'I don't know whether to laugh or cry any more, Nakul. I am so fed up with everyone telling me how difficult this situation has been on them. "You have to understand, Tara" is how each one of you starts a sentence. Why should I care? Not one of you has thought of me, what it's like to be in my shoes, or my mother's shoes, these past few weeks. The hell we've gone through. And you know what this entire experience has taught me? It's that I don't need anyone to prop me up any more. Not my friends. Not your family.'

Her voice dropped to a whisper. 'And not you.' His face crumpled.

She walked five steps ahead of him the rest of the walk home.

He'd been on eggshells since then, at his solicitous best. Life was on autopilot, falling back into old routines. The house ran like clockwork. Nakul, kept fed and taken care of, her in-laws checked in on. And though she was back to looking the same, not a hair out of place and always beautifully turned out, it all felt so forced. She preferred to spend their evenings at home, while Nakul continued as if nothing had changed. A part of her wondered if he had been faithful while she was away or if he'd resorted to his old ways. The strange part was, she wasn't sure if that knowledge would even hurt her in the same way any more.

Her blogging career had come to a grinding halt, the last thing she wanted was to be trolled online any further, and Farah had tactfully suggested that maybe she sit out the next few exhibitions on their calendar to ensure that no one felt 'uncomfortable'. 'Including you,' she added.

And then she found out she was pregnant.

She didn't know what was keeping her from telling Nakul. Was she hoping he'd mess up beforehand and want out? Was she ready to be a single mum? How would his parents react? Would they treat their grandchild with love or cast him or her off, as they pretty much had done Tara? The last thing she wanted was any kind of dispute over this child. *Her* child.

So many questions and such few answers.

And then one night, after a surprisingly nice dinner, where things had almost seemed normal, she'd almost told him.

Almost.

They'd gotten home at the same time as the senior Puris. And right off the bat, Anjali Puri had been in a foul mood. Apparently, at their dinner, the conversation had focused on Mohan Mehta's release and the murkiness of the situation.

'And then Bonnie Melwani said, "So tell us Anjali, is it true that it is only because Arjun Singh's money is involved that your samdhan got bail? Because, my lawyer friends tell me, it rarely happens, and even Tara being allowed back into the country. Shaan must have helped, na?"'

'And then, that cow, Ritu Shrivastava, asked, "I heard that he's got some major leverage on all the big guys. How else would he get out? And even Tara, going back to Bombay and facing no issues. This is the problem with India, anyone gets away with anything."'

'And Meeta Kapoor, who is your father's oldest friend, turns around and asks, "I hear that part of the MohanCity township was actually built on land meant for an orphanage and it was usurped. Is that true, Anjali? How ghastly."'

'The whole time, Bonnie kept adding, you know, Anjali's in-laws, this and Anjali's in-laws, that. It's just so difficult to keep our head high in society any more . . .'

'Bonnie's been eyeing my position at the British Indian Society for eons, and who knows whether they will elect me again next year, with all this hanging over us?'

She shook her head, a lone tear rolling down her cheek. Nakul, on seeing his mother's distress, immediately took her hand.

'How do I tell them that we don't know anything? If we had known, do they think we would have let this marriage happen? We have no choice now but to keep silent,' she wailed, squeezing her son's fingers, oblivious or unconcerned by Tara's presence.

Tara rolled her eyes as her husband continued to console his desolate mother. And just like that, *her* Nakul was gone in an instant.

Over the next few weeks, her husband's hot and cold behaviour continued. When his parents were not around, he acted normally, affectionately, but the minute his mother appeared, always despairing about her fall from social graces, he turned cold.

It was exhausting. Coupled with the nausea and hormonal changes, Tara felt drained, wondering which side of her husband would come home every evening.

And then she snapped.

It was Nakul's cousin's engagement. Anjali's niece Saloni had bagged a Tandon boy, from the knighted family that routinely topped Britain's Rich lists. The entire clan had flown in from Lagos to celebrate.

The engagement ceremony was to be held at the Tandons' Belgravia mansion and it was to be one of Tara's first major social outings post her father's arrest. She was a little nervous, but excited for Saloni, with whom she shared a good relationship.

Surprisingly, her mother-in-law, usually so interfering about her clothing choices, had been hands off for this event, too busy with her sister and ingratiating herself with the Tandon family to be concerned about her daughter-in-law. Not that Tara minded; these days, she went out of her way to avoid her toxicity.

Left to her own devices, Tara chose a mint Benarasi lehenga that she paired with a belted, slip tunic from Anushka Khanna, making sure her slight bump was well covered. She accessorized with emerald strings that had been a gift from Nakul's grandmother. After months, it felt good to dress up. She'd called in her favourite hair and make-up artist, and thanks to the hormones at play, she looked radiant.

She was just putting on a pair of heels when Anjali Puri walked downstairs, took one look at her and remarked with a raised eyebrow, 'You're ready so early?'

'The card said the roka was at 5 p.m.?'

'Nakul,' his mother admonished. 'You didn't tell her?'

'Uh,' he said, not meeting Tara's eye.

What Nakul had failed or rather was too chicken to mention was that the family thought it better that Tara skip the intimate engagement ceremony and instead come for the cocktails and dinner, where there would be more of a crowd and it would be easier for her to blend in.

'It's Saloni's day and we don't want the focus to go from the bride and especially not on such negative things,' Anjali told her, somewhat condescendingly. 'The Tandons are sticklers for propriety, and Maasi doesn't want to do anything to upset them.'

'If anyone asks, we'll just say you had a migraine, and then James will come back and pick you up by 8 p.m.,' she said smoothly. 'Also, avoid wearing the ring,' she said, alluding to the ten-carat pear shaped diamond ring Nakul had given her for their anniversary. 'We don't want you to be showing off, given the circumstances.'

Tara's cheeks burned. She looked to Nakul for support, but her husband seemed transfixed by his cuff.

As gracefully as she could and before the tears threatened to spill over, she turned on her heel, to her bedroom and shut the door quietly. She waited for Nakul to come, hoping that the man she had fallen in love with was still somewhat present in this robot, who gave into his mother's every whim. But the footsteps receded from the door.

She waited until they'd left to collapse on the floor, her shoulders heaving with sobs, her body curled up, unconsciously mimicking the baby's position inside her. Tara cried till there was nothing left, lying on the cold marble bathroom floor.

It was the early hours of the morning when Nakul returned and Tara, who had been lying in bed awake, pretended to be asleep.

When he'd finally surfaced the next morning and made his way to the living room, Tara was sitting by the window, nursing a cup of tea.

'Where were you last night?' He started aggressively. 'James called so many times and so did I. Everyone was expecting you. Mum is *really* upset.'

She stared at her husband's impudence, choosing not to react and instead turned back to looking out of the window silently, aware that Nakul was waiting for her to get up and fix him breakfast. When he realized no help was forthcoming, he started banging his way around the kitchen.

When he finally returned, a smoothie bottle in his hand, she turned towards him, then turned back to the window.

'I'm pregnant.' She paused.

'And I want a divorce.'

20

'Ma'am, can you just turn towards Sir a little more? Yes, yes, just like that. Now put your hand on his shoulder. Yes, beautiful, beautiful. What a shot,' the bald, burly photographer yelled out in encouragement.

'I think we got it,' a young bespectacled woman with close cropped hair and an arm filled with bracelets that clinked every time she moved, stated as Shaan looked over the images on the monitor. 'Shall we start the interview?'

Shaan and Pratap were being featured on *Life & Style* Magazine's Power List, as the Political Change-Makers of the Year. In the course of the next half hour, over tea and sandwiches, they chatted with the writer on their personal dynamics, the call of public service, their hobbies and interests.

'So, Shaan, before we wrap up, I have to ask you,' the writer said. 'When do we hear you announcing your candidacy?'

Before Shaan could answer, Pratap chuckled. 'I think one politician in the family is enough, don't you? Shaan is doing such good work on the ground, I don't think she needs to run for office. And besides, she's such a support on the election trail to me, *aur phir* family *bhi, kahaan* time *nikaalegi.*'

'My husband is right on one front, I don't *need to* do anything,' Shaan replied, smiling, through gritted teeth. 'But, to answer the question you asked ME,' she looked at her husband pointedly. 'I have always had a policy—never say never. And I'm not one to plan ahead. I am known to be impulsive. So, this election is not on the cards, but for the next,' she winked. 'You will just have to wait and see.'

'And what my sweet husband needs to understand is this, that once a woman makes up her mind, no one can stop her.'

Shaan was seething after the writer and her team packed up and left.

'How dare you answer for me? Is that the kind of marriage you think this is? As if you can be the only one to make the decisions?' she said, following Pratap into their bedroom. 'Do not EVER do that again.'

'One second, haan. Since we met, you've never discussed wanting to contest. Now what happened? Suddenly, you've gotten a *chaska*?' Pratap challenged. 'In our family, the women are not politicians.'

'And in my family, I was groomed to be one. How did you think you were going to marry Arjun Singh's daughter and not have her involved? Have you ever even come out and asked me what I thought would be my political future? You just presumed, that in my excitement to marry you, I forgot all about my life's plans?'

She stared him down.

'You know, I'm beginning to realize that you think I should be your plus one—*neta ki biwi,* who dabbles in women's issues, stands next to you while you are cheered on at the podium, and makes sure your home and life run smoothly . . . let me tell you, buddy, YOU have another thing coming if you think I'm going to bow down . . .'

'Arré, now the Shaan Singh I used to hear about is showing her fight,' he said condescendingly.

She shot him a warning look.

'You know, what . . . YOU'VE just made the decision for me. Next cycle, you're going to be standing next to me. That is, if I CHOOSE to keep you around, and I WILL be contesting.'

~

Pratap's refusal to take Shaan's ambitions (vacillating as they may be) seriously was beginning to rankle her. The common ground that they had found was slowly crumbling. Lately, it seemed like they were on their way to becoming one of those married couples who only argued when together, preferring to lead completely different lives.

Pratap was spending more and more time in his constituency, which meant that Shaan was on her own for the majority of the week. When he was home, he was distant and preoccupied, and Shaan, still smarting from the interview, felt that he was keeping her at arm's length deliberately. The monotony of marriage was stifling.

'Fine, fine *bol ke*, I'm going crazy,' she complained to Shiv. 'All the aunties say, how are you beta? Fine. How is married life? Fine. How is Pratap. Fine. How is sex life? Fine. How has my life come to the point where the only way I can describe it is by saying fine?'

In her single days, this would have been the time when she'd send a flirty text to Matt or gotten on a flight to see him. She toyed with the idea of rekindling something, just to get the blood in her veins moving, but whether it was the oppressive Delhi heat or the overbearing lifestyle of a politician's wife, even that took too much enthusiasm.

'When were you in Bombay?' she questioned Pratap at breakfast one morning. 'You had a meeting with Abhimanyu Joshi? What's that all about?' she referred to the young Mumbai MP who was in the running to become the next chief minister.

He'd dismissed it. 'Flew in for a few hours,' he said, not looking up from the paper. 'We had some work to discuss.'

A few days later, she'd asked her secretary to coordinate the dates for the campaign appearances he had previously requested she join. She came back puzzled. 'Sir's team says that there is no need for you to come now.'

When he'd come home, she'd questioned him again, his non-committal responses further irritating her. She was getting ready for dinner at the Khannas, absentmindedly shuffling through a rack of dresses, when she heard a series of muffled pings coming from his navy-blue Nehru jacket hanging on the closet door. Pratap was still in the shower, so she quietly removed the phone, to check who was messaging so frantically.

Pratap always had on hand a couple of devices. The one in his jacket pocket was predominantly used for work in his constituency, where network could often be an issue, or so he claimed. In her occasional sweeps, this was one she didn't check that often, and she was startled to find a series of messages from Serena appearing on the screen.

When do I c u again.

I miss u. xo

Can you call me tonight, please? I'll be waiting.

Can you come back to Bombay, baby?

Shaan felt a wave of anger rush through her. While she was doing her best to make this damn marriage worked, he was doing just as he pleased. Typical. Her eyes smarted—her marriage had become that stereotype, the one she'd mocked plenty of times before. '*Dilli mein aadhein shaadi pocket ki poori barbadi,*' she would cackle about the state of marriages around her. While the husbands were doing everybody and anybody, the wives were trying to fill the voids in their lives with ladies' lunches and shopping sprees at the mall.

'Still deciding what to wear? Come on, Shaan,' Pratap snapped, walking into the closet, a towel wrapped around his waist.

Shaan turned away from him, so he wouldn't see the tears in her eyes. She straightened her shoulders and went back to rummaging through her closet, her mind whirling.

She refused to be reduced to a cliché. Screw him. And screw her father and their bullshit rules.

And so, starting that night at the Khannas, the old Shaan returned. Or rather, the Shaan she had buried in a pledge to make her marriage work. A shot of tequila, a line, dancing on the bar, copious flirting—the sense of freedom was exhilarating and when Pratap left the party early, she knew she had made her point.

When she'd finally surfaced the next morning, he'd warned, 'Watch yourself Shaan, you're going too far.'

But rather than being deterred, Shaan, like a wilful child, acted up even further. For the next few weeks, the partying continued, she would stumble home when the sun was just rising and some nights not come home at all, having found some guy to randomly hook up with.

She was slowly unravelling. She'd shown up drunk to Pratap's school friend Karan's birthday party, getting into a screaming match with Pratap when he'd tried to take her home; she'd taken a bad tumble off the bar while dancing at the Chadhas' anniversary dinner, and had gotten into a loud argument with the hostess's visiting sister at another sundowner. On the occasions that she came home early, she brought the party with her. The morning after found the house littered with cigarette butts, empty bottles and glasses, not to mention dustings of powder on the glass coffee tables; Shaan passed out on the living room couch in her party clothes.

When Pratap came home one weekend, the house was thumping with music, and Shaan was shooting lines in the living room with a group of people he'd never met. He asked them very calmly to leave. Shaan and he had gotten into a heated argument. It was the most they'd said to each other in weeks.

'*Kya soch rahi ho*? It's 9 p.m. The staff is outside, they can see everything that's going on. What the hell, Shaan?'

'As if you've not done it before,' Shaan sneered. 'Let's not pretend you are some good little boy. We all know the shit you get up to.'

'What are you even talking about? Do you hear yourself?' He held her firmly by the shoulders.

'Get your hands off me,' she was now belligerent, shrugging him off. He'd stormed out of the house and she didn't hear from him after.

And then, a few days later, after a particularly wild night, Shaan passed out cold at the Mehras' farmhouse. The couple called Pratap in a panic and he'd driven in the middle of the night to Chhatarpur, with their family doctor in tow. Thankfully, they'd managed to revive her and avoid hospitalization but the next morning Pratap finally broke his silence when a somewhat chagrined Shaan appeared, looking like a truck had run over her.

'How long are you going to keep this up?'

Shaan didn't answer, sitting down shakily on the armchair, focusing intently on the wave of nausea that was passing through her.

He let a few minutes pass before saying, 'I'm done, Shaan. I'm really fucking done. You want to behave like this, you go fucking do it somewhere else, but if you are in this marriage, I will not be disrespected. Bas. It's a joke, YOU are becoming a joke.'

'Listen, you are an adult. And I didn't get married to become a babysitter. But this has got to end, you could have gotten badly hurt last night, and people are already starting to talk. The booze, the coke, the partying, the flirting, it has to stop or else . . .'

Despite herself, Shaan burst out laughing.

'Or else, what? *Bade aaye lecture dene.*'

'What's that supposed to mean?'

When Shaan didn't answer, he continued. 'It's your life, babe. But you're jeopardizing everything with this childish behaviour and I don't want to deal with this shit any more—'

'I'm jeopardizing . . . I'm . . .' she scoffed. 'YOU are the one still doing Serena. You *promised* me it was done. You *promised* me you would give this marriage a chance, but yay for me, you're just another lying fucking . . .,' she shot back angrily, her voice hoarse from the cigarettes and tears.

'Don't look at me like that. I found all those messages. How long has it been going on for? From the beginning? Were you sexting her from the mandap? Our honeymoon? Were you both sitting and laughing at how gullible I was to believe you? To believe that you actually wanted to give this marriage a chance and not just use me for a political alliance?'

'That's why you went to Bombay, haan? "I had some work to discuss,"' she mocked him. 'What work did you have with that . . .?'

'Shaan, I want to talk about this and explain, but I need to tell you this—your parents are on the way,' Pratap said hurriedly.

'You called my father? Are you kidding me?'

'No, I didn't. Calm down. Your drama last night reached him, and he called me at 8 a.m. this morning, furious. I managed to talk him down, but your mother and he insisted on coming to lunch.'

'That's all I fucking need,' Shaan muttered, stomping out of the door.

~

'It's just one small drink,' Shaan said to herself. Hair of the dog.

The clink of the ice cube, a tiny pour of vodka, the fizzle of soda, a splash of lime. Making a drink was a ritual she'd always enjoyed. She took a sip.

She poured a little more. And took another sip.

And now her family were making what was just a de-stresser into something else. Her father had even gone as far to suggest that she needed an intervention. It was like in that Sandra Bullock movie, that she couldn't remember the name of. The entire day had been ridiculous. She took another sip.

By the time her parents had arrived, Shaan's mood was even darker, thanks to the dual effects of tequila and her cheating husband and she was ready to take down even her father if she had to. But Arjun Singh, being Arjun Singh, had gauged his daughter's state and instead of going on the offensive, had lingered over lunch, gossiping, chatting, laughing and behaving like nothing had happened.

Shaan, on tenterhooks throughout, waiting to pounce on the first negative word out of her father's mouth, was exhausted by the time he actually got around to the elephant in the room.

'So, Shaan,' he sipped his tea. 'I hear you've been getting carried away with the partying again.'

Shaan opened her mouth to say something but he put up his hand to silence her.

'I'll say this once and I won't say it again. What you did last night was stupid and irresponsible. You don't care about your reputation or ours, then care about this, you could have been seriously hurt. You got lucky. Next time, you possibly won't be.'

He'd gone on about how her drinking was out of control and he and Pratap had decided that any more such behaviour and she would be sent to a rehabilitation facility to get in order. Shaan had sat stone faced throughout.

'Are you done?' she'd finally asked her father, her voice steady. 'There's no point in me saying anything, because you are not going to let me defend myself. But maybe you and Pratap should ask yourself why I act out this way? Maybe at some point, you both should take responsibility for your behaviour instead of always putting it on me.'

'Shaan, you are not a child any more. You cannot blame everyone else for your tantrums. Handle your problems like an adult. Both of you,' he added, shooting Pratap a look as well.

'It was a stupid night, Papa, and fine, maybe it got out of control. But I don't need an intervention, don't be ridiculous. And Pratap can think whatever he likes, I will do what I want.' Her mouth was set in a firm line.

'Shaan,' her mother spoke up. 'We don't want to get between you and your husband. Every couple has fights here and there, but that doesn't mean you take it to such an extreme.'

Shaan laughed, sarcastically, 'For parents who don't want to get involved now, you all were quite involved in making this marriage happen, hain na?

~

'Drinking again?' Pratap asked with a raised eyebrow, walking in on Shaan standing at the bar.

'Oh, fuck off.'

'Listen Shaan, I need to talk to you about what happened,' he stepped towards her.

'I know I'm at fault. It just happened with Serena. It was one time. I promise you, it's over. It was a stupid mistake and I'm really, really sorry.' The words tumbled out.

Shaan stared at him and took another sip, the vodka burning the back of her throat.

'The thing is, and I know you are not going to believe this, but I really am committed to this marriage. I, I thought, *ki sab theek chal raha hai.*' He raised his palms to the sky.

'I want to make this marriage work. *Bas galti ho gayi.* Come on, let's figure this out.'

Shaan just shook her head, trying to clear the fog. They sat silent for a while.

'Tell me the truth. Were you in Bombay to see her?'

He closed his eyes. 'I didn't lie to you. I was in Bombay on work, but yes, I did see her. Nothing happened, we just met for a coffee and I was trying to tell her it was over. I swear to you, it was only the one time.'

'You're unbelievable. How do I know anything you are saying is true?'

'*Theek hai.* You're right. You don't. Just like *mujhe nahi pata* if you are out hooking up with some guy. But what choice do we have?' he cocked his head. 'So,' he looked away from her, out of the window. 'How many guys were there?' Pratap's jaw clenched visibly.

Shaan narrowed her eyes. 'Jealous?'

'*Sach bolo toh*, I never thought I would be having a conversation with my wife about her affairs. I'm old-fashioned, Shaan. You may not think it, but I don't like all this. Marriage should be about trust and I know I was the one who made the mistake, but I promise you, it won't happen again.'

'Can I ask you something? When we were getting to know each other, you never wanted to get physical. Even now, our sex life is not . . .' she looked at him squarely. 'I always wondered, I tried with you and, I don't know . . . are you even attracted to me?'

Shaan cringed at the vulnerability in her own voice.

'Did you really doubt that?' Pratap came over to the couch and took her hand. 'I was still so confused. I was with Serena, but I also wanted you, but I was confused. And you know, look who you are.' He laughed nervously. 'Have you seen whose daughter you are? I couldn't just hook up. But, no, it wasn't a question of not wanting. Promise.'

'That's honestly the lamest excuse,' Shaan rolled her eyes.

They sat together, side by side, for a little while.

'You're not going to get off the hook that easily. I'm not okay with women on the side. Not Serena, not anyone else. So, let's get that shit clear.'

He nodded and raised his eyebrow at her. 'Fine. But that goes for me too, men . . . and women both.'

'Just covering my bases,' he added, when she shot him a look.

'Also, stop treating me like I'm going to turn into some stupid desperate housewife. I'm Arjun Singh's daughter. My instincts have been honed by him. Use my ideas, use my knowledge, and trust me, you won't regret it.'

'Thirdly, I will do what I want to do with my life and my career. I am ambitious, what I want may change all the time, but I want a husband that supports me.'

'Is this about your seat? *Char saal mein bahut kuch ho sakta hai*, Shaan. First, let me win this election.'

'You want to win this election? I'll tell you how.'

He snorted with laughter. 'Fine, toh step up then. Tell me what I should change. You have to prove yourself, you know. But Shaan, bas. No drinking every day. *And baaki ka toh bhool ja*. If you want to stand for elections, these stories will come back and haunt you. So, let's get serious.'

'Then don't piss me off to the extent that the only thing I can do is get pissed,' she said with a half grin. 'I'll tell you what. Since we never did the whole dating thing properly, let's list our deal-breakers,' Shaan said, getting up and rummaging through the desk drawer for a paper and pen.

'Aria would be so proud of me if she saw me now.'

Pratap looked at her quizzically.

'Never mind. Let's make a contract here and now, deal? I'll give my word, will you?'

21

October 2018, Mumbai

They showed up, dressed in the uniform reserved for such solemn occasions. Starched, designer white chikan and diamonds, gleaming in the harsh Mumbai sun, their faces half obscured by oversized sunglasses.

They came in condolence, but also in curiosity, eager to take a mental roll call of the others present. They seated themselves on white cloth-covered chairs in a windowless room, their necks craning towards the front, to catch a glimpse of the bereaved family—the widow, the pregnant daughter, a spot for the conspicuously missing son, the wealthy, snobbish samdhans from London, the handsome son-in-law.

Their eyes took in the white and green floral arrangements ('tasteful, simple, not showy' they would comment later over chai) framing the photo of the man in question, taken in his younger, more successful days, the black and white image capturing a happier moment in time.

God, when had he become such a fraud? Or had he always been that way? they wondered.

After a polite length of time, they slowly made their way to murmur condolences to the family. Call, if you need anything. We're here for you. He's in a better place. Prosaic phrases uttered in the moment and soon forgotten.

They got into their chauffeur-driven sedans, air-kissing goodbyes, cheerily making plans for lunch at the new Chinese place. As their cars drove away, their drivers navigating through the crush of cameramen present, they looked out the window, at the protesting crowds with their placards, the men in khaki trying to keep a sense of order and shaking their heads in dismay. What a fall from grace!

The cars took a sharp left turn, back to their homes in the Southern part of the island city, their inhabitants marvelling at their own magnanimity; their very presence at the funeral of a disgraced man indicative of their worth as friends, as people, their good deed for the month completed and their minds absolved of any guilt.

~

He died in his sleep. After the din surrounding him the last few months, the end came quietly.

After his release from prison, he'd moved into the second bedroom of his sister-in-law's flat. He would sleep with all the lights on, his nights fitful and claustrophobic, his mind and body still acclimatizing after so many months in the confines of a jail cell. When Bina had gone in with his morning chai, he'd been dead several hours.

A massive heart attack, the doctors said. Given the stress he was under, it was no surprise, they surmised. He'd been out on bail, but the threat of new charges and a probable return to custody loomed. His wife was sedated, his son to be tracked down . . . who would break the news to the pregnant daughter before the media hounds caught a whiff?

Given her niece's delicate condition, Tara's maasi phoned Nakul, who had just about gone to bed after another night out. She had to repeat herself three times before a still inebriated Nakul registered what she was saying and stumbled to their bedroom, to tell his estranged and pregnant wife that her father was gone. He sat on the edge of the bed as she sobbed and sobbed; he took her into his arms, where she lay ragged like a limp doll; he whispered to her to 'stay calm, for the sake of the baby', but the anger and agony on her face made him shrink back. For hours, they both lay there, together but worlds apart—him watching her and she curled up, palm on her belly, body heaving with sobs.

He must have dozed off. The next thing he remembered was being shaken awake. She was dressed, handbag in hand and suitcase by the door, bloodshot and vacant eyes visible behind her spectacles.

He shook his head to wake himself up, wincing at the stale, metallic taste of whisky and cigarettes.

'I'm coming with you.'

~

'Papa is gone. Papa is gone.'

Three words that Tara kept repeating to herself. But no matter how many times she said it or thought it, her mind still couldn't comprehend the finality. She would never see her father again, never hug him, never breathe the musky warm scent of Old Spice, probably the only thing about his old life he hadn't upgraded; she'd never find him late in his study, waiting up for her, to hear all her stories, but also to make sure that she was home and safe; she'd never walk with him down his favourite Bond Street in London, popping into Russell & Bromley to try on a pair of shoes or slurp noodles, his doused in chilli oil, at his favourite Chinese restaurant Kai.

She'd never introduce him to his grandchild.

He'd been thrilled at the prospect of becoming a nana. 'Bitiya, you have made an old man so happy. Disneyland, London Zoo, Hyde Park—I'll take the baby everywhere first,' he promised excitedly, planning ahead, even though it was all unlikely; both were acutely aware that their future, his future, was so uncertain.

In the last few weeks, with him home, they'd spoken every day. She avoided telling him about the situation with Nakul, instead trying to keep the conversation light, often making up stories about restaurants and dinners she'd been to, friends she'd met and events she'd attended, when in reality, most days she hadn't even gotten out of bed. He seemed tired, he'd told her he wasn't sleeping well, and she knew from the press that his bail had caused a huge uproar; pressure was mounting for it to be revoked. He was stuck in a cycle of fear and regret, 'I made so many mistakes, Tara. So many wrong things happened, I promise you, I am trying my best to fix everything . . . to make amends.'

He worried about Bunty, who was miserable and lonely abroad, desperate to come home to resume the life he'd become accustomed to.

'It is only you I don't have to worry about. You are my good girl, you made smart choices.'

She stared vacantly at the sea of white, the faces blurring, as the singer's bhajans turned even more mournful. She felt

Nakul's hand patting hers and she turned her face towards him, as he smiled tentatively. A few seats down, Anjali and Ajay Puri were seated, their hands clasped together, Anjali fanning herself with her dupatta, beads of sweat clinging to her upper lip.

She shook her head. She didn't know what to make of this family. Was she meant to feel gratitude for Nakul showing up, after months of horrendous behaviour?

When she dropped the pregnancy-divorce bombshell, it was like she'd flipped a switch. Nakul had gone from pushing her away to doing everything to make her stay. He'd been adamant about making their marriage work, tearfully proclaiming time and time again, that he'd be a good father, a better husband. This was all that Tara had ever wanted, for Nakul to need her more than she needed him, but circumstances had changed, she had changed.

Typical Nakul. What he couldn't have, he wanted. You're better than the best, his mother would keep telling him, encouraging a false sense of superiority. His whole life had been a quest for more—a fancier car, the latest watch, the best suite on holiday—and fortunately for Tara, pretty, popular and wealthy, she'd fit the bill. Until she hadn't.

It's not that Tara was not culpable. She'd been enamoured by it all—by her good-looking boyfriend, by his illustrious family and the money and trappings that came with them, by the idea that her place in the social order would be cemented. She'd overlooked Nakul's roving eye, his mother's imperiousness, their need to change Tara and fit her into a mould that best served them. She'd gone along with it all, her desire to please and to be a part of his world winning over any doubts. It was her naiveté that she believed all the concessions wouldn't come at a price.

And then there were her in-laws. She didn't have the energy to deal with their vacillations any more. Was this show of strength by his family for real or like everything else her mother-in-law did, a social pretence? They had to be relieved, she thought angrily. Now that her father was dead, they wouldn't have to face the ignominy of being related to a felon. Slowly, as public memory faded, their social superiority would be once again restored.

For some weeks, she'd managed to shut them out, she and Nakul living as strangers until she figured out what came next. But Anjali was not one to relinquish the upper hand. Once her in-laws found out she was pregnant, Anjali had switched to doting mother-in-law mode, popping in with treats and gifts, getting Mandy Smith, their architect, to come up with designs for the nursery, booking Fortnum & Mason for a baby shower. Taking control as usual for 'Nakul's baby', as she referred to her unborn grandchild, smoothly removing Tara from the equation. Divorce was not even an option in their ecosystem, the idea that their precious son would fail at anything, an absolute impossibility.

Her father would be (she just couldn't refer to him in the past tense) devastated by her getting divorced, by her even entertaining the idea of raising a child alone. Truth be told, she was terrified. When she'd first told Nakul, her plan was to move back to India to be closer to her family, but now her father was gone and her brother could no longer return, it was just her mother. In a home that wasn't even theirs, in a city that was filled with harsh memories of her father's failures. Is that really where she belonged? Then, there was the matter of custody. In one of their heated fights, Nakul had yelled angrily that he would bleed her dry, before allowing her to take *his* child. He'd apologized moments later, but she'd been shaken, knowing that her finances could no longer bear the burden.

She looked at her mum on the left, her head bent, a white dupatta partially covering her face. She had spent the last few days heavily sedated; bereft—of her husband, of her son, of her home—she couldn't find the strength to even get out of bed. She'd insisted on keeping a seat empty for Bunty. He should have been here, she cried; the duty of a son is to perform his father's last rites. In the end, it was the daughter who stepped up.

In colloquial Gujarati, when someone passes away, it is often said, 'Off *thaiye gai.*' As children, Tara and Bunty would always giggle at the rather unfortunate choice of wording, Tara nearly always chiming in, 'Like a light?' Decades later, as she sat at her father's funeral, she thought of how achingly accurate her glib reply was. With her father's passing, she felt shrouded in darkness.

The bhajans came to an end. The singers packed up their instruments. The last of the mourners filed past the family, hands folded. Tara rose to her feet, a little unsteady, holding on to the chair for support. She felt a hand around her waist. It was Aria, gesturing for Tara to lean on her.

~

A few nights later, Aria and Shaan arrived at the apartment, armed with containers of food.

'Mum sent all your favourites, Tara!' Aria said, a little too brightly, unpacking the boxes in the kitchen as Tara murmured a quiet thanks. 'You need to eat well, you know. For the baby at least,' she chided.

Her mother was already in bed. She'd barely left her room since the funeral, only making it to the dining table at Tara's coercing, leaving Tara and Nakul to face the handful of visitors who arrived to pay condolences. After a few days in the apartment, Nakul moved to the Taj with his parents. So it was just the three of them now. Her friends set the table and gestured to her to sit, filling her plate.

'I made brownies for you too, extra fudge sauce and tiramisu,' Aria continued, rambling nervously, as Tara hunched over her plate, pushing the food around with her fork.

'Where's Nakul, T?' Shaan interjected, Aria shooting her a grateful look.

'At the hotel with his parents. He wanted to give me 'time' with my mother, he claimed,' she added, with a dry laugh. 'But let's be honest, he just needs his five-star comfort, and this,' she gestured to the boxy living room, 'ain't gonna do it for him.'

Her friends were silent, both at a loss for what to say. There was no guidebook for a situation like this.

What words could provide comfort to a friend whose father had spent the last few months of his life in jail? Who had died an ignominious death? A friend who was battling on all fronts—her own family, her husband, the complex mechanics of the Indian legal system. A friend who was also pregnant.

This was unchartered territory.

'She won't want to see me,' Aria fretted to Shaan, on their way over.

'I want to be there, but the last time we spoke, it was awful.'

After their last interaction, Tara had ignored Aria who, after a few attempts at contact, had stopped trying, believing that she was respecting her friend's need for distance.

'Stop being a twat, Aria,' Shaan snapped. 'This isn't about you, so please quit the BS. Tara doesn't know what she needs right now and whatever happened before, has to take a pause for the next few days.'

For the past half hour, Aria, in a manner very unlike her, had blabbered on, about the most mundane things, anxiously trying to fill the silences with words. She knew their relationship was on thin ice, and she was terrified about saying the wrong thing.

It was hard to be sanctimonious when she saw the blows her friend had been dealt. Aria only hoped it wasn't too late to rectify things.

But what Aria didn't realize was that the events of the last few months had hardened Tara. Everyone had a breaking point, and sweet, naïve, eager-to-please Tara had reached hers. Her bullshit meter, as she told her husband, openly referring to his mother's behaviour, had peaked, and no one was exempt.

'So, Aria,' Tara looked up from her plate, anger flashing suddenly across her face. 'Now that my father's dead, you've forgiven us both for our grave sins against humanity?'

Aria opened her mouth to speak, then clammed it shut again.

'What? If this is a pity party, I DON'T need it. I didn't have you by my side all these months, so a plateful of brownies isn't going to make up for it. Let's be REALLY clear about that.'

'You're right.'

Tara ignored her and continued.

'You know, I realized something the other day. My entire life, I have been *so* dependent. Financially, emotionally, socially. Dependent on my father, dependent on my husband, dependent on you both, dependent on *so* many people, for *so* many things. And it took the ground falling underneath me, for me to realize that I don't need to be any more. I don't *want* to be any more.' she shrugged.

'All these years, I have been a rich little girl, living in a glass cage. Protected, sheltered, cared for. I have never even paid a phone bill myself, never opened a bank account, it was all handled. Someone was handling, it. Someone *else*—my father, his secretary, his accountant, my husband, so many someones, handling my entire life.'

'Until no one was. It was just me left, sitting with lawyers and accountants, attempting to learn and understand financial transactions and legal codes that were beyond me. It was me running to the courts, the government offices and to police stations. It was me who had doors slammed in my face, time and time and time again,' she clenched her jaw.

'And I was terrified. Terrified, that I was going to make some mistake that would prevent my father from being released. Terrified that some decision or move on my part would cause further damage. Terrified, that the authorities would find some loophole and come for me, for my mother. Do you know what it's like to live with that?' She laughed bitterly, answering her own question.

'But how would you girls? You live like I did, you have everything 'handled' for you. And you know what terrifies me now? It is becoming that person again. How crazy is it that I didn't know what was happening in my own home? How crazy is it that the people I loved the most, my father, Nakul, you girls, the people I put on such a pedestal, the people I would follow to the end of the earth . . .'

She took a long, deep breath, trying to steady her voice.

'In the end, who was left when everything went to shit? Who was looking out for ME?'

Shaan put her hand on Tara's shoulder, as tears ran down her face. She wiped them away furiously.

'I don't even know why I'm crying any more. Am I crying because my father died? Am I crying because Aria's been such a bitch? Am I crying because I'm fucking hormonal? Am I crying because my baby will never meet his or her grandfather? Am I crying because a year ago, I was living a life where my biggest problem was whether I was on the Birkin waitlist? Am I crying because I have a lifetime to go, trying to fix all that he did?'

'I'm just *so* tired,' she was now sobbing.

The girls led her to the couch and sat beside her, their arms around her shoulders, as Tara cried, and cried, and cried and cried.

They sat like that until finally Tara, emotionally and physically spent, curled up and fell asleep, her head in Shaan's lap.

They sat without saying a word, the room so quiet that they could hear their breath, punctuated by the sound of the city's traffic below.

They sat like that, Shaan caressing her friend's head, until the late hours of the night, when they decided against moving her, nestled her head on a pillow, covered her with a blanket, turned off the lights and tiptoed out of the apartment.

22

'So, you're really going ahead with it?' Leah asked, as she sat on the love seat in her sister's dressing room, watching Aria get ready. The dressing area had not been spared Roman's dramatic makeover either; the previously pastel-hued room was now stark, a maze of all white marble and mirrors, the only pop of colour, a red silk Oscar de la Renta blouse that Aria had selected for dinner.

'To really see yourself, to see your truth,' Roman had philosophized on his minimal ode to the Hall of Mirrors, each reflective panel, magically gliding open, to reveal a section of Aria's immaculate closet.

'Kinkyyyy,' Leah had laughed, taking in the mirrored ceiling. The overall effect was more disorienting than calming.

Aria had a date. With a Parsi boy. Set up by her cousin Ayesha, though it could have pretty much been her parents, given how close Ayesha was to them.

Now, in response to her sister's question, Aria shrugged and went back to lining her eyes.

She didn't want to admit to Leah that she was lonely, that she missed Rohan so much that there were days she couldn't breathe, that maybe a rebound relationship or, if nothing else, a fun date was just what she needed to take her mind off him.

And so, when Ayesha, in town for a few days from Miami, had suggested that she meet Farhad, Aria had surprised herself by agreeing. Farhad, a few years older, was divorced ('a totally mutual, happy one') and a successful banker in Geneva. Ayesha, who had been particularly concerned about Aria's dismal love life, had convinced her cousin that the two would hit it off immediately.

By the end of the evening, Aria was convinced that Ayesha had lost her mind. Farhad had arrived late for dinner at the Japanese restaurant he had picked for the date. Aria was waiting patiently at the sushi bar, sipping on a glass of red wine. He'd been only slightly apologetic, quickly moving on, summoning the maître d' for their table. 'My assistant specifically asked for the window,' he announced, several times, his voice a little too loud in the small restaurant.

Later, when she described him to Leah, her sister knew exactly the kind of person she was referring to. As the daughters of a wealthy, powerful man, they had grown up seeing two different kinds of reactions to their family—either obsequious and ingratiating or a flex of wealth, power and position, often quite volubly. Farhad fell under the latter.

'The entire dinner,' Aria sighed, nibbling on her coconut chia pudding the next morning, 'was an exercise to show me how cultured he was. His taste in wine—if he had sniffed and swirled the glass any more . . .'

Leah laughed.

'And then, the sushi was just *too* subpar for his liking. The salmon not fresh, the tuna, not sliced properly. Poor Robert, he sent it back four times. I was mortified. And he kept calling Robert, Garcon!'

Through the dinner, Aria kept trying to steer the subject to neutral territory but soon realized that for Farhad, one-upmanship was an extreme sport.

When she mentioned that she'd just returned from a business trip to London, he'd gone into a critique of airlines ('They really send the worst planes to India,' he'd sniffed. 'The first class I flew here was abysmal'), not failing to mention his new business contract had a clause that he would only fly private.

When she turned the conversation to tastes in music and film, reminiscing about an incredible U2 concert she had seen, it was a story of how his friend, 'he's like one of the world's biggest music producers', had invited him to Bono's afterparty.

The name dropping was enough to make her head spin.

'He's smart and clearly very successful. But he was throwing numbers and figures at me like we were on some reality business show,' she rolled her eyes. 'And all I really wanted was a nice glass of wine and some easy conversation.'

'But you know what really pissed me off? Throughout dinner, 'You know, in Geneva we . . .' was how Farhad began every sentence. 'In Geneva, the sushi is better, in Geneva, the service is better, in Geneva, the roads are cleaner, in Geneva, the air is better, in Geneva, excuse my language, but the shit doesn't stink . . .'

'All valid for sure, but what is it about people who move out of India and come back only to bash it? I mean, you grew up here, your parents still live here! And the entire time he behaved like my only wish in life was to be some kind of mail-order bride. Did he forget that I went to Harvard?'

Leah laughed, tears streaming down her face. 'You know Ari, you can be pretty funny sometimes.'

'Finally, I had to tell him that I've been to Geneva multiple times and I'm sorry it's the dullest place on earth! Wild horses couldn't drag me there.'

And that was the end of the night.

But Ayesha, buoyed by the fact that she'd managed to get her rather reserved cousin out on one date, wasn't one to give up so easily.

Ayesha Adams was the free-spirited, blue-eyed daughter of Rusi's cousin Behroze and her husband Sean, who had died in a tragic helicopter crash off the coast of Africa, when Ayesha was in her first year of college.

Behroze and Rusi had been incredibly close and he'd been devastated by her sudden passing. Even though, technically, Ayesha had been an adult, Rusi had become a de facto parent, making sure that he and Meher were involved in every part of Ayesha's life and she, in theirs.

An only child, Ayesha was very fond of her little cousins and had been there for all their milestones—from smoking their first joints to their college graduations.

Now that she had set up base in Miami, running a successful boutique PR firm, Ayesha made at least one annual trip to Mumbai to spend time with the Mistrys, usually around Christmas, and often en route to some party destination to spend New Year's Eve.

It was a joke in the family, that you could spin a globe and any country your finger rested on, Ayesha would have a friend (and often a suitor!) there. As a by-product of her being schooled in Switzerland, New York and then in California, coupled with an outgoing personality, Ayesha seemed to have adopted the #friendsasfamily mantra and was almost always jet-setting off for some friend's celebration. It was either a fortieth birthday in Mykonos or a wedding in Istanbul; then there were the summers in Capri and the winters skiing in St Moritz. In her constant quest for the offbeat, in February, she was heading to Peru for an Ayahuasca retreat, much to Rusi's consternation.

'Ayawhatta?' he asked, perplexed. 'Now, come on Ayesha, it's time you got a bit serious. What do you tell your clients if you're never in the office?'

'Oh, Uncle Rus,' Ayesha laugh, 'This *is* how I run my business. My new client is a wellness guru who wants to set up an Ayahuasca retreat, so you could say this is research,' she added with a wink.

She had no interest in getting married ('Why on earth would I limit myself to being with one guy?' she said, horrified, when Rusi had once brought it up, leaving him red-faced. He'd never asked again) but had a steady stream of paramours who all fell hopelessly in love with her to only have her lose interest when things got too serious.

Every year when Ayesha visited, Rusi and Meher would put together a big welcome home party. The guest list included old friends of Behroze's, the extended family and Ayesha's always extensive list of friends, both visiting and local. It was a fun night, one the entire family looked forward to, and usually ended in the early hours of the morning with someone jumping in fully clothed into the pool. Meher always marvelled at how much Ayesha could get away with in Rusi's eyes.

This year was no different and given her new self-appointed role of playing cupid, on Ayesha's list was Zayn Mody, the young architect who was being noticed for his sustainable design practices. He and Ayesha had met and bonded at Art Basel, and she was convinced he would be a good match for Aria.

'Ayesh, the world only tells us how we are decreasing in numbers. Yet, like Houdini, you manage to pull out these Parsi boys out of thin air!' Leah laughed. 'Are you planning to start a Parsi shaadi.com next?' she riffed on her cousin's serial entrepreneurship.

'Not a bad idea, Li. Look at my success rate. It seems my job with Aria may just be done,' she batted her baby blues in the direction of Aria and Zayn, who were laughing away in the corner. 'I think a glass of bubbly is in order, and now, let's see who we can find for you.'

Aria had to give it to her cousin. After that disaster of a set-up, Zayn was actually cool. Slightly taller than Aria, he had this easy hipster vibe, his skinny-jeans-striped-tee-beat-up-Converse-kicks look setting him apart from the preppy navy blazer crowd.

Aria found herself drawn to him and the fact that he hadn't taken his steel-grey eyes off Aria all evening, showed that the attraction was mutual. And as a bonus, he hadn't flinched when meeting Rusi; he'd been unfailingly polite, answering all his questions with ease, but the level of intimidation Rusi often commanded, was either missing or very well-disguised.

He'd been more fascinated by the home, although he admitted to Aria that his style was far removed from crown mouldings and Chippendale. Aria, in a move that was quite unlike her, had taken him on the full tour, including her newly renovated bedroom; he'd nearly spat out his drink when she'd extrapolated on the concept of 'monastic minimalism'.

'Come ON, what is that,' he threw his head back in laughter, the dimple on his right cheek deepening. 'You didn't seriously buy that pseudo-design bullshit? You're SO much smarter than that.'

She'd blushed, changing the topic. They hung out for a little while longer, sitting side by side on her bed, until Leah had come looking for them. Later, she'd cringed at the impropriety, spending the rest of the evening stressing that she'd come on too strong.

They were inseparable that night, which made avoiding Farhad so much easier. Despite their disastrous date, an invitation to Rusi Mistry's house and the future stories he could tell were too tempting for him to turn down.

By 4 a.m., only a handful of guests remained, Zayn included. Ayesha was the first one into the pool, stripping down to the bikini she was wearing under her slinky red dress. Meher, anticipating this, had stocked the dressing rooms for the guests with new swimsuits, flipflops and beach towels.

Swimming under the moonlight sky, giddy from the champagne and with a cute boy by her side, Aria surprised herself by agreeing to forfeit the usual New Year's Eve plan skiing with her parents in Gstaad for one that was way out of her comfort zone.

And that was how Aria ended up in Phuket, with her cousin Ayesha, ten complete strangers and a boy that she was kind of interested in.

~

'God, this flight is at such an unearthly hour,' Ayesha grumbled as she and Aria walked through a deserted Bangkok airport enroute to Phuket. 'I still don't get why you only fly commercial.'

'Every time I fly with either you or Shaan, you always ask me that. You know Dad,' Aria shrugged.

From the time they were young, Rusi had made a concerted effort to ensure his daughters were aware of their privilege.

'There's no room for princesses in this house,' she and Ayesha said in unison, mimicking his stern baritone. They burst into laughter, raising a few eyebrows in the quiet airport lounge.

This trend of his friends' young children jumping on private planes was one he was flabbergasted by—what a ridiculous sense of entitlement! His daughters should be grateful that they could travel as often as they did, and he had made it clear early on that his plane was off-limits when it came to their personal jaunts.

'When you earn your position at the company, then we will revisit your use of the plane,' he had told them categorically.

'Sigh. Uncle Rus and his rules,' Ayesha rolled her eyes. 'You could have at least let me book one so we wouldn't have to schlep through this unending airport!'

'You'll survive. Now, tell me,' Aria turned to her cousin. 'What's the real story with Zayn? And what's the scene in Phuket?'

~

It was impossible not to be floored by the home Zayn had designed. The client's brief was to design a functional, modern tree house, and he'd seamlessly merged elements of Geoffrey Bawa's tropical modernism with the proportions and simplicity of Philip Johnson's famous Glass House in Connecticut, one of his favourite sites.

It was a place Aria had visited while at Harvard, and she was amazed at how beautifully Zayn had translated that vision in such a unique way. Situated on a hilltop overlooking the azure bay, the steel and glass cubed structure, which in some kind of architectural magic, only had a single beam running through it, had three sides covered in lush green vines, while the fourth gave an unobstructed view of the water. For the building, Zayn explained, he'd only utilized wood, glass and minimal metal—he wanted to mimic the feeling that the interiors and exteriors were in complete harmony. The lawns outside were pristinely landscaped, the only interruption to the green was a bio-filtered wet edged pool, just adding to a feeling of limitlessness.

It was liberating to live with so little, Aria thought to herself, as she took in the airiness of the place, her mind already redecorating her rooms at home.

'This is incredible, Zayn. It really is the polar opposite of Windsor Villa,' she laughed, as he took them on a tour of the sparse interiors, passionately pointing out every detail. The furniture was commissioned with an emphasis on repurposing or reusing waste materials, Zayn explained to Aria and Ayesha, and this, along with its solar panels and energy efficient electricals, made it a smart, eco-friendly home, the future of design.

The client, a wealthy NRI family from Hong Kong, had been so pleased with the result that they had insisted Zayn spend a week enjoying his masterpiece, and it was here that Ayesha and a few of his friends were staying.

Aria had demurred at the invitation, it was a little too much for her to live in such close proximity to strangers; instead, she'd checked into a hotel a short drive away.

'You're really okay staying alone?' Zayn and Ayesha asked her multiple times.

Zayn had flown off to Thailand post the party and in the days that followed, he and Aria exchanged a few flirty texts. The more they chatted, the more he fascinated her. He seemed to be ambitious, but not in the way the other men she knew were, his ambition seemed to grow out of his desire to really have an impact on how people lived. There was a self-awareness to him that she found appealing; like her, he had clear boundaries, and for the first time since Rohan, she was actually excited at the prospect of getting to know someone.

The rest of the gang were flying in the next day, so it was only the three of them for lunch. The villa's private chef whipped up the most delicious Thai food, and along with the G&T's Zayn kept mixing her and dips in the pool, Aria spent the afternoon feeling every worry of the last few months melt away.

That evening, Ayesha was hanging with friends from Miami at a beach club but Zayn and Aria had both begged off, instead choosing to opt for a quiet dinner at a jazz bar he loved. They sat, side by side, at the bar, as the band played. Over bowls of steaming pasta and glasses of red wine, Zayn told her about his childhood. Though he'd grown up in South Mumbai, their paths had never crossed, more likely because he left for Florida early on in high school, on a swimming scholarship.

He was a restless soul, he said, he loved to travel and his father, also an architect, had planted the bug for adventure—

thanks to his father, their holidays were not at Disneyland or in London but were always spent in the most remote places, learning about nature. 'We went to Lakshadweep before it became what it is now, and it was just incredible, how untouched it was,' he told her. He'd been diving, hiking and camping since he could remember and that's what had sparked his obsession with designing spaces that were in sync with their environment. 'My dream home, which I'm hoping to build before I'm forty, will be up in the mountains,' he grinned.

He asked Aria, 'So, if you didn't have this massive company, what would you have done?'

'You won't believe it but no one's ever asked me that question. It's so much a part of our lives and who we are, that there was never really even a moment that I thought there would be something else.'

'I can understand how incredible a legacy it must be, but a company isn't who you are.'.

After dinner, and a few turns on the dance floor, where Zayn had twirled and dipped her till she was nearly dizzy, they'd driven back to the hotel on his Vespa, Aria part terrified, part thrilled, her arms circling his waist, holding tight.

'Want to go to the beach?' she asked, somewhat tentatively when they reached, not wanting the evening to end. That's how they'd ended up on the hotel's private beach, under the stars, chatting quietly.

It was nearly midnight, when he got up, brushed off the sand and reached for her hand to lift her up. Under a full moon night, as the waves crashed around them, Aria surprised herself and kissed him first.

~

Missing you girls. Weird being here without you two.

Aria sent the photo of the view to The Originals and leaned back on the beach chair. She was exhausted, but happily so. It had been a fun few days and she'd found herself going with the flow—she relaxed her rigid routine, stayed up late, drank copious glasses of wine, ate her weight in pad thai, danced more than she'd ever danced before—and she'd enjoyed every single minute. There was something liberating about being with strangers who didn't know anything about you, she'd discovered.

And then there was Zayn. They talked, they laughed, they flirted. It was easy with him. With them.

This morning, though, she was happy to have some time to herself. As she sprayed sunscreen liberally over her bare shoulders and belly, she found herself missing Tara and Shaan. At one time, they'd have spent hours here on this line of deck chairs, sunning themselves, playing game after game of Monopoly Deal, going into the ocean for a dip when it got too warm. Those were the days—when their only problems had been whether to take a nap or get a massage.

It had been so long since they all just hung out without any of the tensions that now clouded their relationship. She and Tara had spoken on and off since the funeral, but she knew that their friendship was a long way from being rehabilitated, and the thought had occurred to her several times, with sadness, that maybe their relationship was just one that had run its course. She was conflicted by everything that had transpired between them. Where would they start again? Could adult friendships even restart? If nothing else, the past few months had shown them just how different they really were. Could they find common ground, as they had all those years ago?

Her thoughts were interrupted by a server bringing her coconut water. She murmured thanks and took a sip of the sweet, icy drink. It had been some year—highs and lows with Rohan, the arguments with her father, the fallout with Tara. Her relationships this year had been rocky, and she wasn't one to make resolutions, but in the new year, she wanted to, she *needed* to, make sure that her personal life was a little steadier. She could definitely do with a lot less drama.

If the last few days were any indicator, things were off to a good start. She smiled, thinking of Zayn. They were in the sweet early stages of dating and she was enjoying how uncomplicated it was. Relationships, like this, I can handle, she thought, taking another sip of her drink.

Tonight, to bring in the New Year, he was having a party at the house. 'Good food, some good friends and music, so much better than braving the crowds at some awful club,' he said, and Aria was surprised at how much she was looking forward to being with him and their motley holiday crew.

But at the moment, she was enjoying her alone time, with a good book for company, some time in the sun and an afternoon at the spa to help ease the way into a long, hectic night ahead.

~

'Wow, dollface, you look gorge,' Ayesha gave her cousin a warm hug, enveloping her in her signature jasmine scent. In what was a daring look for Aria—a tropical print dress with cut-outs that showcased her tiny waist and her tanned skin, beachy waves and statement gold earrings—she was looking undeniably sexy. Zayn clearly thought so too, he put his arm around her waist and kissed her gently.

'You clean up good,' he whistled.

'Learned from the best,' Aria winked at her cousin, who was quite visibly thrilled by the appreciation. Ayesha, in a vintage white Alaia dress, showcasing her brilliant tan and her voluptuous curves, had forgone her five-inch heels for a pair of gem encrusted flats, her hair tied back in a slick ponytail. She looked sensational and was keenly aware that all eyes were on her.

'Look at this place,' Aria held on to Zayn's arm around her waist, as the trio made their way to the bar. It was a full moon night and there was a light fragrant breeze, scented by the sea and the floral arrangements. Luminous white lanterns dotted the lawns, and right in the centre, parallel to the pool, a long table was set for dinner.

'That's a massive seating. Who else is joining?

'Half of Bombay seems to be in town,' Zayn laughed, handing her a glass of champagne. 'Before I knew it, word got out about the party. The caterers have had to really scramble to accommodate the numbers. The bar is overstocked though, so I'm hoping that everyone's so drunk, they forget to eat!'

Aria smiled as he kissed her again, tasting the salt on his lips. She played with the multicoloured beaded necklace that he wore around his neck, a gift from his ten-year-old niece. She wasn't ready to face people she knew from back home, but she was determined not to let any worry cloud her evening.

Tonight was going to be great. And with the promise of a new year in the perfect setting, with a very affectionate Zayn, she was more than ready to end what had been a tumultuous year on a good note.

Aria was two glasses of champagne and quite a few turns on the dance floor down, when she felt a tap on her shoulder.

She'd been in the middle of an intense conversation with Zayn's cousin Noor and her partner Lindsay. In the course of the last few days, Aria had become fond of the couple and also somewhat envious of their relationship. Both incredibly successful, Noor in private equity and Lindsay in real estate, they seemed to balance each other out in the most ideal ways. While Noor brought passion to her opinions; Lindsay got her message across with diplomacy and tact. While Noor was a stickler for order and routine, Lindsay was a lot more easy-going, happy to let the universe lead her. Beyond their lively banter, there was a healthy mutual respect and understanding. At the moment, they were hotly debating where they should have their upcoming wedding and they'd brought Aria into their conversation.

Aria's heart dropped when she turned, and she took two steps backward, stumbling in the process and stepping on Lindsay's toe.

'Ouch!!'

Aria shot her an apologetic glance and turned back to the person standing in front of her.

He looked good.

He had a stubble. His nose was peeling a little from the sun.

He looked good.

Rohan Rawal flashed a full-toothed grin at his ex-girlfriend, cocked his head to the side and pushed his hair out of his eyes.

They both stood there, waiting for the other to speak. Aria was aware of Noor and Lindsay looking at her curiously. But before she could break the silence, Zayn swooped in.

'Ro, my man,' they fist-bumped, chest-bumped, back-slapped, the de facto bro-hug that seemed to characterize male greeting. 'You made it!'

'I've been here for a while, man. Loookkkkk at THIS place,' he let out a long, admiring whistle.

'I really wanted you to see it, it will give you an idea of what all we can do,' Zayn waved over a waiter, to get Rohan a refill.

'Oh, where are my manners? This is my cousin, Noor, her partner Lindsay and . . .' he winked at Aria. 'And THIS is Aria. Guys, meet Rohan.'

Rohan raised his eyebrows, as Zayn drew her to him.

'Oh, Aria I know,' Rohan's face had a strange smile. He did not take his eyes off her bare waist, where Zayn's arm was resting.

Aria felt her throat dry up and she took a gulp of her champagne.

'How do you guys know each other?' she said, her voice at a high pitch.

'Oh, I'm doing Rohan's new house in Goa. It's going to be sick!'

~

So far, Aria and Zayn hadn't classified their relationship. Things had progressed while in Thailand, but Zayn was non-committal. They were dating, but were they exclusive? For the first time, Aria was holding herself back from putting a label.

She liked him, she *really* liked him. He brought in a sense of fun. She'd gathered from conversations with Noor and Ayesha that Zayn had been single for nearly a year. They told her that when his last girlfriend had moved away, the distance had been a mutual deal-breaker, though they were still in each other's lives.

Their dynamic was entirely different from what she'd had with Rohan and Aria knew a lot had to do with her. She was more relaxed with him, less on edge, the fact that they could explore their relationship without millions of prying eyes was not a privilege she would ever take lightly again. In many ways, he ticked all of the boxes—Parsi, ambitious with a passion for his work—but, if she was being really honest, there were moments when she couldn't help but wonder if they were on the same page.

'I don't want to sabotage this before it even gets somewhere,' she told Dr Shroff. She'd called her from Thailand, as things between her and Zayn had started heating up.

'What constitutes sabotage for you?'

'I don't know. Putting him into a box, putting my expectations on to him, scaring him off . . .' she winced.

Rohan hadn't come up. Or rather, she hadn't brought him up.

That is, until she could no longer ignore her past. Or, at the moment, her present. Looming larger than life, as always, the attention, centring on him, even here, where the guests were all too cool, (or pretending to be too cool) to be enamoured by a Bollywood star. Even on a lawn of this size, every time she turned to say hello to another friend or make her way to the dance floor, he seemed to be there. At times, her skin prickled at how close they were; that familiar frisson returning.

Did Zayn give her that same thrill?

She shook her head, annoyed at her mind's questioning.

Why now? She'd spent so many months trying to forget about him. And she was *finally* in a good place. And yet, despite everything, what she felt for Rohan was still very much a part of her. She'd pushed her feelings aside, built a wall around them, so she could move on the only way she knew best, but all it took was seeing him again to send her down that rabbit hole.

And that's how Aria Mistry found herself over a span of a few hours, kissing two men as the year turned.

23

'Oh Em Gee!!' Ayesha cackled. 'Aria Mistry, you little vixen. Who would have thought?'

Aria looked around red-faced, shushing her cousin, lest anyone at the cafe hear her. Ayesha knew she shouldn't laugh, but seeing the total misery on her strait-laced cousin's face, was almost farcical. For the poor child, her indiscretions were, in her mind, tantamount to a social death.

Aria had woken up this morning, alone in her hotel room, hungover, guilty and filled with remorse for the night before. She was furious at herself. What had she become? She, who prided herself on being so virtuous and correct. She, who had judged (silently, more often than not) everyone around her if they didn't fit her standards. And here she was kissing two men. In one night.

Her cheeks burned with embarrassment as she recounted the story to her cousin.

Seeing Rohan had unnerved Aria; so she spent the evening trying to pretend he wasn't there. She'd stuck by Noor and Lindsay as Zayn got progressively more, how could she put it, 'spirited'.

395

'He was so attentive,' she told Ayesha, hugging her, kissing her, pulling her on to the dance floor. 'And then suddenly, it was like a switch had flipped. He wouldn't stand still for a second, he was all over the place, his hands were all over the place, and it was making things very awkward. And you know how uncomfortable I get. I realized, then, from the frequent trips he was making to the bathroom, that he was wasted, in every sense of the word.'

They'd had a blowout, any kind of substance abuse was a deal-breaker on Aria's list. 'How can you be so stupid?' she found herself yelling. 'We're in Thailand, do you know what trouble you can get into, for god's sake!' He had just laughed, denying it. 'Chill babe, have a drink. It's all good,' infuriating her even further. As the night progressed, she tried several times to talk to him, but he shrugged her off. As a final straw, he had yelled at her in front of a group of people. 'You're not my effing girlfriend or mother, so back off.'

Aria's face burned as she remembered how embarrassed she'd been. She was furious at herself again, for what now seemed to be a bad judgement call. She walked back into the house, her hands shaking, as she called her driver to take her back to the hotel. She was done with this night, with this year. She'd gone up to Zayn's room to grab the bag she'd left there, and when she'd come out, Rohan was waiting, arms crossed, leaning against the wall.

'Are you okay?'

Aria groaned silently. Of course he had seen it all go down. This night couldn't get better.

She just nodded, unable to get the words out.

'Can I drop you home?' she nodded again.

They hadn't said a word to each other in the car. When they pulled up into the driveway of the hotel, he walked her to her room. At the door, she hesitated for a second, and at the same time, they'd both spoken.

'Want to come in?'

'Want company?

They laughed, the awkwardness dissipating a little.

Aria led him out to the deck overlooking the ocean, kicking off her heels and stopping to grab glasses and a bottle of champagne on her way. 'It's New Year's Eve in a little while,' she shrugged, as a way of explanation.

They sat on the oversized daybed, their shoulders nearly touching, looking out on to the undulating waves. In the distance, they could hear the festivities continuing, as revellers across the island counted down to the New Year.

'Ten, nine, eight . . .' he turned his face to hers.

And then he kissed her. And she kissed him back. And they kissed. And kissed. And kissed.

They'd had sex right there out on the deck, and after, he sat with his arms around her till the sun came up. It had been a beautiful night, but the morning brought a new wave of realization and anxiety for Aria.

'No one can ever know, Ayesh. Swear on me, you won't tell anyone. Not even Leah,' she pleaded.

Ayesha took her cousin's hand. 'Ari, honey, it's okay. You're young! This is what young people do—we kiss many boys or girls, we break hearts and we get our hearts broken. We all do things we may not be proud of but you can't live like a nun forever, you know? And if it makes you feel better, it's not like you and Zayn were that serious. It was a casual thing—a holiday hook-up.'

'It's NOT okay. I don't behave like this,' Aria wiped away the hot tears spilling down her cheeks. 'I'm . . . I'm not some tart,' she said, unable to use the word that came to her mind.

'I don't know what it is about him. He drives me to do things that I've never done before.'

'But isn't that what being in love is really about?' Ayesha asked. 'Someone who you can push your boundaries with and for?'

'Not like this. God, I can't even look at myself. I'm so pathetic. Imagine if my parents found out!'

'Aria! You gotta stop, honey. You cannot live your life by Rus's rules. How happy has that made you so far?'

'You ended it with this boy, who you are still clearly in love with, because he didn't fit your father's idea of what the right husband should look like for his daughter. To me, it's the most absurd thing. FIGHT for who and WHAT you love or you are going to spend the rest of your life unhappy. I love you and I sometimes worry how you seem to be okay living within these constraints.'

'I didn't end it because of my father . . . Rohan knows what he did. And honestly, it's easy for you to say I should go against my parents,' Aria started, her eyes widening, as soon as the words left her mouth.

Ayesha was momentarily taken back. 'Why, because mine are dead?'

'No, no, Ayesh,' Aria stammered. 'I'm sorry, I'm sorry, I don't know what I'm saying,' she reached over to hug her cousin.

'You're right, maybe I don't have my parents here with me, to worry about their reactions to my every move, but I always have their voices in the back of my mind, Ari,' she said gently. 'But would I live by their every diktat at the expense of my happiness? I don't think so.'

'So what, I go against everything I've grown up being taught? What if Dad disowns me? What if no one at work takes me seriously because my husband makes a living singing and dancing and kissing other women on screen? What if I don't want to live a life where I'm waiting for him, while he is frolicking on some movie set for months at a time? What if I can't handle all the starlets and bimbos throwing themselves at him? The newspaper articles? The paparazzi? I've always been secure with myself, with who I am, and what I am capable of. I don't want to become some insecure wreck, questioning my worth. And you are forgetting, who knows if he really hooked up with that co-star of his? I can't be with a guy who cheats, what kind of life is that?'

'What if you just don't want to trust him? What if you can't handle the fact that you're not the only star in the relationship?' Ayesha said quietly.

Aria looked at her cousin, annoyed. 'Don't even go there. That's ridiculous.'

Ayesha put her hands up in defeat. 'It's not like Leah and I have not said that to you before.'

'Well, it doesn't make it any truer now.'

They sat in silence, as Aria twirled a paper straw over and over between her fingers.

She hadn't told Ayesha that Zayn had left a dozen missed calls and messages for her late last night and this morning. She wasn't ready to talk to him—she didn't know if she was more furious with his behaviour last night or embarrassed by hers.

She'd also woken up to a one-line message from Rohan that made her stomach do flips. *God, I've missed you.*

'My life coach back in Miami,' Ayesha said, bringing back Aria's focus to the present, 'says that some people come into our lives for a reason and some come for a season. So which category does Zayn fall into, and which one does Rohan? You need to ask yourself that.'

'But you also need to know what makes you happy. What are you willing to live with, and what are you willing to let go?'

~

'Wow, I've really grown up,' Shaan chuckled to herself as she rang for her morning chai. Pratap was still sprawled out beside her asleep. She let her fingers trace the muscles on his upper back lightly, wondering, not for the first time, how her life had come to this.

It wasn't a complaint but more a source of amusement. Not for the first time, she felt like she was looking into the windows at someone else's life. Who would have thought five years ago, heck, even one year ago, that she, Shaan Singh, Delhi party girl, would have spent New Year's Eve at her farmhouse with four other couples around a bonfire? Not to say that there hadn't been bottles of wine and straight tequila, but it had been pretty tame. She went over her past escapades in her head—she hadn't even told Pratap half the stories.

Rio de Janeiro, 2008: The first time she had ever made out with a girl. At a nightclub, on the table.

Las Vegas, 2012: When she won 15,000 dollars on the blackjack table. Only to lose it again the next night. What happens in Vegas, stays in Vegas, and thankfully her father had been too distracted to notice that dent in his bank account.

St Moritz, 2014: Ryan Gosling. Skinny dipping in a hot tub. Okay, so it wasn't really Ryan, but a close lookalike, at least when she squinted, and they'd been busted by her Delhi crew. Which, if she hadn't been that wasted, would have been mortifying.

And here she was, bringing in a new year. The fact that she had woken up at 9 a.m. without a raging hangover, or in a stranger's bed, was testimony enough.

She tiptoed around the bed, with a mug of tea in her hand, out on to the terrace, breathing in the fresh crisp air.

What would this year bring?

In the last twelve months, she'd gained a husband who was seeming less and less like a stranger. She and Pratap were finding some sort of equilibrium. She still hadn't completely forgiven him for the Serena incident, but she could see him, in his own, often confusing way, trying to make amends. Not that there weren't moments when she questioned everything.

'Maybe this is who you are. And that whole party girl thing was just a phase? Have you thought of that?' Aria had remarked.

She couldn't deny that the past few months had been about a sharp learning curve. Internally, she struggled with his infidelity. She questioned how, as someone who claimed to be so entrenched in promoting the rights of women, wasn't she actually a feminist fraud?

Her parents decided who she would marry, and without much of a fight, she'd acquiesced. Pratap cheated on her, she'd taken him back. Even if a little voice argued that she hadn't been faithful herself, she still couldn't rationalize that she had become *that* woman, who 'compromised'. In that same spirit, she'd let her career and her work take a back seat, happy to play the supportive wife, to be one half of a power couple.

Was that adulting? Or was that just copping out?

She could blame Pratap all she wanted. She could call him out on his traditional views, on his often myopic stubbornness, but the fact remained that she was playing right into them. Where was that feistiness she was known for? That independence she prided herself on?

Last week, she announced her decision to campaign for a Legislative Assembly seat. When the incumbent in her father's constituency had announced that he would be retiring by the next cycle, she'd taken it as a sign. This was her chance to prove herself, to create her own platform, separated from her father's and Pratap's, and to work for what she believed in. Till the election, she was determined to put everything aside and to focus, with the same zeal she had when she'd just returned from college.

She'd clipped the newspaper article out, left it on the breakfast table, for Pratap to see.

'I'm running,' she'd said with finality, when he sat down.

'I got that.'

'I'll have to discuss it with Papaji,' he added later. 'He's going to have reservations, but . . .'

'Discuss all you want. It's happening,' she'd responded firmly.

Pratap had just smiled, that same cryptic smile.

She was beginning to realize that as impulsive her decisions could be, Pratap was on the opposite end of the spectrum—he needed to ruminate, and mull, and overthink every single step.

'I'm convinced it's why his conversation is so stilted, there's just too much going on in his head!' she laughed to Aria.

He could be incredibly kind, to people he barely knew. 'I mean, I'm not defending him at all, but he was such a douchebag, to you and to all my friends. Oh god, remember how struck he seemed with Rohan? And then look how he came through with Tara.'

'Shaan Singh Sharma, am I wrong in saying that you seem quite in love?' Aria teased.

Shaan rolled her eyes. 'It's only Shaan Singh,' she retorted. 'Not taking on anyone's name. Ever. Actually, thinking I should just go with Shaan, like Madonna, and that pastry guy you love. And Pratap still can be kind of douche-y.'

It wasn't like she was crazy in love with him. 'Not like you and Rohan were, or still are,' she told Aria. This was not how she had imagined how she would feel about the man she would marry. But Pratap, he was growing on her.

'You make him sound like moss,' Aria scoffed.

He wasn't one to gossip, he'd pretend he wasn't listening, but he heard every piece of news she shared.

He looked at things very differently from her, and it was unnerving, especially for someone who had so far coasted by with the motto of 'my way or the highway'.

He could be moody, obstinate and irascible at times.

He expected those around him to revolve on his axis— and that's where he and Shaan constantly batted heads.

'God, Shaan, the same chicken curry again,' he pushed his plate aside. 'You have to teach the cook some new recipes.'

That's all it took to get Shaan riled up.

'Let's get this straight. If you want that kind of wife, you are looking in the wrong direction. You want a new recipe, look it up yourself,' they'd squabble like children.

'God, sometimes I feel like I married my father,' she groaned to Aria.

'Better you than me, friend,' Aria said. 'Imagine if I had to live by another version of Rusi Mistry and all his rules.'

Shaan poured herself another cup of tea and reached for her phone to text the girls.

Happy New Year bitches! Who did what and who last night? :P :P :P

A few minutes later, her phone pinged. A direct message from Aria. She'd been doing that a lot lately, sidestepping their group chat for one-on-one conversations. Shaan sighed. She was so done with this underlying tension between her two friends.

Happy New Year. Can you talk? It's been a night.

Forty-five minutes later, when Shaan hung up the phone, she still couldn't get over her conversation.

'You little tartlet,' she cackled when a tearful Aria had recounted her shenanigans of the previous night.

'It's like we switched bodies or something. Here I am being *Biwi No. 1*, and there you are playing Helen.'

'Helen?'

'Never mind. Tell me more.'

'Wild. Wild. Wild,' Shaan shook her head, as Pratap walked out on to the terrace rubbing his eyes.

'In some countries, talking to yourself is a sign of madness, you know,' he flashed her a cheeky grin, as he poured himself some tea.

'You will NOT believe what happened last night,' she said.

'First day of the year and already gossip *shuru*,' he leaned back on to the floral cushioned armchair across from her.

'Whatever. You know you want to hear it. So, little miss perfect Aria went and . . .'

~

Tara stared at her reflection in the bathroom mirror.

'New year. New me?' she thought wryly. There would have been a time, in the not-so-distant past, that on New Year's Day, she would have had a list of resolutions, mostly around diet and exercise, that she would put into practice.

But here she was. Exhausted. Physically. Mentally. Emotionally.

She wasn't the same Tara; that's what she kept telling herself, but she was living in limbo, her mind in constant conflict. There were days when she found herself slipping back into her old ways and then snap, she'd remember all that had happened and spiral again.

Every day, she vacillated between staying in her marriage and walking out. How could she bring a baby into her complicated, unhappy world? She caressed her belly; the only part of her life that seemed to be in control.

She'd gone to a therapist at Aria's urging, but had come away dissatisfied, unable to find the answers she was looking for. As an exercise, the therapist had suggested she write a letter to her father, sharing her unresolved feelings. Tara had sat down at her kitchen counter, with all intention; four hours later, all she had was smudged ink and a tear-soaked sheet.

She struggled to put into words the extent of her feelings. The fear and the exhilaration she felt for her unborn child; the need for space and the need for support that characterized all her relationships at present; the anger and the regret that she felt that he was gone; that despite all that had happened, she knew he was a good man, she wanted the world to know he was a good man. That she missed him, missed him desperately.

So she walked. She laced her sneakers, put her headphones on and walked. She walked through Hyde Park, she walked through the streets of Mayfair, she walked along the Thames. She just kept walking. She didn't know where she was going, but the act of moving, physically at least, quietened the constant noise in her head.

She rubbed her belly again. In the last few days, it had grown, the walk turning into a waddle. She wrapped her robe loosely around her bump and walked out to her bedroom. Nakul was still asleep, and she was grateful for a little more alone time before she would have to rehash their conversation from last night.

Tara sighed. She knew she wasn't being fair to him, with her constant dithering. But did she really owe him anything? What was keeping her here any more?

Nakul had been shockingly patient with her, but most days, everything he did seemed to get on her nerves. He was suffocating her with his solicitousness, a case of too little too late.

She walked out on the terrace, breathing in the cold January air. There wasn't a cloud in the sky, it was a perfect winter morning and the entire city seemed to be still in bed, nursing their hangovers.

Last night, she'd grudgingly accompanied Nakul to a New Year's Eve party at a restaurant in Mayfair, booked by their, well, *his* friends. When the news had broken about her father, most of the Mayfair Mrs, had frozen her out. But last night, they'd all pretended everything was normal, glossing over the past few months, too self-involved, to even feign any guilt or remorse at their treatment of Tara. She sat through the interminable evening, with lengthy discussions over upcoming holidays, mother-in-law issues, new diets and their free flowing, unsolicited advice on baby shopping and child-rearing. But her patience soon wore thin. She wasn't really in the mood to deal with them or her suddenly overbearing husband, who was getting drunker and more physically attentive, constantly pawing at her. She needed air, and so when Nakul headed to the bathroom, she snuck out. The plan was to walk home, but halfway there, she had realized she was hungry, and as the clock struck midnight, she found herself sitting on a bench in the middle of Oxford Street, eating McDonald's french fries, as drunken revellers walked past her.

In hindsight, it had been incredibly foolish for so many reasons—Nakul had been furious, waiting when she'd finally gotten home—she was pregnant, it was freezing out, London on any night wasn't the safest place, let alone on New Year's Eve. And yet Tara had found a strange sense of quiet, sitting there, in the middle of the mayhem.

~

Tara did not want a baby shower. She made her wish explicitly clear. And Nakul had concurred.

So, despite the advance planning, Anjali Puri, in what was probably the first and last time, had backed down.

Still, at the end, the baby shower went on as scheduled. But it wasn't her mother-in-law, but her mother who insisted she change her mind.

'Tara, it's mother's duty to have *godh bharai*,' she said sadly. 'But god has other plans. So let mummyji have this party. *Papa yaha hote*, even he would want it like this. And what fantastic plans she has, *itni* fancy party, *unhone* plan *ki hai*. She has spoken to me, and she is planning small puja beforehand. I'm telling you, this baby will bring *raunak* back into all our lives.'

Tara tried to argue but her mother played every emotional card. Tara knew that for her mother, the very fact that the Puris would host such a major celebration, would signal to the world that all was right in their family, despite everything that had happened. And for her mother-in-law, well, her benevolence would be on full display.

And so, everyone had won. Except Tara, that is.

She'd kept the details about the state of her union from her mother, but Bina, still somehow, continued to exhort Tara to make the marriage work, if not for her mother's sake, at least for the baby.

And so, Tara swallowed all her misgivings.

As a gesture of support, Anjali downsized the event. After the small puja at home with just family, her mother, on video call, 150 close family and friends, would attend a champagne brunch. In her trademark style, Anjali had gone all out with the Peter Rabbit theme, Nakul's favourite childhood books.

Welcoming guests was an archway of pasted-hued balloons and eight-foot-tall floral bunnies; the centrepieces were cane baskets filled with bunches of flowers tied with ribbons ('to look like they came straight from the garden!' Anjali exclaimed) and life-sized chocolate bunnies. 'Nibbles' circulated, each petit four, made according to theme—carrot cupcakes, the tiniest pot pies and quiches, rabbit-shaped cookies, cheese plates and rainbow-hued crudites—all followed by a sit-down brunch.

It was beautiful, and her mother-in-law was beaming at the party's success. Surrounded by people she'd considered family and friends until several months ago, Tara had never felt more alone. By the time the speeches rolled around, she had reached a breaking point. So, when her mother-in-law and Nakul presented her with a new emerald (the baby's birth stone) necklace, she looked at them, horrified, and burst into heaving sobs, in front of their guests.

Later, Anjali smoothly explained away the outburst, ascribing it to Tara being overwhelmed by the family's love. When the reality was, that now, nothing sickened Tara more than empty materialism.

~

Hi, girls, I just wanted you to hear it from me first. Nakul and I are separating. I'm moving out. I don't really want to talk about it at the moment, so please don't ask me any questions. But it's my decision and I should have had the guts to do it a long time ago.

Tara typed the message to the Originals and turned back to her notebook.

Next, she exited The Mayfair Mrs. Check that off the list too. Then, the Puri family group, the Puri cousins group . . .

She didn't feel like getting into long discussions, answering all the endless questions, rehashing what Nakul had done and not done, what she had said and not said, listening to all the commentary and advice on being a single mother.

'What kind of life will that child have?'

'Doesn't your child deserve the best?'

'It's not like he was cheating on you or treating you badly, think of your child, Tara, of his or her future, of your future?'

'They are such a good solid family.'

'He's not a bad person, Tara, people make mistakes. It was such a strange time.'

'Arré, these things happen in a marriage. What matters is that he is so loving and takes care of you.'

'What is your biggest issue—that he wasn't there for you? Your generation reads too much into these things. You are being too dramatic.

'If there are problems, it's okay, sleep separately, so many couples do that, but stay together, for your child, for YOURSELF. For *your* happiness.'

'Without Nakul, you are nothing, Tara. We have only taken care of you as a family, god knows what all we have had to deal with, and now you are taking our only grandchild away from us. For what, for your selfishness.'

She'd heard it all. The last two comments on repeat, courtesy Anjali Puri. Her mother had been inconsolable, initially retreating from Tara completely, spending her days in prayer, refusing to speak to her.

But Bina was slowly beginning to come around. She'd called Tara tearfully the previous night and said sadly, 'I don't understand, Tara. Why do you want to take such a serious step? You don't know what it is like to bring up a small child,' her mother had started.

'Mama, I know, but I just am not happy.'

'Happiness, is state of mind, Tara. You have to make yourself happy.' Bina sighed, the lines on her forehead deepening. 'Guruji says that happy comes from us inside, and only we can make our happiness. We cannot expect anyone else to make us happy or sad or angry.'

Tara had closed her eyes and exhaled loudly.

'But, you are all I have left. Only god knows when I will see my Bunty again. I want to be with you. So, whatever you decide, I will support you. But please, please promise me this, Tara. Please think. Papa is also not here. If something happens to me, who will be with you?'

Avoidance had become Tara's armour. And lists. Lists kept Tara sane. As she packed up her life into cardboard boxes, having a to-do list gave her a sense of control that prevented her from spiralling. It prevented her from breaking down. It prevented her from listening to all the voices in her head, that were pushing her towards the safer option.

Nakul had been furious when she'd told him her decision. It was on the second day of a surprise weekend he'd planned at a luxury estate in the countryside. They'd had a perfect day. A long walk, afternoon tea by the fire and a personalized five-course dinner. They'd talked, laughed even, reminiscing about their dating days, the fights they had, that now seemed so trivial, they'd talked about their future and their dreams for their unborn child. It had been all that she'd always imagined.

After a very long time, Tara had gone to bed in peace.

But the next morning, when she was woken up by the baby kicking furiously, she'd turned on her side, to look at her sleeping husband. And she'd known. She'd known that she'd moved on. She knew that if she stayed, she would never truly be living the life she now wanted. She'd known that the love that she'd once felt for Nakul was as a different person, a naive Tara. And she'd known, that while she'd struggle as a single parent, she wouldn't—couldn't—have it any other way.

But to Nakul, even after all that had happened, her decision had come out of nowhere. Whether it was denial or disbelief, he just couldn't comprehend the idea that Tara would *ever* leave him, leave the life that he'd given her.

'I don't understand. Are you crazy?! We're good right now, aren't we? We're good! We're having fun!' he said, his tone changing from anger to pleading.

'You're not thinking straight. It's the hormones. Come on, Tara, we can work through this.'

'I know you are frustrated, I know you are angry right now,' she said, as calmly as she could.

'But before we hate the sight of each other, I think it's best. I only have love for you, Nakul, for this baby you have given me. But too much has changed. I'm not the same girl you married. And I'm tired of working so hard to meet your expectations.'

'So, now it's all my fault? You will NOT blame this marriage breaking ON ME,' he'd gotten into her face.

'It's not about pointing fingers. It's about changing priorities. In the last few months, I've come to accept who you are, who your mother is, and who I am.'

She exhaled.

'We want very different things. We are very different people now. It took all that happened for me to realize that. I was in awe of you, of this entire world. I was okay to let you and your family create a life for me. My father had done it, now my husband would. I wanted the picture-perfect life, no rough edges. But if I've learned one thing, it was all a bubble, and bubbles—they burst.'

'We have our whole lives ahead of us, to be happy. To be with people who love us unconditionally. And to be good parents to this baby,' she'd pleaded.

'So there's someone else? You're cheating on me?'

'Nakul, don't be ridiculous. I'm six months pregnant. The only men I'm cheating on you with is Ben & Jerry,' she laughed sadly.

'The shock on his face,' she would later tell Shaan. 'It was heartbreaking and at the same time so infuriating. He's always been made to believe how special he was and that any girl would be so lucky to have him.'

'You wouldn't dare divorce me,' he sneered. 'What will your life be? I'll give you nothing, NOTHING. I'll take the baby, I'll take away your accounts, you'll be left all alone. Who's going to believe you versus me? I have the best solicitors in the country, and they'll destroy you . . .' he'd gone on and on, yelling, screaming, throwing pillows across the room.

But Tara remained as calm as possible. She knew she had to be, to reason with him, while he'd worked through his anger.

'I really felt I was watching someone else's life, someone else's marriage. You know, when you hear someone say they had an out-of-body experience, you can never imagine. But I felt . . . so removed from the scene. To be honest, I've felt removed from every scene in my life for a long time now.'

Nakul had stormed out of the room. Hours later, he reappeared, surprising Tara, who had been convinced he had driven back home to London in anger. She'd been sitting on the leather armchair, wrapped in a blanket, looking outside at the falling snow.

His eyes red and swollen, he'd dropped down to his knees, nestled his head on Tara's growing belly, his shoulders heaving. Tara stroked his head as they both cried, holding each other.

They cried for the past few months that had been filled with so much anger and resentment, they cried for the good times they'd had together, they cried for what might have been, they cried for their baby, who would never know a life with the two of them together.

And they cried out of relief. Relief that they could both move on, relief that they could both find that great love—theirs hadn't been that great after all—and relief that they could finally stop pretending.

24

If this had been one of Rohan's films, the hero and the heroine would have found their way back to each other, against all odds; convinced their warring parents to come around to their great love affair and danced their way into a lifetime of beautiful sunsets. A nice tidy ending.

But this wasn't a movie unfortunately, and real life rarely mimicked reel.

In real life, Aria and Rohan were back together, her father wasn't close to coming around, and at the moment happily ever after seemed to be a big question mark.

But as Oprah would say, what Aria knew for sure, was that no one had ever made her feel this way. It was the kind of love that was maddening, exhilarating, the kind of love that practical, pragmatic Aria had never really dreamt of having, the kind of love that was all consuming.

The kind of love that came with pitfalls, the realist in her wouldn't fail to remind her. But Aria was trying her darndest to suppress all the negative voices. She wanted more than anything to be with Rohan, and for the moment, she was letting herself go along with it.

What had caused this switch? She hadn't figured it out yet.

She couldn't really pinpoint an aha! moment (thank you again, Oprah) but their time in Phuket had made her realize that she was fighting a battle of her own making. If she considered herself such a modern, independent woman, then wasn't it time to stand against the parochial notions that may have worked for a different time? But what she also knew, was that Rohan would have to earn her trust, that wasn't a compromise she was willing to make.

She'd come clean with Zayn without going into detail, but his reaction had thrown her off balance. He'd been clearly pissed, of course, but she couldn't figure out if it was because of Rohan, his star client, or because he had feelings for her.

He'd brushed it off with a dig, which had rankled her.

'Who would have thought you'd be a player . . . but it's all good.'

Clearly, it was. He had called Rohan the next day to suss out whether the house plans were still on track. Rohan, being Rohan, had decided to string him along.

'Hmm, some would say that you were jealous,' Aria teasingly remarked, drawing circles on his bare chest. They were curled up on the deck. Aria had extended her stay in Phuket and Rohan had moved into her villa. For the last seventy-two hours, they'd talked, they'd made love, they'd laughed, they'd walked on the beach, they'd swum in the ocean, they'd fallen in love, all over again.

Rohan gave her a look and pulled her closer. 'Who won in the end, though?'

'Excuse me, I'm not some kind of prize that you both were fighting over,' Aria said reddening again, the memory of the night still a fresh source of embarrassment.

The days that followed were incredible. When Rohan and she were in their own bubble, it was like everything around them ceased to exist. She still marvelled at how much she still had to discover about him.

But reality had to set in. And the minute they set foot into Mumbai, they'd had to snap out of their loved up reverie. They'd been papped exiting the airport together, and before Aria could even tell her parents, a grim-faced Rusi Mistry had cornered her the next morning, wordlessly handing over the day's papers.

But this time, Aria hadn't cowered. She'd been rehearsing what she would say all night and before she lost her courage, she knew she had to come clean.

'I didn't want you to find out like this. I guess you can tell that Rohan and I reconnected in Phuket. Before you say anything,' she said, as her father opened his mouth to interrupt. 'Please hear me out.'

'It wasn't planned, which I'm sure is your next question. We crossed paths on New Year's Eve and over the next few days, we realized how important we are to each other—correction—I realized.'

'The thing is, Dad, I never stopped loving him,' Aria said, eyes shining with tears. 'But I've been so caught up in what you would think, what everyone around us will think, I've been so consumed by responsibility, and legacy, and roots . . . words that that really sound so outdated and archaic when you think of it.'

'I understand some of your reservations, I've had them too. I understand he is not what you've wanted for me, for whatever your reasons.'

'But he's what I want, for me. At some point, Dad, I have to start making my own choices, even if you think they are mistakes. Have you ever thought of the fact that you are okay with me making decisions that involve millions of dollars but you don't think I'm equipped to make a decision about the man in my life?'

'Maybe you are not equipped to make any decision at the moment, Aria,' Rusi's voice was cold. 'Is this your way of informing us that you plan to marry this chap?'

'I'm not saying anything like that. I'm saying, you have to give him a chance, and let me give this a chance. It's what I want.'

'Are you done?' he'd asked her, before pushing back his chair and striding out of the room.

'Mom!' Aria exclaimed.

Her mother put her coffee down with a sigh, shaking her head.

'I know, Aria, I know. He is being unreasonable. I will speak to him, I promise you.'

'You kids, I tell you,' Meher joked feebly. 'Who needs caffeine—when I'm guaranteed a dramatic wake-up call every morning.'

'Aria, this is what you want, darling? You've thought about all the issues and concerns you had before, you've thought about everything that comes with being with him, you've really really thought . . .'

'I love him, Mum. I do, and yes, I know it's going to be filled with many challenges. But right now, my biggest challenge is getting Dad on my side. I don't want to lose my father, either,' she'd said.

'Oh darling, you could never lose him. It's a lot for him to take in. You're his little girl, he wants to protect you, and yes, he's not used to having his way questioned. You both have that in common. But you have my support, wholeheartedly, if you know that this is right for you, then I will do everything in my power and stand by you.'

But despite her mother's exhortations and arguments, Rusi remained unmoved.

Aria didn't know what was worse, Rusi's blistering anger or the iciness he had now adopted. He kept their interactions short and to the point, both in the office and at home.

'He'll come around darling, give him time,' her mother said. Meher had made an attempt to have Rohan over for a meal, further rankling her husband, who avoided showing up for dinner that night.

Meanwhile, Aria was taking baby steps in merging their lives. Baby, baby steps. She and Rohan were spending all of their free time together, but she still was resisting moving out beyond the four walls of his apartment.

When they had gone out for dinner, they'd been spotted by photographers, by excited fans, who thought nothing of crowding around their table, in hysterics, asking for a selfie.

Seeing her photo each time in the paper and reading the comments online unnerved her. An army of super fans were furious at what they saw as Aria's role in the demise of #Rolika, and the hateful trolling was beginning to wear her down.

'Ignore it,' Rohan had advised. 'They'll lose interest once another romance happens.'

She stayed off the internet as much as she could, but wherever she went, in the corridors of the office, on site visits, at the salon, getting her hair done, she heard hushed whispers about them. At lunch with her sister, Aria had been mortified, hearing the women on the next table, whisper incredulously.

'*That's* Rohan Rawal's girlfriend. She's not *that* pretty.'

'He and Malika make a much better pair. What does he see in her?'

She'd had to restrain Leah from making a scene. They'd left without having dessert.

At the office, one of her father's oldest managers had come to her with a big toothy grin.

'Ariaji. You will call us all no, for the wedding? My daughter is a big fan of Rohanji. His last picture was too good.'

It had taken every ounce of her being to accompany Rohan to the screening of his latest film, the one he shot with Malika in New York. She'd walked in through the back and was guided to the first-row seat, which had been reserved for her, while Rohan and Malika walked the press line outside. When they'd finally made it to their seats, Malika had ignored Aria, seating herself on the other side of Rohan. For the rest of the evening, she'd used every opportunity to flirt with him.

Her blatant disregard set Aria off, and she lashed out at Rohan later that night.

'You have to trust me, Aria. She's just acting up for the cameras, that's what she does.'

'The cameras were off, Rohan. It was a dark theatre. Did she really need to be whispering things into your ear, through the film?'

'Oh god, who am I?' Aria paced the room. 'This is not me, this needy, jealous, insecure person. You and your life make me behave demented.'

She'd left his house shortly after, refusing to stay the night.

Back home, she was striding up the stairs, taking them two at a time, when she heard her father call out.

'Aria,' his voice boomed, stopping her mid step.

He was standing at the door of his study, he gestured for her to join him.

She braced herself for yet another argument, as she made her way inside, sitting primly on the sofa in front of his desk.

'You were out?'

'Yes, Rohan had a film screening.'

'How was the film?'

Aria was surprised at this line of questioning.

'Rohan was good. It's a sweet love story.'

Rusi just nodded.

'Do you feel proud seeing his work?'

'I'm not sure how to answer that. He's clearly good at what he does, he works hard, and . . .'

Her father leaned forward and sighed. He removed his glasses and pinched the bridge of his nose.

'Aria, you know how I feel about Rohan. But you don't know why I feel that way. I know you think it's my way of controlling you, at least that's what your mother keeps telling me. And you believe it's my archaic snobbery and elitism, am I correct?' He arched his eyebrow.

'Maybe you are right. Maybe it is all of the above. Maybe I am too old-fashioned, maybe I have my mind set on a certain path, on certain social codes, but to be frank, that's what's seen me through life.'

He exhaled.

'But my issue with Rohan is more than just a blanket dislike for all he represents. It's personal and it's not a conversation I wished to have with you. But here we are, and I feel that I must. At Tara's wedding, I found him . . .'

Aria furrowed her brow, as her father, haltingly, recounted the incident with Rohan.

25

Summer 2019, Ibiza

Shaan caught Pratap's eye as he followed the tall, sexy blonde in a string black bikini as she made her now hourly lap around the pool.

'Yes?' she said archly to her husband, peering over her diamanté studded sunglasses.

Pratap laughed heartily. 'What? *Dekhne mein kya hai.*'

His buddies high-fived each other. Shaan rolled her eyes and turned back to her magazine.

It was quite the scene at the Nobu Hotel pool in Ibiza—great music, flowing drinks, beautiful people. The last time she'd been on the island was with Rohan Rawal and his then girlfriend, the actress Karishma, hooking up with random guys she met at the clubs. Now, she was the girl who took couples' holidays. Pratap and she had spent the last few days with his school friends—a blur of dancing till dawn at Pacha and lazing by the pool in the afternoons. It seemed that besides the ghazals and shayaris, Pratap was quite the EDM lover and dancing at Ibiza's famed nightclubs was exactly the kind of holiday he was game for.

They'd crossed the first-year hurdle and their relationship, with its many speed bumps, had been quite the path of discovery. Theirs wasn't some torrid love, but they were slowly building their own version of a marriage. She'd been drinking less, he'd ended it with Serena, and while they were still treating their marriage with kid gloves, they were finding a rhythm.

This trip had been a short break from the political machinations of Delhi and Shaan was enjoying the downtime. Pratap had won the election by a landslide, and Shaan was taking a break from her candidacy to hop over to London, to be there with Tara for the birth of her godchild.

'Shaaan, Shaan, *dekh*,' Rina, one of the wives nudged Shaan to look up from her magazine. 'Isn't that George Clooney?' Their entire crew shaded their eyes to see the silver fox and his wife Amal saunter into the restaurant. '*Chalo*, Instagram *ke liye* photo *ho jaye*,' Samira added, already halfway across the pool before the others could join her. Shaan hung back, a little embarrassed, but not enough, and surreptitiously took a photo of the couple to send on The Originals.

OMG! Tara, your favourites—Amal and George are at the Nobu, she typed out, furiously adding heart emojis. She immediately got a reply from her friend.

Uff, I love her. They seem perfect . . .

But then again we know how that works out! :P:P:P

Amal ki kamaal. Now, see, she's the kind of woman I want to be, so smart, so beautiful, she makes George Clooney look like a pappu.

Ha, Shaan. I don't know if Pratap will be happy to be called that.

BTW, last night, we saw Sienna Miller at Pasha. She's smokin'. These boys were going nuts! Shaan added.

I can't wait to see you, T! And my sweet little baby! Aria, come to London!

When she got no response, Shaan typed . . .

Now bas, we really need a trip together. Just us three. Just like old times.

Come what may, this year, she was going to make this trip happen. She was going to get The Originals back in form.

But in the meantime, she stretched languidly, put her phone away and turned back to watching George and Amal, who were now surrounded by a gaggle of over-excited Delhi girls.

26

Roman Shaw was back in Aria's life.

But, this time, with a different brief.

As Aria walked through the cozy, warm rooms that he had created in her new home, she felt immediately at ease.

Her very own apartment. Aria was thrilled at how it had all come together.

When Granny Shelley had passed, along with her binder of recipes, she'd left Aria this apartment in a small Art Deco building, nestled in a quiet cul-de-sac just off the city's busiest thoroughfare.

And when Aria made the difficult decision of moving out of Windsor Villa, she knew that the place where Shelley lived happily for so many years would be the perfect new home. She said a silent thank you to her grandmother, grateful for the safety net she provided.

As Roman proudly walked her through all the little details—he'd kept some of the apartment's vintage features and mixed her grandmother's antiques with some more contemporary pieces—she could picture having her morning coffee on her grandmother's cane rocking chair, mixing batter for brownies on the large kitchen island, or lounging on the grey sectional sofa with her friends.

'It's turned out just as you wanted, Ari.' Rohan hugged her from behind. 'Though I still don't know why you wouldn't just move in with me,' he pouted dramatically. 'But the good news is, there's enough space in that walk-in wardrobe for all my stuff.'

She smiled, turning to face him and kissed him gently.

After that evening in her father's study, Aria had been mortified by the story he'd recounted. For the first time, since Rohan and she started seeing each other, they'd managed to have a civil conversation.

'I'm not going to pretend that I'm not embarrassed and furious that you had to see that, Dad,' she said, her voice shaking. 'And it is something that I am going to discuss with Rohan. But at the end of the day, and there's no excuse for his behaviour, it was before we got together.'

'It doesn't make it okay, but everyone has a past. We've all done stupid things when we were younger, that we're not so proud of.' She laughed, trying to lighten the mood. 'Well, maybe not you, Dad? But I've had some moments, especially in the last year, that have been hurtful and selfish, and behaviour that I would not condone, otherwise, with anyone else . . .'

'I love him Dad, and whatever he did or didn't do, I have to take a less judgemental view, for my own happiness. I saw what that did to my friendship with Tara and even with Rohan, and I am trying really really hard, to not constantly expect everyone to live their lives by my value system.'

Her father said slowly, 'You are an adult, Aria. As much as I don't want you to be, you are. And I have to face that,' he gave her a grim smile.

'But I have to tell you, that I don't know if I can accept your relationship with this boy.'

And so, they reached an impasse.

While the conversation thawed some of Rusi's iciness, Aria found her father had built a wall between them. He no longer asked for her opinions, or called her into his meetings, he no longer spent hours chatting with her over breakfast about new projects, or asked her to accompany him to new site visits. His secretary set up weekly updates with Aria, so she could apprise him of new developments in their hospitality division that she was overseeing and update him on the progress of their portfolio of hotels, under the Smith Group.

He left her to her own devices to run her end of the business, occasionally asking for updates and passing on messages through other company executives.

On the occasion that Rohan came to dinner, Rusi would offer a cordial greeting, but then shut himself away in his study.

'He won't come around. Not for a long time. I know my father, he takes forever to get over even the smallest slights and this . . .' Aria said to Rohan, after she'd recounted the conversation they'd had.

'Fuck Aria. I didn't even know you. I didn't even know that was your father. It was a stupid night and a stupid, stupid mistake. Honestly, I don't even remember it. That's not who I am any more.'

'All deal-breakers for me, Rohan. This is not a conversation I ever want to have again.'

And then her father called her into his office one day. He was seated behind his desk, several of the company's senior management sitting on the leather couch across from him.

'Aria, we've had a substantial offer from an investor, for our stake in the Smith Group. I've taken it to the board, and they agree that we should accept it.'

Aria looked at him, horrified.

'What offer? What are you talking about? We are just finishing the renovation on the Scotland property, our opening date is in three months. I'm leaving for London at the end of the month, to work there till the opening. We're in the final stages. How can you suddenly decide to divest our stake? You know what we've, what I've put into it'

Her father shrugged.

'It's a business decision. It makes financial sense. You cannot get emotional about it.'

'Emotional? You are the one who told me how this deal was going to continue Granddad's legacy in hospitality. To bring us on to the global stage, with one of the most diverse portfolios. How it was a full circle, given that I was going to head this?' Aria was incredulous at her father's U-turn.

'And now you are telling me NOT to be emotional? You didn't even consult me! You took it straight to the board. So it's a done deal, then,' the bitterness crept into her voice.

'It makes sense, Aria,' the company's CFO piped up. 'It was too good an offer to ignore.'

She glared at her father, shaking her head in disgust. 'Let's face it, Dad, that's not what this is.'

'And what will I be doing at Mistry & Sons, now that you've taken away my project?'

'That's not a conversation for now,' Rusi said firmly, as the others in the room shifted in their seats. 'But there are possible roles that have been earmarked that can use your skill set and expertise.'

'Great. I can't wait to hear your decisions on my life,' Aria turned, as calmly as she could, and walked out of her father's office, tears streaming down her face.

~

A few weeks later, she walked back into her father's office, a letter in her hand.

She stood in front of his expansive wooden desk.

'What do you need, Aria?'

'I don't know what the protocol is. But I have put a great deal of thought into this, and I think it's best I step away from Mistry & Sons. I will always feel a responsibility to this company and to what our family has built, and I hope one day I can be back here, having earned my place, and earned your respect.'

She paused, swallowing.

'But right now, I think I need to go out there on my own. I need to make my own mistakes, make my own decisions, emotional or otherwise . . . I need to find my own path. For my sake and for the sake of our relationship, I think it's best that I resign from the day-to-day operations.'

She put the envelope on the table.

'I want to thank you for all that you've done for me. For all that you've taught me. I don't think I could have asked for a better teacher,' her voice cracked.

She exhaled. 'I love you, Dad. You have been the most important person in my life, but I think what the last few months have shown us is that our relationship needs to evolve. I am not a little girl any more, I need to have my own voice in my own home, in my workplace. And that's why I think it's best, for both of us, if I move out too.'

She could see her father clench his fists.

'I don't think it's fair on us, or on Mum, or Leah, to live in a house with so much tension. I want Rohan to be welcome in my home, and I don't want to be treated like I am a child any more. I hope you can understand where I am coming from . . .' she trailed off.

Rusi pursed his lips. 'Well, it seems your mind is made up. I will not stand in your way.'

Aria was taken aback at how quickly he'd come around.

'If you're expecting me to add that you'll always have a home here,' he pointed around the office, 'or at Windsor Villa, well, I can make no such promises,' he said, his tone cold.

'Because, let's be clear on one thing, this talk of independence is rather rich. Do you know what it is like to be really independent? Without the safety net that you have?' he raised his eyebrows at her.

'So, let's call this what it is. This is possibly you throwing away your life and future for that chappie. But if that's what you want, so be it.'

~

'I read somewhere once,' Aria played with the piping of the ikat cushion, folding and unfolding the edges, 'That you can't have both professional and personal happiness at the same time. One has to give. Do you think that's true?'

Dr Shroff peered over her glasses at the young woman sitting in front of her. She said gently, 'It doesn't matter what I think, Aria. Do you believe in that statement?'

A pause. The cushion, folded and refolded again, Aria's fingers rhythmically repeating the action.

'I don't know. I wonder. On one hand, I'm really excited about what this new venture will bring . . .'

'Tell me a little about that.'

Aria brightened, sitting up straighter. 'So, I realized, that there's this incredible influx of talent across fields, these young entrepreneurs who are starting cool businesses, experimenting with concepts and ideas, bringing in new services. And I wanted to, in my own way, be a part of that. Of course, I have access to some funds, and I wanted to use my experiences as a woman in business and apply all that I've learned from my father to incubate young talent, who may not have the ability to scale their dreams,' she was now talking rapidly. 'My first investment is this young patissier who wants to put a modern spin on the Indian sweet shop. It brings together my love for desserts and hospitality, and it's a fitting ode to my grandmother, so ta-da! The first ShellProof Investment.'

'Wow. You really seem so connected to this project. So, we have the career aspect, that seems to be going in the direction you'd like it to. Now, what about your personal life? You mentioned your father, how are things between you?'

Aria massaged that sweet spot at the base of the skull that her acupuncturist promised would release the tension headaches, now an almost weekly occurrence.

'Status quo. He's holding on to his end of the deal, he's not getting involved in anything I do. To be honest, he's not saying much to me either. My mum tells me that he watched one of Rohan's films the other day, so I don't know, maybe he's coming around?'

'And what did he think of it?

Aria, laughs. 'I was too scared to ask.'

'It's a long process, and I'm a realist—I don't expect for it to change overnight. His favourite can-never-do-wrong daughter moved out, stepped back from his company and is with a man he doesn't approve of, so I can see how difficult that must be to comprehend. I am not angry with him any more, I'm just sad. I just hope one day he sees that I'm happy and my reasoning behind it.'

'And you are happy.'

Aria smiled. 'Yes, I'm getting there. You know, I have seen a whole new life, one with me in the centre, having my own agency in all aspects, and I can't unsee that. This past year has shown me that. But to go back to your question, yes, Rohan and I are in a good place, I'm opening myself up to setting a dynamic and boundaries that work for us. I'm enjoying living on my own, and I know it sounds really New Age-y, but I feel my grandmother is with me, at so many times. I have a small, but steadfast circle of friends . . . so yes, I would say that things are looking up.'

'And Tara? Is she part of this circle?'

Aria sighed. 'Tara will always be a part of my life. At least, I would like her to. But I know that a great deal has happened between us, and I want to give her time.'

She folded the piping of the cushion again. 'I think, this year has taught me how to have more perspective and to not be so rigid. I criticize my father for the same faults, but I need to work on it as well . . . work in progress!' she said with fake cheer.

'Complicated relationships seem to have been my forte last year. Time for that to change,' she rued.

Before Dr Shroff could pose another round of 'whys?', a buzzer rang, signalling the arrival of her next appointment.

'And that's what we'll work on. Honing that perspective. Let's get into that on Thursday, Aria,' Dr Shroff made a note in her little book. 'See you at the same time?'

Aria replied in the affirmative, put the cushion back in its place, instinctively plumping it up. As she walked towards the door, she stopped as if wanting to say something.

'Yes, Aria?'

'Nothing. Nothing. Thank you, doctor.'

Aria left the office smoothening her ponytail, adjusting her shirt and shaking off the emotions of the last hour with her therapist. If she didn't hurry, she would be late for her one-on-one with the patissier.

It was time to get to work.

27

Tara licked her lips nervously. She took a sip of her ginger tea, grateful for its warmth, squared her shoulders and opened her laptop.

'You can do this,' she chanted over and over again, her fingers poised over the keyboard, a now familiar mix of gratitude and apprehension infusing her every thought.

It had been a few months since her father had died. Six weeks since she'd had the courage to move out of the home she shared with Nakul and her in-laws. And just two weeks since she'd moved into an apartment at the end of Pitshanger Lane in Ealing, just fifteen minutes by tube from Bond Street, but miles away from the life she had been leading.

When she'd visited this ground-floor apartment, seven months pregnant, heartbroken and a shell of her former self, she'd immediately fallen for its beamed ceilings, French windows and sizeable backyard that had just enough space for a swing set and a small herb garden that she'd already started working on. She'd put in an offer almost immediately and in the last few weeks, in setting up this home, she'd found her equilibrium.

She rubbed her expanding belly. The baby was due any day now and making Tara wait patiently. In a few weeks, she wouldn't be alone, she'd have a teeny baby and, if all went according to plan, her mother to start a new chapter with.

'A new beginning.' Those were the words she focused on, as she extracted herself from the only life she'd known and took a massive leap of faith.

But for her to really start afresh, there was something she needed to do. She needed to come clean.

She turned on her computer, unlocked her Instagram account, took a pause, and then started typing slowly . . .

Hi. I'm Tara. Now, I'm sure you are wondering, why after so many years on this platform and hundreds of posts later, I'm reintroducing myself. See, a few months ago, my father died. The death of a parent under any circumstances is devastating, but my father died while he was out on bail, for a crime that hurt the lives of many families. All these months, from the moment he was arrested, I have grappled with the implications of his actions—both on society at large as well as personally. As his daughter, and one with such a public profile, I feel that I owe you all, and all those who are hurting from his actions, an apology. I know words may not be enough, but when I say that from the bottom of my heart, how deeply sorry my mother and I are for the pain, I do hope you will believe me.'

She took a deep breath and continued.

As many of you have commented, I led a gilded life. This platform only enhanced that perception. I was friends with all the right people, I hung out at all the right places, I wore all the right clothes. I led a life of great privilege. When my father was arrested, it all came crashing down. Now, before the trolling begins, let me say it—I'm not expecting sympathy, but know this, as an adult, I can admit that my father was a deeply flawed man, but as his little girl, he will always be my hero.

I've had a great deal of time over the last few months to evaluate all that is important to me. I've seen my marriage break up, friends come and go, my mother and I lost our home, our individual identities; our names will now be forever associated with the word 'scam,' our lives will always be fraught with the legal, emotional and social implications of what my father did. What is that saying about the sins of the father . . . But they say even in the darkest clouds, you find some silver lining. Just before my father died, I found out I was pregnant.

What my father did took from me the only life I had ever known. And what my daughter did is give me a life back. In many ways I'm still the same Tara—do I still love fashion? Hell, yes. Do I love nothing more than an evening out with good friends? Who doesn't? Do I still love to travel and discover new places? Yes.

I can be clumsy, sometimes ditzy and make the best healthy-ish banana bread.

BUT . . .

I'm also finding a strength and resilience in me that I didn't know existed. I've found the courage to say enough is enough; to take my life into my own hands. To create a world that I'm proud of, to embark on a journey that I can call my own. Your vibe attracts your tribe, they say. And that's exactly what my hope is for my life and by extension, this platform. I wasn't prepared to parent on my own, but I'm taking it a day at a time. My only hope is that my daughter will forgive the mistakes I make.

So, Hi again. I'm Tara. I'm thirty-two and live in London. I'm a soon-to-be single mum to a baby girl. This is my story. And I'd love to hear yours.'

Tara took a deep breath and hit enter. She turned off her computer and walked out barefoot into the backyard, the cool, wet grass tickling her toes.

It was the first few days of summer. The rose bushes the previous owners had planted were in full bloom, just in time for her daughter's arrival. She held her belly, still amazed that she would soon be a mother.

She headed back inside a little while later, brewed a fresh cup of tea and turned on her computer with trepidation.

She stared at the screen, her hand over her mouth. And the likes just kept climbing.

ACKNOWLEDGEMENTS

As far back as I can remember, I dreamt of being an author. I'm pretty sure it all started when, at the age of eight, my mother gave me an iridescent unicorn journal, with lavender pages and a lock (essential to keep away from the prying eyes of a nosy younger sister), encouraging me to put into words all that I saw and experienced. For that, the bookshelves that filled our home and for giving me the world, I will always be grateful. Love you, Mama and Papa.

It's taken countless cups of coffee and an incredibly supportive community of individuals that's brought me to this very moment.

Karan Johar, for always being the strongest shoulder for me to lean on, and for the best, no-holds-barred advice. This book is better because of you.

On a very muggy July day in Rome, the ever-encouraging Nonita Kalra suggested I try my hand at fiction. A few months later, she introduced me to Chinmayee Manjunath, who would go on to become my sherpa for this entire experience (she also gave this book its title!), a sounding board for all my neuroses, writing and otherwise, and is now a good friend. Thank you to both.

I didn't leave my cousin Sid Aney, a fantastic writer, much choice in teaching me the finer details of financial dealings and political campaigns. I'm not sure how good a student I was, but it's Sid's insightful comments on my writing and his key additions that helped craft the Singhs back story and also improved this manuscript in general. Thank you, Sid! Waiting on your book now.

I turned to a roster of experts for this story. Any errors you see here are mine, not theirs. I'll forever be indebted to them for their advice and time:

My lawyers, Vivek Vashi and Amanda Rebello, for breaking down the legalese in the book, answering all my naive questions and helping navigate the entire publishing process.

So grateful to my close friend Praniti Shinde, who was as always generous with her time, insights and support.

My fellow school mum, friend and legal expert Kanika Premnarayen Kapoor, along with her team, Abhimanyu Kaul and Rajbir Singh, also aided me in fact-checking all the legal elements.

Mohit Bhalla, a senior editor and journalist, who took time out of reporting the real news, in helping me create the fictional financial irregularities in Mohan Mehta's story.

I turned to the inimitable Punit Jasuja, the man behind the country's most spectacular weddings, to create Tara's multi-million Euro big fat nuptials. It has to be said: The stories Punit told me have given me enough fodder for multiple future books.

Ria Talati Advani, besides being one of my oldest friends, is a brilliant interior designer. With her help, I designed the homes of the Mehtas and the Mistrys in full glory.

I relied on my friend Ashika Poohomul Mehta, psychotherapist, MSW, to take me through different scenarios in the therapist-patient interaction.

Soon-to-be-published author Ambika Vora's generosity with her experience and her network only underlined, for me, how powerful women supporting women is. I am so touched by all you did.

I finally got to be shot by one of my favourite photographers, Hashim Badani, who very kindly took my author's portrait. Ashwin Thadani of Galerie Isa kindly lent us his amazing space to shoot in.

I wouldn't be writing this very page if it wasn't for the team at Penguin Random House India. Milee Ashwarya took a chance on a very eager debut author. I hope this novel is all you had imagined. My editor Dipanjali Chadha's attention to detail and enthusiasm for these characters makes this story a much smoother read. Saloni Mital ran a fine-toothed comb over my pages. Roshni Dadlani, who very kindly read an initial draft, gave me a lot to work with. A shout out to the PRHI marketing and design teams, for their efforts.

My superlative agents, Hemali Sodhi and Ambar Sahil Chatterjee, of a Suitable Agency, went beyond the expected to bring this book to life. Your patience and guidance means the world to this debut author.

It took me over a decade to even work up the courage to take on long-form fiction. I wrote most of this novel while I was working at *Vogue*, and over the years, I was fortunate enough to learn from some whip smart writers, editors and individuals. Priya Tanna impressed on me, among many things, the power of a good story and the importance of solid writing; fellow novelist Anindita Ghose, Manju Sara Rajan, Aishwarya Subramanyam, Renuka Joshi Modi, all exceptional writers, who edited (and bettered!) so many of my *Vogue* pieces over the years. My colleague and friend Megha Mahindru read an early draft of this novel and was right on point with her feedback as was Priyanka Kapadia, who made my week by reading it all in one sitting. Thank you, Anaita Shroff Adajania, the keeper of secrets (!) and Arjun Mehra, who continues to be a guide.

The Originals, for letting me borrow their names and for listening to my stories all these years.

At its heart, this is a book about female friendship. And I'm lucky to have a tribe that cheers me on. Aneesa Dhody and Neha Samtani read the first twenty pages and encouraged me to keep going after. Aneesa, my oldest friend, took on so many roles through this journey—from patient listener to event planner. Thirty-five years later, Nyrika Holkar and Nisha Anand Kothari still laugh at my stories. Fellow author Megha Kaushik took time away from her own manuscript to read mine. Petals Deas Kaji, Antara Marwah, Archana Walavalkar, Rishna Shah Mehta, Ria Grover, Amrita Parekh,

Gayatri Hingorani Dewan, Namrata Doshi, Hemali Lathia Dalal, Kajal Fabiani, Arati Juneja, Farah Nathani Menzies, Tina Narula, Sonali Gogia, Freyan Neterwala, Shagun Ajmera, Neha Gandhi, Simeen Colabawalla are just a few of the incredible women I learn from and I have in my corner. Batasha Varma Mathur generously and whole-heartedly stepped in at such a crucial moment. I will never forget your kindness.

Daneesh Davar, my hype woman, who added the sweetest touch to the launch. Hina Oomer Ahmed marked my book's debut into the world in such style, as did Sravanya Rao Pittie with her gorgeous design. Gauri Nayar reached out to her network and shared her expertise.

As a working mother, I'm surrounded by a strong ecosystem that gives me the space and time to fulfil all my dreams.

Hiroo Johar, for all her love and encouragement.

Kanubhai Sheth and the late Jaswantiben Sheth treated me like their own from day one, as did Rekha and Narendra Sheth, Rima Seth who continue to provide my children and myself a safe space and strong emotional support.

My gorgeous babies Vedika and Vedant, who, I hope in the future, understand why I spent so much time chained to a desk. Maybe, just maybe, at some point, they will think that their mother being a published author is cool.

Rahul Mirchandani, brother from another mother, who among other things, brings humour, tech skills and the ability to mix a great G&T to our family.

Anushka Khanna, lifeline, sounding board and problem solver. To have a sister who makes your dreams her own, is a blessing beyond imagination.

And finally, Rikin Sheth, my partner of the last nineteen years, who provided me with the tough love and encouragement I needed, who read countless revisions, and who continues to inspire me to *do* better and *be* better. With you, my glass is always full. I lucked out, babe.